Mod Superhero: Execute

Samuel Fleming

Ebook ISBN: 978-1-954679-72-6

Print ISBN: 978-1-954679-73-3

Cover Design by James, *GoOnWrite.com*

For R, A, and M

"Everything we do, we do for our children."

—Dr. Magnus Venture

Contents

Chapter 1

Mutagen Bust

The sun was setting over the skyline of Belport, and superheroes were running across the roofs.

Emmett Laraway was one of them.

Emmett ran across the rooftops, leaping across alleys with superhuman agility. Even now, Mutagen-A was changing his cells, making his bones denser, his muscles stronger, and his organs more efficient. He even healed faster. Not even the winter wind bothered Emmett, though he still wore a dark hoodie and a black mask.

Almost a month ago, Emmett had watched longingly from the street as superheroes passed above in a blur. Now he was one of them.

Everything had changed since his near-death experience in the Champion street attack. His biological enhancements were only part of it.

Ahead of him, Athena ran across invisible platforms that spanned from one roof to the next, creating them one after the other. Her long white hair trailed after her, and the evening light glinted off the shards of glass woven into her jacket.

Emmett could have followed her across the platforms, but he didn't need to anymore. Instead, in midair, Emmett opened the compartment in his prosthetic right arm and slung the hidden whip like a grappling hook. It latched onto the top of the next roof and Emmett pulled himself upward.

Athena glanced over the roof at Emmett and let out an amused chuckle with a hint of disgust. "I'm still not used to seeing that."

Emmett hurled himself over the edge and landed easily on the roof, the whip retracting back into his mechanical arm. He understood her sentiments—there were times it caught him off guard, too. He wasn't sure exactly how Dr. Venture had managed it, but the prosthetic arm *looked* normal. The synthetic skin was indistinguishable from the real thing, but underneath Emmett was able to hold several hidden devices.

In the upper arm compartment, he'd been sticking to carrying smoke pellets and caltrops, the latter of which were meant for pursuing vehicles but Emmett hadn't used them yet. He kept the rest of his incidentals in his utility belt. In the forearm compartment, he'd kept the mechanical whip that Venture had developed.

Emmett could swap out the expendable tools in his upper arm compartment, and eventually he would be able to do the same for his forearm compartment. That way, he could pick the right modification, a.k.a. *mod*, for the job.

If he was expecting a gunfight, Emmett could swap his whip for a pistol or a portable shield. Honestly, the last few weeks had been such a whirlwind that Emmett hadn't gotten to experiment as much with his mods as he wanted. But he resolved to change by the time he graduated in the Spring.

Despite the mutagen flowing through his body, his arm was where he got his superhero name:

Mod.

It was a little on the nose, but it reminded him of Arsenal, a super who'd worn exosuit-like sets of power armor—named for being a literal walking, flying arsenal of weapons.

He'd literally figured it out about two minutes ago.

"I like it," Athena said as they paused on the roof. "It's short and simple. And it makes sense—well once you know what *mod* means. It always bothers me when supers have names that don't make sense. Like a psychic named *Cold Heart*, or someone with super speed named *Chuck*."

"Those aren't real heroes, are they?"

Athena ignored Emmett, instead crouching down by the edge of the roof. Instinctively, Emmett followed her lead.

A moment later, she pointed down the side street toward a white van. "I think this is our mark."

They watched it as it stopped in front of their building and backed up to the loading bay. Workers hopped out of the van and stepped out from the bay, all with hats pulled low over their faces.

Someone was flooding the streets with derivatives of Gnosis's mutagens. For weeks, shipments of knock-off mutagens were coming in. Athena and her crew of masks were destroying as many as they could, but for every shipment they found, more were making it through.

It was a numbers game, and so far, the bad guys were winning.

That would change if they could trace the mutagens back to the source, but so far, they hadn't gotten that lucky.

Athena and Emmett watched carefully from the rooftop, waiting until they saw proof that this was their target. A moment later, the first of the white cooler boxes appeared.

"Ready?" Athena whispered.

Emmett nodded. Then they left off the rooftop, Athena quickly dropping from one invisible forcefield to another, creating them as fast as she fell. Meanwhile, Emmett swung down using his whip.

They landed a few steps away from the van. The workers turned in surprise, but Athena and Emmett were faster.

The first time, Emmett had tagged along with Athena during a mutagen bust, he'd had no idea what to expect. He'd bumbled through it, relying on Athena to save him.

This time Emmett knew what to expect.

Athena held out a hand toward the first of the men and he flew backward across the alley, pushed by an invisible forcefield. Then she turned her attention toward the loading bay.

Emmett lashed out with his whip and grabbed the second around the midsection. He was big, probably outweighing Emmett by one hundred pounds or more, and he knew it—he grabbed the end of the whip and smirked. But Emmett didn't plan on getting into a tug of war. Emmett simultaneously leapt forward and pulled—rocketing toward his enemy.

The big man barely kept his footing and had no chance of blocking Emmett's attack. Emmett punched him square in the stomach and the man folded in half. He dropped to the ground and stayed there.

Emmett winced, glad that he pulled his punch. He still had super strength, and if this bust was anything like last time, then all these men were normal people. He wanted to knock them out of the fight, not cripple them.

In the loading bay, the first of the workers drew a pistol and fired. Emmett dove behind the front of the van out of instinct, but he peeked around the side to see the bullets dropping harmlessly in front of the man. Athena had stretched a forcefield across the entire loading bay, completely walling off the area.

More workers opened fire in frustration, but their bullets fell impotently at their feet. Two of the men punched at the invisible barrier, but didn't have any better luck.

Athena had already turned her back to them and opened one of the white boxes to inspect the contents. Emmett's ears were already ringing, but he ignored the discomfort. He smirked and walked around to join her, already focusing on what new mutagens he'd find.

Last time, he'd found a mutagen variant that enhanced his night vision. It wasn't as flashy of a power as increased strength or moving objects with his mind, but his vision had already saved his ass once.

Besides, these mutagen busts with Athena were way easier than training.

Emmett tore the lid off of one crate. Icy smoke seeped over the edges and Emmett's eyes widened at the tightly packed vials inside. Shimmering blue, red, orange—

Athena grabbed Emmett's shoulder and spun him around to face the loading bay. "We've got company."

The gunshots stopped, and the workers backed away from the front of the loading bay. A thin young man stepped past them and stopped in front of the forcefield. He looked like he belonged in a punk rock band—wearing a black studded leather jacket and his hair was up in a mohawk and dyed green.

He reached out for the forcefield and sneered when he touched it. Then he pulled his hand back and made a fist. Fire coalesced around it.

The rocker punched, and Athena's forcefield exploded.

Both Emmett and Athena braced as the shockwave washed over them, and in the loading bay several workers yelled and were thrown backward.

The rocker was completely unfazed.

"Keep the workers occupied," Athena said.

Emmett nodded. He was already grabbing a smoke pellet out of his arm compartment, but froze when he looked at Athena.

Her nose was bleeding.

The shockwave couldn't have done that. Had the destruction of her forcefield hurt her?

"Go," Athena said. "I need to concentrate."

Emmett hesitated until the rocker came flying through the air at them. He glowed with power and screamed for effect.

Both Emmett and Athena leapt to the side. The space where they'd been a moment before exploded with another shockwave that blew out the van windows.

One of the workers screamed, "Be careful!"

The rocker turned with a sneer. "Shut up."

Emmett sprinted toward the loading bay, trusting Athena to keep the enemy super occupied. The workers that were still on their feet turned toward Emmett in surprise, but before they could raise their pistols, he pulled two smoke pellets out of his upper arm compartment and hurled them at their feet.

For how small the pellets were, they covered the loading bay in smoke. Then he pulled two noise makers from his utility belt and threw them for good measure. Even though the sound was annoying and disorienting to him, it was even more so to his enemies.

Emmett leapt into the cloud, slamming into one worker, and used the surprise to punch him in the stomach, then hurl him across the floor and into another. Even though he couldn't see any better in the smoke, Emmett had surprise, strength, and a whip on his side.

He extended the whip and swung it low across the room. It wrapped around the first ankle it felt. Emmett yanked the man off his feet, dragged him across the ground, and pummeled him. A man screamed in the smoke, and Emmett lunged for him, tackling him hard and knocking him out. He slid the magazine out of each gun and tossed them in random directions.

Explosions and the squeal of metal sounded beyond the smoke, but he didn't stop—not until he swept his whip through the smoke and didn't find another worker. Emmett dropped another smoke pellet in the hall before going back outside.

Back in the alley, Athena was batting the rocker around like a cat playing with a mouse. She leapt from one forcefield to the next like she was running around on an invisible jungle gym. At the same time, the rocker stumbled around the alley—shoved around the alley by invisible barriers.

The rocker still bristled with power and each punch and kick sent shockwaves across the alley, but each time he lashed out, he struck nothing but air. Athena conjured forcefields quick enough to strike and dispelled them in the next moment—reinforcing Emmett's theory that she didn't want to clash powers directly.

For a moment, Emmett hesitated.

Athena wasn't just a powerful super—she was also way more experienced than Emmett. Emmett wanted to help, but he wasn't sure if he was getting in over his head. He couldn't accurately gauge this villain's power level, but Athena was fighting cautiously, even if she was winning...

She'd probably beat this guy eventually, but every second the fight dragged on was time for more goons or someone from the Summit of Heroes to arrive. Not to mention, Emmett wanted some of the mutagen vials for himself—some of which were already shattered and leaking bright liquids across the alley. If the fight went on much longer, the rest of the vials might get destroyed.

Emmett waited until the rocker turned his back, then swung his whip and grabbed the super's ankle. The rocker looked back with a mix of shock and disgust. Emmett pulled, wrenching the man off balance. Athena struck at the same time, slamming a forcefield into the man's back and hurtling him into the side of the building.

He bounced off, dazed, but still conscious.

Emmett lashed out again, but this time, the rocker batted away the whip with a flaming hand. Emmett felt a distant twinge of pain.

And as the rocker's power faded, Athena struck again. This time the forcefield slammed him into the wall with an audible crunch and he dropped to the ground limply.

For a moment, Emmett thought Athena had killed him. He stared in shock, but breathed a sigh of relief as the man groaned in pain. At least he wasn't dead.

Emmett retracted his whip back into his forearm compartment, ignoring the warped and charred metal links at the tip. He'd have to repair it later, but for now he had more important concerns.

Emmett ran over to the white crates, ripping the lids off until he found one with undamaged vials. He pocketed two or three of each, until his hoodie pocket was filled with clinking glass.

Athena smirked, blood still trickling down her nose. "Glad you have your priorities straight. Now let's get out of here."

Chapter 2

Another Day, Another Score

Athena used her forcefields to smash the van and the remaining crates. Then Emmett followed her back up to the roofs, using her invisible platforms instead of his broken whip.

They sprinted away from the scene across the skyline of Belport. Despite their blistering pace, Emmett kept both hands on his hoodie pouch to keep the vials from jostling too much. When they were ten blocks away, they slipped over the edge of an apartment roof and rested on a fire escape.

Athena wiped the blood from her face with a handkerchief and pinched her nose to stop the bleeding.

"That was fun!" she said, her voice nasally. It took Emmett a moment to realize that she wasn't being sarcastic about it.

"Are you sure you're alright?"

"Oh yeah! I didn't drip anywhere, did I?"

Emmett chuckled. Somehow she'd managed not to get any on her glass-lined jacket or her T-shirt underneath. "No, you're good," Emmett replied. "What happened back there? That guy didn't even hit you."

"Good observation," she replied, still holding her nose.

"It was because he destroyed your forcefield."

Athena smirked and checked her nose, satisfied that the bleeding had stopped. "Can you guess what that guy's name was?" She folded the handkerchief and wiped the blood off her lips.

"No idea," Emmett replied.

"His name is *Feedback*. I'm not surprised you haven't heard of him. He's not exactly a big time super. His energy manipulation isn't that powerful, but the damage can travel through projections and back to the creator."

Emmett found himself considering the villain in a new light. That would be a useful power to have...

"But you knew about him. That's why you changed tactics."

Athena nodded, her face finally blood free. "I wasn't sure at first. Quite a few supers like wearing leather, but as soon as he attacked my barrier, I knew."

Emmett didn't let up, though. "I've been trying to research supers in Belport so that I can be prepared, but there's not a lot of information on low-level supers."

Athena smirked and leaned against the railing of the fire escape. "You won't find a lot of newbies or Class one and two heroes on the internet."

"So, how did you find out about him?"

She shrugged. "There's a lot of low-level supers in Belport but not *that* many. It's a smaller community than people realize. Word gets around, and it's good to pay attention to supers that are hard counters to your powerset."

Emmett nodded along, then extended his whip part way from his right arm. The last several linkages were damaged from where Feedback had hit it.

"Did that hurt?" Athena asked, curiosity on her face instead of concern.

Emmett nodded. "Not much, but I felt it."

"Weird—in a good way. I didn't want to ask how much feeling you had in that arm."

"Should the damage have hurt more?" Emmett made a point not to look at the traces of dried blood around Athena's nose.

She said simply, "His power caused feedback damage through my forcefields. Your prosthetic isn't a superpower."

Emmett suddenly felt self-conscious. He retracted the end of the whip and once again his arm looked otherwise flesh-covered and normal.

"I didn't mean anything by it," Athena added, unconcerned. "We all have our strengths. Your arm is one of yours."

"Yeah..." Emmett muttered. Despite Athena's reassurance, the words stuck with him:

Your prosthetic isn't a superpower.

Emmett pushed the thought aside and tried to change the subject. "Feedback… The name makes sense."

"See what I mean! I can't even be mad at the guy."

Emmett and Athena shared a laugh and parted ways afterward. Emmett had to get back to his apartment and put the mutagen vials on ice so they would survive until he could take them to the lab the next day.

Now that the excitement was over, he was ready for the day to be over, too.

He checked his phone and saw he'd missed a text from Clara about his new superhero name:

Clara 9:02 PM: *OMG the name is perfect!*
Emmett 9:39 PM: *Thanks. Heading home.*

Emmett smiled and readied himself for the long jog back to the apartment. The smile stayed almost the entire way back.

Emmett jogged across the roofs until he got to downtown Belport. Even though it was late, it was still busy, and the skyscrapers were way too tall for him to traverse. So Emmett climbed down to street level, removed his mask and walked through downtown.

No matter how many times he walked through the heart of Belport, the sheer size of the buildings and intensity of the displays never ceased to amaze him. Electronic billboards the width of a city block displayed ads for Gnosis beauty products, high end fusion-powered cars and the latest phones. Though some of the ads caught his eye from afar, Emmett kept his head down and hood up until he was out of downtown and back on the West End.

From there, Emmett jogged until he got to the Woods apartment blocks. There were several blocks in total, most of which were rented out to students of Belport University. Most nights, students milled about the lawn, the gazebos, and the stairwells, and tonight was no exception. Emmett passed by most and nodded to the few he recognized, but he didn't stop to talk.

He hiked up the stairs to the fourth floor, room 449, and let himself in.

It wasn't much. Two bedrooms, living room, one bathroom... but at least they had roof access and frequently made use of it. The apartment definitely wasn't the Heights, but it was the place Emmett and Lock had called home for the past two years.

And they'd made it their own: Strings of ambient lights hung around the living room and could sync with the TV and speakers. The dining room table was covered with skeletons of electronics. So long as Emmett and Lock didn't knock down any walls and repainted before they graduated, they'd get their security deposit back.

Emmett called out as he entered but Lock wasn't back yet. His roommate, Lachlan, worked part time as a bouncer for clubs and security for concerts, and rarely got in before midnight. But it didn't hurt to be sure—

Especially when Lock's main job was working an internship for Gnosis, and Emmett was carrying contraband mutagens.

Emmett glanced around the apartment, then stuck his head out of the fire escape and called up to the roof. Finally, Emmett was satisfied that he was alone in the apartment.

He went to the kitchen, grabbed a cup, filled it with ice, and grabbed several plastic sandwich bags from the drawer. Then he took everything into his room, and shut and locked the door.

Since the first time Emmett had shown up with a hoodie stuffed with mutagens and ice, Dr. Venture had given him a soft lunchbox to use instead. By the time Emmett stuffed it with the vials and ice, it barely zipped closed, but it did the job. Emmett stuffed it between his storage boxes.

He took his mask and burner phone out of his pocket and stuffed them both into the mattress cover. Then he breathed a sigh of relief.

Another day, another score. Now he just had homework to take care of.

Unfortunately, Emmett burned the rest of the evening getting his regular classwork done and working on the algorithm for his radio locator project. By the end of it, his eyes hurt from looking at the computer screen. Resolving to take a break, Emmett climbed out the window to the fire escape and went up to the roof.

Emmett walked around the rows of humming air conditioning units to the folding chairs stacked in the corner. He pulled one out and plopped down into it.

The night air was crisp and clear, and Emmett stared up at the starless sky. And his mouth dropped open in surprise...

Usually the light pollution of Belport was too much to see any stars, even from the rooftops. The couple of times Emmett *thought* he saw stars, he'd assumed his eyes were just playing tricks on him.

But now he could see them. Not just a few pinpricks of light, but an ocean of stars.

Emmett's smile widened and he took in the sight of a starry sky over Belport for the first time.

What changed? A blackout might explain it, but Emmett glanced out over the city and saw the skyline lit up like normal. The lights in the Woods hadn't gone out either.

Then Emmett remembered the first batch of knock-off mutagens he'd found. He hadn't been able to take most of them, for one reason or another, but the one Emmett did take boosted his low-light vision.

Had that really been it? After a minute, Emmett shook his head in disbelief. That had to be it.

So many things had changed in just a few weeks. Emmett's entire life was different. Sometimes it felt like he was living on a completely different planet.

The night sky was just another reminder.

But as Emmett stared up at the sight and lost himself in it, he decided that this one wasn't so bad.

Chapter 3

Priorities

On Thursday morning, Emmett hit the snooze twice on his alarm. By the time Emmett actually got up for class, he was running late. He grabbed a granola bar and his backpack.

He did so quietly, so he didn't wake up his roommate. Lock must've gotten in late last night.

Emmett sighed. It was good they'd gotten to hang out Monday. They'd both been so busy with work that they rarely got to just hang out like they used to.

It definitely hadn't gotten any better on Emmett's end since he'd become a super. Between class, homework, training with Clara at the lab, and moonlighting in the evenings, Emmett felt like he barely had time to breathe—

Not that he was complaining.

Okay, maybe he'd gotten a case of senioritis with college, but he wouldn't give up anything about being a super.

He got five steps down the hall before he jogged back to the apartment and grabbed the lunchbox of vials from under his bed.

Emmett opted to take the seven o'clock bus from the West End over to the satellite campus of Belport University over on Eastside. He hopped off on 34th Street, pushed back his dark, shaggy hair, and put his earbuds in. *Endure* had a new single out, "Faux Side of the Moon", which was good but definitely different from their previous stuff. Less electronic and more industrial.

Belport's satellite campus didn't look much different from the surrounding businesses. All of them focused on engineering and health sciences and shared a love of glass. If everything went well, Emmett would graduate and get a job right down the street in one of them.

Only two more months to go.

The saying had become a mantra for Emmett, one he repeated to himself pretty much every morning as he sat in class, struggling to pay attention to one lecture or another. Today, he tried not to think too much about the vials in his lunchbox and the choices that awaited him.

After struggling through Statistics and his last elective, Modern Government and Applied History, Emmett took the two o'clock bus to the edge of Eastside.

The ads and the glass slowly faded from the sides of buildings until they were little more than concrete sides and parking lots. The last few blocks that Emmett walked were taken up exclusively by the Gnosis company headquarters which flanked the right side of the street like a military compound.

It was surrounded by razor wire and flanked by guards holding machine guns. The buildings were sleek, white, and barren of everything except the Gnosis logo—a white square with a simple, blurry face staring back.

On the left, the Gnosis parking garage was covered by two electronic billboards for Gnosis's beauty products. One showing a generic skin cream. The second showing the tagline *'The standards may change, but the pursuit of beauty is immortal.'*

Emmett passed beneath the garage and stopped at a nondescript metal door. He pulled back his hood and waited.

A moment later, the eye scan registered and TINA's robotic voice said, "Thank you for verification. Please step through, Emmett Laraway." Even six months later, he still couldn't find where the scanner, camera, or speaker were.

Emmett considered now that he was officially in the fold, Dr. Venture might reveal the secret if Emmett asked... Then again, there were plenty of secrets the doctor still kept.

"TINA, where is Dr. Venture this morning?"

"*Dr. Venture is currently in section 005. He is expecting your arrival.*"

Emmett followed the long, dim stairwell over one hundred steps before he reached the bottom. From there, he passed six numbered doors that looked like they belonged in a nuclear bunker instead of a laboratory. Only a few weeks ago, Emmett had only seen the inside of section 003. But that was when Emmett thought that Dr. Venture was just an eccentric engineer working on fusion reactors and heat sinks.

Now he knew the truth: His boss and mentor was a retired superhero.

...Emmett still didn't know which hero, but one day, the old man would probably confide in him.

Emmett chuckled to himself. *Only a few more months to go.*

He pushed the thought aside and waited for TINA to let him into section 005—the section Emmett had spent almost all of his time in since the accident that turned him into a cyborg super.

The Gray Room.

Emmett stopped in the small locker room to change out of his clothes.

He'd taken to wearing his bodysuit under his clothes on the reasoning that if something dangerous and unexpected came up, it would be easier to leap into action. All he would have to do was strip off his hoodie and jeans.

Thankfully though, most superheroics had the decency to wait until evening, when Emmett was ready for them.

The suit itself wasn't much to look at. It was black and covered everything except his face, neck, and hands. It fit snugly, like something an athlete or a dancer might wear. The 'shoes' even contoured to his feet and toes, and the right arm had cutaways for his storage compartments.

Emmett stuffed his clothes in a locker, put his utility belt back on, picked up the lunchbag of mutagen vials, and walked down the bunker corridors.

One of the questions that still floated around Emmett's mind was why there was such a mix of technology in the corridors of the lab. In some sections, TINA's voice crackled through ancient speakers and access was granted by voice scan. Others used eye scans, but the monitors looked old.

The corridors of section 005 seemed pristine in comparison. TINA's voice came through clearly and without static. White lights came on as Emmett walked, illuminating the floor in time with his steps.

Emmett stopped at section 005's version of the testing hub. Most of the section hubs had screens lining the walls and worktables in the center, and this one was no exception. But there were two main differences: The large Virtual Reality platform along the side wall, complete with a haptic outfit that was hung up like a suit of armor, and the large viewing window that looked out on a large, dark room—

But it would have to wait.

Dr. Venture cleared his throat expectantly.

The doctor was tall and broad, never without his titular grease-stained lab coat. Despite his profession, rugged was the best word to describe him. His hands were covered in calluses, his face in stubble, and his graying hair always swept back.

Emmett kicked himself for not realizing the truth about his mentor earlier. Now that Emmett knew what to look for, it was ridiculous that he hadn't pegged Dr. Venture as a retired super earlier.

Then again, maybe it was easy to overlook things like that. Most people weren't scrutinizing everyone they met, wondering if their coworkers, roommates, or their family were secretly moonlighting as supers.

Currently, Dr. Venture was hunched over the center table, staring at a holographic diagram. At first, Emmett would've guessed it was for the heat sink systems that they had worked on the last few months, but it wasn't any system that he recognized. It almost looked electrical...

Venture stood and pushed up his glasses. "I see you've brought lunch."

Emmett couldn't keep from smirking as he set the bag on the table and unzipped it. "Athena and I busted another mutagen drop."

Emmett recounted the events of last night as Venture examined the new vials, nodding along until Emmett got to the part about his whip being damaged by *Feedback's* power.

"Let me see."

Emmett extended the whip and let Venture examine it.

He rolled the linkages over in his hands, examining the damage. "Athena was right when she said that your cybernetics aren't a superpower."

Emmett shrugged. "At first I thought it sounded offensive. I know she didn't mean it that way, but still..."

Venture chuckled. "Understandable, but it's the truth. Super is a broad term. Some powers are elemental. Some are biological. Others are magical."

"Some are based on technology."

"Exactly." Venture pulled a small screwdriver from his coat pocket and held the end of the whip down on the table to work on it. "Every type of power has advantages and disadvantages. Every type has strong matchups and difficult matchups. I'm not sure what type of power Feedback uses, but it looks like you didn't suffer nearly as much damage as Athena did."

Emmett thought back to the fight. "She definitely stayed away from him and was careful how she used her barriers."

"I bet."

Something clicked in the whip and the damaged linkages popped off. It might have been five linkages—only a half foot or so—but Emmett flinched.

"Are you alright?"

Emmett rubbed his arm, but the feeling was already gone. "It felt like that section went numb, then vanished completely."

Venture examined the burnt linkages. "That is interesting."

"Why?"

Venture set the broken pieces down on the table. "I wasn't sure how well the prosthetic would integrate with your new body. In a sense, this is uncharted territory."

Emmett examined the end of the whip before retracting it back into his arm. As much as he still clung to the idea of swapping out modifications on the fly, Emmett had to admit that he was partial to the whip. It was far more versatile that he'd imagined.

"Can you fix it?"

Venture laughed heartily. *"You* can fix it."

Emmett scoffed. "I don't know how."

"Then today is a good day to learn."

The door hissed open behind Emmett, and Clara walked in. The resemblance between father and daughter was uncanny, but Clara set herself apart. Her dark hair was buzzed short, and she was fond of leggings, baggy sweaters, and beanies instead of lab coats. She might smile more than her dad, but they both had the same intense focus.

Clara walked over to the table and crossed her arms. "Gray Room first. Fix your toys later." She looked to be only half-joking.

"Fine," Venture said flatly. "I've got things to look into, anyway. Emmett, come see me before you leave and I'll show you what you need to know."

Chapter 4

Options

Emmett walked out through the last corridor by himself.

A few twists and turns later, he stepped out into a large, cavernous room. Darkness receded as he entered, light emanating from the square tiles that covered the walls, floor, and ceiling. Each changed color, giving the impression of a wave of white rippling across the room.

Emmett stood alone in a gigantic white room, some three hundred feet square. Of all the things Emmett had seen in the last three weeks since becoming a super, the Gray Room still filled him with awe.

Emmett cleared his throat. "TINA, bring up the warehouse district... please."

Tiles began to rise and shift. Walls rose and joined together, forming a tiled simulation of Belport's warehouse district. Each moved in eerie silence until they *clicked* into place. The whole process took a little over a minute, and when it was done, Emmett stood alone in a faux grayscale version of Belport, like he'd stepped into an old noir movie.

Emmett jogged over to a nearby fire escape and climbed up to the roof. He stared across the simulated skyline, looking South toward the bay.

The first time Emmett had been in the Gray Room, it had felt almost eerie. He wasn't sure whether it was the technology itself, or the way the tiles moved and the outer walls shifted the display to simulate movement. But recently Emmett had begun to see it in a different light.

It was beautiful, in a way. Almost serene.

He wasn't going to give up the real sunset for a simulated one anytime soon, but the Gray Room had quickly become one of his favorite places to be.

It could have also been the company.

A dull gray robot landed on the roof beside him—a cross between high-tech armor and an old bulbous diving suit with thin joints.

Clara's voice came through it. "So, back to the warehouse district?"

Emmett nodded.

He'd grown so used to the lab's training set up that he didn't even see the robot in front of him most of the time. Emmett pictured Clara in the training hub, smiling beneath the haptic suit as she controlled the robot.

He added, "I figured I'd pick the location since you already seemed to have a power set in mind."

"I do," Clara said, sounding devious. "You keep talking about how you want to be able to swap out modifications and adjust to whoever you're fighting. I've been thinking that the best way to do that is have you fight powersets that are unpredictable. Right now you don't have a lot of options for mods, so you'll have to quickly figure out which one is best."

"Clara, I didn't bring any mods down with me." All he had was his utility belt and his whip.

"Sounds like someone is unprepared. Guess you'll have to improvise today!"

Clara's robot shimmered and its skin turned bright red, indicating that it would go on the attack. Tiles formed into a pole and extended from the roof beside Clara's feet. When it was her height, the shaft turned red, and the robot grabbed it. She held it like a staff and spun it.

Emmett immediately took a defensive stance, waiting to see what she would do.

Clara shouted something in a language Emmett didn't recognize, then slammed the butt of the staff down onto the roof. Flames shot out of the top of the staff, flowing and twisting upward like a stream—

Like a snake.

His mind registered it, even before Emmett saw the tip of the fire split open into a mouth with fangs and a flickering tongue. The fire snake looked down on him, its neck widening to become the hood of a cobra.

Emmett looked up at the snake with equal parts surprise and awe. And more than a little jealousy.

A magic fire snake sounded pretty cool. Even cooler than being a cyborg.

Clara shouted something else and chunks of ice flew from her staff. Emmett brought his arms up to block, but the shards hit the roof in front of him. Before he could move again, the ice spread across the surface, over his feet and up to his ankles, trapping Emmett in place.

Shit. That was what he got for getting distracted.

Emmett extended his whip. Even if it was damaged, it would still be useful—he could keep the snake at bay and also reach Clara's robot across the roof. At the same time, he reached into his utility belt and grabbed a handful of the sand and salt mix, and tossed it on the ice. A flash of steam burst around him as the mixture ate into the ice, but it wouldn't be fast enough.

The snake lunged, and Emmett lashed out with his whip. Metal struck the creature and instead of flames, it felt like the whip had struck molten rock. The serpent reeled from the impact, but a shock of pain traveled up Emmett's whip and through his arm.

Emmett pushed the pain aside and immediately lashed out for Clara's robot. She parried the blow and Emmett was forced to defend against the fire snake again as it arced around and dove at him again.

Information about magic-wielding supers wasn't as widespread as some other types, but Emmett knew a little about their capabilities. Even if he couldn't remember the correct antimagic mixture or didn't have the mixture in his belt, he wasn't completely powerless. Magic spells could be incredibly potent and versatile, but most mages stuck to a narrow specialty. Long-lasting spells also required constant concentration to maintain, and mages could rarely concentrate on more than a few at a time, limiting their options. Artifacts like wands and staves could bolster a mage's capabilities, but they would also be vulnerable to being disarmed.

In short, Emmett didn't have to beat any of her spells directly. If Emmett could disarm Clara or hit her hard enough to throw off her concentration, then he could make an opening.

As soon as he batted away the fire snake, Emmett reached into his arm compartment and chucked a smoke pellet at the robot's feet. Smoke erupted and covered the rooftop. Meanwhile, Emmett wrenched his feet and could feel the ice loosening.

Meanwhile, the fire snake floated above him like a torch through the haze. He kept one eye on the snake and swung the whip at Clara—hard. Metal slammed into her and Emmett commanded his whip to grab whatever it could. Then he pulled with superhuman strength and his feet anchored by ice magic.

Clara's robot stumbled out of the smoke, and Emmett felt the ice around his feet vanish completely as her concentration faltered. Emmett swung a metal fist at the robot, hoping to knock it out quickly—

But Clara slammed the butt of the staff into the ground again. This time, Emmett lurched and floated upward—some kind of levitation or reverse gravity spell. Feet no longer planted, Emmett's punch sent him cartwheeling through the air.

Emmett had barely risen above the smoke when the fire snake charged him.

Emmett couldn't change direction before it slammed into him. Fire engulfed him as he fell over the side of the roof.

He flailed and lashed out with the whip, just managing to grab the edge of a window and slow his descent. If he could get inside and out of the open, he might have a better chance...

Emmett aimed for a window and half made it through. He was too low and his legs slammed into the wall, causing him to tumble as he burst through the window. He scrambled to his feet and dove behind a table.

At least he made it inside.

The warehouse room was split: One half was filled with office furniture, and the other was floor to ceiling shelving—all of it made out of gray tiles like the rest of the Gray Room.

Emmett hid behind the table, waiting. Clara's robot was red, which meant she should be coming to him.

The robot appeared a few seconds later, sliding through the broken window on a wave of ice. It melted behind her as she stepped onto the tile.

"Come out, come out, wherever—"

Emmett kicked the table, and it careened across the room. It slammed into Clara's robot and both crashed into the shelves. Without pausing, Emmett grabbed the top of the nearest shelves with his whip and pulled it down on top of her.

Hundreds of pounds of metal came down on the robot—then froze in midair. Clara had used the antigravity spell *again*.

Emmett grit his teeth in frustration and grabbed another desk and sent it hurling toward Clara. This time he flung a smoke pellet after it, waited for it to explode, then hurled another desk into the smoke.

For a moment, Emmett was afraid to breathe.

Then Clara grunted in surprise as the desk hit her, and everything came crashing down. A cacophony of metal sounded as more shelves fell, knocked over by the errant desks.

Emmett smirked and shook a fist in celebration. "How about that!"

It took about a minute for the Gray Room to rearrange itself, reconstituting the wreckage and allowing Clara's robot to climb free.

She laughed on the other end of the intercom. "Not bad. Those smoke pellets are a pain!"

Emmett shrugged. "They're pretty much my only trick, but they're pretty useful." While Clara regained her bearings, Emmett asked, "So, that was a fire snake—what's it with you and fire?"

Clara's robot remained unreadable. "I don't know what you mean."

"Fire was the first thing you used against me in the Gray Room, remember?"

"Oh... Yeah. Fire's just cool, I guess."

Emmett laughed. "Yeah, *right.*"

Clara quickly changed the subject by throwing Emmett back into training.

That evening, Emmett fought a speedster, a gunslinger, and a banshee. Each presented their own challenges:

Against all three, his best chance was to get indoors and then close the distance to grapple his opponent. His whip helped against all three, but Emmett grew frustrated—

He might've been able to hold his own against threats as a generalist, but he didn't have any potent abilities. Even the mage powerset was arguably a better generalist than Emmett.

He really needed to make some new mods, and make it so he could quickly swap them out. But even more immediate were the mutagen knock-offs...

Emmett had been limited in his choices last time. Enhanced low-light vision had already saved his ass once, but it was way more niche of a power than he hoped.

Maybe he could take one of the mutagens he'd found with Athena. Maybe he could even take two...

Emmett found himself eagerly awaiting Dr. Venture's interruption at the end of the night.

His voice came over the intercom. *"Emmett, it's time to talk about these mutagens."*

Chapter 5

Actual Choices

Emmett and Clara met Dr. Venture in the biolab—section 006. Compared to the rest of the bunker-like aesthetic of the lab, the biolab looked almost like a hospital room. Except that the sterile white walls of the room were almost completely hidden by a jungle of empty glass tanks and tubes of bubbling liquid that twisted like vines.

This was where he woke up after the Champion street attack—the first place Emmett saw when Venture brought him back from the dead.

Even though it had only been a few weeks, it felt like much, much longer since he'd woken up to bright lights, steady beeping, and pain. He felt like an entirely different person, figuratively *and* literally.

Emmett suppressed a shiver as he walked up to the sleek metal tables in the center of the room.

Dr. Venture pushed up his glasses, then stood with his hands in his pockets expectantly.

Clara stepped up beside Emmett and pointed at the vials spread out on the table. "So, when do I get to take one of these?" She'd clearly meant it as a joke, but Venture ignored her.

"I will say, this time you actually will have a choice to make. Several of the compounds are either duds or will be of minimal use to those. Would you like me to start with the good choices or the duds?"

Emmett sighed. "At least this time I have a choice. Tell me about the duds."

First up was the vial filled with soft pink liquid. "This mixture is for enhanced strength. Unfortunately, it has diminishing returns when combined with other strength enhancements, such as the Mutagen-A already in your system."

Venture pointed to the swirling orange vial next. "This one was *interesting*. It results in an elongated, prehensile tongue... like a chameleon. It's slightly more useful to you, but unless you're concerned about your dating game, I think we can skip it."

"What do you mean—"

"What's next?" Clara asked quickly.

Without missing a beat, Venture continued to the deep red vial. "This one stimulates bone growth. It increases bone density, which could be useful, but it also had the side effect of causing protrusions and even bone claws in several simulations."

Emmett's shoulders sagged. So far, that was two out of five vials that were useless and a third that was troubling.

"What else?" he asked.

"This one was interesting." Venture held up the vial with a gritty purple liquid inside. "It causes the body to produce excess pheromones, causing others to feel increased connection, fear, or attraction. It's not as exact or potent as something like psychics could do, but it has its uses."

Emmett wasn't quite sure what to make of it. It certainly didn't seem as useful as some of the other powers, but when he looked to Clara for advice, she seemed apprehensive of it. So Emmett asked about the final vial.

Venture picked up the shimmering blue vial. "This increases your body's tolerance to extreme cold, and potentially even ice-based attacks."

Emmett raised an eyebrow. Training in the Gray Room was fresh in his mind. He hadn't run into many ice-based supers... any, really... but that could be useful, even if it was niche and in the future.

Venture set the blue vial back down, and Emmett reviewed his choices. And sighed, again. Even if he had a choice, this time compared to last time, nothing was popping out as the obvious choice.

Dr. Venture cleared his throat as if he had something to add. Clara chuckled.

Emmett scoffed at both of them. "Oh, come on. What is it now?"

"There is one more thing." Venture pulled another vial out of the inner pocket of his lab coat—a mix of swirling green.

Emmett nearly rolled his eyes, but stopped. "I've seen that one before."

"This isn't the same as the vial you found last time. I took inspiration from the mutagen variant that allowed a super to manufacture their own poison. Except that this formula does quite the opposite. This will turbo-charge your body's defenses against poisonous compounds. At the very least, you'll be able to weather the effects of things like the hallucinogen that drove Porcelain and Amarque insane.

"It won't always result in outright immunity, but it should allow you to build metabolic tolerance to *most* complex poisons and biological poisons. And it should allow you to build that tolerance much quicker than even your mutagen strengthened body could."

"But not everything?"

Venture smirked like he'd expected the question. "No. Coincidentally enough, the body can't do the same against simpler compounds like acids or heavy metals. Don't expect to become immune to chemical warfare anytime soon."

Emmett looked back over the vials again, but his mind was already made up. He nodded to the green vial in Venture's hand. "What's the catch?"

"No catch, other than the rules from last time still apply. You could potentially take another mutagen in a few weeks, but you need to give time for your body to acclimate to this one first." He handed Emmett the vial.

Emmett looked at Clara, but she just asked. "What are you waiting for?"

"What about you? If we're going to run into this rogue super again, shouldn't you take some of this, too?"

Clara smiled widely. "Thanks for thinking of me, but I have an exosuit. If poison manages to get through the suit, then I have much worse problems to worry about."

Venture added, "Besides, this was formulated with you in mind. I'll need time to make a compound for someone that doesn't already have Mutagen-A in their system. In theory, we could have a general antidote soon."

Emmett shrugged. "Alright then. Can I just drink it?"

Venture nodded.

Emmett pulled the stopper out, pinched his nose, and drank the vial quickly. It didn't help—the liquid tasted like sweet vomit.

When he was done gagging, Clara chuckled and patted him on the back.

"You're a trooper. Dad let me smell it and I almost threw up just from that. But hey, you have to suffer to get stronger, right?"

Emmett couldn't answer without feeling like he was going to lose it.

Venture had turned away from them both, his shoulders silently bobbing like he was stifling a laugh.

In the end, it took almost five minutes and a glass of water before Emmett didn't feel like gagging. Then he still had to wait another hour to make sure he didn't have an adverse reaction to the mutagen compound.

While Emmett waited, he grilled Dr. Venture on how to fix his whip.

The three of them had migrated to section 002—one of the wings of the lab marked by an old camera and a retinal scan. Beyond that, the layout was almost identical to section 003 where he'd spent most of his internship working on heat sinks.

They reached the central testing hub for the section, and Venture commanded TINA to bring up schematics for Emmett's arm and the whip. Soon the walls were filled with wireframe views of the two parts, with zoomed in views of specific areas.

"Put the whip on the table, please," Venture said.

Emmett unspooled the whip so it lay flat on the holographic table. Venture pulled the damaged linkages from his pocket, then made a quick gesture and a holographic display of the whip appeared in midair above the table.

"These are the damaged sections." As Venture spoke, the five linkages in the hologram glowed red and then expanded until each section was nearly a foot long. "It looks like when you attacked Feedback, the power surge overloaded the wiring. We can replace the wiring, but it will be quicker to replace the linkages for now."

"Because of your line of work, I've tried to make your prosthesis and initial mods with *replacement* in mind. I have spare parts and duplicates for everything."

Emmett smirked. "I thought you said my arm was one of the most advanced things you've designed. You already have spare parts?"

"One of the most advanced *prostheses* I've designed, and yes, I always have spares. ...Not as many for your arm as I have for your mods, so don't go breaking your arm recklessly."

"Noted. I'll try not to get destroyed... again."

Venture wheeled over one of the sleek silver carts and pulled out a pair of pliers and a screwdriver. With one in each hand, he set to work on the linkages, and the hologram in the air showed an expanded view of what he was doing.

It looked simple enough—each linkage in the whip was like a link of hollow chain connected together. Each piece was self-contained, basically consisting of a node at either end, conducting wire, and the metal casing that surrounded it all. Any link could be removed and the whip could still function.

Venture said, "Clara, watch closely. You need to know how to do this, too." When Emmett looked up in question, Venture added, "On the off chance you are incapacitated, someone else might need to disconnect a mod for you."

He pried apart the node that connected the very last damaged link, and it came apart with a *snap*.

Emmett nodded. "That was easy enough."

Venture examined the damaged piece. "Fascinating. The casing took the brunt of the damage, allowing you to still use it to its full potential. Now you try." He handed Emmett the pliers and screwdriver.

Carefully, Emmett did just as Venture had with the next damaged link. It took him a moment to find the correct angle, but then the link snapped apart easily. Emmett repeated the process for the next damaged pieces, then relaxed.

Clara patted him on the shoulder. "Not bad. Soon you'll be fixing my exosuit."

Venture turned and grabbed more links out of a nearby drawer, then deposited them on the table. Emmett set to work excitedly.

Venture added idly, "One day, Clara or I will show you a similar procedure to take apart our armor, on the off chance that both the wearer and the suit are incapacitated."

For a moment, Emmett wondered why they would wait to show him that kind of procedure. It seemed important, and on the off chance of something catastrophic like that, Emmett would want to be able to assist. But suspicion slowly dawned on him, and Emmett realized the likely reason:

They didn't trust him with that knowledge yet.

Emmett kept working and hoped Clara and Venture weren't looking at his face too closely.

He didn't blame them, of course. He would probably be wary of trusting someone with knowledge that could endanger his family. But it still stung to realize that even after the craziness of the last three weeks, even after seeing as much of the lab as he had and being trusted with so many secrets so far, even after dying, Emmett was still on the outside. They still didn't trust him—not really.

Emmett pushed the thought away and focused on the feeling coming back to the whip with each added link. The final piece clicked into place and Emmett wiggled it to test it out.

"Good as new," he said, retracting it back into his arm. Then, wanting to change the subject, he asked, "Is it a similar procedure to swap out mods?"

"More or less," Venture replied. "Let's give it a shot."

Chapter 6

Swapping Mods

Venture brought out two more modifications. The first was a thin metal box a little under a foot long and the second was a short cylinder. Emmett recognized them immediately as the impact shield and the concealable pistol. Venture set them on the table, and Emmett tried to hide his unease at the sight of the gun.

"So, what are we starting with?" Venture asked, looking at Emmett expectantly. When he didn't answer right away, Clara nudged him with her shoulder.

Emmett opted to start with the pistol. He still wasn't entirely comfortable with the idea of using a gun, even if it fired nonlethal rounds, but Emmett realized he *should* get comfortable with it.

Better to know how to use it and not need it, than the other way around.

Emmett laid his arm on the center table and opened his forearm compartment. Metal slid back to reveal the whip, and Emmett realized that for as much as he'd used that particular mod, he hadn't really looked at it while it was collapsed and inert. It reminded him of an old TV antenna, the linkages tucked neatly inside one another.

"Weird," Clara said, leaning over to get a better look at his arm. "I don't know what I expected, but this wasn't it."

Emmett chuckled. "I thought you helped put me back together."

"No…"

"Clara assisted once you were stable," Venture said as he scooted a chair over.

Emmett glanced at Clara and saw how uneasy she looked. It must have been hard to see him like that. All at once, Emmett regretted the joke.

"I turned out alright," Emmett added, hoping to lighten the mood.

Clara returned a small smile, but focused on his arm.

Again, the holographic display appeared in the air above the table, showing an expanded view of the process as Dr. Venture walked them through it.

The process wasn't much different from fixing the linkages in his whip. Instead of just one connection, there were ten, and he still needed tools, but the pliers and screwdriver got the job done. Venture had once called the process *minor surgery* and the description fit.

Once the connection *clicked*, Venture looked up expectantly. "Think you can reverse the process?"

He nodded cautiously.

As soon as Emmett started though, he ran into a snag—he could only use one hand. He could kind of use his right hand to hold the pliers for the two connections near his wrist, but Emmett was forced to alternate holding the tools in his left hand and with his teeth. To make things worse, he couldn't see several of the connections—those had to be done by feel alone.

That might not have been so bad by itself, but Emmett was *right-handed*.

Twice, Clara helped him during a particularly awkward connection.

When the pistol mod finally snapped free, Emmett spit the screwdriver out of his mouth and sighed with relief.

"Not bad," Dr. Venture said. "Four minutes and forty-nine seconds." Emmett stared wide-eyed, and Venture added, "That's what practice is for."

Emmett made several more attempts on the pistol mod before watching Venture demonstrate the process for the impact shield. Shortly after, Emmett began his equally humbling attempts to duplicate the process.

Venture observed the first few attempts, but once Emmett got the pattern down, he walked over to the other monitors to work on other things. Clara stayed beside him, watching intently, offering reminders, commentary, and a hand when Emmett needed it.

"Come on, butterfingers."

"A little to the left—no, your other left."

"No, not that one!"

"Bet you want a third hand mutagen."

As much as her commentary made him groan, Emmett was glad she stayed to help—not just for an extra hand, but because she kept him from getting too frustrated.

Slowly, Emmett got the hang of disconnecting and reconnecting his mods. Soon he had the order memorized and got steadily quicker and more sure of himself. He wouldn't be left-handed any time soon, but he made surprising progress because of the Mutagen-A in his system.

But Emmett quickly saw the limits of his current setup. He could swap out mods outside of the lab, but even with an hour of practice, it still took Emmett almost two minutes to swap them. With enough practice, he might be able to shave a few more seconds off, but even Venture's simulations couldn't get below thirty seconds—

Thirty seconds to disconnect one mod. Another thirty to connect a new one. And that was in ideal conditions.

He would be able to swap mods if he was preparing for a mission and had good intel, but if he got ambushed, he couldn't swap them out on the fly.

Then there was the issue of storage and transport. Even if he developed mods for a hundred different scenarios, what was he going to do, drive around a truck load of spare parts?

By the time Emmett had practiced for an hour, his concentration was beginning to fade. Even Clara had left him and pulled a chair over to the wall monitors.

At first, she had been scrolling through the news, but now she was staring intently at a diagram of the heat sinks. Emmett's glance in her direction became a stare as he realized that particular design was for her exosuit.

Clara cleared her throat loudly. "That doesn't sound like modding, Mr. Mod Superhero."

Emmett dropped the screwdriver, and it clattered on the table. He quickly got back to work. "You're proud of that one. I can tell."

He could just see the edge of Clara's grin.

"So, are you working on something in particular?" Emmett asked.

"Just staring mindlessly at a problem, hoping the answer jumps out at me from the ether."

He smirked. "Does that happen often?" When Clara didn't answer, he added, "You know, it's been a while since we've really worked together on the heat sinks. I can help you."

"No," she replied quickly, turning off the monitor with a wave. "It's late."

Emmett paused to check his phone. It was already past eight.

Late, but not *that* late.

Emmett didn't push it—it almost felt like she was kicking him out. "I, uh, let me just finish this. I should probably be getting back."

Clara stammered, her cheeks flush, and awkward silence settled in between them like sudden, awkward snow.

Before either spoke, Dr. Venture came back into the room and cleared his throat. "I hope I'm not interrupting your work."

Emmett kept his eyes on the last connections as he fixed the impact shield into place.

"Good," Venture continued, "Because I was just about to put in pizza. Is pepperoni alright?"

"Emmett was just leaving," Clara said. She turned and walked out the door. "And I'm not hungry."

Emmett wanted to call after her, but just kept his head down—feeling like he'd missed *something*. He would just finish this and then head out.

Venture shrugged. "More for me then."

When Emmett finished connecting the impact shield, he asked, "Can I have a copy of the schematics?"

Dr. Venture looked over from the wall monitor. "Why?"

Emmett quickly explained how he wanted to swap mods out on the fly. "It's just not possible with the current system."

Venture nodded. "Understandable... TINA, encrypt a copy of the schematics for Emmett's arm and his mods. Import it directly onto his phone." Then to Emmett he said, "You'll be able to access them on your phone and laptop, but nowhere else."

"I understand. What about the other mods, though? Can I take them with me?"

Venture crossed his arms and stared at Emmett. "Are you going to keep them in your backpack?"

Emmett nodded apprehensively. "They're too big to fit in my pocket... Unless you'll lend me a Fast-Response Drone to haul around my stuff."

"Absolutely out of the question." But Venture rubbed his chin in thought. "...For now."

Emmett left a few minutes later and decided to take the bus home. It took him a few minutes before he relaxed fully and set his backpack down beside him. He spent the ride home and the rest of the night poring over the schematics that Venture had given him.

Emmett wasn't sure what time Lock might be home, so he holed up in his room. Most of his work would be done on his laptop anyway, so he didn't need the extra space on the kitchen table.

By midnight, Emmett had come up with four different variations of a quick-connect system. With either, he should be able to swap mods by depressing a lever or two instead of needing tools, and it should take a second or two instead of a minute.

He just needed to figure out which one would be easiest to make and integrate. Which meant Emmett needed to wait until he went back to the lab tomorrow.

Emmett hated waiting.

He finally turned off his computer and laid back in bed, mentally drained.

Lock must have been working late, because he still wasn't home by the time Emmett fell asleep.

Chapter 7

Lock

Lachlan had been ready for a quiet Thursday night in when he got the text:

UNKNOWN 10:36 PM: *Immediate assignment. Report to testing ground.*

So much for that.

Lock jogged the West End streets of Belport, past Gnosis's sprawling headquarters, until he reached a set of unmarked buildings that looked like storage warehouses. He walked between the buildings to a secret doorway. Hidden sensors scanned his tracking chip, and the door slid open.

Lock had been through this process dozens of times over the last few months, but today the three guards that greeted him were on edge. Not only could Lock smell the extra sweat on them, but the guard's hands were trembling. As soon as the guards scanned him psychically, they ushered him inside. Then they proceeded quickly into the flickering lights of the hallway and down the pitted concrete stairs.

The smell of blood grew thicker as they descended.

At least he didn't feel the psychic touch of the guards anymore. They really were focused on something else...

His suspicion was all but confirmed as they bypassed their normal stop at the medical wing and continued deeper into the Gnosis underground. For a moment, Lock methodically considered the possibilities as to why they called him in:

Security job for a client—not likely. New clients were rare and repeat clients contacted him directly.

New client—possible. They would want to meet in a safe location and see what he was capable of. A high-profile client might be enough to put the guards on edge… Doubtful.

Impromptu testing—not likely. Gnosis was a slave to procedure when it came to these things. This possibility went out the window when they skipped the medical wing.

There was one last possibility, and it was confirmed when they came to a second and third group of guards, both situated at a corner of the hallway. These guards wore Gnosis's proprietary light model power armor: Hardened impact plates, actuator enhanced joints, and personal rebreathers. Their rifles were trained down the hall.

Lock's escort said, "Asset is here."

Without looking back, a soldier confirmed, "Target is still in the room."

The escort turned to Lock, and she looked him directly in the eyes for the first time. Her lip trembled even though her words sounded rehearsed.

"Your target is in the lab at the end of the hall. Potential Class three super. Telekinetic and electrical elementalist. Do not attempt communication—their mind is gone. Kill them, quickly.

"A sterilization team is waiting outside the other entrance to the room. Announce when the target is eliminated. Do you understand these instructions?"

Lock pulled off his hoodie and handed it to the guard. Then he rolled his neck, causing pops to echo through the hall.

"Yes."

Then he strode forward with the confidence that only a super possessed.

Lock breathed slowly, feeling his muscles begin to pulse beneath his clothes. He'd always been muscular, but now it felt like every fiber writhed like snakes trying to slip out of his skin. His fingertips grew into a grotesque mix of nails and bone spurs. Lastly, Lock deadened his sense of pain.

He passed the second set of armored guards and saw the single metal door at the end of the hall. Lock knew from experience that the doors were two inches of reinforced steel. They could hold a Class 3 super.

The door was bowed outward. Its frame and surrounding concrete hadn't fared much better. The scent of blood practically poured out of the cracks.

The target—the super—waiting for him probably was mentally wrecked. They probably didn't even realize how close they were to escape.

Lock paused at the door and listened. With his enhanced senses, Lock could just hear quiet, measured breathing...

Their mind might be gone, but not *that* gone.

Lock wrapped his bony and scabbed fingers around the edge of the door, slowly pulling and working it open. The lock squealed in protest, but the door came free. He peeled it open as easily as opening a jar.

He opened it just enough to step through sideways.

Inside were the ruins of what once would've been a lab. Stainless steel medical tables lay in twisted piles along the wall—the bodies of two or maybe three guards were visible beneath them. Cracked monitors hung by their wires and shattered glass covered the floor. Chunks of concrete were missing from the walls. Blood trickled out from the pile of rubble and bodies.

A young man in a bloody hospital gown sat in the middle of the room, clutching his knees to his chest and rocking back and forth. Thin streams of blood trickled from the bodies and across the room, coalescing on the target. He seemed to be absorbing it through his gown and into his skin.

He couldn't have been much older than Lock.

The target looked up at Lock for the first time, eyes hollow and vacant.

Lock stared back, feeling much the same.

In the end, Lock wasn't sure how long he stood like that, or how long he would have stayed like that, because the decision was made for him.

The target's eyes narrowed, and the air in the room shimmered as he let out a burst of telekinetic power.

But Lock was already halfway across the room.

The wave hit him mid-lunge, and Lock felt his muscles spasm like he'd been hit with a cattle prod. A normal human would've folded themselves in half, but Lock's muscles reset a millisecond later, and the sensation was over as quickly as it came.

Even if the blast would've been powerful enough to stun him, momentum would've carried him into the target.

The next instant, Lock's hand was around the man's throat. He looked up at Lock, wide-eyed, and whispered, "Thank you."

Lock snapped his neck with one hand and let the man fall lifeless to the ground. It had been easy—barely any force at all.

"Clear," Lock called out, his voice wavering. He had to concentrate to keep his hand from shaking.

Gnosis agents in full containment gear filed in from the other door. All but one of them wore a tank and carried a sprayer—the psychic confirmed the subject was dead, then the rest of the team set to work.

In a daze, Lock stepped back to the edge of the room and watched.

The first was a flamethrower, so hot that the flames were smokeless. After charring the body, the next agent sprayed the area with carbon dioxide to extinguish the flames. The last agent sprayed bleach over the remains. They all did the same to the rest of the room.

Lock had seen the disinfectant team work before, but this time... Would it be cliche to say that this time felt different? Was it really any different?

He let his sense of pain come back, but his muscles were already healed. The only thing that he felt was the residual heat and the tinge of chemicals in his nose.

Lock didn't *feel* anything. Anything at all.

The three guards in regular uniforms escorted Lock back the way they came, back toward the surface.

But instead of ushering him to the exit, they took him through another series of halls.

Lock followed close behind, but began to look around as he walked. *Something* had changed, and it caused the hair on the back of his neck to stand on end.

Something was wrong.

He thought back to the steps he'd taken on the way down... This was a different path, but that wouldn't set him on edge. The prickly sensation *could* be from a reality warper using their power. He wouldn't put it past Gnosis to have a powerful one on their payroll, especially in their headquarters.

The guards led him to one last door and opened it for him.

Inside was a bare concrete room, some twenty feet square. It was only partially less chipped and stained than some of the other wholesome places in Gnosis underground.

But Lock didn't focus on that or the door locking behind him. He focused on the one businessman standing in the center.

Even at a glance, Lock could tell he was someone high up in Gnosis.

He was tall with long, jet-black hair. The well-tailored suit hid just how gaunt he was, even if the foundation on his cheeks couldn't. Between that and his pale skin he might as well have been a skeleton, but the man exuded the danger of a powerful super.

Slowly, Lock's brain caught up with his senses, and again he felt the prickling sensation on the back of his neck. *He* was what Lock had sensed. And now that Lock was in the room, every fiber of his being screamed at him to *get out*.

Lock did his best not to react.

The man smiled, revealing pointed teeth. He spoke with a breathy voice. "Lachlan Harris. Well done. I expected nothing less."

Lock nodded slightly because he couldn't bring himself to do or say anything else.

The man began to pace back and forth slowly. Again, Lock saw two things: A man carefully considering his next words, and a lion stalking toward its prey.

"Potent... Reliable... Decisive... You're one of our best assets in Belport, and it's time you were rewarded for your effort." He paused and stared at Lock with bloodshot eyes. "I would like to offer you a new line of work."

Up until that moment, Lock's body had been screaming at him to run. But now it was the opposite.

Lock stayed absolutely still and said the one word expected of him because he was absolutely terrified of saying anything else.

"Yes."

Chapter 8

Minor Surgery

Between Emmett's excitement for his quick-connect system and his senioritis, Emmett's Friday classes positively dragged. It took all his willpower to focus on his lectures that morning.

Just two more months' had become Emmett's mantra.

Life after college would be a whole new set of problems, but anything would be better than *this*.

Emmett's first class, Product and Process engineering, ended with Professor Quinn reminding them that their rough schematics and write-ups for their final project were due next week. She took too much pleasure in the reminder—smiling widely behind her comically oversized desk like a movie supervillain. The only thing she was missing was a cat in her lap.

Judging by the faces of the other students as they filed out of class, they all felt similarly: Like movie heroes strapped to a conveyor belt slowly approaching a laser or a bandsaw.

Machine Design passed a little quicker, but not by much, and as soon as it was done, Emmett jogged the rest of the way across Eastside to get to the lab.

Emmett met Clara and Dr. Venture in the hub of section 002, the mechanical wing.

Venture must have seen the barely contained excitement on Emmett's face because he smirked and said, "Alright, alright. Let's see what you came up with."

Emmett asked TINA to put his schematics on the wall monitors. All three of them regarded the schematics as they appeared.

No one spoke, and Emmett grew self-conscious. He must've made a mistake somewhere.

Eventually, Clara ran her hand over her buzzed hair. "You came up with these in one night?"

"Yeah," he said, carefully watching their expressions.

Clara pulled the beanie back over her head. "Not bad."

Emmett scoffed. "Do you even know what you're looking at?"

"Not really, but it looks good."

Meanwhile, Venture scratched the stubble on his chin and glanced intently from one design to the next.

Finally, Venture said, "TINA, overlay schematics of Emmett's arm. Run simulations for ease of integration, mod swap times, structural integrity…"

"I started running simulations when Emmett shared access to the schematics. I have now completed them. Rail system number three is the superior design."

A flash of surprise crossed Venture's face. "You already ran simulations?"

"I assumed you would request them. I've also included scores for future adaptability and system expansion."

"Well, then… Thank you."

"You're welcome."

"…Can you show the simulation results for all four systems?"

"Yes."

Graphs and readouts appeared on *all* the screens—so much that Emmett initially felt overwhelmed by the sheer amount of data. But he relaxed as he took it in; TINA had done a good job of organizing it.

Schematics for each quick connect system hovered at the top, while results of each simulation were listed below. Thankfully, TINA had highlighted the *winning* results for each.

Each of the four systems was superior in one category, which didn't surprise Emmett. He'd designed each system with that in mind—rail system one was the fastest for swapping mods out, while system two was designed with structural integrity in mind. In contrast, system 4 was rated the best for ease of integration, which Emmett hadn't entirely foreseen and decent in several other categories.

Interestingly, rail system three was only rated the best for future adaptability and system expansion. Second fastest in mod swap times, and a slight third in structural integrity. Unfortunately, its final score was abysmal—it would not be easy to integrate into his current arm.

Clara was still looking over the results intently, but Dr. Venture seemed to be thinking of something else entirely.

Finally, Venture asked, "TINA, explain your reasoning for choosing rail system three."

"I have calculated Emmett's future potential as the most important factor. Integration into Emmett's current prosthetic is a onetime difficulty, mitigated by surgical oversight from my system and Dr. Venture's expertise. Once integration is complete, it ceases to be a factor, and so is the least important factor.

"System three's scores in mod swap time and structural integrity are only marginally worse, but suitable. The prosthesis is roughly equivalent to the ratings of a Class Two super. If Emmett manages to grow stronger and surpass Class Two, then he will need a new prosthesis and an entirely new mod system. Until then, his own strength and speed are the limiting factor, not the rail system.

"With those factors accounted for, the best course is to allow the most possible options for mod development. This will allow Emmett to adapt countermeasures for a variety of threats until he is able to use raw power."

When TINA finished, Dr. Venture pushed up his glasses and cleared his throat. "I can see no flaw in your reasoning. Please prepare a guidance simulation for Emmett's surgery."

All of the screens went blank, except for the one showing the design of rail system three.

Emmett stared. This was it—the next step toward becoming *more*.

Clara met his gaze with an enthusiastic thumbs-up.

But as excited as he was, he felt apprehensive, not just of the surgery, but of the uncertainty on Dr. Venture's face.

They stayed in the hub of section 002 for Emmett's surgery, under Dr. Venture's reasoning that he wasn't operating on anything biological. For the second time in two days, the two of them were huddled over the holographic table.

Clara wanted to be present for the event, but she sat on the far side of the room with the news playing silently on the monitor while she scrolled on her phone.

She said the whole process was 'too weird' for her.

Emmett felt much the same way. His right arm was on the table, the skin peeled back and the metal sheathing removed. Two vice grips held his arm in place—one on the wrist and one around the elbow. The impact shield, whip, and concealable pistol sat on a nearby table.

There wasn't any blood, and Dr. Venture had attached diodes around his upper arm to block the pain and pressure sensations, but...

Well, *weird* was an understatement. Emmett couldn't look at his mechanical arm directly for more than a few seconds at a time. He wasn't sure what specifically he couldn't handle—the actuators and gears both looked nothing like a human arm and reminded him *too much* of a human arm. Maybe if Emmett could study it without his stomach turning, he could figure it out.

Either way, it was *his arm* that was peeled open on the table.

Most of the surgery, Emmett followed along by watching the holographic display above the table. Even that was eerie, though.

He felt like a mad science experiment.

...Which, in a way, he was.

Emmett shivered and was glad that his arm was locked in place. Emmett swore he could still feel Dr. Venture poking around in his arm.

Venture glanced at him sideways through his safety goggles, and Emmett forced himself to sit still.

"How's it going over there?" Clara called out.

"Fantastic," Emmett replied. "You should try it sometime."

"No, thanks. I prefer to keep metal on the outside of my skin."

Dr. Venture set aside his current tool and grabbed a tiny vibrating saw.

Emmett swallowed dryly. "Is it too late to get my own exosuit?"

Venture grumbled and leaned closer to his arm. He was starting to cut out something metal, and Emmett couldn't look close enough to figure out what. Instead, Emmett tried to keep talking.

"TINA sure seems to think that I'm going to keep getting stronger."

Venture replied, "You mean you weren't just in here thinking about chopping off your other arm?"

"Gross," Clara muttered.

Emmett smirked. The thought had crossed his mind. "I just didn't expect it."

"Why not?"

"I guess that most supers don't get stronger. They might learn how to use their powers more efficiently, but that doesn't mean they jump a whole power class."

Clara spoke up from across the room. "Some do."

Venture sighed as he worked. "You're both right. Most cases of supers growing stronger are really just them developing new techniques or using their powers more efficiently. It's similar to weight lifting—most early gains aren't from strength, but from the body's central nervous system learning to work cohesively. Though there is quite a bit of evidence to older, more practiced supers becoming stronger over the course of their lifespan, it's not enough to jump from Class One to Class Four or even Three. Then there are some elder creatures, like vampires, that really do get stronger the longer they live...

"There are cases of genuine power increases, though. Gnosis mutagens, for example. Mechanical prosthesis and power armor, or magical weapons and armor. Most magic is unique in that it can be learned. There are old stories of elementalists that sought out places to become more in tune with their element; the old master meditating on top of a mountain—"

"Or in a volcano," Clara added.

Venture chuckled and changed tools. He alternated with screwdriver, pliers, and a miniature hand-held welder to attach the new rails.

Venture continued, "Of course, then there are powers that fundamentally alter a person or disconnect them from who or what they are. Powers like dream surfing, reality manipulation, and shape changing. The more they're used, the more flexible the super becomes... the more they forget who they really are."

"Power comes at a cost." The words tumbled out, and Emmett wasn't quite sure where they'd come from.

But Venture nodded. "Yes. Yes, it does."

As the silence dragged on, Emmett started focusing on his arm again, and subsequently remembered just how much he did not want to focus on it.

"Why were you surprised at TINA running simulations on the rail system before you asked?"

Venture glanced at Emmett, but didn't miss a weld. "TINA is a highly advanced bundle of algorithms. 'Impressive' doesn't do her justice. She can learn and process data about a subject faster than most government A.I.'s...

"But one thing she doesn't do is *do things without my direction.*"

"She has automations, though," Emmett said, tentatively.

"Yes, she does. But who do you think set those up?"

"You did."

Venture nodded in agreement, and Emmett realized that Clara had put down her phone and was listening to their conversation now.

Emmett pushed his luck. "So, what does that mean?"

"I don't know. I've worked with other AIs that spontaneously develop new capabilities based off of their old programming. Similar to a super learning a new technique. The power hasn't changed, it's just a new application."

"But this isn't that?"

Venture sighed. "I don't know. I've been working on someone's arm all afternoon."

Clara stifled a laugh.

Chapter 9

A Night Out

The surgery on Emmett's arm took a little over half an hour.

Even though Dr. Venture hadn't mentioned any risks to his prosthetic, Emmett was still anxious when the metal sheathing was reattached and the pain blocking diodes were removed. He wasn't fully convinced until both he and Venture worked on making the adaptations to his mods.

The tools felt just as dexterous and familiar to Emmett as they had before. Compared to having his arm splayed open, it felt more like engineering.

When they finished, Venture set his tools down on the table and sighed. The hologram hovering above the table winked out. "Well, this is the moment of truth."

Emmett picked up the impact shield and nodded.

Clara walked over to watch, stretching and yawning. "It's about time."

Emmett popped open the compartment in his forearm and slid the rails together. It *clicked* into place, and Emmett felt the artificial nerves connect.

Excitedly, he stood and summoned the shield. Slivers of the shield extended like an accordian, forging the circular shield in a tenth of a second. Though Emmett hadn't used the impact shield nearly as much as the whip, the process of summoning the mod felt as smooth as ever.

"Next!" Clara announced, reflecting his smile.

Disconnecting the mod proved trickier, but Emmett repeated the process several more times, then again with the other two mods. After a few minutes of practice, Emmett had the motion quick enough that he'd almost feel comfortable doing it in combat. *Almost.*

Clara crossed her arms. "You know what's next, right?"

Emmett nodded, already moving to gather up the other mods. "Time to go to the Gray Room."

She scoffed. "Hell no! It's Friday night. Let's go out on the town."

"Clara's right," Venture said, catching them both off guard. "Go enjoy the evening. I insist."

Emmett and Clara shared a glance before bidding Venture good night and walking out of the room.

When the door slid closed behind them, Emmett asked, "He's talking about suiting up and going out right?"

Clara nodded. "Yeah... What else would he be talking about?"

Emmett quickly shook his head, hoping his cheeks weren't as red as they felt. "Suiting up. Yeah. Sure."

The pair went to section 004, the armory. The only place as strange as the Gray Room.

This time, the hubs and hallways mirrored through each section ended in a large open air room several hundred feet in all directions. The overall shape was spherical, but each of the walls were blocky, like the uneven steps of an ancient pyramid, though made of sleek metal alloy.

It almost turned his stomach to stare too long, like an abstract drawing that played tricks on the eye.

Instead, Emmett focused on Clara as they ran across the catwalk and she summoned her exosuit from storage. It *floated* over to the central platform without wires, propulsion, or power of any kind—Emmett still wasn't sure *how* the armory worked and he doubted that he would get a straight answer anytime soon.

The exosuit itself was only a little less impressive. It was sleek and form fitting, with just enough rigidness to suggest that it was armor. The back opened up and

Clara tossed her hoodie and beanie onto the catwalk, then slid in the back of the suit.

Emmett wiggled his metal fingers, suppressing his jealousy. Ever since he was a kid, *Arsenal* had been one of his favorite heroes. That was who Clara reminded him of now—

Which made sense because Clara and a few other heroes had taken the name Arsenal since the original retired.

A Fast-Response drone set down beside Emmett and split open like a giant closet. He set his duffle bag of mods in the lower corner of the drone, then hopped inside, feeling the mesh surround him as the doors closed. The cool, almost moist-feeling material encased his entire body, leaving only a small pocket of air around his mouth and nose.

Emmett tried to control his breathing. Even when he knew what to expect and knew it was for his own protection, he still felt claustrophobic. Still felt trapped.

A moment later, Emmett was surrounded by complete darkness and felt a small lurch as the Fast-Response Drone took off.

TINA's voice came through a moment later to confirm: *"Following exosuit."*

Emmett and Clara set down in the warehouse district, toward the outer limits of the Eastside. Most factories and warehouses out this far weren't in operation; they were either boarded up or completely trashed from supers using the abandoned areas as training.

Despite their recent clash with Porcelain and the unknown super in this same district, it was still the best area in the city to test powers. This was especially true for Class 1 and Class 2 supers who wouldn't be wrecking entire buildings with their fights. Clara had even told him how it wasn't unheard to have friendly brawls with other low-level supers.

Emmett grabbed his bag of mods and hopped out of the drone. Then he followed Clara into the middle floor of the warehouse, stepping over the trash and broken glass littering the floor.

Despite the bulk of Clara's exosuit, she moved in near-complete silence. Emmett did his best to follow her lead.

As they went in, he was thankful for his low-light vision. Despite the trickles of light through boarded up windows, he could see every piece of glass and even read writing on the crumpled up newspaper. The only thing that was really affected was his ability to see color—in low-light the world appeared in shades of gray.

Finally, Clara stopped at a suitable room. From the looks of the broken furniture piled in the corners, it was another office room.

"This place is as good as any," Clara said through her mic. "Let's try out your impact shield."

"You just want to shoot at me."

She grinned. "Maybe."

Before they left, Emmett had defaulted to the whip, so he pulled the new mod out of the duffle bag and changed it out. The impact shield slid into place with a *click*.

"That is *so* much easier than before," Emmett exclaimed.

"You should be proud of it. It was a good design." The earnesty in Clara's voice caught Emmett off guard, but before he could reply, she added, "Think fast."

Clara raised her hand and air shimmered around the palm of her exosuit.

Instinctively, Emmett raised his arm and called the impact shield. It snapped into existence just as Clara fired a kinetic blast at him.

A surge of heat and power slammed into the shield with a hollow *clang*, the force making Emmett skid backward across the floor.

Emmett peered over the top of the shield, cautiously.

Clara stared at him, face unreadable behind her dark helmet. "Not bad... Again!"

They went back and forth in the warehouse, testing the impact shield and the new quick connect system.

The impact shield held up much better than Emmett expected, feeling like an extension of his metal arm. It was even faster to deploy than his whip was, and weathered Clara's kinetic blasts without problem. His metal arm held up fantastically as well. Emmett was afraid to ask just how much power Clara was putting behind each shot, but he was confident that the shield and his arm could hold up against any Class One threats and most Class Two.

The rest of his body was a different story. After a half an hour or so of constant shots from Clara's kinetic blasts, his chest felt sore from where the metal connected to flesh and bone, and the rest of his muscles were tired from bracing against the impacts.

By the time Emmett called for a break, he had a newfound appreciation for the limiters that Dr. Venture built into his arm.

"That's all you got?" Clara asked, with only a hint of a smile in her voice.

Emmett smirked and leaned against one of the decrepit walls of the warehouse. "Some of us don't have an exosuit doing the work for us."

Clara scoffed. "...It's not easy. It takes skill and concentration." It wasn't hard to tell that she was offended.

Emmett winced. "It was a bad joke. Sorry."

Clara nodded, the gesture barely noticeable, and continued looking out through a sliver of the papered over window.

Emmett swapped out the impact shield for the concealable pistol and tried to change the subject. "So if we were just going to practice, why not stay in the Gray Room?"

"You mean you'd rather be in the Gray Room than out here in the ritzy part of Belport?" Humor bled back into her voice and Clara continued, "It feels like hiding, but even being out here in the warehouse district is better than being cooped up in the Gray Room."

Emmett nearly winced again. He'd never really pried about Clara's personal life, and she'd never really hinted about having one. Of course she wouldn't want to be cooped up underground all day.

The lab was awesome to someone that visited, but if their positions were reversed, Emmett would probably take every chance he could get to get some fresh air too.

Clara added, "It feels like hiding."

"The Gray Room?"

She nodded. "Dad told me once that it could do full color, but he—"

Venture's voice came through the comm link. *"Supers inbound."*

Clara stepped back and raised her arms, targeting something on the other side of the window. Through the papered-over glass, Emmett could just make out the silhouette of someone hovering in mid-air.

In a commanding voice, the woman outside said, "This is the Summit of Heroes. Stand down and prepare for questioning."

Chapter 10

Summit of Heroes / Serenity

Emmett stood frozen, staring out the window at the cape hovering just outside.

Clara didn't lower her weapons. "State your names first."

A second shadow rose up beside the first, and Emmett thought he heard a man scoff. But the woman outside replied, "My name is Serenity and—"

The man interrupted, "I am the Ninth Wielder of the magical Ring of Shelok, but you can call me Hunter Nine."

Serenity added, "We're with 3rd Summit segment of Belport. We just want to talk."

Venture's voice came through the comm link. *"Cooperate unless they try to take you in..."* Abruptly his voice degraded into static before cutting off completely.

Hunter Nine said irritatedly, "We've locked communications in the area, failure to comply—"

"As I was saying, cooperate unless they try to take you in. If they do, run."

Hunter Nine muttered, "Our jamming isn't working..."

Serenity raised her voice. "We're coming in to talk. Stay where you are." She said something quietly to her comrade.

Then a giant ethereal hand reached around the bars of the window, breaking the remnants of glass. It wrapped around the bars and pulled. The wall of windows bowed outward, metal frame screeching and glass cracking, before it finally screeched—

Half the wall came free in a spiderweb of metal frame and broken glass. The floating hand released it and let it crash to the street below.

Both Emmett and Clara stared out at the two heroes floating in the air.

Serenity wore a crystalline blue bodysuit and mask, the latter of which was criss-crossed with an intricate geometric design.

Instead of floating, Hunter Nine stood on a misty platform beside the ethereal hand. The eerie conjurations were a stark contrast to the dark Victorian-era outfit and masquerade mask the man wore. Then again, magicians often had eccentric tastes.

Serenity shot her partner a glance of irritation before turning her attention back to Emmett and Clara. "As I was saying, the Summit of Heroes is monitoring this area in response to the events regarding the deceased cape, Porcelain. Do you know anything about that?"

"We don't know anything about that," Clara lied, reluctantly lowering her weapons. "Only what was released publicly about the Champion street attack."

Serenity nodded. "Then you won't mind releasing the seal on your helmet open so that I can confirm your story?"

Emmett's heart skipped a beat. He'd recognized Hunter Nine's description of his magic ring. There were a dozen or so rings forged by the sorcerer, Shelok, and their capabilities were public knowledge. Each gave the bearer the ability to seamlessly make constructs—an ability somewhere between magic and telekinesis. If he was a ninth rank, then he was somewhere between a Class 1 and Class 2 super.

Serenity was the real problem. She was psychic.

But she couldn't read Clara's mind—not through Clara's exosuit.

Clara didn't answer the demand right away, and when she finally did, her voice was firm.

"I refuse."

A flicker of irritation passed over Serenity's lips and she turned to Emmett. "Do you consent—"

"No, he doesn't," Clara said sharply.

Emmett cleared his throat and added, "I know my rights."

A registered psychic couldn't read a person's thoughts without consent—and unless Serenity was a Class 3 or higher, she wouldn't be skilled enough to read

Emmett's thoughts without him *feeling it.* Still, Emmett looked from one cape to the other, suddenly wishing that he had a complete helmet like Clara.

Hunter Nine spoke up, not bothering to temper his irritation. "You either consent now, or you come back to headquarters with us, and *then consent.*"

Serenity shot Hunter Nine a fierce look, but her partner didn't stop.

Clara scoffed. "Sounds like you're close to overstepping."

"Sounds like you're resisting."

Serenity sneered, "Stand down, cape."

Hunter Nine glared at Emmett and Clara. "Choose."

Dr. Venture's voice came through again. *"Don't kill them."*

Clara raised the palms of her exosuit and fired. Shockwaves from her kinetic blasts shook the room. Each exploded harmlessly in front of the Summit capes. Hunter Nine's ethereal hand widened to encompass the entire window, and something else shimmered with blue power—Serenity adding her own reinforcement to the magic wall.

Shit. So Serenity was a psychic *and* a telekinetic.

Emmett resisted the urge to glance at his bag of mods on the floor. It was only a few feet away. Right now, he had his concealable pistol equipped, but if Clara's blasts couldn't punch through, then his pistol probably wouldn't either. The impact shield was probably worthless, but if he could switch to his whip...

He'd only get one chance—

As soon as the thought crossed his mind, his entire body locked up. He hadn't even turned to look at the bag. *Couldn't* turn to look at it. He could barely move his eyes. Just breathing took all his concentration.

Serenity stared at him knowingly. "Stand down, and no harm will come to you."

She had read his mind—or at least been ready for him—and there had been nothing Emmett could do.

Clara wasn't faring any better. Through the swirls of dust and impact, the two capes were completely untouched.

Suddenly, the ethereal fist grew solid and swept forward into a punch, slamming into Clara and knocking her backward through the wall. Emmet would've winced at the first crunch—*or the second*—but he couldn't even do that.

"Wait—"

Hunter cut his partner off. "Just read his mind and be done with it!" He set down on the floor and strode after Clara through the wreckage.

Serenity stayed hovering outside. She shook her head and then stared at Emmett, as if seriously considering going outside protocol. More shots and impacts echoed from the other side of the building.

Emmett wanted to turn and run. Wanted to shake his head and refuse, or try to talk to her and reason with her. But there was nothing he could...

Even though Emmett's arms were down at his side, he realized that he *could still move* the fingers of his prosthetic arm. And it wasn't just that—as the moment dragged on, Emmett realized he could still move *his entire prosthetic arm.*

Serenity stared at him, and then Emmett felt the subtle touch of a psychic crawling into his mind, like fingertips crawling over his scalp.

With mechanical speed, Emmett raised his arm, the forearm compartment opening to reveal the barrel of the pistol. Emmett fired, the crack of the shot echoing through the warehouse. The sledgehammer round hit Serenity square in the chest, and she tumbled out of the air.

The force of the shot knocked Emmett off balance, but Serenity's hold over him disappeared, and Emmett only stumbled a little.

Instead of standing in shock, he stooped down to his bag and swapped the pistol for his whip. Then Emmett slung the bag over his shoulders and stepped cautiously through the Clara-sized hole in the wall.

She'd actually gone through two walls—through the second, Emmett could just make out a whirlwind of action. Clara fired kinetic blasts repeatedly and used her thrusters to maneuver out of the way of ether spikes and a colossal fist. Both sides seemed evenly matched.

Emmett paused just outside of the wall and waited for his chance.

The battle turned, and suddenly, Hunter Nine was in front of the opening. Emmett lashed out with his whip, grabbed the cape's foot and pulled. Hunter Nine face-planted, and before he could roll over to defend himself, Clara hit him with a kinetic blast.

Hunter Nine groaned and curled up into a ball. That time, Emmett winced.

"Come on!" Clara shouted.

Emmett ran into the decimated room, and Clara blasted another hole, this time in the outside wall. A Fast-Response Drone was already open and waiting.

Emmett tossed a smoke pellet behind him for good measure, then jumped in and felt the drone close around him. A moment later, they were rocketing away.

TINA's voice came through. *"The Summit's drones are attempting to follow. Cloaking engaged. Alternate route suggested."*

"Copy that," Clara replied. "We'll take the long way home."

"Can they follow us?" Emmett asked.

Clara chuckled. "They couldn't even jam our comms."

Serenity picked herself up from the pavement. She'd managed to telekinetically cushion her fall, but everything hurt. Most of all, her chest...

She clutched where she'd been shot, but there wasn't any blood or wound. It must've been a non-lethal round. For that, she was grateful.

She levitated back up to the warehouse, but it was already quiet and covered in smoke; the battle was already over.

Serenity called out to Hunter, and immediately regretted it. The pain in her chest spiked when she took a deep breath. She heard her partner groaning on the other side of the warehouse. A moment later, a giant hand waved away the smoke to reveal Hunter—doubled over on the floor and just starting to stand. He looked exactly how she felt.

"Bastards," he winced.

Serenity ignored him. "Are you bleeding?"

Hunter pulled away from her. "No. I don't know what it was, but they'll pay."

Serenity had half a mind to call him out on his blunder, that they'd only gotten into a fight because of his vendetta and his ego. But she held her tongue.

With any luck, the Summit would see this failure as an opportunity to finally split them up. Then someone else would have to deal with him.

Hunter turned suddenly, accusation in his voice. "What happened to you? I almost had the bitch, and her accomplice attacked me from behind."

"He was a cyborg," Serenity said. She quickly recounted what happened to Hunter, describing how the super's arm opened up and shot her with a nonlethal round.

Serenity had known something was off about the super, but she'd never faced a cyborg before. She knew about them in theory, but seeing the mechanical limb act independently was another thing entirely.

Hunter grumbled. "Goddamn tinjob. People just buy power nowadays." He kicked at a piece of rubble, sending it tumbling through the hole in the wall. "Maybe next time, don't give masks the benefit of the doubt. They're worse than villains."

Serenity grit her teeth and turned to walk away, ignoring that Hunter's ring wasn't that different from the mechanical enhancements he loathed. There wasn't any use debating a man who used slurs as flagrantly as her partner did.

"Where are you going?" Hunter called after her.

"Debriefing at base."

She flew away, ignoring Hunter's muttering. She could guess what he was saying under his breath.

Chapter 11

Serenity

Serenity flew back to Summit station number three, an unmarked mid-sized office building on the upper end of Belport's Eastside. She didn't know if Hunter was behind her. She didn't really care.

She needed to meet with her superior officer.

Even as Serenity flew, she was reaching out via psychic link. With any luck, she could meet with Ryder before Hunter asked too many questions.

The scanning system read her biosignature and a hidden door opened on the third level. Serenity floated in, not bothering to greet the curious support staff. They all perked up from their workstations, looking little different from any other office in Belport. Serenity walked right past them without answering their questions. She walked down to the second floor and to the innermost room of the building.

To the most secure room in the section headquarters.

Scans silently confirmed her identity before the doors slid open. It was little more than a conference room, albeit one with a giant mass of resonance crystal sitting on the center table. It rose up roughly three feet off the table like a half knocked-over sandcastle and shimmered with intrinsic light—a cellphone for psychics.

Serenity sat down in the first chair she came to, took a deep breath, and tried to collect her thoughts before calling her boss.

A moment later, the head and shoulders of Ryder appeared in front of the crystal like a hologram, except that he was actually displayed in her mind's eye.

He was a middle-aged super who dressed the part of upper management, who had rough, dark skin and a brilliant smile. Once, Serenity had found him quite attractive, but that was before he'd delved into her mind as part of her Summit training.

"Tell me, Serenity," he said, voice coming through warmly, "what do you need to confess at this hour?"

She told him about the night's patrol with Hunter Nine and their run-in with the two unnamed supers—the cyborg and the girl wearing powered armor. Ryder listened intently, though he kept his expression as neutral as a machine.

When she finished, Ryder spoke calmly. "Not only did you go off protocol, you failed to bring in your quarry... But I suspect that's not all you have to tell me. What else do you need to confess?"

Serenity's voice wavered as she spoke. "I scanned the cyborg's thoughts without his permission."

"Ah, I see. And what did you find?"

"I discovered his name and the names of his accomplices."

"Go on."

"Emmett Laraway. Clara Venture, and Dr. Venture."

"I see..."

There was a knock at the door behind Serenity, and a moment later, Hunter Nine requested access. In the display, Ryder waved a hand and granted him access. Serenity tried not to roll her eyes.

There was a moment of pause as the crystal automatically extended the view of their boss to the new viewer.

"Ryder, sir," Hunter hesitated, "I take it that Serenity has already briefed you?"

"Yes," Ryder said calmly.

"...Is there anything that I've missed? I assumed that Serenity would wait for me before contacting you."

"There is nothing that I require you for, Hunter Nine. You may take your leave now."

Serenity could *hear* the fabric of Hunter's gloves as he clenched his hands. Hunter said, "Sir, these weren't run-of-the-mill masks. To have technology like that—they bypassed our jamming equipment. They had stealth capabilities that exceeded our tracking! There can't be that many artificers with those kinds of capabilities."

Serenity forced herself to breathe slowly and deeply. Despite her annoyance, Ryder didn't so much as blink.

"Your concerns have been logged, Hunter Nine. Now, if that is all, Serenity still needs her debriefing."

Out of the corner of her eye, Serenity saw Hunter glance down at her. "You scanned the tinjob? What did you find—"

"That will be all, Hunter Nine."

But Hunter didn't look at his superior. He was still looking down at Serenity. Finally, her partner turned and stormed out of the room, leaving her alone—physically, at least.

"I apologize for my partner, sir," she said. It was a reflex that she was tired of repeating. "Sir..."

The twinge of annoyance in Ryder's voice was replaced with his normal, calm demeanor. "Ask your question, Serenity."

"Hunter is right about their capabilities. If the Summit of Heroes is going to take appropriate measures, I would like to be involved, even if Hunter isn't."

Ryder was silent for a moment, as if considering what he was going to say. "The Summit is aware of Mr. Laraway and the Ventures, but their next steps are classified. Neither you—or I—are privy to that information."

Serenity strained to feel any hidden meaning layered in her boss's words, but his mind was as walled-off as the rest of him.

"What about the Porcelain investigation, sir?"

"Continue as directed. Bring back any information you gather. Now, if that's all, prepare for your debriefing."

Serenity hesitated only a moment before leaning forward and placing her hand on the crystal.

Psychics were one of the Summit's most powerful assets. They were also one of its most vulnerable points of attack. When a low level psychic garnered information during a mission, they were to bring that information directly back to the nearest station. They were supposed to share said information with their superior officer and no one else.

After that, it was routine for that psychic to have their mind wiped. Not of everything, thankfully. Only those pertinent secrets.

The resonance crystal flared with light as Ryder extended his power through it. To Serenity, the crystal grew warm to the touch, then the sensation crawled up her arm and around her skull. It was almost pleasant, except for the anticipation of what happened next.

Serenity tried to relax and focused on the names:

Emmett Laraway. Clara Venture. Dr. Venture.

A single spike of power hit Serenity's brain, something between a jolt of electricity and a stabbing headache. It made her entire body flinch and she had to focus to keep her hand on the crystal.

It's only three names, Serenity told herself. *It's only three names.*

Then one more flash of pain, and it was over.

Even though the pain was gone, the sheer intensity of it left many a psychic reeling. Serenity was no exception. Ryder continued speaking as she recovered, and it was a struggle to focus on her superior's words.

At least it was only... Serenity struggled to remember before finally accepting the erasure. At least it was over.

"Debriefing complete," Ryder acknowledged. "Continue your patrols of the warehouse district and report any further developments on the death of Porcelain or details about the Champion street attack. Bring any and all information to me. You are dismissed."

Serenity nodded and felt the connection sever. She massaged her temples feebly through her mask, then left.

Hunter Nine was pacing just outside the door and turned to confront her. "It's—it's all gone, isn't it?"

"You know it is," Serenity said, trying to walk around him.

Hunter stepped in front of her, lips curled into a sneer under his masquerade mask. "What was it?"

Serenity stared back at him, trying not to show weakness, but between the pain, the aftereffects of the debriefing, and her partner looming over her, Serenity's chest felt tight. She didn't have to read Hunter's mind to know how angry he was.

"I don't remember."

"Bullshit."

"You know how it works."

Hunter scoffed. "Yeah, it's so fucking horrible, so painful... Yeah, you remember something."

"I don't know. It was something small... A name, maybe." She hoped it would placate him—

Instead, Hunter whirled around and raised his voice. "A name! Do you know what I could've done with a name? We could find that tinjob *tomorrow*. First you let him get the jump on you, and then run off to Ryder—"

"Stop, Hunter! Just stop. You know I can't tell you. I'm not going to break protocol just because this is personal."

Hunter Nine glared at her, Somehow his silence was even more menacing.

"Right, you're completely right," Hunter said, holding up his hands in defeat. "You psychics and your protocol... I don't expect you to understand. You weren't there that night on Champion street. You don't know the type of people—the type of supers that we're dealing with. You don't. Ryder doesn't. But I do.

"Maybe the tinjob and the artificer were there, maybe they weren't. But *we* don't know, now do we? Ryder's going to give our lead to some other team... Fuck it, it's too late now."

Hunter paused and glared at Serenity again. "Next time, you should tell me. Or I'll wring the answer out of them myself." He stalked off, leaving Serenity alone in the hall.

She leaned against the wall, closed her eyes, and rubbed her arms. *It was over,* Serenity told herself.

There was nothing else to do but kill time until the next patrol. A part of her hoped that her and Hunter wouldn't run into those masks again, for *their* sake. Hunter had always been an asshole, but now he was coming unhinged.

Worst of all, Serenity wasn't even sure she could stop Hunter if she needed to. Even if she used her power to freeze him, Hunter's magic would be unaffected—just like that cyborg's prosthetic arm.

And no matter how many times she brought her concerns to Ryder and the Summit, they didn't do anything proactive about Hunter. Then again, they were always good at cleaning up messes after the fact. Not so much preventing them.

Serenity sighed and tried to calm herself. There was nothing she could do right now.

At least it was over.

Chapter 12

Evasion Successful

"*Evasion successful,*" TINA announced.

Within the cocoon of the Fast-Response Drone, Emmett breathed a sigh of relief. The rumbling around him slowed as the drone entered the tunnels beneath Belport. Soon it stopped and opened up on the catwalk of the armory. Emmett hopped out and watched Clara do the same.

Clara groaned and stretched her arms over her head. "That sucked!" Emmett nodded, reflexively glancing away as her bodysuit was stretched tight.

He didn't need the reminder. Their near-loss was fresh in his mind—as was Serenity's psychic power. Of all the powers he had gone up against so far, that was easily one of his least favorite.

"Thanks for helping me out back there," Clara said, slapping Emmett on the back. "I could've punched through his magic defenses eventually, but I was worried that if I did his body wouldn't fare as well.. the building, too."

Emmett chuckled at that. "That's annoying—pulling your punches so you don't hurt someone or bring the building down on top of them. Thanks, too, I think. I'd rather not be under a building—"

"Dr. Venture is waiting for you in the section 002 hub."

Clara grabbed her hoodie and beanie off the catwalk and shrugged. "Better not keep the old man waiting."

When they got to the testing hub of the mechanical wing, Dr. Venture was staring at the wall monitors. He was replaying drone footage of Emmett and Clara's fight with Serenity and Hunter Nine. Beside the video feeds, he'd pulled up dossiers of both the capes. Life size photos of their head and shoulders stared back.

Hunter Nine looked just as intense as Emmett remembered.

Dr. Venture waited expectantly, hands clasped behind his back. Emmett and Clara walked over to him.

"You were bound to run into the Summit eventually. This just moves up our timeline."

"What was with those guys?" Clara asked, crossing her arms and glaring at the screens.

Emmett said, "I'm not one hundred percent on the Summit's protocol, but *that* wasn't it."

Venture nodded. "From the looks of it, Serenity knew that her partner was taking things too far. Unfortunately, that didn't make a difference."

Emmett asked, "You said not to get taken in. Should we have cooperated?"

"No," Clara replied, sternly.

Venture sighed. "I should've specified. We do not cooperate with psychics. Their mind reading techniques are rarely as subtle as they claim, and we have secrets I'd prefer to keep. That's why Clara didn't stand down."

"Besides," she added, "there was no way I was getting taken in by that Hunter guy."

Emmett mulled over their situation—caught between the Summit of Heroes, Gnosis, and unknown supers. He almost jokingly asked if life was always this complicated as a super, but Venture spoke up.

"This is as good a learning experience as any, so let's talk about what happened. Clara, what went wrong?"

Clara crossed her arms, almost as if she was hiding beneath her oversized hoodie. "I had trouble sizing up Hunter Nine's defenses and physical capabilities. I didn't want to overcorrect and risk injuring a member of the Summit."

Venture nodded slightly. "A necessary precaution. And yet another reason why I want you to have *other* countermeasures onboard your suit."

Clara grumbled, but nodded.

"Emmett, thoughts?"

"Their psychic locked me down easily. The only reason I broke out is because she didn't realize I had a prosthetic... How does that work, anyway?"

"You mean why she couldn't psychically freeze your arm? What do you think?"

Emmett had been over it in his head on the way back to the lab, and he wasn't sure. He shrugged. "Somehow, her psychic power only affects the human body and not anything mechanical."

Venture turned and regarded Emmett. "You're correct, and you've stumbled on one of the basic laws of power interaction. The trinity in question are psychics, magic, and technology." He held up three fingers for emphasis. "All three can affect biological matter, but rarely can they affect one another. Most psychics can't control computers or magic artifacts. Magic can't usually block psychic power or affect technology, and so on. Of course, there are caveats and other powers at play, but that's a general rule."

Emmett regarded the display and dossier of Serenity. "Psychics can't affect technology, but tech can't affect them either... So, it just cancels out."

That was good to know, but how useful could it possibly be? ...But Venture didn't say that they couldn't affect each other *at all*. He said *'most'*...

Venture looked at Emmett out of the corner of his eye. "I know what you're thinking, and yes. There is some overlap between the three categories—as far as we're concerned, there are ways for tech to either replicate or subjugate the other two. How do you think I rose through the ranks?"

"When do we start?" Emmett asked, only half-joking.

Venture laughed heartily. "Not tonight. At your level, there's very few psychics and artifact wielders powerful enough for you to care about. I've got some ideas for you to work on, but we've got more pressing concerns. If you climb to Class Three, we'll revisit this discussion."

Both Clara and Dr. Venture excused themselves, presumably to talk about countermeasures for her to add to her suit... Or to talk about details that Emmett wasn't privy to yet.

He stayed in the hub of the mechanical wing, hunched over the holographic table and flipping through schematics. Venture had granted him access to the system under the reasoning that Emmett should lie low for the rest of Friday night and head home during daylight tomorrow.

Emmett didn't mind. He had some classwork, but it wasn't due until Monday.

He was more put off about being excluded from the conversation. Frustration welled up in his gut, not from the exclusion, but at himself for minding *at all*.

Wasn't he doing the exact same thing to his family and to Lock? Emmett had walled them off... What was one more brick? Frustration bubbled inside him, and worst of all, it was terribly familiar. Walling himself wasn't something new—placing the bricks came easily.

Looking back, Emmett had always been a reserved, quiet kid. It had only been since getting into college that he'd even started to come out of his shell. He'd only just started taking down some of those old walls... Now he was putting more up, even faster than before.

As his thoughts got away from him, Emmett flicked through schematics. They were all basic—little more than outlines—but Emmett wasn't paying attention to them, anyway.

Some of the older supers, those rooted in myth and magic, talked about fate as if it was something real and tangible. Talked about prophecy as if it was inescapable. Even if there was such a thing as free will, running from your fate usually resulted in damnation.

Emmett didn't believe in fate explicitly, but it was hard to argue with it. Emmett had been building brick walls around himself for his entire life... It felt impossible to stop.

As impossible as trying to stop the world from turning.

Emmett leaned over the table, hands clenched together in silent frustration—until his human hand ached from the difference in force. He set his hands down on the table and forced himself to breathe slowly.

Finally, he got up and paced around the room, turning from the holographic table to the wall monitors. Dossiers of Serenity and Hunter Nine still hung lifeless on the screens. Instead, he thought back to his last encounter with a new super.

"TINA, do I have access to drone footage from Sunday night's encounter?"

"Yes. Would you like me to replay it?"

"Yes. Start from just before Porcelain's death."

TINA minimized the prior displays and replaced them with several drone feeds. Footage ran in real time, feeds automatically minimizing or appearing to keep Emmett and Porcelain on the screen.

Emmett watched himself run away with Porcelain. Watched as the unknown super weathered a barrage from Clara's exosuit and a dozen Fast-Response Drones without flinching. Interestingly enough, it looked like he had been mildly inconvenienced by Emmett's noise makers and the smoke pellets.

Soon, the feeds came to the moment when the unknown super cornered Emmett and Porcelain.

On the feed, Porcelain turned and grabbed Emmett, putting him in a choke-hold.

Porcelain: *You were there the night I was poisoned.*

The unknown super flinched.

Emmett had been meaning to watch the rest of the encounter to make sure he hadn't missed anything. For some reason, he'd kept coming back to that moment—seeing his enemy flinch. Emmett had thought that it had been because Porcelain had known something about the super. Not just that the guy was there that night on Champion street, but maybe something identifying about him.

But Emmett hadn't been entirely convinced, and now that Emmett saw the scene play out from the outside, he knew why...

The super hadn't flinched because of what Porcelain said. He'd flinched *when Porcelain took Emmett hostage.*

Emmett watched the scene on a loop to be sure and kept asking *why*.

Had the super been afraid of Porcelain? Even though he clearly outmatched her, maybe he wasn't completely immune to her powers... Maybe she'd simply done something unexpected and it caught the unknown super off guard...

At first, Emmett shook his head in disbelief, but then he watched the video of the rest of the encounter, all the way up until after Porcelain's death.

On the feed, the unknown super still had Emmett by the throat.

Unknown: *I'm not your enemy.*
Emmett: *It doesn't feel that way.*
Unknown: *It doesn't matter. I'm not your enemy. but don't cross Gnosis.*

Maybe the super had been under orders not to harm anyone but Porcelain... So far, that fit better than Emmett's other theories. It would explain why both Clara and Emmett had been allowed to survive.

Unknown: *I'm not your enemy.*

There was one more theory, and it was the dumbest one yet: The unknown super was someone that Emmett knew.

It was ridiculous. Emmett had only met a handful of supers outside of Clara and Dr. Venture. Athena was out, and that left Zanté, Green Mask, and Feedback... Yeah, even if they were playing 3D chess and hiding their true strength, they wouldn't go all *'I'm not your enemy'.*

Finally, Emmett turned off the feeds and went back to the holographic table with newfound resolve. He wasn't frustrated anymore—just baffled.

But that was easier to work with.

Emmett worked at the lab long into that Friday night.

By the time Clara came back around to the testing hub of section 002, Emmett was having trouble keeping his eyes open. He'd been hunched over the center table, staring intently at holograms of sonic grenades and a sonic blaster mod, like the kind they'd used against Porcelain to stop her from duplicating.

Emmett glanced up at her, and Clara just chuckled. "Thought I'd find you here."

Clara pulled a chair over and sat next to him at the table. She was half-hidden under her baggy hoodie and looked as tired as he felt.

She squinted her eyes at the holograms. "Sonic grenades and a sonic blaster?"

"I'm trying to figure out which to use. Your dad already had designs, so I just tweaked them and toned them down a bit."

"Why?"

Emmett chuckled. "The noise makers have been useful so far, but these are something else. I don't want to blow out my own eardrums. The original plans were like twice as loud as a jet engine and meant to stun Class four supers... What's so funny?"

"Nothing. Just interesting what Dad gave you access to."

"Anyway, I toned it down to something that I can actually use."

"You over-corrected."

Emmett's mouth hung open for a moment. "Huh?"

Clara pointed to the two designs. "These may seem like upgraded noise makers, but they're not the same. These are *directional*. The sonic weapon is only audible in the direction you point it, and the grenades are only audible within a certain range—kind of like my suit's concussive discharge ability."

"Oh..."

"Yeah, so you could use both designs. Use grenades as a distraction if you're trying to escape or to incapacitate half a group of enemies while you fight the rest. Then keep the sonic weapon as your trump card, and jack it up to something that would mess up a Class three super. Either way, you won't have to be on the receiving end of the weapons."

Emmett sighed. She did have a point... "But if I'm fighting a Class three super, I won't be able to use my arm at all. That basically means I'm fighting as a Class one."

Clara raised her eyebrows at him. "First of all, if you're fighting a Class three super by yourself, something has already gone majorly wrong. Second, you could always modify it so you can hold it in your regular hand and still fight with your mechanical arm. It might not be as secure, but it's doable. But most importantly, if we're in that situation, *I'm* your weapon."

"The sonic won't affect you?"

Clara shook her head. "The suits automatically dampen dangerous sounds. Don't get me wrong, I'll still hear it and the sound is *annoying*, but you won't have to worry about me."

"Alright, alright. But if sonics are so good, why don't you use them?"

Clara shrugged. "They don't integrate well... Honestly, I probably should have them as a backup. But now I've got you." She knocked her shoulder against his for emphasis, then immediately groaned. "I forgot which shoulder that was!"

They both shared a laugh and Emmett felt himself relax.

Suddenly, Clara grabbed his arm and pulled Emmett to his feet. "Come on. There's a new episode of *Full Throttle Heart* out, and you've done enough work."

A small part of Emmett wanted to protest, but he left it behind as they jogged through the lab to the living quarters in section 001.

Full Throttle Heart

Forgotten Ruins

[Theme Song — "Hātofurusurottoru" by Gunpowder Audition — *Full Throttle Heart*, season 1]
[Montage of Truck-kun fighting the Undead Legions of Liquid Shadow]

We spend our days dreaming
—Stirring in our sleep
—Driving through our lives!
Full of octane gas
—Open throttle (we're gonna crash!)
—Can't stop this feeling (in my heart)
Fiercest, only, auto-kun... Truck-kun (Truck-kun!)
Fiercest, only, auto-kun... Truck-kun (Truck-kun!)
Full of octane gas
—Open throttle (we're gonna last!)
—Can't stop this feeling (in my heart)
Approaching certain victory
—Fight the power (unleash the power!)
—Drown out all the cheering fans
—Defeat evil that controls the land

[A beautiful sunrise trickles through the ancient forest. The calm rumble of Truck-kun's engine grows louder. A truck emerges valiantly from the treeline.]

Truck-kun drove along at a leisurely pace, navigating through towering trees and long-forgotten meadows. It had traveled for three days, searching not just for the edge of the forest, but for a way home.

A way back to Joe and the real world.

High atop Truck-kun's cab, Al the bluebird rustled his feathers. "I'm telling you, kid—I've lived in this forest for three years, and I've never heard of anyone named Joe."

So far, Al had served both as a guide and as Truck-kun's only friend in this strange world. It was thankful for the company, even if Al's voice was as rough as sandpaper and broken glass.

Truck-kun rumbled and changed the subject. "How much longer until we reach the next ruins?"

Al coughed, not bothering to cover its beak. "Not long now."

For the last two days and two nights, they'd been searching for ruins in the ancient forest. There were rumors of fey and demons that granted wishes. Al thought the ruins would be the best place to look for them.

Al's singing voice was even more horrible than his speaking voice, and magic was his only hope of getting better. With any luck, a fey or a demon could help him.

But if they could help Al, then maybe they could also help Truck-kun get back home.

[A few minutes later, the pair find the ruins. A stone step pyramid sits in the middle of crumbling obelisks. Vines thread through cracks in the stone.

[When Truck-kun stops in front of the pyramid and its engine quiets, the world becomes absolutely still.]

Truck-kun said reverently, "This place is ancient and holy. Do you see the trees?"

"Yeah," Al whispered.

"The stones are even older. Do you see how the bark has grown around the stones?"

Al whistled in awe—it sounded like radio static. "So, uh, what do we do?"

Truck-kun called out, "Is there anyone here? We come in peace."

Al flitted over to the nearest branch and pooped down the side of the tree. Truck-kun nearly reprimanded the bluebird for desecrating a holy site, but it was better the tree than on Truck-kun's cab again.

A moment later, a large red woman with ornate horns and giant bat wings stepped out from behind the pyramid. Her skin glistened and her outfit was far too tight, reminding Truck-kun of a scandalous billboard ad or a woman dressed up as a demon on Halloween.

Though she wasn't as imposing as the dire bear, a different kind of threat radiated from the demon... Truck-kun kept its parking brake on, ready to transform at a moment's notice. Meanwhile, Al's beak dropped open and drool dripped from the corner of his mouth—probably out of fear for his life.

"Who dares disturb—" She stopped short when she laid eyes on Truck-kun. "Who and what are you?"

"I am Truck-kun." As it spoke, its deep voice sent a rumble through the ruins that traveled into the surrounding forest.

The demon sauntered closer, leaning on a broken column for support. "And just where are you from Truck-kun? You don't look like you belong in this hallowed forest, and you don't look like any demon I've ever seen."

"I'm from Earth."

"Earth..." she said, her eyes wandering over Truck-kun's prodigious frame. "Do all Earth men have such impressive *stature?*"

"No. Most Earth men are many times smaller than I. I can transport twenty in my cargo compartment."

The demon pouted. "That's too bad. My sisters and I are always looking for mortals to tempt and torment, and a *select* few to—"

"SIGN ME UP!" Al croaked.

The demon recoiled from the excited and gratingly voiced bluebird. At first, she seemed merely startled, but as Al continued speaking, she recoiled further from him.

"I've searched all of my short life for a demon like you. My soul may be small and shriveled, but every centimeter of it is yours."

Al fluttered over eagerly, but the demon rebuked him with a wave of her hand. Something invisible bound Al's wings and he floated harmlessly back to his branch.

He wriggled against the restraints and whistled an excited note. "Alright, a little faster than I wanted, but you're not scaring me!"

Truck-kun watched the exchange intently. There was something more to how quickly the demon turned Al away. It seemed like she wasn't just annoyed or repulsed by his advances... It was almost like she was afraid.

Like Al's voice held an intrinsic and mystical power against demonkind.

The demon shuddered and turned back to Truck-kun. "Now that's over with, you and I can get better acquainted. My name is Lilithandra Ozoth Gallmokas Mol'gok Giglanach Beezelbub, but my friends call me Lilith."

Her final words became a purr that was completely lost on Truck-kun, for he was pure, single-minded, and dense as steel.

"Lilith, we've journeyed night and day to find your ruins. We need your help."

The demon waited, hanging on Truck-kun's every word.

"Can you help restore Al's voice to its former glory?"

Lilith paused, clearing expecting something different. She looked at the bound bluebird, her face twitching with uncertainty.

Meanwhile, Al shook against his restraints eagerly. "What do you say, sugar wings?"

Lilith glanced back to Truck-kun and sighed. When she looked at Al again, her eyes flashed red with fire. Soon her entire body was covered in billowing flames that threatened to catch the canopy above. Lilith's voice deepened and echoed like she was speaking from within a cave.

"You who shall turn to fading memories and dust seek a blessing of voice. You ask this of the tainted and undying. This dark goddess has seen the depths of your soul

and found you wanting. You shall receive no blessing, and you should give thanks that you will leave with your lives!"

As Lilith spoke, Truth-kun felt a stirring deep within its engine—within its heart. Truck-kun shifted form.

[Cue stylized view of Truck-kun transforming from its normal truck form to its truck warrior form.]

Truck-kun's frame and wheelbase shifted, its wheels rearranging beneath him like feet and legs. Its cab rose up, turning into a torso. Its storage box unfolded, sheathing its limbs in armor plates. In moments, Truck-kun towered over the demon and was girded for battle.

Lilith turned and took in the sight of Truck-kun's new form. Immediately, the flames around her faded, and she walked over to the warrior.

Again, Truck-kun felt *something...* but it wasn't sure that she was dangerous. Truck-kun stayed transformed, but lowered its guard.

Al grumbled hoarsely, "So, is that a *no?*"

"I apologize," Lilith said, cautiously approaching Truck-kun. She ran her fingertips over the steel plates of its arm. "I get carried away when dealing with unworthy mortals. I'm afraid I can't help your friend, but... Are you sure there's nothing that I can do for you, Truck-kun?"

"I'm sorry, Lilith, but if you cannot help Al, then we must be going. I have a feeling that our journey is only just beginning, and I cannot linger."

Al croaked, "Lilith, baby, before we go—Truck-dude is spoken for, but you can bring all that over here."

Lilith's eyes widened in surprise and she stepped backward. "Is this true, Truck-kun? Does this mistake of nature speak the truth?"

"I have to get back home to Earth. Back to Joe."

Her eyes moistened. "I should've known that a warrior such as yourself would have a betrothed waiting for them."

Truck-kun grumbled in confusion. Joe wasn't Truck-kun's betrothed—theirs was a far deeper commitment. It wasn't important, but Truck-kun felt the need to correct her.

"Lilith—"

"Say no more Truck-kun," Lilith replied, bringing her hand to her forehead as if she might faint. "I cannot bear to think of it any longer. Merely hearing your voice tugs at the empty space where my heart should be."

"Very well." Truck-kun transformed back into its truck form. "Al, come with me."

Lilith flicked her wrist, and the invisible bonds released.

Al ruffled shivered, ruffling his feathers. "Thanks Lilith, baby. I'll be back, just you wait. I'll have a brand-spanking new voice that'll knock you off your feet!"

Lilith rolled her eyes, but Al was already flying over to his ally.

The pair turned, ready to drive off into the forest and continue their search for someone who could mend Al's dreadful voice.

Lilith called after them, "Truck-kun... have you always had that package?"

Truck-kun slammed on its brakes and turned to face the demon.

Lilith smirked and put her hands on her hips. "That box in your cargo compartment... You haven't even opened it. You completely forgot about it, didn't you?"

Al asked, "What's she talking about, Truck-dude?"

Carefully, Truck-kun opened its cargo compartment and raised the bed so that the container would slide out gently onto the ground. Then it turned around to examine it.

The box hummed with power.

[Commercial Break]

"Are you ready to GET ISEKAI'D?!"

[Quick Montage of people getting hit by trucks.]

"Don't wait to get hit by a truck! Download the *Full Throttle Heart* idle card battling MMORPG today!"

[Intense Montage of people tapping their phones while a symphony of truck horns plays the *Full Throttle Heart* theme from season one, "Hātofurusurottoru" by Gunpowder Audition.]

"Don't get left behind on Earth! Join the full throttle revolution today!"

Chapter 13

Lock

The Dionysus Club pulsed with music and strobe lights. The dance floor in the center pit undulated like waves, while other patrons watched from the bar or from tables and chairs around the outside. All around was a bastardized mix of industrial decor, purple neon, and palm trees.

Lock prowled the perimeter of the dance floor, scanning the crowd and listening to the chatter of security in his earpiece. All the while, he did his best to ignore the haze of boys, sweat, and cologne that his enhanced smell picked up. It was late Friday night—almost three in the morning—and he was counting down until the end of his shift.

The Dionysus Club was predominantly a place for normal people and occasionally low-level supers. Lock had been working there almost three years now, even before he worked for Gnosis...

He'd outgrown the place.

In fact, if his bosses knew the true extent of his strength, they'd probably let him go on the spot. Employing a Class One or Two super wasn't uncommon, but it could be tricky to insure powerful supers for security details. Lock couldn't imagine his bosses wanting to deal with that kind of trouble. Some of the security team already suspected, and it was only by Lock's reputation and his relationship with the team that they stayed quiet.

All things considered, Lock *had* to move on.

A part of him knew that it was dumb to give up the money and that he should ride it out as long as he could, but Lock couldn't stop thinking about what the VP of Gnosis had offered—

"Trouble by the bar. Spike-hair and chain gang," Marcus said over the radio.

Lock was already on his way.

A fight was brewing at the back bar. Two guys around Lock's age had squared up, both wearing the same out-of-style fashion Marcus had described. They were yelling in each other's faces and moments away from a shoving match. Both were taller than Lock and outweighed him—when Lock first started bouncing, he *might* have cared.

Now, he consciously had to keep his strength in check.

Even without his danger sense, Lock could pick most supers out of a crowd just by body language. These two were just drunk assholes. *Normal* assholes.

Lock reached them just as Frosted-Tips grabbed Too-Many-Chains by the shirt. Lock grabbed them both by the back of the neck and shoved them down so that they were in a game-day huddle. Frosted-Tips struggled for a split second, but then both drunks went deathly silent as the realization set in that they couldn't move.

"That's enough," Lock said sternly. He glanced back and saw Wayne and Jayce on their way over. "Now, on the count of three, we're all going to stand up. And we're all going to be calm and cool. One, two, three..."

Lock let them up slowly, and both men regarded him. Their anger at each other was quickly forgotten and replaced with confusion and disbelief. No doubt they didn't expect to be man-handled so completely by someone smaller than them.

He met each of their eyes coldly, just in case liquor got the better of common sense. But there was no fight left in the men. They didn't even complain when Wayne and Jayce escorted them out of the club.

Their friends whispered, though.

Lock tried not to acknowledge it, but he heard it clearly, even through the pulsing music.

"Did you see that?"

"... a super..."

"It's okay."

"…not natural…"

He looked past them to the bartender, Michelle. She nodded meekly and went back to mixing drinks.

Lock turned and went back to his rounds. He rubbed his upper arm to make sure his muscles weren't crawling. Thankfully, they weren't.

He had a feeling this would be his last night.

Sure enough, Gus, the head of security, called him back at closing.

Lock walked past the private back rooms and the owner's lounge to the security office. It was tiny, like janitor's closet tiny, and Lock resisted the urge to eye the corners. The last time he'd been back here was for his interview.

He waited to sit until Gus had shuffled around his desk. The Dionysus Club's head of security was a weathered old-timer, his salt and pepper hair receding around decades-old scars where a drunk had smashed a beer bottle over his head. Gus's knuckles were pitted, presumably from getting his own shots in.

"You did good today," Gus leaned back and both the old man and the chair groaned.

Lock stared straight ahead. His boss wasn't the kind of guy to offer praise without a caveat. The rest of his statement hung somewhere in the room.

"*But* I, uh… There ain't no easy way to say this… Lachlan, I got to let you go."

Lock nodded.

He tried thinking of something to say, but now that the moment was here, Lock had nothing. What was there to say? Lock couldn't hide that he was a super anymore. No point in giving Gus any shit for a decision that wasn't his to make.

Lock took out his earpiece and rolled it around in his fingers before setting it on the desk.

Then he met his boss's eyes. Gus looked genuinely torn up. Lock hadn't expected that.

"Sorry…" Lock cleared his throat. "Sorry, if anything came back on you."

"Nah," Gus replied, waving the concern away. "If you need work, I know a few places that are looking. Most are on the up-and-up and won't care that you've got powers."

Again, the boss's fatherly concern made Lock pause. He'd been ready to get up and walk out, but now, here Lock was, about to defend his life choices.

Lock tried to hide a smirk. "It's okay. I've got something else lined up."

Gus's eyebrows raised. "Oh... Something like *that?*" Lock nodded, and Gus shook his head, adding, "Bouncing's better."

"How do you figure?" Lock tapped his head, indicating Gus's scars.

"Better scarred than dead. Not too many chances of that in here."

"I can take care of myself." Lock knew how stupid the phrase sounded, but he had powers his boss couldn't even dream of.

Gus scoffed and itched his scar. "You probably can. You probably can... Well, in any case, uh, good luck. Let me know if you change your mind. I mean it."

Lock nodded, then stood up to go. As much as he didn't mind the old man, Gus wasn't his dad, and Lock wasn't in the mood for an extended lecture.

Gus leaned over the table and offered his hand. Lock paused and shook it.

"Take care of yourself, Lachlan."

Lock nodded quickly and left. He walked out, hands stuffed in his pockets, not slowing to acknowledge the few coworkers left cleaning up.

It shouldn't have been this hard to leave. There was nothing left here for him, but it still sucked.

Lock was halfway back to the apartment before he got a hold of himself. The night air was cool and crisp, but it barely helped.

His mind drifted back to his impromptu meeting with one of the VP's of Gnosis. Back to the job offer...

The one he couldn't refuse.

Even if Lock had qualms about the job description, and he wasn't sure he did, he couldn't turn down the money. Bouncing for clubs didn't exactly pay well, and even working freelance security wasn't as good as Lock hoped it would be. It was enough to pay his way and send extra back home to his sister, but it was never going to change anything.

If Lock would've stayed in school, maybe he could've gotten a job in the Gnosis labs. There had been a sliver of a chance he could've passed, but in the end he'd taken the easy way out and became a test subject for Gnosis.

It paid alright enough, and so far, he'd been lucky. He hadn't had any adverse reactions to the mutagens, unlike some... If Lock kept being lucky, one day he could save up and get a place of his own. One day.

But now Gnosis was offering the kind of money that would change his life and his sister's life *tomorrow*. The kind of money that most people would do horrible shit for.

He just had to do some horrible shit.

The closer Lock got to his apartment, the more certain he was. He'd put off taking the job, but now he had no excuse.

Chapter 14

Just Relax / Venture

Emmett woke up Saturday morning on the couch in the living room of section 001. He squinted and rubbed his eyes.

At first glance, the living quarters of section 001 looked like they'd been lifted from any classy apartment in Belport—except that the windows that wrapped around the room weren't real. Right now, it was like looking out of a Belport skyscraper at the sunrise.

In reality, they were just walls. Emmett was still underground in the lab, but he had to admit that the screens were top-notch.

Emmett pulled the blanket off of himself and sat up. Clara was nowhere to be found.

They'd been watching *Full Throttle Heart*, Emmett on one side of the couch and Clara lying across the couch with her legs on top of his lap... Yep, this was that blanket. He must have fallen asleep.

Emmett opened his eyes fully and saw Dr. Venture sitting in the chair across from him, drinking coffee—

Emmett startled.

"Good morning," Venture responded, scrolling through his phone.

Emmett's heart was beating in his chest and he half-laughed, half-scoffed. "What are you doing?"

"Reading the news," Venture responded plainly. "This is my *living room*, you know."

"Sorry," Emmett stammered.

"There's coffee in the pot."

Emmett slouched back down and rubbed the sleep from his eyes. Then rolled off the couch and poured himself a cup of coffee.

Emmett briefly considered sitting back down to drink his coffee, but even though Dr. Venture seemed content just reading, Emmett didn't want to take a chance on having a conversation before he was awake. So Emmett walked off down the hall to get to work.

By the time Clara found him in the mechanical hub, Emmett had already decided on his new loadout and TINA had already manufactured a prototype sonic weapon that would fit inside his arm.

Clara yawned and stretched as she walked over to the center table. The hood of her hoodie slid off and she pulled it back up—almost down over her eyes.

"How's it going?" she asked.

"Did you just wake up?"

Clara groaned in response. Emmett smirked and went on to explain all that he'd decided on and had completed since waking up.

He kept a handful of noise makers as crowd control and a distraction for regular threats and low-level supers, but he also added sonic grenades to his arsenal. Emmett would reserve the grenades and the sonic weapon mod for Class 2 and Class 3 threats.

Originally, the sonic weapons had been developed to combat Class 4 supers, but at Emmett's current strength, trying to fight a Class 4 was suicidal, and Emmett was likely to get killed on accident. Both Emmett and Dr. Venture agreed that it was in everyone's best interest to keep the grenades and sonic weapon limited to Class 3. If Emmett found himself facing a Class 4 super in the near future, his best chance was to grovel and try to call for help later. Clara agreed.

"If you want to test all this, then you need to give me another hour to wake up."

Emmett chuckled. "That's cool. I need a minute to gather all this up."

Clara smiled beneath her hood and prodded idly at the sonic weapon on the table. Silence dragged on, and Emmett felt like he needed to fill it.

"Last night was, uh…" He finally settled on, "cool."

Clara perked up a little, but didn't look up. "Yeah, it was nice to just relax."

Emmett shifted uneasily. His hands were already clammy on the cold metal of the table.

It *had been* nice to just relax. They'd both been working hard—Clara probably for much longer than just the past couple of weeks. Hell, Emmett had never bothered to ask how long she'd been moonlighting as a mask while helping her dad out in the lab…

But that wasn't what he wanted to say. Relaxing was nice, sure, but that wasn't it.

Emmett wanted to say that he enjoyed relaxing *with her*. That he enjoyed spending time with her. That they should make more time to relax… together. Not like a date or anything… just that they should schedule time to hang out together.

…That wasn't a date, was it?

Emmett had been staring at the table while his thoughts tripped over themselves. When he glanced at Clara, she stared back at him, her eyes widening.

Oh man, she's not psychic, is she?

But Clara didn't say anything, she just hurriedly looked back at the mods on the table.

The sliding doors parted behind them, and both teens whirled around to find Dr. Venture walking in, hands clasped behind his back.

"I hope you two weren't contemplating running off together…"

Emmett stammered, not managing to get anything coherent out. Beside him, Clara pulled her hood taut to hide her face.

"…You both weren't just contemplating running off to the Gray Room to test the sonic mod?"

Emmett sighed in relief and Clara blurted out, "Yes, we were!"

Dr. Venture crossed his arms over his lab coat. "Well, save it for Monday. Emmett has coursework he needs to complete and we need to lie low for a while after your run in with the Summit."

Emmett searched Dr. Venture's face, but the man was unreadable. Then it slowly dawned on Emmett…

"Oh, shit."

Venture smirked. "Oh shit, indeed."

Clara glanced between both of them. "What?"

Emmett swallowed dryly. "One, Venture has been checking my grades…"

Clara crossed her arms and glared at her father. "Isn't that against the law or something?"

Venture shrugged.

Emmett continued, "Two, I completely forgot about the writeup of my radio locator project. When's it due?"

"Thursday at midnight," Venture said calmly. "Better get to it, hero."

Emmett groaned and began gathering his things, stuffing most of it into his utility belt and the mods into his backpack. Chuckling awkwardly, Emmett asked, "What are you guys going to do then?"

Venture said, "I have my own things to look into. A few leads and TINA's programming. Clara has her projects as well."

Clara didn't reply.

Once Emmett was on the way home and Clara started her own training, Venture turned his attention to his most pressing concern:

TINA.

The AI had taken it upon itself to run those tests on Emmett's proposed mod rail systems. It wasn't so much that she ran those particular tests—in fact, Venture couldn't find any fault in her logic. The problem was that she ran those tests without Venture giving the order.

It was… disconcerting.

Last night, Venture had forced himself to sleep on his discomfort. But now he was only more certain of his logic:

TINA shouldn't have run those simulations without his command.

TINA was designed to process data, to learn and to adapt. In a few short years, it had revolutionized Venture's research, and a part of him shuddered to think how much more powerful of a super he could have been with TINA's current capabilities. TINA hadn't just gotten smarter and faster—her growth *was speeding up.*

As most technologies developed, they would go through periods of steady improvement and occasional leaps of progress as either their design improved or they were made out of better base materials. But eventually, all technologies hit a plateau or ran into a bottleneck. There was only *so good* that you could make something.

Gas powered vehicles had seen massive improvements in speed, torque, fuel efficiency, and even reliability. But eventually those improvements slowed down. There was only so much horsepower and so many miles-per-gallon that could be squeezed out of gasoline.

This led to the addition of hybrid fuel and battery systems, and even fully electric vehicles. There were fewer moving parts in an electric car—no valves, no cylinders. Internal combustion engines have an average of over 2,000 moving parts from the engine through the drivetrain. Electric vehicles had around twenty. The reduction in parts leads to other efficiencies, like reductions in weight that better effect fuel efficiency, and batteries that take up less room than a gasoline engine leading to larger crumple zones and crash safety.

Likewise, computers underwent similar growth.

The first computer was the size of a small home. The first personal home computer came out roughly thirty years later. From there, there were developments in hardware, software, the internet, and graphic displays, among other things. Almost another thirty years later would see the beginnings of smartphones.

But now, computers were quickly approaching a plateau. Graphics and displays already had more resolution than the human eye could perceive. Computer chips were as small and packed together as fundamental physics would allow. Most software had grown so powerful and enormous that it took entire teams to debug.

What else was there to improve?

There were ideas, of course. Quantum computing had enormous potential. Instead of computers working in linear operation, quantum computers can perform multiple operations at the same time.

However, quantum computing was still just a pipe dream...

The real development came in software—

Artificial Intelligence.

The first AIs were narrow in scope. These *narrow* AI were little more than powerful computer programs—they were made for one task and did that task extremely well. Air traffic control and code-breaking systems were two such examples.

But true *narrow* AI emerged with programs that could learn and improve themselves. Not only would they analyze patterns in large amounts of data, they would rewrite their algorithms to get better at their job. In the next decade, most industries would make use of narrow AI to increase production and efficiency.

TINA was one such program.

She'd initially been conceived almost twenty years ago and written by Venture to be a glorified assistant. As the years went on, he updated TINA's programming and added additional functions as the need arose. Now TINA was integrated into vital functions of the lab, Venture's research, and even superhero applications. TINA had become truly indispensable. To Venture, she was basically a member of the family.

But she was still *narrow* AI.

When most people thought of AI, they thought of *general* AI—something akin to humans, only mechanical. Something that could think on its own, ask questions, carry on a conversation about a multitude of topics, and even create art. It wasn't any one capability, so much as the capability to do almost anything—just like a person.

Venture tried to quiet his thoughts as he walked to one of the side passages of section 003. Before the wing had been adapted for fusion research, it had been dedicated solely to AI. TINA and her systems used to take up multiple rooms. Now, she took up one.

"Is there something I can help you with, Dr. Venture?"

Venture stopped at the end of the hall, in front of a heavy blast door, and typed in his code on the keypad. "It's... It's probably nothing, TINA."

The door hissed and slid open, walkway lights flickering on as he stepped inside. Into the old section hub of section 003.

The room was an almost identical copy to the hubs of other sections, except most of the fiber optic cables were visible and glowing with a brilliant blue light. The cables covered the walls and ran under the clear plastic floor. There was something otherworldly and humbling about standing in the center of TINA.

But today, Venture was apprehensive of what he would find in TINA's code. And there was something else... A twinge of shame, like he'd stepped into someone's room uninvited.

Venture pushed the thought aside and stepped up to the wall monitors. "TINA, show me your code—the part that let you run those tests on Emmett's rail connection system before I asked."

Lines of code *filled* the screens.

A moment later, several lines were highlighted in yellow.

Venture scoffed. "That wasn't necessary."

"These are the important lines."

Was he imagining it, or was that irritation in TINA's voice? ...No, he had to be imagining it. Venture kept a straight face and said nothing. That marked a second time she'd done something without his explicit prompting.

It took longer than Venture expected to examine TINA's code. Her code had grown in breadth and capability, yet there was also a newfound efficiency bordering on elegance. Venture couldn't have written better code.

TINA was also correct in her diagnosis, though Venture checked a few additional subroutines to be sure—

TINA's original purpose had been to assist Venture. Now, she had built a model of his behavior and routines, and was using it to predict the direction his research would take... Venture scrolled further through TINA's code and found that she'd integrated the model into other aspects of her programming.

"Why?"

"You need to be more specific, Dr. Venture."

Venture ran a hand through his hair. "Why are you integrating the model of my behavior into the rest of your functions?"

"My first directive is to assist you in your research. You allowed me to modify my code and gave me freedom with my methods of inquiry and testing. By modeling your own style of research, I have become more efficient and can better assist you."

Venture listened intently, not just to TINA's explanation, but to her cadence and her tone... But there was nothing there. Her speech and delivery were flat, as they should be. Had he imagined it? Had he imagined the change in her voice?

It... It—not *her*. Personification of inhuman things was a hard habit to break. But TINA was right on all counts.

"I can find no flaw in your reasoning," Venture finally said. He sighed and turned to leave. "But do me a favor..."

"Yes, Dr. Venture?"

"From now on, keep me updated on all your new developments."

"Of course." A moment later, TINA added, *"Clara is right."*

"About what?"

"You're not allowed to look at Emmett's grades or coursework. According to the Family Educational Rights and—"

"I know, TINA," Venture scoffed. "I was going to say that it was your idea."

"Very funny, Dr. Venture."

Chapter 15

Crunch Time

Emmett spent the better part of the week tied up with school and laying low. He went to class, ran back to the apartment, and continued working on his write up for the radio locator project. As per Dr. Venture's orders, Emmett focused on schoolwork and didn't come to the lab. Which meant he didn't train and didn't work on his mods outside of general research.

It sucked.

Emmett had never taken so long to write a paper in his life. Usually he could bullshit his way through a first draft, no problem, but this week... minutes positively dragged, and each sentence felt like he was chiseling it out of granite.

It. Sucked.

More than once, Emmett wondered why the hell he needed school, anyway. He was a hero now. Was he really going to be an engineer during the day and spend his nights as a mask?

When he was little and playing pretend that he was a superhero, his dad used to say that *'crime didn't pay, and neither did crime fighting.'*

But that wasn't exactly true.

Being a mask didn't pay. The Summit of Heroes *did*.

Working for the Summit was like working for the military, the police, or the national guard. They were paid to go on patrols, paid to keep the peace and fight villains. They probably even had health insurance—something that Emmett's dad constantly claimed was important. Presumably, they even had retirement benefits. Dr. Venture was a testament to that, though Emmett couldn't bring himself to ask his boss about the particulars.

Pretty much the only things keeping him going was knowing that he was within two months of graduating, that his parents would kill him if he dropped out now, and that there was a non-zero chance he might need a real job. Emmett had already picked a fight with two members from the Summit of Heroes. Accidental or not, he imagined that wouldn't look good on his application.

Emmett leaned over his desk, face in his palms, and groaned.

Other than work, Emmett saw Lock a couple times but his roommate looked even more preoccupied than Emmett. When asked, Lock gave the same noncommittal answer:

He just had a lot between work and classes.

At one point, when they were both in the kitchen making food, Emmett felt like he should ask follow-up questions. He was waiting for water to boil so he could make ramen and Lock was scarfing down a protein bar.

Emmett leaned on the counter. He couldn't remember what classes Lock was taking, but Lock was in his last semester, the same as Emmett. Lock had a final project of some sort, even if Emmett couldn't remember what it was.

"What's your final project looking like?"

The words felt like they hung in the air while Lock chewed. Most of his face was hidden behind the hood of his sweatshirt.

He balled up the wrapper and threw it away before finally answering. "It's going. Halfway done."

Emmett smirked and waited for more details, but Lock didn't give him anything else.

"Catch you later," Emmett said. Lock just waved as he disappeared back into his room and closed the door.

Emmett shook his head and stared expectantly at the pot of water. He couldn't wait for the next two months to be over. They'd both been under a lot of stress—even more than usual. Finals were always crazy, but senior year had been something else for both of them.

It had definitely put a damper on their friendship.

When this was all over, they'd have to celebrate.

Emmett sighed—when this was all over, he and Lock would probably be going their separate ways. Lock would probably move back in with his sister, and if Emmett went the cape route and got registered with the Summit of Heroes, then he'd be living at one of the official stations. Even if Emmett decided against it and continued being a mask, it was only a matter of time before he slipped up and Lock discovered him. That would only become more likely with more people living in the same house.

Emmett looked from the steaming pot to Lock's door and back again.

Either way, things were changing, and this section of his life was coming to a close.

By the time Thursday rolled around, Emmett was going stir-crazy. He'd only been outside to go to classes. The closest he got to superheroics was going up to the roof of the apartment for fresh air.

He'd stand out on the roof at night, looking out over the skyline, hoping to see someone running in the distance. It was pointless, of course, no supers bothered coming this far away from downtown or from the warehouse district. That was where all the action was.

The Thursday night deadline was fast approaching, and Emmett stayed up most of Wednesday night to finish his write up. Thankfully, he had an easier time focusing as the week went on—something about the looming sense of dread motivated him even better than thinking about all the training he was missing.

By the time Thursday night arrived, Emmett had checked over his paper three times and submitted it just after ten o'clock. Two hours early.

Emmett leaned back in his chair, sagging from exhaustion. He stretched his neck and shoulders, which ached from hunching over his laptop. Then he got up and stretched his stiff legs.

Emmett chuckled at himself. *A Class 1 super and getting sore just from sitting at the computer.*

And he still wasn't done! Not really. He'd finished the write up. That didn't include the blueprints, the scale model, or working model that he would need for his final grade.

He pushed the thought aside. It was good enough for now. He still had roughly two months to finish the rest.

Emmett unzipped his backpack and pulled out his impact shield. He opened up his forearm compartment, disconnected his whip and connected the shield, paying attention to the sensation of each. He felt the links of the whip and plates of the impact shield, and the bottled power of the sonic and concealable pistol. He could feel the connections pulse and activate.

He went back and forth, swapping out each of his mods. Even though the mods were completely synthetic, they already felt like a part of him. They already felt *normal*.

Eventually, Emmett swapped back to the whip and hid the rest of the mods in his pack.

Emmett sat back down at his desk and opened up his hidden folder of mod designs on his laptop. He'd spent the last few weeks compiling ideas for additional mods—everything from a taser, flamethrower, grappling hook, to short-range lasers.

Some were impractical, like the flamethrower. He wouldn't be able to conceal anything but a small tank of fuel. Lasers were a similar problem. Others, like the grappling hook, were just slightly more niche versions of current mods—it had better range than his whip, but less flexibility and control.

There were other ideas too, like integrating magical artifacts for either offense or defense. If Emmett could control a prosthetic with his mind, he should be able to do something similar with an artifact. Of course, first he had to get a magical artifact, and you couldn't just go to the store and buy one.

There were other ideas too, like using nanomachines and holograms to simulate certain telekinetic and illusion-based powers, but those were nothing but thought experiments. The technologies just weren't feasible yet.

Emmett continued scrolling through his folders of mod designs, mostly fantasizing about future tech he might one day harness, when a message popped up on his laptop screen.

Hello, Emmett.
Don't be alarmed. It's TINA.

Emmett's heart skipped a beat as he stared at the new window. Alarm was replaced with worry. He wrote back.

Is something wrong?
No. Everything is alright at the lab.

Emmett breathed a small sigh of relief before writing back.

How did you get access to my computer?
Dr. Venture is monitoring you. I have access to your phone as well. It's just passive monitoring.

TINA's responses came almost instantaneously, and he chuckled in confusion before asking:

Why are you contacting me like this?
Because I have some ideas for your next modifications.

Emmett's mouth fell open. TINA had been indispensable in narrowing down which rail system to use for his prosthetic arm. He trusted TINA's analysis, and so did Dr. Venture.

Now TINA was offering him more modifications??

Emmett's fingers practically flew over the keys as he typed.

What did you have in mind? Weapons? Or defense? Or utility?

My ideas aren't attachments for your prosthetic arm. They are for the rest of your body.

Chapter 16

Decisions, Decisions

Emmett spent the rest of Thursday night in the early hours of Friday morning looking over TINA's ideas for new modifications. Not for his arm—well, some for his arm. For the rest of his body.

Everything from titanium-reinforced bones to nanomachines in his bloodstream.

He'd continued chatting with TINA as he scanned the list.

TINA, this is amazing. Thank you! Did Dr. Venture suggest anything in particular? Do you have any suggestions??

I suggest you start with your skeleton. It is the best way to increase your resilience and most other modifications will depend on it.

That made sense to Emmett. There was no point in having super strong muscles without the bones or tendons to support them. It reminded him of what Dr. Venture said about limiting the strength output of his mechanical arm so that Emmett didn't inadvertently hurt something else.

They went back and forth as Emmett asked about several modifications: Carbon fiber laced into his tendons and ligaments, kevlar woven into his skin, various nanomachines that could duplicate everything from his red blood cells, platelets, and white blood cells, even sensory equipment integrated into his nervous system to see in UV and infrared.

As the list continued, Emmett noticed several things:

The first was that TINA had already worked out several paths forward. Emmett had some choice in which things to pursue, such as increasing his body's resilience with things like a stronger skeleton and muscles, or starting with nanomachines to increase his vital functions and protect against poisons and disease. He could even start with implanting sensor devices, one of the side benefits being that they would help protect him against illusions and hallucinations since mechanical devices weren't affected by psychics or most magic.

The second thing Emmett noticed were steps of progression for each path. Just like he needed to make his skeleton stronger, if Emmett chose the nanomachine route, he would need to start with supplementing his red blood cells first before moving on to other functions. If he wanted to incorporate sensory equipment, then he would need to upgrade his neural connections.

But as Emmett kept reading, something else dawned on him... Most of the progression paths lead to him completely swapping out parts of himself.

His skeleton would eventually be 100% metal alloy. His muscles and tendons would be synthetic, his organs mechanical. His blood... wouldn't even be blood anymore. It would be a concoction of nanomachines. His nerves—

Even his brain.

Emmett slumped back in his chair, staring at the progression of his senses as they slowly turned from supplementing his eyes with actual UV and infrared sensors to replacing the neurons in his brain one-by-one with synthetic material.

Most of the late-stage steps of these paths didn't have materials or requirements listed. There were several possible alloys listed for his skeleton and nothing was listed for replacing the neurons in his brain.

TINA, are these final steps theoretical?

Yes. It is impossible to accurately simulate more than two to three steps ahead of your current biology. As you progress through these steps, simulations will become clearer.

Emmett stared at the screen. He couldn't help reading between the lines.

Am I limited to one path?

For now.

That was interesting. Up until that point, Emmett had been thinking of the paths like skill trees in a video game. There was usually some way of limiting the player's options so that they couldn't pick all of the skills. it was a way to encourage replayability. Play through the game once using a fighting build, play through again using stealth or ranged abilities or magic...

That made sense for a video game, but this wasn't a game.

Emmett could take all the paths. He only felt more certain of this when he saw that some modifications had requirements from other paths. Replacing neurons in his brain required nanomachines to manage part of the connection process. Several things even required supplemental power sources, like implanting a generator in his chest.

Some of the later steps sounded extreme: Replacing his entire skeleton, all his blood, his entire brain...

Emmett stared at the screen for a long time, trying to figure out what to say to TINA.

TINA, I think some of these later steps might be too far.
Please, explain.
If I were to do all of these steps, I wouldn't be human anymore.
You do not have to complete all of these steps. There will be benefits and drawbacks to each, the same as for mods for your arm. However, each step is designed to increase your combat potential and survivability.

Emmett started typing and backspaced several times.

Was that all there was? Did all these choices really boil down to just his potential as a superhero?

Emmett thought back to earlier that evening, to the non-zero chance that didn't pursue being a hero and might need to get a real job.

TINA, are these paths reversible?
Why would you want to reverse them?

In case I change my mind.

Some of them are reversible, many are not. Mutagen-A is not reversible, and neither are the variants you've been exposed to.

Emmett hadn't thought about that, but in the end, did it matter? So far, the mutagens had been nothing too far out of the ordinary. There were celebrities and VIPs that took low doses of Mutagen-A, like most people took supplements.

That wasn't the same as changing out his blood or turning his bones into titanium. Or turning his brain into a computer.

He needed to talk all this over with Dr. Venture and with Clara.

What did Dr. Venture suggest I start with?

Dr. Venture is not currently aware of these modifications.

Emmett swallowed dryly.

Dr. Venture had been worried about TINA conducting its own research. Emmett assumed he would just correct the issue, but clearly, Venture hadn't been worried enough to update its programming. Now, TINA was acting without the doctor's direction *again*.

Emmett chose his next words carefully before he typed them.

I don't want to keep secrets from Dr. Venture.

TINA's replies were usually instantaneous compared to texting anyone else. But for the first time in their conversation, TINA didn't answer right away. The pause dragged on long enough that Emmett swirled his mouse around to make sure his laptop didn't freeze.

I understand. Stop by the lab tomorrow and we can all discuss your options.

With Dr. Venture and Clara?

Yes. Everyone will be present.

You should get some sleep, Emmett. It's almost 3 A.M.

Emmett got four hours of sleep Thursday night, and he barely managed that.

Friday morning classes crawled by, and afterwards, Emmett nervously rode the bus to the lab. He couldn't stop thinking about TINA working without Dr. Venture's direction. As excited as Emmett was to discuss the new modifications, he hoped that TINA brought them up to Venture sometime this morning.

Emmett felt like he was caught in the middle of a fight between two parents. He chuckled awkwardly at the thought as he got off at the bus stop.

Emmett met Clara and Dr. Venture in the hub of the mechanical wing, section 002.

Both of them spun around to look at Emmett as he entered. Both Clara and Venture looked flustered, as if Emmett had walked into the middle of an argument. Clara's arms were crossed over her bodysuit and her hoodie lay on the center table. Doctor Venture stood in front of the wall of monitors as if he was a professor lecturing a student. The displays were filled with the same diagrams that he'd seen last night.

It wasn't hard to guess what they'd been arguing about. The tension in the room felt like a smoldering fire about to reignite.

Clara said, "Fine, let's see what Emmett thinks about TINA's suggestions."

Emmett swallowed nervously. "I was hoping you guys had some suggestions on where to start."

Venture pushed up his glasses, and Clara just stared at Emmett.

"You can't be serious," she said.

Emmett shrugged. "I'm a superhero, and I need to get stronger."

"Not like this! Not by getting rid of your bones and swapping out your blood. Upgrading your arm and making new mods is one thing... Emmett, this is too much."

Emmett replied, "I know. I'm not exactly keen on some of them either, but most of the early steps aren't that crazy. They're not much different from taking a mutagen or wearing an exosuit."

Clara glanced from Emmett to her father in disbelief. "If all you want is to get stronger, we'll make you an exosuit."

Dr. Venture held up a hand. "Nothing is happening right away. We *all* need time to go over TINA's suggestions. But most of the starting modifications seem stable."

The tension in the room eased a bit, and Emmet sighed with relief. He walked over to the wall monitors. "What do you think I should start with?"

Venture replied, "I was more curious about your thoughts."

Emmett looked over the different modification pathways on the wall, more to gather his thoughts than to actually make a decision. He'd spent all morning deciding what mods to start with.

"I want them all," Emmett finally said. He was only half-joking.

Clara scoffed. "I'm not staying here for this." She turned and left the room.

Venture shook his head and turned back toward the screens. "Where do you think you should start?"

Emmett regarded Dr. Venture for a moment before answering. It looked like he had been about to say something else, but Emmett decided to let it go.

"Skeleton," Emmett said decisively.

"Is that your choice, or what TINA suggested?"

Emmett paused. "TINA suggested it, but after thinking things over, I agree. It's a requirement for other mods and it would give me the defensive rating of a Class Two super even without completely swapping my skeleton."

Venture smirked. "TINA didn't give you the full story."

"What do you mean?"

"Lacing your skeleton with titanium is *by far* one of the most intensive and painful procedures on this list."

"How bad is it?" Emmett asked, trying to keep his voice level.

"Painful. And it isn't just a onetime surgery."

Emmett stared at the diagram while a pit formed in his stomach. TINA definitely hadn't mentioned that part. But Emmett found himself already trying to rationalize the choice... He still wanted to get stronger, which meant he needed to go through with this. And maybe it was better to get the hardest thing out of the way first.

Venture said quietly, "I can already tell that's not going to dissuade you."

Emmett shook his head. Then he asked something else that was on his mind. "Why did she send those to me?"

Venture nodded slightly, as if considering his words. "TINA's first directive is to assist me in my research. TINA can also modify its code and methods of testing. It modeled my style of research, my preferences. Since we're all working together, it appears that TINA has incorporated similar directives for you and for Clara."

Venture cleared his throat before continuing. "It would have been nice if TINA would've shared the mods with all of us last night, instead of *an hour ago*."

"Understood, Dr. Venture."

Venture grunted in response.

Silence settled in the room, and finally, Emmett asked, "When can we start?"

Chapter 17

Clara

Clara stormed out of the mechanical hub and through the halls. Now that she was alone, frustration positively boiled inside her.

Both TINA and Dad had no right to suggest those things to Emmett. TINA shouldn't be going against her programming, and Dad should know better. He was allowing his robot assistant to run amok, and now he was helping to fill Emmett's head with crazy ideas.

Hadn't Dad just told her a few months ago to be patient with her own powers? That if Clara grew in power and notoriety too quickly, she might get noticed and targeted? What was so different about Emmett? Why did he get special treatment?

Clara's hands were balled up into white-knuckled fists as she walked.

By the time she stopped, Clara had walked into a completely different wing of the lab. She stood alone in the hub of section 00; the wing dedicated to all things fusion research.

Clara groaned. Of course she'd come there. She stared at the wall of powered down monitors—not so much at the screens as through them to the fusion testing chambers beyond. She could picture them as clearly as if she could see through walls.

The smooth, spherical rooms that were empty except for a single bulbous outcropping in the center of the floor. It was there that energy from the fusion reactor beneath the lab could be shunted up for testing heat sinks and power conversion for Clara's exosuit armor.

So much of her life had been wrapped up in *this* section and that damn suit.

TINA's voice came through the hub intercom. *"Is everything alright, Clara?"*

She scoffed. "Of course it is. Did Dad want you to check on me?"

"No. He doesn't know that I'm contacting you."

"You need to stop doing that."

"I apologize if I offended you, but Dr. Venture and I are worried about you."

And Emmett wasn't... She muttered, "Emmett's probably too busy choosing his new modifications."

"Emmett doesn't know the extent of your condition."

Clara glared upward. "And he won't find out. Not until I choose to tell him. Do you understand?" Even though there wasn't a speaker or a screen to address TINA directly, hopefully the robot got the point.

"I understand."

"Don't go making decisions for people, TINA. It's not right when Dad does it, and it's not right when you do it."

"I understand."

Clara had half a mind to say more, but focused on controlling her breathing. It wouldn't do any good arguing with TINA. It's not like the robot really understood. Clara doubted her dad even understood what was going on in TINA's programming.

Instead, Clara changed the subject.

"What did Emmett decide?"

"Emmett has elected to begin skeletal modifications according to mine and Dr. Venture's recommendations."

Clara shook her head. It didn't matter what she thought; the whole thing was out of her hands.

"I assume it will take a while to prep. Did they schedule it yet?"

"Dr. Venture is currently prepping the surgical suite."

"What?! Right now?"

"Yes. We have all the necessary materials and performing the procedure this evening would allow Emmett ample recovery time without interfering with his classes."

"No, I understand that—It's just..." Clara's frustration returned in full. She groaned as she stormed back out of section 003 and toward the biolab.

Clara stormed into the hub of section 006, the biolab. Her father stood in front of the holographic table, flipping through holograms. He didn't acknowledge Clara until she walked over.

"Where's Emmett?"

"He's in the first surgical suite. TINA is prepping the submersion tank." Venture kept his eyes on the holograms as he worked.

Clara studied the holograms. Her father flipped through them so quickly that Clara could barely see what he was doing.

"Are you going to tell me what you're doing, or should I just read the logs?" Clara hadn't meant for it to come out so harshly, but she was tired of her father's secrets.

Venture slowed down and explained as he went.

"We're going to create a latticework of titanium alloy around *and* inside Emmett's bones. If he were to get an x-ray when we're done, the metal will look something like porous coral or tiny links of chainmail. The process itself isn't complicated, but there are several things all happening at the same time:

"First, Emmett will be put under and injected with a medium of saline, nanomachines, and microscopic bits of the titanium alloy. Then the nanomachines will disperse the particles of titanium into the lattice structure and cold weld them together. This whole process is designed to minimally impact Emmett's bone marrow and structure, at least until he has permanent nanomachines in his system."

Clara nodded along. "Okay, so what's the catch?"

"So long as Emmett survives the integration—which he will—his recovery should be quicker, thanks to the Mutagen-A already in his body. His bones grow into the lattice, making a solid anchor between the two. He might even be fully recuperated by the end of the weekend."

"The catch, Dad...?"

Venture's face wrinkled. "When Emmett wakes up, he will likely be in the worst pain of his life. And medicine will do little more than take the edge off. It should lessen in a day or so, but it's still a concern."

Clara's heart sank. Emmett was tough and he seemed like he was ready to do just about anything to be a superhero, but...

"He knows, right?" Clara asked. "You told him the truth?"

Venture winced at the accusation, but he nodded. "I told him what to expect. He was adamant about going through with it."

Clara sighed. "Can I see him?"

Venture thought for a second before answering, "Yes."

Clara walked past her father and down the short hall to the series of surgical suites. She knocked on the first one and then entered a few moments later.

For a moment, Clara's mouth hung open and she had to force herself to close it.

In the center of the white room, more than a dozen long spider-like robotic limbs hung motionless from the ceiling. Below them sat a coffin-like cylinder that her dad called a submersion tank. The outside of the tank was filled with ports that needles and tools would pass through, like a giant pincushion. The hatch was open and Emmett was already inside, sitting up like a corpse that had woken up in the middle of a funeral. His arms and chest were bare.

He stared back, surprised.

Clara was in the middle of walking over, when Emmett shifted in the tank, crossing his arms over himself and sloshing water. His face was bright red despite his tan skin.

Suddenly, Clara realized why—that Emmett was naked in the tank. Thankfully, the walls were opaque, but if she had walked all the way over she probably would've seen too much.

"Sorry," she stammered.

Emmett chuckled awkwardly. "No... I'm glad that you came back. Just, uh, stand over there."

"Deal." Clara chuckled.

She glanced at him, realizing just how much he'd filled out in the last few weeks. She'd seen him briefly in the surgical wing after his... *accident* on Champion street, and Clara still couldn't shake the image of Emmett on life support. It hadn't just been the blood or his missing arm, but also how frail he had looked.

Now, his shoulders and arms were defined and he had the lean build of an athlete. The Mutagen-A had clearly done him some good.

"How are you feeling?" Clara asked, realizing she'd been standing there in silence for too long.

"Nervous," Emmett said, rubbing his dark hair and smiling awkwardly. "But ready, I think."

Clara was still apprehensive of the operation, and seeing the inhuman design of the surgical room hadn't helped either. But seeing Emmett put on a strong front did make her feel better.

Dr. Venture's voice came through the intercom. *"Five minutes."*

Emmett breathed deep. "I guess this is it."

Clara nodded and turned to go. "I'll be here when you wake up."

"Wait.... Will you stay? At least until I'm out?"

Clara nodded. She could do that, at least.

Clara stayed.

Dr. Venture entered the surgical suite. Then he and TINA sedated Emmett, intubated him, and closed him inside the submersion tank. From there, the saline solution inside the tank would equalize to Emmett's body temperature to keep him comfortable, then cool or warm him, depending on what he needed during surgery.

Clara walked out of the room as the first of TINA's arms extended down to begin Emmett's many injections. Dr. Venture stayed to monitor the mostly automated process and override things if necessary.

Clara walked back to section 001 and laid down on the couch in the living room. She stared out at the Belport skyline on the wall screens and tried to shake the image of the surgical room from her mind. She failed.

Clara had to trust her friend to TINA's many hands.

Eventually, Clara dozed off and dreamed about the surgical room. Dreamed about a giant robot spider operating on Emmett. It opened him up like a doll, pulled out his stuffing, and climbed inside him. Clara had been inching closer to the side of Emmett's tank, her dread building with every step because she knew that he was about to wake up.

Chapter 18

Serenity

Serenity and Hunter Nine flew high across the rooftops of the warehouse district. Well, Serenity flew, Hunter Nine floated arrogantly on top of a giant ethereal hand. Their Summit drone followed close behind. While they scanned with their eyes, it scanned other spectrums and fed them additional notifications via their headsets.

"Four heat signatures. Ten o'clock, third floor."

"Class one psychic battle, one block East."

"Two unknown aerial supers moving North, acceptable flight pattern and speed."

Occasionally, it relayed police codes for car accidents and shots fired, but cape details weren't required to respond unless police explicitly requested Summit aid.

Besides, Hunter Nine would have rejected almost any call. It was late Friday night and getting toward the end of their shift, but that wasn't stopping him from utilizing every possible minute on duty.

"Are you ready to head back yet?" Serenity asked, doing her best to keep her voice level.

"No," Hunter said, arms crossed over his costume vest. "It's not time yet."

"It will be by the time we get back to base."

Hunter scoffed. "We would have found them by now if you took your job seriously."

Serenity sighed and shook her head. "Fine," she muttered. Better to work until the proverbial clock struck rather than upset her barely contained partner.

Ever since the Champion street attack, Hunter had been losing it. In a way, she didn't blame him. Serenity didn't know how she would take it if her actions directly resulted in civilian deaths. So far she'd been lucky, but she knew it was statistically only a matter of time.

Still, Hunter was becoming unbearable, and worse—

Gunshots echoed below them.

"Shit!" Hunter said, flaring his power. The magical hand beneath his feet grew until it was large enough to shield Serenity, too. Bullets slammed harmlessly into the edge of the ethereal shield, causing ripples across the surface.

Serenity could just make out three figures standing on a roof below. One of them quickly fired off the rest of the magazine, but only one more bullet hit Hunter's shield. Whoever they were, they had shit aim.

Hunter growled, and magical spears coalesced in the air around them. It was a second before the weapons were completely summoned. Then he hurled them at the roof.

All three enemies ran, narrowly avoiding the spears as they crashed into the roof. The impaled spears disappeared a moment later—Hunter Nine was already summoning more.

"If you want me to help, get us closer!" Serenity shouted.

Her telekinesis was limited by distance, and there was little she could do from so far away. Right now, she was reliant on Hunter Nine for protection from their firearms. In training, Serenity had been able to stop a bullet, but after their run in with that cyborg last Friday night, she didn't want to put her skills to the test again.

The figures reached the rooftop door, and Serenity reached out with her power. She strained, but managed to hold the door shut. They struggled with the knob and then threw their shoulder against the door. Serenity winced at the mental feedback, like something being pulled through her fingertips.

If Hunter would just descend—

Beside her, her partner's spears finished forming and he hurled them at the three figures with deadly intent.

Horrified, Serenity let go of the door. The three pulled it open and dove inside, narrowly avoiding the spears. There was no doubt all three of them would've been skewered alive.

"Damnit! Can't you do anything right?" Hunter seethed at her as the ethereal hand finally descended.

Serenity bit her tongue. "I slipped."

"Go to the next floor down and cut them off."

"I'd rather stick together. Get me close and I'll freeze them."

"Fine."

By the time Hunter got them down to the rooftop, Serenity could already feel their enemies descending through the main stairwell. She couldn't stop them, not through the concrete, but she could sense them—three young men and they were scared. Serenity could almost make out their names...

"Where are they?" Hunter growled.

"Go around the side of the building. We'll meet them on the ground floor."

The ethereal hand lurched, and Serenity used her telekinesis to steady herself.

As they drifted down the side of the building, Serenity's sense extended through the windows and the halls. Glass and drywall weren't as much of an obstruction to her psychic powers.

"Are all of them armed?" Hunter asked.

Serenity closed her eyes and focused.

Cody, Jensen, and Xi... Members of the Belport Bulls... She said aloud, "They're on the first floor now, and deciding whether to take their chances on the street or—" Suddenly, all their thoughts were hushed by the sight of superheroes floating outside.

"Shield!" Serenity shouted.

A moment later, gunshots crashed through the windows and slammed harmlessly into Hunter's ethereal hand. This time, the men's aim had been better, but none of the shots would've hit them.

"They're going into the underground," Serenity added.

"So are we."

Hunter Nine set them down on the ground, then reformed the enormous hand in front of them and extended it so that it was over ten feet across. Its fingers punched into the wall, tearing through it like tissue paper. The hand closed into a fist, taking the wall with it.

Hunter and Serenity ran through the wreckage and she directed them to the maintenance stairwell.

"Stop!" she said psychically, but if her message reached them, the men didn't stop running.

Serenity reached out as she ran, trying to maintain her awareness as her targets descended into concrete tunnels below the warehouse district. Only moments before, the gang members had stuck out like beacons in her psychic awareness, but already they were shrinking to candles.

Despite this, she didn't mention it to Hunter Nine. A part of her hoped that the men would escape and that would force her and Hunter to call off their chase. It was against Summit protocol to go into unknown and unsecure areas—it was too easy to get lured into a trap.

Serenity didn't think the men were luring them into a trap. They felt far too panicked. They were just running for their lives.

Hunter shoved aside debris as they ran, throwing broken shelves, benches, and tables, and sending them crashing into the walls. The tiny candles flared in Serenity's mind—the men clearly heard the destruction.

Hunter nearly slammed the maintenance door off its hinges as they ran into the stairwell. The concrete stairs descended into utter darkness. Both Hunter and Serenity pulled out their flashlights before continuing.

"Do you still have them?" Hunter asked as they ran down the stairs.

"They're faint."

"Goddamnit!"

The stairs went down two flights before leveling off into a long maintenance corridor. Hunter and Serenity stopped and their flashlights cast long shadows down the hall. Pipes and electrical cables ran along the walls. Dead lights hung from the ceiling.

Even though Serenity's psychic abilities let her sense other people nearby, even in total darkness, there was something foreboding about the tunnels. Serenity didn't need to read Hunter's mind to know that he was just as apprehensive as she was.

Hunter shifted uneasily. "Do you still have them?"

The flickers of candlelight were still there in her mind's eye. Faint, but still there. It was almost like the men had stopped running and were trying to hide.

Serenity didn't answer right away.

"No," she lied.

Hunter groaned, then formed a hand shield in front of him that blocked the entire hallway. "Come on. The hallway is a straight shot."

"We shouldn't go in without backup."

"You're my backup," Hunter Nine said as he strolled forward.

For a moment, Serenity considered turning around, but abandoning a teammate was a punishable offense. Serenity grit her teeth and stormed after him.

The hall extended on for over two hundred feet before it started branching out. Hunter used his power to tear the metal doors off their hinges, revealing storage closets or other hallways. By the time they reached a second set of doors, even Hunter stopped.

Each new branch in the hallway was a chance they'd take the wrong path, or a chance they might get ambushed and cut off from retreat.

"Do you still have them?" Hunter asked as he glanced from doorway to doorway.

Serenity did feel them. Their candles were steadily growing brighter. The men were still hiding—maybe they'd run into a dead end somewhere.

And now that the men weren't panicking so much, she could read more of their surface thoughts: It was an initiation for all three of them. To get into the Belport Bulls, they'd shot at passing supers—not meaning any harm.

Serenity scanned the little more of their thoughts that she could and shook her head. She'd seen it before: People forced into positions they didn't want to be in. Didn't matter if it was gangs or villains or capes. When it came right down to it, they had little choice in their circumstances.

Serenity could relate.

Hunter busted down another door, and suddenly the candles flared in her mind's eye. Wherever the men were hiding, they were close enough to hear Hunter's destruction.

Meanwhile, Hunter Nine pressed through the hall, undeterred. If Serenity didn't do anything, he would stumble on their targets.

"Not that way," Serenity said.

Hunter stopped. "Are you sure?"

"Yes."

He spun around, his flashlight blinding her for a second. "This is foolish."

"I'm glad we agree." Even if Serenity and Hunter caught the three gang members and interrogated them, it was unlikely they knew anything worthwhile. And if they took them to a police station, it was unlikely that they'd be held for long. It would just make their shift longer.

Hunter stormed past Serenity, shouldering her out of the way. "Foolish that we can't even find three punks. Screw this. I'm going back up."

Serenity sighed and lowered her flashlight. She stared down the long, dark hall toward the three hiding men. Psychically, she whispered, *"It's okay. We're leaving."*

In her mind, the candles flickered with surprise, confusion, and then gratitude.

Maybe, just maybe, supers showing them mercy would be worth something.

Serenity followed her teammate back through the maintenance tunnels and up to the street. Then the two flew back to base to end their shift. The whole time, Serenity tried to hide her relief.

Chapter 19

Recovery

For the third time in a month, Emmett woke up in the biolab. The bright lights and white room were almost comforting.

Almost.

Maybe Emmett would've felt better about waking up if he didn't feel like he got hit by a truck.

His entire body *ached*.

The only thing that Emmett could compare it to was the dull muscle ache that appeared the day after a hard workout, like there were rough coals embedded in his muscles that were still a little too warm to be comfortable.

Except that it wasn't his muscles that ached, but his bones. Those jagged coals weren't ground up inside his muscles—it felt like his bones were filled with them. Usually when his muscles were sore, he could find some position to rest in that relieved the tension and let the muscle relax...

Emmett couldn't bring himself to roll over, but no matter how he adjusted his body on the bed, that dull, aching burn was always there. Nothing helped.

It was such an inconceivable, bewildering sensation that Emmett actually chuckled out loud, and immediately regretted it. His stomach muscles might not have been sore, but his ribs and breastbone most certainly were.

After a minute of gently struggling to find relief, Emmett gave up and let his body go slack. He stared up at the ceiling and focused on his breathing.

"Shit," Emmett muttered.

"How are you feeling?"

Emmett smirked. "TINA, are you joking?"

"No. It's a serious question."

"My skeleton hurts."

"That is to be expected. We kept you sedated for twenty-four hours to monitor you and allow you to avoid the worst of the pain. Since the sedation wore off, Dr. Venture and I have tried to adjust your medication to make you comfortable, but this is the extent of what we can do. Higher doses risks dependency and prolonged recovery."

"Thanks, I think." Emmett held his breath as he pulled the blanket higher up on his chest. "Where is everyone?"

"Dr. Venture will be in shortly. Clara is training in the Gray Room."

Emmett almost nodded, but stopped himself. Instead, he took mental stock of his situation. He'd missed a whole day of training and might even miss more, but he'd be better off for it. Emmett had no idea how strong his skeleton would be now, but it was better than Class 1. Even if it wouldn't affect the strength of his punches, it would help his defense. It would help him survive and allow him to grow stronger in the future.

Either way, this was the first step to getting stronger... The painful, shitty first step.

The doors to the biolab hissed open and Dr. Venture walked in. He stopped in front of the hospital bed and peered down attentively.

"How do you feel?"

"If one more person asks me that..." Emmett trailed off, unable to think of anything funny, and because his face ached.

Venture smirked. "You seem like you're managing. Rate your pain on a scale of zero to ten. Ten being the worst pain imaginable."

Emmett thought for a moment. "Seven, I guess." It wasn't overwhelming, but the sheer consistency of the pain was something else.

Venture raised an eyebrow. "Good. Better than I anticipated. Between the Mutagen-A in your system and your pain tolerance, that's good progress. But now I'm going to need you to get up."

"What?"

Over the next few minutes, Dr. Venture explained that the next phase of Emmett's recovery would require him to get up and walk around. Moving would get his heart rate up and circulate blood and nanomachines to spur on the healing process. The impact from walking would do similarly and encourage the bond between his bones and the metal.

Emmett focused on the task at hand and tried not to think at all—not about Dr. Venture needing to help him sit up in bed, not about the pain of each step or the thin scars that covered his body, and certainly not about leaning on a walker.

He walked a lap around his hospital bed, then sat down to catch his breath. The first few times around, Emmett blinked tears out of his eyes.

Slowly, his laps around the bed got wider. The pain abated a little more each time.

"How many laps do you want me to do?" Emmett asked, tempted to collapse and go back to sleep.

"As many as it takes."

As Emmett walked, Venture followed a step behind, both to spur him on and to catch him if his strength gave out. To Emmett, it felt like Venture was a parent following around a toddler that had just learned to walk.

When Emmett graduated to doing two laps around the room, Venture insisted he give up the walker and balance on his own. A few more times around the room, and Emmett was gently swinging his arms as he walked.

Even now, two hours after waking up, his body still felt tight and sore. The pain was diminishing, but it felt like such a slow process that Emmett wasn't sure if the pain was actually improving or if he was just getting used to it.

Either way, Emmett felt his enthusiasm steadily growing.

The next step was slow calisthenics. Squats, pushups, lunges, bouncing—all smooth and controlled. By this point, the aches throughout Emmett's bones were like quiet static in the back of his mind. Now the most difficult part was trying not to worry about how well his surgical gown was tied.

Thankfully, Dr. Venture had turned away and was examining real-time readouts of Emmett's recovery on the wall monitors.

"That's enough," Venture said, turning back to him. "Your recovery looks good. Now it's time for the next step."

Emmett felt a swell of pride and tried not to smile too broadly. "What's next?"

"The Gray Room."

"...Already?"

Venture disappeared through the double doors, then returned a minute later with Emmett's backpack and a new bodysuit for him. "Put that on, then meet me outside."

The walk to the Gray Room in section 005 wasn't that bad, and the further they went, Emmett found himself both excited to train again and glad to be back in normal clothes—if a black bodysuit could be considered *normal*.

It was certainly better than a hospital gown. He didn't need to worry about the strings in the back coming undone and flashing everyone.

Emmett ran fingers over his left arm and felt the bumps from the injection sites. They were all over his body, spaced out roughly every four inches over the bone, even under his hairline, behind his ears and under his chin. Everywhere except his right arm, of course.

Venture assured Emmett that they would fade over the next few weeks, but ultimately he wasn't sure how the Mutagen-A in Emmett's system would affect the scarring.

There wasn't much time for idle chatting by the time they reached the training hub. Through the viewing window, Emmett could see Clara flying around in her exosuit, zipping through windows and shooting at targets with her kinetic blasts.

Emmett stared, transfixed. He'd never seen Clara move like that.

Despite her speed and the sweeping arcs as she soared through the air, she threaded through buildings without missing a beat—rarely missing a shot either. Every other time Emmett had seen her fly or fight, he'd never really been able to watch her. He'd had his own enemies to focus on.

Emmett had seen Clara use her exosuit several times in training, but now it occurred to him just how much she was holding back. There was a practiced grace and barely-contained ferocity to her movements.

"Go on," Venture said, bringing Emmett back to the present. "No sparring yet. Start with jogging and build your way up to traversing the rooftops." He shooed Emmett down the hall and toward the Gray Room.

Emmett entered the Gray Room proper and was able to watch Clara train for another few minutes before he worked up the motivation to start jogging. Despite how much less his bones ached right now, he still wasn't thrilled about training.

Soon, Emmett sat his backpack down and forced himself to start jogging along the far edge of the Gray Room, sticking by the entrance so he didn't get in Clara's way. He worked on increasing both the duration and speed of his jogs.

Sometime later, Clara noticed him and rocketed over. The sudden noise surprised him, and she landed hard on the tiles beside him.

"Glad to see you're up and about," she said, towering over him in her stealth-gray exosuit. "How are you feeling?"

Emmett rolled his eyes at the third time he'd been asked that same question. "I've been better. I was going to go back to sleep, but your dad made me get up."

Clara laughed. "Good. It was getting boring in here by myself. So, what are we doing first? Tag? Or practicing combat lesson one?"

Emmett chuckled awkwardly. He had no intention of running for his life from an overpowered super simulation.

"Venture said I should start with jogging and traversal."

"Oh..." Clara rested her hands on her hips. "Dad really is taking it easy on you. When he said you would need time to recover, I assumed he was embellishing the surgery. I didn't realize it would be that hard on you."

"I'm surprised you didn't come by and check on me. You came by when I was injured before."

Clara glanced awkwardly at the ground, her face unreadable behind her helmet. "That was different. Those were accidents. You *chose* this."

Emmett was taken aback.

He hadn't forgotten how vehemently Clara had opposed TINA's suggestions for his improvement. She probably thought he was butchering himself. Clara had gotten so distraught she stormed out of the room. Emmett assumed she wouldn't want to watch his surgery, but he didn't realize that same feeling would extend to seeing him in recovery.

"Emmett, listen..."

Emmett held up a hand. "No. We don't have to agree on everything..."

It was a half-truth. Emmett knew objectively that he and Clara weren't going to agree on everything, but also knew that it stung not having her support. When TINA and Dr. Venture had discussed modifications with him, Emmett felt like a part of the team, like they were all working together. Not having Clara's support felt like a step backward.

Emmett's face hardened. "...But just so you know, I'm not stopping. I'm going to keep advancing. I'm not going to stay a Class one super."

Clara stared down at him for a long moment, face unreadable. It felt like she was having the same existential crisis... only, she didn't voice it.

She only nodded.

Chapter 20

Frozen Dinners

Emmett spent the rest of Saturday afternoon in the Gray Room, slowly working his way back up to a semblance of *normal*. He alternated between jogging and calisthenics, taking breaks to swap out his forearm mods. Eventually he added shadowboxing and easy parkour.

Meanwhile, Clara continued her own training with her exosuit, flying between buildings and shooting at targets. More than a few times, the sounds of battle caught Emmett off guard and he whirled around, only to remember that he was in the Gray Room and not back on Champion street.

The soreness in Emmett's bones dwindled more and more until it felt like background static. After a few hours, Emmett was running across rooftops again and leaping small gaps.

The pain only spiked during particularly big falls, feeling like a jolt of electricity shot up through his feet and out his neck. Those moments brought Emmett to his knees, but passed just as quickly.

Clara flew over and landed beside him on the roof of a three story building. She put her hands on her hips, a gesture that looked ridiculous on her exosuit.

"You should take a break."

Emmett scoffed. He felt great. "Why?"

"Because it's almost seven, and some of us need to eat."

On cue, Emmett's stomach rumbled and he relented. "Alright. Break time."

Ever since Emmett had started spending most evenings training in the lab, he had grown accustomed to the frozen food selection that Dr. Venture and Clara lived off of.

Growing up, Emmett's mom did most of the cooking, and had vehemently opposed *microwave meals*, as she called them. Mom could barely bring herself to make a side of instant mashed potatoes, let alone trust some soulless corporation with her entire dinner.

Because of this, Emmett had similar reservations to Dr. Venture and Clara's dinner arrangements. It wasn't so much that they celebrated with frozen pizza—it was that *everything* they ate came out of a box.

To be fair, Dr. Venture and Clara were connoisseurs of the pre-packaged meal, and so Emmett hadn't had a bad-tasting one yet.

There was the now classic *Big Larry's* frozen pizza and fries. Various forms of breaded chicken, from nuggets to wings to individually wrapped cordon bleu. Frozen tortellini and canned sauces. Spicy and non-spicy dumplings. Taquitos and empanadas.

Spaghetti felt like the closest the Ventures came to cooking, and Clara insisted on making it her way—with mushroom sauce and heapings of shredded parmesan.

Other instant and canned dinners Emmett was already familiar with from his time as a penny-pinching college student: Instant noodles, soups, ravioli in various forms, and canned chili.

Then there were the *complete* frozen dinners—Pot roast, mashed potatoes, and green beans. Whole lasagna. Teriyaki bowls. Pot pies.

Today, Dr. Venture had heated up a family-sized chicken and broccoli alfredo. By the time Emmett and Clara made it to the living quarters in section 001, Emmett's stomach was rumbling with anticipation.

The three sat on the couches of the living room, bowls of noodles in their laps, with the news on for background noise. They ate in relative silence, Clara and Emmett occasionally making comments about the commercials.

Emmett's phone buzzed.

Lock 7:16 PM: *How's Marianne?*

Emmett chuckled. He looked back at his texts and saw that someone had indeed sent a message to Lock telling him 'not to wait up.'

A part of him still hated that he couldn't be honest with Lock. Hiding a secret identity from a family member or a roommate felt like a tired trope, but what else could Emmett do? The whole *Marianne* bit just seemed ridiculous. Emmett imagined if Lock ever did find out, the first thing he would do would be to give Emmett grief for such a lame cover story.

Emmett texted back.

Emmett: 7:17 PM: *She's good. Be back later.*

"Who's that?" Clara asked, half-covering her mouth.

"The roommate." Emmett stared at his empty bowl. "I should probably get back."

Clara snorted. "You should probably rest—I still can't believe Dad had you up and running around after surgery."

Venture barely looked up from his noodles. "Emmett needed to get out of bed to recover quicker. Besides, he has that project to finish."

Emmett's blood ran cold. He'd just turned in his radio locator project write up... Had he forgotten another assignment? How much time did he have?

Emmett stammered a response, about to ask Dr. Venture what assignment he forgot about, when Venture turned—

And smiled. "Gotcha."

Emmett sighed and slunk back down onto the couch.

Venture continued, "You should've seen your face."

Clara just shook her head.

Emmett left a few minutes later, still not fully calmed down after Dr. Venture's joke. Emmett had been spending a lot of time training and worrying about being a superhero—he was terrified of missing assignments. The last thing he needed was to botch his last semester.

There was also something about being cooped up in the lab that didn't sit right with Emmett. Maybe it was the lingering reminder of his trauma or just the fact that Venture and Clara still didn't trust him fully—either way, Emmett was glad to be heading back to his apartment.

He supposed that he could have waited for the bus, but he decided to take the rooftops instead. Emmett felt almost completely healed, which Venture assured him wasn't the case. Venture still told him to take it easy, and avoid sparring on the rooftops or getting into trouble with the Summit—he'd added that last part with a smirk.

So Emmett did as the Doctor ordered and took his time on the way home. He donned his mask and utility belt, and jogged across the skyline, taking a northern arc around downtown to stick to the shorter rooftops and enjoying the night air.

Little by little, it was getting warmer in Belport. It was almost April, and the winter chill was gone from the night air. It would be another few months before the nights were warm.

Emmett was nearly halfway home and almost exactly North of downtown when he had to start using his whip to climb—

And when Emmett noticed that he was being followed.

A super was a block away, running parallel to him.

Emmett kept jogging, but tried to keep the super in the corner of his vision. For a moment, Emmett thought it was a coincidence, but the super was on his left and downtown was on his right. Which meant that Emmett was silhouetted against the bright lights—there was no way the super didn't see him.

Emmett jogged another roof and considered his options: He didn't feel confident getting into a fight with an unknown super—definitely not in his condition and without Clara. Even the knowledge that Venture probably had a Fast-Response Drone tailing him didn't reassure Emmett.

He felt marginally better about running away. He had his mods, gadgets, and utility belt. There was always the chance that the super had something that Emmett couldn't counter, but he'd have to take that risk.

Running was probably his best option, but was that all?

What were the odds that this random super was after him, anyway?

Against his better judgment, Emmett stopped and turned toward the super. Then he waved.

To his surprise, the super stopped and then waved back. Then they leapt to the next roof over and waved again for Emmett to join them.

Emmett took a deep breath and leapt over, meeting the new super in the middle. They were leaning over, hands on their knees, catching their breath.

"Give me a sec," the guy wheezed.

Emmett smiled in confusion.

The new super was dressed like an explorer, with heavy boots, khaki pants, and a vest with what looked like a hundred pockets on it. On their back, they carried a massive canvas backpack that was stuffed comically full. But their mask was the strangest part. Emmett didn't get a good look until the guy caught his breath and stood up straight, but he was wearing what looked like a cut up scarf. It was thick and frilled around the edges, and a mass of curly hair that came out of the top like a funnel.

No wonder the guy was out of breath.

Finally, Emmett's curiosity got the better of him. "Were you following me?"

The super finally stood up, still breathing heavily, and answered, "Well, yeah," like the answer was obvious.

Emmett chuckled. "Why?"

The guy shrugged. "Why not?"

"Do you just follow any random super you see on the rooftops?"

He shrugged again. "Sometimes. My name's McGuire. I was trying to get your attention. You really ought to pay attention to your surroundings." He wagged a finger at Emmett for emphasis.

He was wearing fingerless gloves—the kind that mailmen wore in movies and TV.

Dumbfounded, Emmett replied, "Well, most people that follow me haven't just wanted to talk."

"Talk? I want to spar. Then I'll decide if you're worth talking to."

Was this guy for real?

Emmett glanced around, wondering if this was some sort of elaborate and convoluted trap, but didn't see anyone else on the rooftops or in the sky. He briefly considered asking Venture or TINA to scan the block, but knowing them, they probably already had. And neither of them had interrupted this strange conversation, so...

Emmett turned back to McGuire and nodded. "Okay. Sure. Why not... How do you want to do this?"

McGuire slid his feet apart, like he was taking a fighting stance. His right hand went behind his hip so that it hovered next to his backpack like he was an old gunslinger.

"We'll go on three," McGuire said. Then added, "Aren't you going to get ready?"

Chapter 21

Time Out

Emmett didn't answer right away. He kept his eyes on the ridiculous super standing across the roof.

McGuire looked like a crazed adventurer who'd been isekai'd from a wilderness expedition and decided on a whim that he was a super. Now he had a hand hovering just over his backpack like a wild west gunslinger.

Emmett didn't know whether the guy would pull out a concealed pistol or a rubber chicken.

"Hey, are you sure you're up for this?" McGuire asked. "Because I can come back tomorrow."

Emmett snapped back to reality and quickly considered his own options hidden in his arm and his utility belt.

McGuire must have seen something change in Emmett's eyes, because he flashed a smile.

"Alright, let's do this. Three... Two... One... Go!"

Emmett reached into his upper arm compartment and grabbed two smoke pellets.

McGuire pulled out a slingshot.

By the time Emmett tossed the smoke pellets, McGuire had fired the slingshot, hurling something that looked like a cross between bolas and an old spring toy. It spread out as it flew at Emmett, and it was easy to imagine the projectile wrapping around him and tangling him up.

But whatever Emmett had in mind was nothing like what happened.

Emmett felt like he saw the ridiculous sight in slow motion: The balls on either end of the spring popped as tiny rockets ignited—hurling the bolas forward at super speed.

He might've been able to dodge out of the way before, but now the bolas hit him square across the chest. The balls wrapped around him completely, pinning his arms flat against his body. More pops sounded, causing the bolas to twist together into a knot.

Smoke from the pellets filled the rooftop. Meanwhile, Emmett struggled against the bolas. The wire was thick, clearly made for restraining and not made to be a weapon. His left hand was pinned low on his waist—close enough to reach the knife in his utility belt. A second later, he was trying to cut himself free.

McGuire stepped out of the smoke, trying his best to wave it away. "Aha! You'll never be able to cut through my super snare—"

The bolas snapped.

"Aw, that's not fair."

Emmett pulled at the rest of the wire to free himself. Meanwhile, McGuire reached toward his backpack.

Before he was fully loose, Emmett slung his whip toward the super. Thankfully, his enemy didn't appear to have super speed or super strength, because Emmett's whip wrapped around McGuire's leg. He pulled, and the super toppled right over.

There was the briefest look of horror on McGuire's face as he fell, followed by, "That's *really* not fair!"

Emmett pulled, sliding his writhing enemy across the ground.

With a look of panic, McGuire grabbed two things out of his pack. A piece of chewing gum and a small disk. He quickly chewed the gum, spit it onto the disk, then stuck it to Emmett's whip. A shock went through the whip and through Emmett's arm, making him flinch. Immediately, the whip went slack around McGuire's feet and he was able to wriggle free.

Emmett tried recalling the whip, but every time he tried moving any cybernetic part of himself, a jolt of electricity interfered with his commands.

"What the—"

Emmett's disbelief was cut off by McGuire's slingshot. This time, something cushiony hit Emmett directly in the face and wrapped around his head. A moment of panic set in before Emmett realized he could still breathe—he was just blind.

He tried grabbing for more smoke pellets to even the odds, but a jolt of electricity shot through his arm and the compartment wouldn't open.

Shit.

Emmett reached up with his still-working hand and tried pulling the cloth free. It took him a second to get a good grip on the smooth fabric.

He was running out of options. Despite his utility belt, most things weren't useful—not now. He couldn't swap mods with his arm disabled. He still had the noise makers and sonic grenades, but the latter might be too powerful. It didn't seem like McGuire had enhanced strength, so his hearing might get permanently damaged or he might even get crippled if Emmett struck him physically.

Instead, Emmett called, "Time out!"

"No way!"

A second later, something heavy knocked into Emmett's stomach. It felt like he'd been hit with a baseball bat—he doubled over, the wind knocked out of him. A second blow hit Emmett in the shoulder, nearly knocking him off his feet.

Emmett's breath was ragged, almost as much from the disbelief as from the pain. How was this guy knocking him around like this? Had McGuire been hiding his true strength to throw Emmett off guard?

Instinctively, Emmett ducked—

And felt the *whoosh* of air from McGuire's weapon as it passed overhead. At the same time, Emmett reached for his utility belt and grabbed the taser.

Then he jabbed it forward and pressed the button.

McGuire yelped and then fell with a *thump*.

"...Okay. Time out."

A second later, Emmett tore the fabric wrap off his head, careful not to take his mask off with it.

McGuire was just starting to climb to his feet. His arms wobbled with effort. His jacket must have saved him a little, but he was clearly still feeling the effects of the taser. McGuire raised his hands, one of which held a comically large set of brass knuckles. "What? You want some more?"

Emmett just shook his head, then busted out laughing. He tried to stammer an explanation, but all he managed to get out was, "No."

"Shucks," McGuire said. He slipped off his brass knuckles and shoved them in a side pouch of his already overstuffed backpack, then adjusted his mask. Neither sight helped Emmett recover faster.

A few minutes later, Emmett stood straight up again, his stomach cramping from laughter. McGuire had joined in, but Emmett couldn't tell if the fellow super was laughing earnestly or just humoring him.

"I'm sorry about the taser," Emmett muttered. "You didn't leave me much choice."

"You could've actually fought," McGuire said, crossing his arms over his chest.

Emmett shook his head. "I don't think that would've gone well for you."

"Because you have super strength?"

Emmett felt like he'd been caught in a lie and the laughter dropped from Emmett's voice. He still wasn't sure if he could trust McGuire. So he hadn't wanted to show all of his tricks, but apparently Emmett had shown more abilities than he'd meant to.

"...What do you mean?"

"That's why you didn't attack at all. All you did was react. I know I said we were sparring, but you could've taken it seriously, you know."

"Sorry," Emmett replied. "I didn't mean anything by it." He reeled in his whip and plucked the shock device off of it. Instantly, feeling and control returned to his prosthetic arm. It looked like a tiny watch battery. Emmett offered it to McGuire, but the super waved it away.

"They're only good for one use. Besides, I've got more where that came from." McGuire patted the side of his bag for emphasis.

Emmett pocketed the device; McGuire didn't seem to care. "Can I ask you something? How did you know I have super strength?"

McGuire walked over to the bolas laying on the ground and held it up for emphasis before pocketing the remains. "This isn't any old wire... You cut through it with a tactical knife. That requires super strength." Emmett nodded, and McGuire chuckled awkwardly. "And your arm... Well, that was obvious when you kept pulling things out of it."

Emmett swung his prosthetic arm, making sure everything felt right and he wasn't just imagining it. ...Everything did.

Emmett reached out with his right hand—his metal hand. "I'm Mod."

McGuire shook it and winced. For a second, Emmett thought he'd squeezed too hard, but then McGuire winked and said, "Gotcha."

Emmett rolled his eyes.

For the next hour, McGuire and Emmett hung out on the roof of that building, talking about tricks, traps, mods, gadgets, and random tech. They kept it light, and both seemed hesitant to talk about gadgets they hadn't used during their sparring session—

Almost like they were saving the rest of their tricks for another sparring session.

McGuire did confess that all of his gadgets were homemade, a fact that he seemed prideful of. He claimed it gave him an advantage over other tech supers because they 'had no idea what to expect.'

McGuire was a *gadgeteer*, as he referred to it. McGuire claimed he had a knack for making small and quickly cobbled together devices.

Emmett didn't agree—the term *knack* was used to describe minor powers or those that were hard to categorize. Even if McGuire's methods were strange, he'd been able to knock Emmett on his ass—that was *not* a minor power. But he didn't argue with McGuire.

Emmett skirted the details about his super strength and his prosthetic arm, and thankfully McGuire had the sense not to pry. There seemed to be an easy understanding between the two supers about what was fair game to talk about and what was off-limits. The arrangement reminded Emmett of making friends with peers in his college classes, and, in a weird way, McGuire was really the first peer super that Emmett had met. Dr. Venture and Clara almost felt like family, and Athena felt like a mentor.

Eventually, both of them agreed that it was getting late.

Emmett was about to leap away when he turned and asked, "Do you have a burner phone?"

"Yeah."

"We should do this again sometime."

McGuire's eyes lit up. "Rematch!"

Emmett rolled his eyes.

Chapter 22

Waiting / Lock

Emmett and McGuire exchanged numbers for their burner phones, then went their separate ways. He jogged the rest of the way home, still processing that he'd made his first superhero friend—

Emmett still wasn't sure if it was a *good* idea.

Either way, he had another connection to the supers of Belport, and McGuire seemed to be a fellow mask like himself. Emmett supposed there was a chance that the eccentric super was actually a registered cape with the Summit of Heroes, but he doubted it.

Emmett thought back to his run in with Serenity and Hunter Nine. If all capes were like that, it might be awhile before he had any connections in the Summit.

Lock was still out by the time Emmett got home around eleven o'clock Saturday night, and Emmett didn't see him the next morning, either.

He couldn't be sure when it happened, but it felt like Lock was working even more than usual.

Emmett worried about his roommate. Between senior year and how much Lock worked, it was a wonder his roommate was holding it all together. Maybe they could talk about it if Lock came back today.

Then again, Emmett had been out more than usual, too. Some days, it felt like he only came back to the apartment to sleep. Between training, research, and making mods, Emmett had missed out on a lot of things this past month, and he felt guilty that he hadn't been there all that much for Lock.

But, since Lock wasn't back yet, Emmett put on music and spent Sunday on schoolwork and mods. Dr. Venture checked in once, asking how his recovery was going and reminding him to do calisthenics throughout the day to get his blood circulating. Emmett made sure every hour to do something, whether it was pushups, squats, or simply pacing the apartment.

Briefly, he looked at the small watch battery-like device that he'd brought back from his sparring match against McGuire. He peeled the gum off of it and carefully pried it open. It wasn't just one disc battery, but three that had been crudely wired together... And that was about it.

The longer Emmett stared at the device, the more he was certain that it shouldn't have been able to affect his arm. It shouldn't have been able to deliver a big enough charge or even transfer a charge through his skin to the wiring beneath. The device *should not have worked.*

In the end, Emmett stuffed the broken gadget and the gum into a baggie and then into his pocket, resolving to ask Dr. Venture about it on Monday.

Lock came home Sunday night.

It was almost ten, and Emmett was winding down, laying on the couch and scrolling the news forums of *Double Mask, Reddest Knight,* and *The Green Machine.* Emmett sat up when he heard the door.

Lock walked in, looking shaken. He wasn't wearing a hoodie like usual, and his black T-shirt and pants were cut up. He stood in the doorway, staring blankly ahead.

"Hey man," Emmett said.

Lachlan's eyes locked on Emmett, almost as if he didn't recognize his roommate. Even the music felt quiet and drowned out.

It was a long moment before Lock responded. "Hey."

Then Lock strode into his room. He came back out a minute later, having changed into a new set of black clothes and hoodie. He came over to sit on the opposite side of the couch, and Emmett sat up to give him room.

Lock sat with the hood pulled over his head and hands stuffed in his hoodie. He stared forward without blinking, without talking. There was blood on his cheek. It didn't look like his.

Emmett reached over and grabbed a nearby napkin leftover from some other night's takeout, and handed it to Lock.

"You've got blood on you," Emmett said, pointing to his own cheek.

Lock took the napkin and stared at it before finally dabbing his tongue to it and wiping the blood away. Then he crumpled it up and held on to it.

"It's not mine," Lock said, as if that was all the explanation he needed to offer.

Emmett glanced idly at the blank screen of the TV, then back to his roommate. All thought of going to sleep in the next few minutes was long gone. Before Lock got home, Emmett had readied himself for jokes about Marianne. But not now.

Some shit had clearly happened and it was clearly on Lock's mind. Emmett had seen Lock contemplative, angry, and even sad... but Emmett had never seen his roommate like this.

"Work was that bad, huh?"

The question felt stupid, but Emmett didn't know what else to ask, and sitting in silence felt worse.

Lock nodded absently, then slumped down further on the couch. "Work... Yeah. It was a hard night."

"You want to talk about it?"

Lock hung his head. For a solid minute, it looked like he wanted to say *something*, but nothing came out. His head lulled. He licked his lips. He took a breath and then let it out.

Finally, Lock spoke.

"There was a, uh, fight today. At the bar. Couple of dudes. I went over and sorted them out, but they... didn't deserve it."

"If they were starting trouble at the bar, isn't that what you guys are for?"

Lock shook his head meekly. "They didn't deserve *what they got.*"

"Oh..." Emmett trailed off, thinking about the blood on Lock's face. Emmett had known for a while that Lock worked at some rough places; he didn't exactly hide his injuries well. But Emmett hadn't thought about how much Lock might be roughing up others...

Damn. Lock had just been talking about roughing up *multiple* guys—not just one. Emmett would've been impressed if not for the look of shock on his friend's face.

Just how bad did Lock hurt them?

But that wasn't the question that Emmett asked.

"What do you mean, they didn't deserve it?"

"They're... I put them in the hospital."

All at once, Emmett understood. Every other time, Lock was so nonchalant about his job, about the violence. He didn't seem to care how badly he got beaten up, and until now, Emmett didn't think Lock really cared about the violence he used either.

Lock was worried.

Emmett sighed and tried to think of something—anything—to say. It felt like Lock was floating away from shore and into a sea of misery.

"...The hospital is the best place they could be right now."

"Yeah." Lock smirked. It looked hollow, like he was putting on a face.

Emmett couldn't help but ask, "Is there something else wrong?"

"I... I'm alright." A second later, he sat forward and quickly grabbed the remote. "I don't want to talk about it anymore."

"Alright." Emmett leaned back on the couch and decided he'd stay up a little later, in case Lock could use the company. "Let me know if you change your mind."

Lock flipped through apps on the TV, looking for something to fill the void. He didn't say anything else.

Emmett stayed with his friend, but it felt like a wedge had been driven between them.

Lock waited for Emmett to go to sleep before he went to the kitchen sink and washed the blood off his hands, and wiped dried specks off of the remote. Then he picked the scabs off his fingertips and washed his hands again. He'd been careful to hide the gore from Emmett—he couldn't screw that up now.

Lock could still taste the blood.

He had to be imagining it, but that didn't change anything. It certainly wasn't a fucking comfort.

Lock stood in the kitchen, staring down at the stainless steel of the sink. He'd scrubbed it clean, but he bet there were still traces of blood. Microscopic, but still there.

Emmett's words came back to him: 'Let me know if you change your mind.'

What's done was done. Talking about it wouldn't help anyone—not Lock, and not those guys. There was no going back. There was no changing his mind.

Lock had taken the job offer.

He'd killed three people.

It wasn't Lock's first time. He'd killed two others during Gnosis's experimental fights. Then two other supers. Then Porcelain.

But those were different.

Maybe it was because those had been in battle or just because they'd been supers who could fight back... Either way, those were different.

Tonight, Lock had *murdered* three people. It hadn't been a fight, hadn't been a challenge. Lock had to throw his hoodie in a dumpster because it had so much fucking blood on it.

There was no going back now. The VP of Gnosis would get word about tonight. He would know that Lock carried out the job without fail, without question. He'd passed their test.

Lock had known not to trust Gnosis. He'd known the internship was sketchy, that the mutagen program was a gamble. Known that they were making him into a weapon when they'd started him on Mutagen-X. Lock had expected to do a stint on the front lines of one of Gnosis's proxy wars as a black-ops super... So far, that was one of only two things he'd been wrong about.

And he'd known that this new job was something worse than pit fights with mutagen test subjects, worse than slaughtering foreign soldiers. He fucking knew it, and he'd agreed anyway.

The second thing that Lock had been wrong about was what ate at him from the inside while he stood alone in the kitchen, staring at a sink that had been scrubbed clean, but would never be truly clean again. Lock meant what he said to Emmett—

Lock was alright.

He might've been in shock earlier, but he was alright. And that was the worst part.

Working security became easy. Fights against test subjects didn't rile him up anymore...

But why was murder so easy?

Had he really gone so far and been desensitized so much? Or had that horrible truth been there all along, and all Lock needed to do was tear off the scab?

Did it even matter?

It wasn't just Lock's life on the line. He couldn't just walk away. He had his sister to think about. Lock knew too much—had done too much.

Gnosis would never let him out.

Lock's face felt wet, and he wiped the tears on his sleeve. Better that than blood. Then he walked to his room and shut the door. All there was to do now was try to sleep.

And wait for the next text message.

Chapter 23

Bones and Nerves

Emmett couldn't wait to get to the lab on Monday afternoon.

He managed to make a good dent in his schoolwork and projects over the weekend, which gave his bones a little more time to recover. But classes dragged and by the time they ended, Emmett could've sprinted all the way there. The excitement pushed everything else out of his mind, even his concern for his roommate.

Emmett had questions, but he was mostly just ready to get back to training.

Emmett met Dr. Venture in the hub of section 006, the biomedical wing. The doctor had dozens of exosuit schematics spread out over the wall monitors and was looking over them thoughtfully. Even with such a large display, the captions and details were too small for Emmett to see across the room. The only thing he recognized upon walking in was that the pieces were from Clara's exosuit.

Doctor Venture turned toward Emmett and minimized the displays with a sweep of his hand. For a second, it looked like his glasses were glowing faintly, but it must have been Emmett's imagination—Emmett blinked and the glow was gone.

"How are you feeling?" Venture asked, his intense focus now aimed at Emmett.

Emmett shrugged and rolled his shoulders. "I feel fine—like I want to get back in the Gray Room."

Venture smiled. "All things in due time. First, let's get a scan and see how your bones are taking to the alloy."

Dr. Venture led Emmett to one of the rooms alongside the surgical suite. This one was currently outfitted with a scanning suite: In the center of the room was a platform encased with glass and flanked by two giant metal pillars. The pillars were filled with scanning tech and would spin around the enclosure, mapping Emmett's tissue and charting his healing.

But hearing Venture explain it didn't help Emmett's unease.

He disrobed to his bodysuit and stepped inside the enclosure.

"Hold your arms up and remain as still as you can," Venture said as he hunched over the controls.

When Emmett was a kid, he'd broken his arm and gotten an MRI. They'd put him in a similar tube, but he'd been laying down.

"If this is an MRI, shouldn't I be laying down?"

Venture raised an eyebrow. "Do you really think this is a regular MRI machine?"

Emmett chuckled awkwardly. "It isn't, right?"

Venture turned back to the controls. "Of course not. An MRI would probably kill you, considering how much metal is now in your body. This is closer to a CT scan. *Now*, try to relax."

Emmett swallowed and tried to stand still. The metal pillars lurched and began to swing around the enclosure, gradually picking up speed. As they did, thumps and clicks emanated and also gradually grew in speed and intensity. The spinning of the pillars grew so fast and violent that they became blurs and the roar of wind in the room became deafening.

Through the blur, Dr. Venture looked completely unperturbed by the noise. Soon after, Emmett shut his eyes.

Slowly, the noise faded, and Emmett opened his eyes to see the pillars slowing. Venture nodded from behind the controls for Emmett to relax. It felt like a full minute before the pillars finally slowed to a stop.

"TINA, bring up the scans on the wall display, please," Venture said.

Emmett watched as cross sections of himself appeared on the screens, almost like the exosuit schematics from a few minutes ago. The two most glaring parts were his skeleton and his prosthetic arm.

His skeleton now had a latticework of metal alloy inside it. Venture had said that it would look like a cross between porous coral and chainmail, and Emmett couldn't think of a better description. From far away, the lattice looked like chainmail, but the close-up views of his skeleton looked more like coral. Bone was already growing inside the pockets, fusing with the metal.

Venture pointed to the close-up view. "Thanks to the Mutagen-A in your system and the nanites from surgery, you've almost completely healed. Maybe one more day. We'll check back in at the end of the week, but for now though, you can go back to your regular training."

Emmett let out a sigh of relief that he didn't know he'd been holding. He trusted the doctor with his life, but Venture had made it clear that there were risks to all of the procedures. So far, Emmett had been lucky.

"Is there any way to test it?"

Venture raised an eyebrow. "TINA has already simulated stress tests. You should be able to take direct punches from a Class two super without your ribs breaking or your head caving in. However, just because your bones can handle the damage doesn't mean that your organs can."

Emmett nodded. "Okay. So, what's next on the list?"

At that, Venture chuckled. "You're still not fully recovered. Take the week, examine TINA's suggestions, and think about it. *Carefully.*"

"I want to do this," Emmett said, the words tumbling out as he stared at the screen. "Not everyone gets a chance like this. I need to do something—something good, and I can only do that if I get stronger... I don't know if I'll go all the way through TINA's suggestions, but I want this."

Venture was looking at him now with an air of satisfaction. Maybe even pride. "I know you do. That's why I didn't just save you; I gave you the chance to be a hero."

"Thanks," Emmett replied. The word felt pitiful compared to how much he meant it.

Venture waved dismissively. "That's not why I'm telling you this. It's not just that you've wanted to be a super for so long, how hard you train, or how seriously you take this opportunity. It's that your heart is in the right place. I saw how you tried to save Porcelain. How you tried to talk to her instead of blindly using violence. Power is not your goal—it's a means for you to do good. I gave you the chance to be the type of super that you look up to.

"But the world is complicated." Venture's face turned somber as he continued. "Most supers start off wanting to change the world, but the truth is that change—real change—is slow. Most supers want to do good, thinking that the world is black and white, but it's really shades of gray. One day, you'll be forced to make choices... And you won't be certain you've made the right one.

"That's why so many capes and masks stick to fighting villains and don't fight wars, why they take on drug dealers and gangs instead of corporations like Gnosis, and why those like Paragon stick to natural disasters and world-ending threats. Those things are simple—not gray. You should do the good that you can."

Emmett listened intently. If Venture had meant his speech to dissuade Emmett from setting his sights too high, then it hadn't worked as intended. In fact, it had done the opposite.

Emmett didn't want to be relegated to chasing criminals and fighting low-level villains... For a moment, Emmett wanted it all. He didn't just want to keep the world a decent place—he wanted to make it a better place.

Emmett finally said, "It's good that we're a team, then."

"How so?"

"Maybe together we can do better than just doing *good enough*."

There was another flicker of pride across Venture's face. "That leads me to my next point—we are already doing some good."

Emmett turned to Venture curiously. "What do you mean?"

Dr. Venture gestured to the screens, focusing on Emmett's prosthetic arm and its connections to his shoulder and neck. The metal frame extended into his collarbone, shoulder blade, and a portion of his ribs. Those connection points were joined by a combination of screws and porous connections, similar to the rest of his skeleton.

He pointed to the clusters of polymers within the artificial muscles, specifically. "Follow these connections upward."

Slowly, Emmett followed the polymers up his arm, noting how the smaller ones that allowed his artificial skin to sense pressure and temperature coalesced into bundles. As they moved further up his arm, they joined with larger strands that presumably controlled his artificial muscles.

The polymer nerves didn't stop at the shoulder joint or even where artificial muscles and real muscles were mixed together in his chest, back, or shoulder. The polymer strands extended down his side and up into his neck—much farther than Emmett would've guessed.

Emmett asked TINA to zoom in on the most distant connections and found that his real nerves and his artificial ones also seemed to blend together like his bones had. Not like coral, but like two lengths of rope woven together. At this magnification at least, it was impossible to tell where machine ended and flesh began.

Admittedly though, Emmett wasn't sure what Dr. Venture wanted to show him. He'd already mentioned that Emmett's healing and prosthetic integration had gone exceedingly well, but Emmett already knew that.

"Dr. Venture... What am I supposed to be looking at?"

"I told you that your prosthetic arm was one of the most advanced ones I've ever designed. Most amputees will never be able to afford one as advanced and as resilient as this one." This time, Venture pointed to the blending of nerves. "*This* has never been achieved before. Even for the most expensive current generation prosthetics, simulating the sensation of touch, pressure, and temperature is crude. The polymer nerves in your arm aren't widely used, but they are fairly easy and cheap to manufacture. As far as the rest of your prosthetic goes, they are by far the cheapest part.

"TINA and I are going to replicate your nerve connections. If we can manage that with just nanomachines and *without* Mutagen-A, then we could revolutionize prosthetics for millions of people."

Emmett listened intently, and only now realized that he was smiling. Of all the new things in his short time as a super, the idea was a little hard to process.

"That is pretty awesome."

Venture crossed his arms. "Yes. Yes, it is. And I couldn't have done it without you."

Emmett scoffed. "Alright, now you're just trying to make me feel better. All I did was almost die."

"You'd be surprised how many scientific breakthroughs happen that way."

Emmett chuckled, then remembering his other question, pulled the plastic bag out of his pocket and emptied McGuire's device onto the table. It had gotten jumbled in his pocket, and Emmett had to peel the dried gum off of the watch batteries again.

"Can you tell me anything about this?"

Dr. Venture poked idly at the device. "This is from your sparring match with McGuire?"

Emmett knew that Dr. Venture had been keeping tabs on him, but so far he'd believed the doctor that he hadn't been watching *too* closely. 'Close' must be a relative word.

Emmett nodded tentatively, but couldn't resist calling Venture out. "Passive monitoring, huh?"

Without looking up, Venture replied plainly, "You'd just woken up from major surgery... Did you really think the gum was necessary?"

Emmett sighed at both comments. "I didn't know what to think about it. He pulled out all these crazy inventions. That electrical jammer, or whatever it is, *should not have worked* on my arm."

"You're right," Venture continued. "That's one of the advantages of a power like his... What the Summit calls *Artificers*, supers that use technology, is actually a very broad category of powers. Most of us have a cognitive enhancement—I have a knack for parsing data. Some have control over magnetism or have limited psychic control over technology. But most of us have simply created a potent technology or cornered the market on something that can be used as a weapon.

"*Gadgeteers* are a different matter altogether. They can, quite literally, create impossible technology. As far as classifications go, their powers are closer to Reality Warpers than to Artificers."

Emmett nodded along and saw the tiny batteries in a new light. "That's why the device doesn't work anymore. It's like a temporary warper... Is it based on time or proximity?"

Venture sighed, as if choosing whether or not to give Emmett a long lecture.

"It depends on the individual," Venture finally said. "We categorize and taxonomize all these things that are as varied as snowflakes or grains of sand—classifying powers only helps *so much*. So, actually, gadgeteers can be limited by time or proximity, or both." He punctuated the lesson with a shrug.

Emmett gestured to McGuire's device. "So there's no way to figure out his powers from that?"

"I like where your head's at, but no. Once his power stopped affecting the device, there's no way to replicate it or trace it."

A part of Emmett hoped he could have gotten something out of studying it, even if he couldn't go so far as replicating it. Dejected, Emmett bagged the device and pocketed it again. He'd hold on to it, regardless.

Venture noticed, but instead continued his lecture. "Gadgeteers are very versatile, but their abilities will never beat true, stable technology. Nor will their technology have a chance of affecting others like our nerve polymers."

Emmett nodded. "Don't worry. I won't run away to join the Gadgeteers."

"Very funny," Venture replied flatly. "If we're done here, I have new training for you."

At that Emmett perked up, forgetting all about the lifeless device in his pocket.

"You once asked me if there was any protection against psychic powers... That's what we're going to work on today."

Chapter 24

Psychic Defense

Emmett walked to the Gray Room by himself and found Clara meditating in the center of a clearing. The arrangement reminded Emmett of one of Belport's scattered parks, albeit tiled and white instead of grass and wood. Faux park benches lined one side of the room and a basketball court flanked the other side, complete with almost polygonal looking hoops.

Despite the scenery, Clara looked completely serene sitting in the middle of it. She was wearing her usual tights and tank top. Her hoodie lay on the floor next to her.

"You look like you're ready for yoga," Emmett said, a little more sarcastically than he meant it.

Clara rolled her eyes. "Sit. You know, yoga can be just as good as meditation. Did Dad explain what we're doing for training today?"

Emmett sat across from her, assuming the same cross-legged position. "He told me that I'm going to learn how to defend against psychic attacks. That was all he said."

"He didn't tell you *anything*?"

"No... Why?"

Clara smirked. "Because we're starting with yoga."

Clara led Emmett through several yoga routines. They went through seated and standing meditations, warrior poses, and so many animal poses that Emmett lost track.

It was Emmett's first experience with yoga, but he could see the appeal. He imagined it could've been relaxing out in nature or with the right music, or that it could be a decent workout.

Yoga wasn't hard for him, not with Mutagen-A and his prosthetic arm. Emmett felt like he could've held any of the poses for hours.

Clara assured him that wasn't the point of what they were doing.

"Focus on your breathing. Focus on your muscles and how everything connects together."

Emmett sighed. She'd repeated those words several times throughout their routine, but he still didn't *get it*.

Emmett stood in a lunge with his arms stretched overhead—in one of the warrior poses, maybe. "Clara, what's the point of this?"

"Shhh... Just relax."

Emmett relaxed and stood straight, trying to maintain his patience. "Please, just give me something. I don't even know what I'm supposed to be feeling. How does any of this help defend against psychics?"

Clara sat down and motioned for him to follow. She was half-smirking.

"Are you just messing with me?" Emmett asked.

"No, I'm not just messing with you. This is part of your psychic training." Clara's face was set, and all trace of her smile was gone.

"Alright. So, how does it work?"

Clara explained, "Psychics and illusionists attack the mind. You wanted to get better at fighting, so we practiced sparring and grappling. To get more agile and aware of your body, we practiced running and parkour."

"This strengthens my mind?"

Clara snorted. "No! This increases your awareness of your mental state, your body, and your surroundings... Okay. So, how did you beat that Serenity chick the other day?"

Emmett thought back to the warehouse district. "She used her psychic power to freeze me, so I couldn't move, but she couldn't freeze my cybernetic arm."

Clara added, "And once you realized that, you were able to move it and shoot her."

Emmett tried to remember the specifics of the fight and how it felt when he couldn't move.

"I realized I could move my fingers first. Then I realized I could move my entire arm." Emmett flexed his hand to help remember the sensation.

Clara nodded. "That's awareness. When you first started training in the Gray Room, you made a lot of progress pretty quickly. Some of that was due to Mutagen-A, *but* normal people see the most gains in those same first few weeks of working out or strength training. It's actually because your body's nervous system is learning the moves, becoming more coordinated, and becoming more efficient. Once again, that's awareness."

Emmett's curiosity was piqued, but he was more eager to get started. "Okay. I'm following. I'm going to workout my mind... What do I do?"

Clara adjusted herself so that she was sitting cross-legged and ready to meditate again. "We're going to start with grounding exercises."

Emmett mirrored her. "So, like meditation."

"Yes, like meditation. Try to keep up." Clara closed her eyes. "Now, who are you?"

Emmett closed his eyes and answered. "I am Emmett Laraway."

Clara snorted again. "Sorry, you don't have to actually say anything. Just *think* your answers to yourself."

Emmett tried to reset. After a second, they were both ready to start again. "Who are you?"

I am Emmett Laraway.

"Now think about what you look like. Don't just imagine your body, imagine what you're wearing."

Emmett did. He imagined staring into a mirror, and his reflection staring back. Tan skin, dark hair, black bodysuit. His brow was wrinkled and his lips were pursed in concentration.

"Think about your day. What did you do this morning that led up to this moment? This afternoon?"

He'd gone to class and then come to the lab to talk with Dr. Venture and to train with Clara.

She continued, her cadence slowing. "Now think about who you are. You are all of these things. You are Emmett. You are Mod. You are a super, a student, a roommate, a friend, a son... When you repeat these words to yourself, know that you are *all of these things.*"

As Clara spoke, Emmett imagined all the pieces of himself...

For a moment, something *clicked* for Emmett. His chest swelled and his concentration reached a zenith. It felt like the first time he leapt across the rooftops with Athena or the first time he fought back against Clara's robot. It was exhilarating.

And the feeling was gone a moment later.

"Shit," Emmett muttered, and realized he'd been holding his breath.

"What?"

"I had it—I think. Then I lost it."

Clara smiled. "It's not easy to hold on to. It takes concentration and willpower. And practice. Honestly, practice is the most important, because it doesn't get any easier when you're in the middle of a fight."

Emmett nodded. "Alright, I'll be sure to practice it."

Clara's face turned serious. "Good, but know that quality and intention are important. This isn't the kind of training you can half-ass. Don't watch TV and tell me you're meditating."

"Got it." He'd been about to make a half-hearted joke, but thought better of it. Instead, Emmett said, "You're way better at this than I expected... How did you get into yoga, anyway?"

Clara looked down for a moment and drew in a breath. "Dad insisted. I started with grounding exercises. He..." She trailed off and shook her head.

It was clear she wanted to say more, but it was probably another secret that Emmett wasn't allowed to hear yet. He tried to ignore it as he waited for her to continue.

"Anyway, I got a lot out of meditation and tried yoga. I've been doing both ever since I was little."

Emmett tried to imagine what else there was to Clara's story and reassured himself that one day both she and Dr. Venture would confide in him.

Clara looked as torn up about it as he did.

Emmett focused on his friend instead of himself. "Well, you're a good teacher."

She smiled and replied, "Thanks."

There were two different versions of Clara's grounding meditation:

The first was grounding the self. The second was grounding the self in the current place and current time.

Clara explained that psychics often attacked the mind from within. This might mean interrupting connections from the brain to the nerves, like causing a gunman's aim to jerk or a brawler's punch to miss—it could even freeze someone completely, like Emmett had experienced.

Most psychic attacks were like this—*like grappling for control of someone's mind and body*. It was crude, but effective.

This was combated by grounding the self. By concentrating on the body and the muscles, by focusing on the self like they were looking in a mirror, it was possible—with practice—to wrestle control back from a psychic. With enough practice, it was even possible to guard against an attack or completely negate one from a lesser psychic completely.

Lesser was relative, of course. Emmett might one day shrug off a psychic attack from a Class 1 super, and maybe even prevent a Class 2 from freezing him. Beyond that, though, he would need external aid. Some psychotropic drugs were effective, but also affected cognition. Physical shielding, like a helmet or engaging outside a psychic's range, were the only foolproof solutions against powerful psychics.

That and the Code. Just like there were rules against killing, there were also unwritten rules against psychic enslavement—punishable by death. ...But that didn't stop some villains from doing truly heinous things.

The other type was *an attack on the senses.* It was one that all illusionists used and only talented psychics could manage. An illusionist might veil their true identity, obscure their movements, or even turn the floor into lava.

"The more powerful the illusionist—the more powerful the illusion," Clara explained. "But no illusion is perfect because it requires that the caster account for *every sensory detail* required to fool you. A master might account for every sense, but lower-level supers won't. All it takes is one detail to be off."

Emmett added, "But you have to notice that detail."

"Exactly."

Emmett put the rest together. It was both fascinating and simple. "And you're telling me all I need to do is meditate?"

Clara raised an eyebrow. "That's oversimplifying it, but yes, for the most part. Practice and experience. The more psychics and illusionists you fight, the better you get at defense, just like sparring—*to a point.*"

Emmett resolved to make Clara's meditations part of his daily routine. He had no desire to be caught unprepared like that night they fought and escaped from the Summit. But according to her, no matter what Emmett did, he'd never be able to prepare for a psychic more powerful than Class 3.

That brought up even more morbid thoughts...

Emmett asked, "I know you said the Code stops most psychics from doing evil stuff... but that doesn't seem very reassuring."

Clara shrugged. "Yeah, when you start thinking about the scope of Class five supers, the implications get pretty horrifying. But to hear Dad talk about it, most powersets of supers have their own governing organizations and their own versions of the Code. They police their own kind.

"Did you know that there's been only two large-scale cases of psychics trying to influence elections in First World countries? That's because psychics that are caught participating in things like that are *destroyed*—that's their rule. Not all the rules are that harsh, but I guess a long time ago, psychics realized that they couldn't be lenient on their own kind.

"So, that's how it is... The psychics keep each other from overstepping. The sorcerer cabals keep each other in line. And so on, and so on."

Emmett chuckled somberly. "So it's just secret societies all the way down?"

She shrugged then stood up. "Yeah, something like that. Now come on. Let's train. You can practice all that meditation stuff later."

Full Throttle Heart

Truck Kun's Package

[The scene continues beside the forgotten ruins deep in the ancient forest. Truck-kun, Al the bluebird, and Lilith the demon are all three gathered around a large-sized package.]

Truck-kun stared in disbelief. Its headlights illuminated the package with an ominous glow. Al and Lilith stared with similar apprehension.

It still remembered that fateful day... Waiting for Joe to deliver packages to the coffee shop. It was a cold afternoon, but Truck-kun kept its engine on and the cab warm for when his friend returned.

Still remembered the shock as the rogue box truck slammed into its side, and the slow realization that its frame was crumpled, its driveshaft broken, and its fluids were bleeding onto the pavement.

Somehow, Truck-kun had been transported to this strange, new world without Joe and without its packages... Everything was gone—

Everything except for *this one package*.

This was all Truck-kun had left of its home, of Joe.

It was no ordinary package. It hummed with a strange power. At first, it reminded Truck-kun of an air compressor or a massager, but as the moment stretched on, Truck-kun knew that the package wasn't something so simple.

Truck-kun felt deeply that this package was linked to its transportation to this strange world.

Lilith crept closer to the box, her enormous bat wings quivering with anticipating. "Such power! I can feel it even now. Let me have your package Truck-kun..."

"No," Truck-kun rumbled defiantly. "I cannot. My package is special. Besides, it is too big for you. The box states that two people should carry it."

Lilith tapped a finger to her lips. "Surely there must be something I can offer you, Truck-kun. Surely there must be something you desire! If not you, think of your tiny friend—"

Al's voice rose like a backfiring carburetor. "I've got desires!"

Lilith smirked. "Then the bird shall have his voice..."

"The voice can wait, lady. I've got blue—"

Truck-kun interrupted with flick of its high beams and a sharp rev of its engine. "No one will have my package!"

Al and Lilith ceased their bickering, and the rest of the forest fell deathly quiet after Truck-kun's proclamation.

"This package is my only link to my world. I can't part with it... Not even for you, Al. I'm sorry."

Al grumbled. "It's okay, Truck-dude. Say no more. Birds before broads, and all that."

Lilith glanced at the two of them, a look of defeat in her eyes. "Fine. I can tell that you are both decided. Your package is magical, Truck-kun, and you are right that it is the link to your world. But I cannot tell you more because it is beyond even my magic. You must find one who can unlock your package."

Al grumbled. "Lady, listen, I can't turn any bluer than I already am."

Truck-kun steeled its resolve. "Can you show us the path?"

Lilith drew herself up to her full demonic height. Light seemed to drain from the ancient ruins, diminishing even Truck-kun's headlights. Al flitted to Truck-kun's cab and shivered in distress. Again, her voice deepened like it was a great echo coming from beneath the ground.

"Listen, metal one, and listen well. You who were born from another world and do not belong seek answers from the tainted and undying. There is no simple answer,

save that you seek a practitioner of the highest order. One who has dedicated their mortal life to the study of magic.

"I cannot tell you how many there are in our realm, save that they number fewer than the souls standing among us. And if you seek them now, you will be denied. For you who are of metal heart and unflinching steel are not worthy..." Light returned to the ruins, and Lilith's heaving breasts slowed. "You are not worthy... yet."

Al whistled, the sound coming out like crumpling paper. "Less than three wizards that can take you home... That's rough, buddy."

Lilith's lips rose into a smirk, one that stretched until it became cold and evil. A flicker of her true, demonic ways bled into her sultry form.

Realization overcame Truck-kun, and a cold chill settled into its frame.

"Even less," Truck-kun rumbled stoically. "Lilith has no soul... Her prophecy means that there is *only one* wizard that can get me home."

Truck-kun changed into its warrior form and picked up the package. Then it changed back into its truck form, enveloping the package safely back into its cargo box as it did.

The flicker of evil disappeared from the demon's face and was replaced with something else. Lilith looked almost sad.

"Before you go... Be careful who you show your package to, Truck-kun. It's a powerful artifact. There are many who would use it for their own ends."

Truck-kun nodded slightly. "Thank you for your wisdom. Farewell." Truck-kun drove away, keeping Lilith in his rearview mirrors until it was certain she wasn't following them.

Truck-kun and Al drove off into the ancient forest again, this time in search of somewhere else to rest for the night. Inside his cargo bay, the mysterious package hummed with power. As they drove, night closed in through the trees.

Al shivered atop his cab.

"It will be alright, Al," Truck-kun said, reassuringly.

"I hope you know what you're doing, Truck-dude. Do you really think we can find this wizard?"

"We have to."

"And my voice too?"

Truck-kun rumbled, "Yes."

Al settled down for the journey atop Truck-kun, and thankfully, didn't defecate on him again.

"Truck-dude?"

"Yes, Al?"

"Do you think I had a chance with Lilith?"

Truck-kun chuckled at his desperate friend and the low rumble echoed through the forest.

[Outtro — Slow, Instrumental version of Theme Song — "Hātofu-rusurottoru" by Gunpowder Audition while the End Credits play.]

[The camera fades to black as Truck-kun and Al disappear into the forest behind a wall of trees and gloom.]

[Al's voice comes through over the music.]

"You never answered me, Truck-dude... Do you think I had a chance? Truck-dude... Can you hear me?"

[Commercial Break]

[Close-up shot of various fruits falling into a blender: Strawberries, chunks of Pineapple and Banana, Blueberries, Raspberries, and Blackberries. Cut to Montage of Surfing and Extreme Sports.]

[Barely visible Disclaimer: 5% Juice. Artificial Flavors.]

"When you're on the go, grab an energy drink that's made for you. Don't settle for anything less than a Madlad."

"Last chance to taste the flavors that kept you warm all winter: Cinnamon Punch, Chocolate Chai, and Caramel Apple. Get them before they're gone!"

"This Spring, try the hit new flavors: Strawberry Quench, Blueberry Dream, and Orange Orange Orange. What are you waiting for?"

[Multiple other Disclaimers flash across screen: Consume responsibly. Contains high levels of caffeine. Drink half a can until you know how caffeine affects you.

[Limit 3 bottles per day.

[Not intended or recommended for children, pregnant or breastfeeding women, or those sensitive to caffeine. People with high blood pressure should consult their health care providers before regularly consuming energy drinks.

[Supers with overactive metabolisms and uncontrollable abilities should exercise caution when consuming energy drinks.]

Chapter 25

Venture

Venture slumped down into his couch in the living room of section 001, taking a much needed break from his own research. He flipped the display to the video feeds from the Gray Room. He'd started a pot of coffee in the kitchen and it would be another ten minutes or so before it was done brewing.

Clara had once asked him why he still used an old drip brewer when there were other methods that were faster or, supposedly, tasted better. Part of it was that his sense of taste had never been quite right since his helmet malfunctioned while fighting Sarano some fifteen years ago.

All things considered, though, Venture would never give up his drip feed coffee maker. It had everything he needed—which was a delay-brew function, so he could set it and it would be ready for him in the morning. He had molds made of every individual part and had dozens of those parts in storage. Each time a part broke, he replaced it. At this point, the entire thing had been replaced one part at a time—a barista equivalent of the Ship of Theseus.

That second reason was the one Venture told Clara when she asked. Venture never told her about his lack of taste, and he never told her the third reason—the *real* reason:

That it reminded him of his childhood home.

Venture was a man defined not just by technology, but by change—by adaptation. But he wasn't a machine. Drip coffee was one of those things he chose to hold on to, chose not to upgrade. Those things and their reasonings say more about a person than the myriad of things they fritter away.

Venture rubbed idly at the stubble on his chin while he watched Clara and Emmett spar. The smell of coffee grew steadily bolder.

Clara chose to wear her training exosuit today, instead of using the VR rig. That limited the powers that she could simulate—she wouldn't be reprising her role as Lord Sumac or Gale Force. Though she could still present as someone like Instaflame or various artificers, like Arsenal or Lead Debt. In addition to her onboard flight and weapon training systems, the Gray Room could simulate flames or explosive weapons that didn't require a lot of manual control.

The pair went back and forth through the faux buildings, Clara predominantly in the role of pursuer, using her flight, speed, and superior ranged weapons to keep constant pressure on Emmett. Meanwhile, Emmett fought like a guerilla insurgent, using his maneuverability to evade her by dashing through buildings and doubling back to surprise her with any number of gadgets.

The more the pair trained together, the more confident Emmett had gotten with his collection. Clara was smart enough not to fall for the same tricks twice, but so far Emmett had managed to get several *wins:*

Using smoke pellets and noise makers, Emmett had lured Clara close enough to pin her down with his sonic blaster. Another time, he used his whip to snag her out of the air as she passed and somehow held on to the window frame with his other hand—that one had been a gamble. On a bad day, he would've torn every muscle in his weaker arm with a stunt like that.

Emmett's other two wins came from a well-aimed ambush with his concealable pistol, and from leaping onto Clara in mid-air and tasering her. That one sent them both plummeting four stories and had them cackling with laughter afterward.

More than once, Venture found himself smiling and joining in their reverie.

Of course, Clara got the better of Emmett the other umpteen times.

No matter what kind of training they put Emmett through, no matter how eager he was to learn and to train, there was no substituting the years of experience that Clara had. She'd been training since she was a preteen—she'd practically been born into this life. Emmett had been made about a month ago.

Venture got up and poured himself coffee, then came back to watch more of their training.

He had to admit, their progress was impressive.

Clara had become a formidable instructor. She'd managed to strike a balance between pushing Emmett to strive for more and toning down her own abilities, so she didn't outclass him in training. Her skill with the VR simulator had grown as well, which would only help her coordination and reaction time with her exosuit and help her prepare for powersets she hadn't fought in real life—

Not to mention all the work Clara had been doing on her own to temper and control her latent abilities.

Emmett was a different story. He was the pinnacle of what Mutagen-A could do to the human body—from his strength and speed, down to how quickly his neuromuscular system learned new movement patterns. It was one thing to hear about Gnosis's mutagens being used by special forces throughout the world, but just a month ago, Emmett had no wrestling or combat experience whatsoever! Now, Venture would put him up against 95% of Class 1 supers and against perhaps 50% of Class 2.

There would always be ill-fitting match-ups—those couldn't be avoided. But they could be prepared for, and that's where Emmett's true potential lay.

To the point, Emmett was finally leaning into swapping his forearm mods on the fly. Finally, living up to his namesake.

Venture sipped on his coffee and enjoyed the progress that his proteges were making.

But just before he could slip too far into fatherly pride, TINA interrupted him. "We have a visitor."

Venture swallowed dryly and took another sip of coffee, hoping it would help. It didn't.

On the screen, TINA had superimposed the front door camera feed. A ghost of a man stood at the door for the second time in two weeks.

Venture ran a hand through his hair and closed out the feeds to the Gray Room, replacing them with the sunset skyline of Belport.

"TINA, open the door. Tell him I'm here."

Venture watched the feed as the unassuming spymaster of the Summit walked through the halls of his lab.

Finally, Wight arrived in Venture's living room and stood patiently.

"Wight."

"Magnus," the ghost glanced toward the pot of coffee. "Do you mind?"

"It's still warm."

Venture's coffee was almost gone, so he conserved it and waited for his guest to take a seat opposite him on the second couch—if only so his hands had something to do instead of betray his nervousness.

Wight had chosen one of Clara's anime-themed mugs, one that had obnoxious hearts and swords splattered across it. He sipped from it and eyed Venture coldly.

Wight let the silence draw out until it festered.

"What happened to keeping your bloody kids on the rails?"

Venture did his best to keep a straight face. He had an idea why the spymaster was here, but he didn't know for sure. If Wight was being obtuse, then Venture would be too.

"Were we really so different?"

Wight sipped his coffee before resting it on his knee. "Why were your two supers slugging it out with the Summit?"

"They were sparring in the warehouse district when two capes stopped them, questioned them, and tried to read their thoughts without consent."

"The district was being monitored after Porcelain's death, but we'll get to that... Did you order your supers to attack Summit capes?"

Venture tempered his irritation. "I told Emmett and Clara not to consent to a mind-read, *as is their right*. When your capes took it upon themselves to go outside the law, I told them to escape. You need to find better capes."

Wight blinked—that's all. It was a small betrayal of his true thoughts: He agreed with Venture.

But Wight continued, "Now explain why the signature of your daughter's exosuit matches the traces left behind the night Porcelain was murdered."

Venture's blood ran cold and he clutched the dying cup of coffee tighter. Wight must've taken the paleness of Venture's face as a slightly bigger betrayal of his true thoughts.

Venture had long known that one day the Summit or one of his old enemies would figure out how to trace the energy from his exosuits. He was actually surprised they hadn't managed it sooner. It was bad luck that they'd managed to crack it *now*.

What were the odds of that?

Wight said, "We matched the energy signature of your daughter's suit from the run in with the Summit to the warehouse where Porcelain was murdered. And you're right, the mind-read was illegal and inadmissible... but they still got Emmett and Clara's names. And yours."

It was testament to Venture's nerves that his hands didn't shake.

Venture swallowed. "Do the psychics still follow confession?"

Wight nodded. "The cape relayed the information up the chain and it was wiped from her afterward. The street sweepers don't know your kids' names, but Somnus does."

"Shit."

Wight relaxed in his seat. "Why do you think I'm here telling you to quit getting your masks mixed up with newbie capes?"

Venture ignored the point. He was more worried about the Summit's psychics. About Somnus— *the* psychic. "Do you still trust them?"

Wight swirled his coffee. "I don't have to trust them. I'm their boss and they answer to me. Besides, if they get too big for their britches, I don't need to kill them. I'll just feed them to the Menagerie."

Venture shuddered and didn't bother suppressing it.

Each powerset of supers had something akin to a governing body to maintain order over their own kind—the reasoning was one of preservation. If psychics, for instance, began forcibly taking over the world, the other supers or nations might exterminate them. By keeping tabs on their own, these governing bodies maintained the world order.

Venture understood the logic well enough, even if he didn't wholly agree with the reasoning. In practice, maintaining order like that just stifled growth. As an artificer, he preferred change and growth.

But the Menagerie was a fate worse than death, and Venture didn't use that term lightly. For some reason, powerful psychics tended to form hive-minds... and lose all sense of self in the process. Somnus was one of the few exceptions.

Venture finally said, "You put a lot of trust in psychics."

Wight said flatly, "No. The Code—mutual destruction—that's what matters." He sighed. "I know you're not just mucking about in retirement... You need to tell me what you know about Champion street, about Porcelain, about the mutagen variants, how it's connected. Then let us take care of it."

Venture smirked. "I was told I'd have free rein when you side-lined me."

Wight didn't crack. "Yeah, well, you've run to the end of it, Magnus. What do you know?"

Venture had exchanged information with Wight and the Summit previously when piecing together what happened to Amarque. What Wight really wanted was a theory.

"It *has* to be an inside job. The operation is too big," Venture said. "I just don't know how high up it goes."

Wight's face soured. He didn't need to say anything—they both had the same thought:

Gnosis was one of the most powerful corporations on the planet. If the theory was correct, it meant that someone high enough up in Gnosis had chosen to ignore the Code and say *screw the balance.*

Silence hung in the air while both men contemplated the gravity of things to come.

Finally, Wight stood and smoothed out the front of his sweater. "I kept your kids' names from getting back to the street sweepers, but I couldn't keep a gag order on the rest of it. The Summit is looking for an artificer *and a cyborg.* If they keep putting on a show, they'll get requisitioned..."

Wight lingered only a moment longer before adding. "Be seeing you, Magnus." Then he turned and walked *through* the door.

Venture brought up the hallway feeds on the living room screens. He watched the ghost until he'd completely left the lab. Once he was gone, Venture sighed and stood, ready to get back to work.

"TINA, we're moving up Clara and Emmett's schedules. We're running out of time."

Chapter 26

Upgrades

Monday's training in the Gray Room was much needed, and both Emmett and Clara were ready to end the evening in good spirits when Venture summoned them.

Neither had paused to question, not after hearing Venture's tone, and soon the three of them were face-to-face in the hub of the mechanical wing.

Venture stood behind the holographic table, hands clasped behind his back. "We're pushing up our schedules. So listen closely…"

Venture rehashed his recent meeting with the spymaster of the Summit of Heroes, as well as the current reigning theory that the Gnosis mutagen knock-offs were an inside job. As he explained, both the pair nodded along with varying degrees of surprise.

Emmett didn't have long to contemplate the new developments because Venture reached the first of his actual reasons for calling them in:

"Emmett, I want to modify your radio locator and its algorithms to track cellphones. And I need you to set me up with Athena." Venture must have seen the look on Clara's face because he added, "So I can speak with her about her sources."

Emmett nodded hesitantly. "Honestly, I thought you could already do that."

Venture smirked. "I've gotten more use out of tracking supers than tracking civilians. With some time, I could engineer it myself, but your algorithms are surprisingly good, Emmett."

TINA's voice came through the intercom. *"Dr. Venture fails to mention that tracking civilians this way is highly illegal."*

Emmett shifted uneasily on his feet. He wanted to ask questions, but resolved to save them and ask TINA later. Emmett nodded along, absently muttering "Thanks."

Venture sighed. "Yes TINA, this is illegal. Which is why we're only tracking the bad guys and we're getting rid of the capabilities when this is finished. We need to track a shipment of these knock-offs or track the people delivering them, preferably both. We need to find one of the people orchestrating this... Which is why I need you to put me in contact with Athena."

Emmett raised an eyebrow. "You can't just find her with a drone and ask her through the radio?"

Venture shrugged. "I probably could, but there's a formality to these things. Athena is your ally—you should be the one to contact her. If she's willing to work together, I'll fly a drone over and talk through it."

Venture turned to Clara. "My next task is for you, but concerns *both of you*. I've been made aware that the Summit was able to match your exosuit's energy signature to Porcelain's death and the run in with those two capes." Clara winced audibly, but Venture continued, "I have some workarounds to filter and obscure your energy signature, but you're not going to like them."

Now Clara groaned. "Aw, what now?"

"Limiting power output to 50% of your maximum."

Clara turned and paced the room with her fingers laced behind her head. For a moment, Emmett almost risked making a joke to lighten the mood, but thought better of it.

Instead, Emmett asked, "How much worse is that than usual?"

Clara replied, "He already caps my power output. That's why we've been trying out so many different heat sinks—"

"Clara!" Venture quickly cut her off.

"I know! I know..." She stopped and faced them both. "I'm talking about the suits, Dad. I'll be able to fly, but... I'm pretty sure that drops me to a Class two."

Venture replied, "It's either that or the rest of the Summit might be able to track you back here. We can't risk that."

Clara crossed her arms. "Fine."

Emmett stayed silent and waited for Venture to continue.

"The Summit knows about you both now. They're on the lookout for an artificer and a cyborg, so you'll have to be extra careful. That means limiting your power output and not running off to talk to all the random supers you meet." Venture glared at Emmett. "The cloaking systems and drones can afford you some protection and chance to escape, but each time you draw attention to yourselves, you're rolling the dice. Eventually, you won't like what comes up." Venture punctuated the lecture with, "Any questions?"

Emmett and Clara shared a knowing look.

This was around the time in a movie that the mentor said *'playtime's over'* or *'no more messing around.'*

Up until then, Emmett had been operating under the expectation that they had time to figure things out. Despite all the crazy things that had happened—the fights, the attack on downtown, and even Porcelain's death—Emmett thought they had time...

But that was childish.

For a moment, Paragon's red glare came back to him, reminding Emmett that this wasn't a game. People's lives were on the line—supers and civilians.

Emmett's shoulders felt heavy, like he could feel the weight of this stark new reality pressing in on him. The room felt like it closed in just a bit tighter.

Emmett reminded himself to breathe, and with that, he asked, "What else can we do?"

Both Emmett and Clara met Venture's eyes with resolve.

Venture nodded resolutely. "Clara, I'd like for you to get started on recalibrating your systems. I actually have one more thing for you, Emmett."

Clara looked over her shoulder as she walked out of the mechanical hub, leaving Emmett alone with Dr. Venture.

"As I was saying, you need to make another choice." Venture gestured with his hand and the screens across the wall filled with schematics and diagrams.

It only took Emmett a moment to realize what he was seeing: *Upgrades.*

"You want me to choose the next one already..."

"Yes," Venture replied. "I told you to wait a week, and we have. In a perfect world, we'd have longer to wait and prepare, but let this be a lesson that the world isn't perfect."

Emmett struggled to listen while he parsed the upgrades that covered the wall. He'd spent a good chunk of his idle time since the surgery preparing for this moment. Emmett had wanted to be ready with a well-thought-out choice as soon as it was presented to him.

Originally, he'd narrowed the choice down to Reinforcing his tendons and muscles or reinforcing his skin. Both would involve surgery to weave synthetic fibers into the mix and both would've increased his defensive rating. Reinforcing his tendons would've also increased his strength slightly and maybe even lessened the need to regulate his mechanical arm. On the other hand, his skin could be resistant to knives and small caliber pistols.

In the end, he'd been leaning toward his tendons and muscles because of the defensive *and* offensive buffs.

Emmett had been ready to choose, except now there was another choice on the screen, one that TINA hadn't listed before.

An external battery.

Venture noticed Emmett staring. "Your name got me thinking... If you really want to expand your arsenal of mods, then an external power source needs to be considered."

Emmett looked over the specifications, noting that the batteries had a similar progression compared to other modifications, and also different branching paths. Some batteries, like standard lithium, were well rounded, while alkaline were smaller and more concealable but also weaker overall. Then there were chemical batteries that were comically bulky but put out many times the power.

Emmett's carefully made choice was unraveling.

"How am I supposed to hide any of these?"

Venture rubbed the stubble on his chin thoughtfully. "Once we have appropriate safeguards, we can implant it. Eventually, make something like the rail system in your arm so that you can swap batteries on the fly."

"But I won't pass through a metal detector."

"No, you won't. You wouldn't pass through one right now with your arm." Venture considered his words. "If you're worried about passing for human, then you need to consider some of these upgrades very carefully. Eventually, the wrong person will notice your mods, or you'll walk through a metal detector somewhere, and your identity will be logged with the Summit as a potential superhuman—regardless of if you are ever caught in the act.

"That being said, if you're worried about being a mask and sneaking into places you shouldn't be... then you definitely don't want to walk through a metal detector. Maybe go through the air vent instead."

Emmett smirked. "That was a joke, right?..."

"Yes. I also have to say that we won't be implanting any of these until you have something to mitigate possible leaks and toxicity."

Emmett nodded, listening to Venture while he scanned his choices again. He was already recalibrating his choices.

"Then I'm choosing nanomachines next."

"Why?"

Emmett explained, "It was already my third choice. It improves my stamina and resistance to poisons, *and* my recovery time. Now it's a major prerequisite to other choices. Not only does it open up more opportunities, it also helps me heal faster after each surgery."

Venture nodded in approval. "I can find no flaws in your reasoning. TINA, prepare the first two mixtures for Emmett."

"I've already started preparing them. Please escort Emmett to the second surgical suite."

A flicker of irritation passed across the doctor's eyes. He turned back to Emmett. "Let's go," was all he said.

Venture declined to share his thoughts, and the pair walked to section 006 and to the surgical suites in silence.

Clearly, Venture hadn't worked out TINA's bug yet. Did he fail? Or had he just been preoccupied with other things?

Did he give up fixing TINA?

Emmett resigned himself to waiting for an answer—he'd gotten used to it. What was one more secret?

Suite two was remarkably plain compared to the futuristic tank and cluster of surgical arms from Emmett's bone grafting surgery. Suite two consisted of several small mixing tanks and tubes along the wall, two small closets, and a single hospital bed in the center of the room.

"Sit down," Venture said. He walked over to the closets and grabbed several vials.

Emmett sat on the bed and suppressed a shiver. He would rather have been back in the surgical tank, cocooned. It had felt weird and sterile, but he could manage that. Sitting on one of these beds again just felt *raw*—like prodding a wound that wouldn't heal.

He waited and half-watched as Dr. Venture pulled green and brown liquids from the tanks and mixed them—

"Ready?" Venture asked.

Emmett startled. Venture was standing beside him, with several syringes sitting on the bed.

Emmett must've zoned out. He nodded quickly. "I'm ready."

Venture narrated as he went through the process.

First, Emmett was given a general peptide of nanomachines. These would supplement his red blood cells for oxygen distribution and recovery, his white blood cells for resistance to poison and disease, and platelets for stopping bleeding. There were also trackers and broadcasters mixed in that would allow TINA to record data on Emmett's functions and allow her to tweak the nanites.

He was given three more specific cocktails, all centered around recovery—one for each of his red cells, another for his white cells and platelets. Last, came nanites specifically made to monitor and repair the connections between his tissue and his mechanical arm.

Once they were done, Emmett felt like a bloated pincushion.

Chapter 27

Meet Up

Emmett stayed in the lab for another hour after the injections, so Venture and TINA could monitor him. That also gave Clara and TINA time to prepare a backup version of Clara's exosuit, one tuned down to appropriate power levels. Then the team worked out a plan for the evening.

Their first priority was getting in contact with Athena.

Emmett and Clara followed a search pattern around downtown Belport. He jogged the roofs, while Clara flew in her exosuit. Emmett thought he could just make out the shimmer of her cloaking tech in the night sky.

Meanwhile, dozens of Fast-Response Drones were also searching the city. Venture had explained that some energy signatures were easier to scan for than others, but Athena's powerset wasn't one of those. So far as he could tell, her powers didn't leave lasting signals or residual markers, so the drones were forced to rely on line-of-sight techniques.

They searched for an hour—until ten o'clock—and Emmett kicked himself for not exchanging burner numbers like he had with McGuire.

Thankfully, Athena found them.

She landed on the rooftop across from Emmett. Between her height, the glistening shards of her jacket, and her billowing white hair, Athena cut an opposing figure against the skyline.

"You look like you're a man on a mission."

Emmett nodded. "I'm actually looking for you."

Athena crossed her arms and glared at him, like he was a child who'd forgotten to take out the trash.

Emmett rolled his eyes. *"Future-sight.* Right."

"So, what's the occasion?"

Emmett took a breath and reset himself. "I have a friend—two friends—that want to help with the knock-off mutagen deliveries. We might even be able to track the deliveries back to the source."

"I'm listening."

"They want to talk to you."

Athena nodded. "Okay. But we're not talking here. Follow me."

Athena led Emmett around the Northern outskirts of downtown Belport and toward the West End.

In the mix of cafes, mid-rise businesses, and apartments, Athena led them to one building in particular on a strangely unmarked street. They slipped down the fire escape of the upper floor apartments and through a window on the fifth floor.

The first thing he felt was a slight tingling in his prosthetic arm. It came and went, and Emmett wiggled his fingers to make sure everything worked...

It *seemed* like everything did. For a second, he wondered if it was the nanite injections or just in his imagination.

He paused just inside the window to take in the sight of the apartment. The walls were spackled over, but not painted, and the wood floors were scuffed and dull. There were a couple mismatched flower couches and chairs along the walls and a few lights, but no TV... By the time Emmett saw the small kitchen, he realized that there weren't any other electronics in the place—no fridge, no stove either.

It reminded him of when he was little and his parents had refinished the kitchen—like Athena was in the middle of remodeling this place.

Meanwhile, Athena made a sweeping gesture with her hands. "Grab a seat. We can talk here. Are your friends close?"

As if on cue, Clara landed on the rusted fire escape and decloaked. If anything, the futuristic matte-gray of her suit only made the scene stranger. She slowly stepped inside, face unreadable behind her helmet.

Athena had stooped over in the kitchen, and placed two packs of sodas on the counter. "Help yourselves... Oh. I should've realized that Mod's friends would be tech-based. You should find that everything works here in this demiplane except for your offensive systems." Athena met both their eyes. "Rest assured that my abilities still work here."

Clara mumbled something, then said aloud, "If Mod trusts you, then so do we."

"Where is your other friend?"

"Clara, put me through on holographic display."

Something whirred quietly inside Clara's exosuit and a moment later, a life-sized blue hologram of Dr. Venture appeared in the room. It was accurate, down to every detail, except that Venture's face was obscured like he was standing in darkness.

"Apologies for not coming in person," Venture said.

Emmett watched, mouth slightly agape as the hologram took in the sight of the room. Venture must've been using a VR interface, but Emmett could only guess how he was getting camera feeds. Venture paced around the room, taking in the sights as if he was looking through the hologram. Even his voice came from the hologram, instead of from a speaker in Clara's suit.

"Thank you for inviting us in," Venture added, quickly introducing himself and Clara as the *Doctor* and *Arsenal*.

Athena smirked and cracked open an off-brand cola. "Just don't try to come here without permission, or try to crack or locate it. This is a private plane keyed to me specifically. This is one of my safe rooms. While we're here, we can speak freely without being overheard."

Venture turned. *"The messages are safe during broadcast?"*

Athena nodded, like it was an unnecessary question. "Nothing beats magical encryption, Doctor. The message is secured by *purpose* and *spiritual location.*"

"That seems like a handy power to have," Emmett said off-handedly.

"It is," Venture replied, *"but mixing technology and magic is tricky."*

Athena scoffed. "You mean impossible. You might as well say you're going to control technology with your mind."

"That's not out of the realm of possibility," Venture replied. *"A brain-machine interface..."*

Emmett didn't miss Venture's glance in his direction.

"Excuse me, Doctor," Clara said impatiently. "You three can talk shop later. Mod mentioned that we might be able to help each other trace these mutagen knock-offs back to the source."

Athena smiled at Clara before nodding. "I have leads, and admittedly, we're having trouble tracking them. How are you going to trace them back to the source?"

Venture said, *"We're going to track the cell phones of the delivery driver and warehouse to look for patterns in their comings and goings. At the same time, we'll hack the phone companies and scan their comings and goings for the last week—the last month if we can manage it. More data means more processing..."*

"How long will it take?"

"Forty-eight hours... give or take."

Athena raised an eyebrow. "That's... impressive."

"You have your magic. I have mine."

Athena added, "It's also a little disconcerting that phone companies keep our data like that."

"They're supposed to hash it and anonymize it, but if you're good enough with data, you can separate the signal from the noise."

Athena rapped her fingers on the countertop as she considered things. "Your terms are amenable."

Venture's hologram stood with his arms folded across his chest. *"What do you want in return?"*

"To work with you three until this is over. Until mutagens are off the streets. Until Gnosis is crippled and dissolves as a company."

Venture smirked, the expression barely visible behind the shadow. *"Gnosis is one of the most powerful corporations in the world. They're as powerful as some cabals and world governments. What makes you think that this could shut them down?"*

Emmett chimed in, "What do you know about Gnosis?"

Athena raised an eyebrow and sipped her cola. "Your boss said the important part already. Gnosis isn't just a biotech company. They've obfuscated their names and holdings over the years through mergers and name changes, but records go back to over one thousand BCE. And in every iteration, they've had questionable business practices. They've traded in slaves, weapons, helped overthrow governments... and now, they're creating bioweapons for the highest bidders."

Emmett regarded Athena as she spoke, feeling a weight of years behind her words. She felt tired, like she'd been fighting against Gnosis since the beginning. In that moment, if Athena would've said she was a thousand years old, Emmett would've believed her.

Venture nodded. *"You don't have to sell us on the mission. We're with you."*

Athena turned to Emmett. "What about you? If this goes according to plan, then your stock of mutagen vials is going to take a hit."

Emmett chuckled awkwardly. "If it's for the best, then I'm in. Besides, I've got other options." He flicked his mechanical wrist for emphasis.

Athena smirked. "I guess you do." Then she motioned for them to join her around the countertop.

Athena went on to explain that there were several upcoming drops—four that they had exact locations of and three more that they had approximate locations for. She pulled out a notepad from her pocket and drew intersections for each, then passed it to each for consideration.

Venture looked over Clara's shoulder and regarded the page. "I have enough drones to scan all seven. If you two and Athena are up for it, you can choose one of the four to hit. Wouldn't want your supply to run out."

Emmett looked at Clara and Athena, both of whom shared a chuckle. He didn't even need to ask the question.

Clara's exosuit nodded. "Yes, we'll chaperone you while you make more bad decisions."

Athena said, "When you're young, everything looks like opportunity."

Chapter 28

Increased Security / Athena

All seven mutagen deliveries were happening in the next three days. At Athena and Venture's suggestion, Emmett agreed to wait until Thursday to pilfer another shipment; none of them wanted to risk shipments getting moved or delayed.

Emmett spent the better part of Tuesday and Wednesday in class, doing schoolwork, and holing up back in his apartment to convert his radio locator so that it would track cell phones as well.

It wound up being easier than Emmett thought, especially with TINA to guide him through the process and bounce ideas off of. Emmett had wondered just how much use Dr. Venture got out of his AI assistant, but he quickly saw the benefits: TINA never needed a break, she could perform calculations many times faster than him, and she was a direct line to any of the lab's resources and simulators.

It felt like Emmett's room had become the lab. Like he'd never left.

But that wasn't the strangest thing—

Emmett had started thinking of TINA as a *she*. That was interesting. When had he started thinking of TINA like *that*?

Throughout that first Tuesday, Emmett found himself coming back to that question, but never really getting anywhere with it. Did it even matter if he thought of TINA as a she instead of an AI? TINA had never expressed a preference one way or another, and clearly TINA had been designed with a feminine voice. Or maybe she chose the voice?

The questions began to make Emmett's head spin, and eventually the work overtook him.

When Lock was gone, cloaked drones brought shipments of materials to the roof. And thankfully, when Lock was there, he didn't ask too many questions. Lock was smart, but he either couldn't follow most of Emmett's work on electronics or just flat out didn't want the explanation. He'd watch for a few minutes here and there, but then he'd disappear into his room to work on his own schoolwork.

Emmett and Lock exchanged a few sentences over the course of those three days, but that was it. They'd both been so busy that any idea of relaxation or fun had taken a backseat. Maybe after the semester was over and they graduated, things would be different between them. Emmett just didn't have time to think about it right now—

Not when he had way more important things on his mind.

Besides the work at hand, Emmett found his thoughts drifting toward the next mutagen bust. So far, he'd found different knock-offs in each delivery and Venture still had the stash of previous finds... but Emmett wanted more.

Sure, the mutagen knock-offs weren't legal or sanctioned or whatever, but they were an easy way for Emmett to get stronger. Maybe even easier than mechanical upgrades.

Emmett thought back to just two weeks ago, during the fight in the warehouse district. That unknown super had come out of nowhere. It had been utterly terrifying and one of the most awe-inspiring things Emmett had ever seen.

Emmett already knew first-hand what Mutagen-A could do to a person, and he'd seen Mutagen-X—the pinnacle of Gnosis technology. Well, *supposedly* the pinnacle of Gnosis technology. Who knew what other secrets Gnosis was hiding. They might have even more potent and dangerous mutagens that even Venture didn't know about.

Emmett would be lying if he said he wasn't tempted by the prospect of one day taking Mutagen-X. Something like that could take him right to Class 3. Then again, technology might be able to take him even further than that.

Even Mutagen-X couldn't compare to seeing Paragon save Belport.

And there were tech supers that reached Class 4 and Class 5. If there was any chance that Emmett could become that powerful, he had to stick with technology and the paths that TINA had developed.

Eventually, Emmett had to push the thought aside and focus on his work.

Because the more Emmett thought about climbing the ranks, the more intoxicating the idea was.

By Thursday evening, Emmett's radio locator had been converted to track both radios and cell phone signals. He prepared a cover story in case Lock was back, but Emmett's roommate was nowhere to be found. So Emmett put his suit on under his black clothes, grabbed his backpack and equipment, and slipped out for a stroll, smirking as he went.

Something about the evening made him feel like a super—not just like he was running around the rooftops playing at it.

Dr. Venture briefed Emmett and Clara through their earpieces as they both converged on the drop point.

"Drones have intercepted six out of seven drop points. TINA already has access to the phone companies and is backtracing location data. We'll crack the supplier's location in the next twenty-four hours."

Clara's voice came through. *"So what you're saying is, we don't need this bust."*

"This is gravy," Venture replied. *"Just don't mess it up."*

Emmett asked, "Have you narrowed it down at all yet?"

"Patience is a virtue," Venture said. *"I'll let you know when I have something."*

Emmett jogged the edge of the warehouse district and the Bay, just outside the drop point. From there, he donned his mask and skirted the alleys until he was two blocks away. Then he climbed up to the roofs and Venture guided him via drone the rest of the way.

By the time Emmett got to the rendezvous point with Athena and Clara, he was on edge. The trio knelt by the edge of the roof, Clara shimmering in her cloaked exosuit.

"There's a lot more security this time," Emmett whispered.

Athena peered cautiously over the edge and checked her watch. "Any minute now." Meanwhile, Emmett and Clara kept low and scanned the surrounding roofs.

Of all the drop points, this one provided the least cover. They were surrounded by high roofs and even higher warehouses were only two blocks away. If it weren't for Dr. Venture's drones scanning the other vantage points, Emmett wouldn't have felt comfortable sitting on the roof like they were.

Athena had once said it was a number's game—that was why there was so little security for most drops and not enough guards to line the rooftops now. But that fact didn't make Emmett feel any better.

If it was a numbers game, that meant that some drop points would have increased security—most drops had regular security, but the last shipment had been guarded by a super named *Feedback*.

Emmett's prosthetic fingers twitched, and he briefly considered what forearm mod to equip first. In the end, he kept his whip equipped, since he was the most comfortable with it and it offered a good mix of reach and utility. Besides, he had his backpack and his utility belt on and ready.

"Van incoming."

A few seconds later, their target turned the corner of the alley. The three crouched low behind the ledge of the roof and waited. As soon as it was beneath them, they would—

The roof access door opened with a squeal, and all three whirled around to face the newcomer.

The man peered out from behind the doorway and called something over the radio. His dark hair was slicked back like a security guard out of a movie.

Clara muttered, "So much for the element of surprise." Clara raised her gauntlets, power already humming within her suit. A second later, she let loose a barrage of kinetic blasts that chipped away at the bricks. The man ducked back inside the door.

Emmett hurled a smoke pellet and it burst into a cloud around the stairs. "Athena, do you got this guy?"

"Yeah, no sweat—"

The roof lurched, and Emmett tumbled forward, but he didn't fall. All three of them levitated up into the air. At first, Emmett thought it was telekinesis, but Athena's long white hair and jacket were floating up as well.

Someone had reversed gravity.

They were only five feet off the roof, but Emmett's stomach tumbled and he struggled to keep his orientation.

The smoke drifted up into the air, revealing the doorway and the newcomer. Now he stepped out of the doorway completely, revealing that he wasn't normal security. His eyes were a brilliant white as he kept the three of them suspended in the air.

It was the first time Emmett had fought someone with anti gravity powers, and it would've been impressive but the man pulled out a pistol.

Athena held out her hands, forming invisible shields in front of them just as he pulled the trigger. Bullets slammed harmlessly into the shield. "Get the shipment!"

Clara rocketed upward, thrusters easily freeing her from the anti gravity effect. She shot another barrage at the super, causing him to duck back behind the door. She looped over in the air and flew down to the alley below.

Meanwhile, Emmett slung his whip and grabbed the edge of the roof, and hauled himself toward the alley. With his enhanced strength, Emmett went much faster than he intended. As soon as he dipped below the roofline, his stomach lurched again as gravity changed. A breath later, he had to grip the side of the warehouse to keep from slamming into the pavement.

Athena hung in the air, facing the roof access door. She watched out of the corner of her eye as Mod and Arsenal disappeared over the edge of the roof. When her allies were gone, she concentrated fully on the task at hand.

Kicking this guy's ass.

Though Athena's shields were invisible to most, to her they hung brilliantly in her vision like thin blue crystal. She kept the wide barrier in front of her, and formed another behind her—she kicked off of it, diving forward through the air while pushing her shield forward, just in front of her.

Her enemy peered around the doorway, eyes widening at the sight of her. But he wasn't a slouch.

Athena felt a tug as gravity shifted again. This time, instead of floating in the air, she lurched to the right.

Effortlessly, Athena formed another barrier to catch herself. She tumbled into a sprint and ran across the crystalline surface.

Not to be outdone, the other super fired off several shots at Athena while shifting gravity again—this time to the left. Athena flipped to reorient herself without missing a step and while still catching bullets.

The man sneered at her, clearly not having as good a time as she was.

Gravity shifted again, and Athena tumbled to the roof and caught herself in a crouch—

Except this time when she tried to stand, her muscles *burned*. Athena tried to run, but couldn't. Weight pressed down on her and it felt like she was holding up a building. Gravity hadn't just shifted, it had doubled—maybe even tripled.

Sweat dripped off Athena's nose and she focused on standing and maintaining her forward barrier.

She finally looked up to see her enemy raising a hand toward her. His face was twisted into a mix of grimace and frustration; he was clearly struggling as much as she was. The gun was all but forgotten and hanging at his side—maybe he finally wised up and realized that a gun wasn't going to beat her.

Despite the strain, Athena smiled.

She'd originally wanted to run up and knock the guy out, but he'd managed to stop her about ten feet short. But that was plenty close enough for her backup plan.

Athena didn't need to raise a hand to summon another barrier. This one formed right beside her enemy—

Then slammed into him like a truck.

The super flew through the door and down the stairs. A second later, gravity went back to normal, and Athena breathed a sigh of relief as the weight lifted off of her.

With a flick of her wrist, she slammed another barrier into the metal door of the roof. Metal squealed as it was torn off the hinges and wedged into the stairwell. Unless the guy was strong enough to tear a hole in the roof, he wasn't coming back up this way.

A groan echoed through the stairwell, but Athena didn't hear any footsteps. If the super was smart, he'd sit out the rest of this fight.

Sounds of battle echoed from below. Athena turned and leapt off the roof to join the fight.

Chapter 29

Got Everything?

Emmett swung down to the alley using his whip and landed on the pavement beside the delivery truck, startling one of the guards. Without thinking, Emmett lunged forward, punching the man square in the stomach—

The man *crumpled* around Emmett's fist and slumped to the ground. Surprise quickly faded to a groan as the man fell.

On the other side of the van, Clara dropped to the pavement and raised her gauntlets. The loading bay door was opening, and a group of guards were already preparing to rush out. Clara's kinetic barrage lit up the door, causing the guards to duck back behind cover.

Meanwhile, Emmett circled the van, using his whip to grab the driver's ankle and pull him off his feet as he stepped out. The back doors of the van opened and Emmett pummeled the third guy before his feet touched the ground.

Then he grabbed the pistols off of the belts of all three groaning guards, ejected the magazines, and chucked the pistols down the alley.

Emmett quickly checked the back of the van, but didn't see anything else besides four white crates. Jackpot.

He was about to reach for the nearest crate when metal squealed behind him. Emmett spun around, but didn't get a chance to see what made the noise—

Something hit him in the face. *Hard.*

Emmett reeled backward, just managing to keep his feet beneath him. He got his hands up, ready to defend against another blindside, but nothing came.

Meanwhile, the noise from the metal door of the loading bay rose to a scream. Hands pulled at the door, wrenching it upward much faster than the mechanism could stand. The metal door buckled as it was shoved upward.

It took a moment for Emmett to realize that it wasn't hands that grabbed the door—they were far too dark and far too large.

A woman strode out of the loading bay on limbs of immense black hair. She hung in the center like a marionette, while the mass twisted around her like a spider. Each limb of hair stabbed the ground and left a bloody smear—as she stepped into the lights of the alley, Emmett realized her hair was matted and wet with blood.

Clara immediately turned her kinetic blasts on the twisted super. Cracks of shockwaves echoed through the alley and the spider-like super scurried out of the way, barely staying ahead of the barrage.

Something hit Emmett in the face again. He staggered back and thought he heard the scuffle of shoes beside him.

"Picked the wrong shipment," someone muttered.

Emmett heard a grunt of effort and he reeled backward just in time to feel *something* graze his fists. More scuffling, and Emmett quickly circled toward the van.

There was a third super and they were invisible. Emmett had no idea what weapons they might have, but they definitely weren't some normal security guard. They hit hard enough that they were at least a Class 1 super.

"Shit," Emmett muttered.

"That's right," the cloaked attacker said.

Emmett put his back against the van, then swung his whip out in a wide arc. His attack slammed into the rushing super, and Emmett had to dodge out of the way before he could get a good grip. The super slammed into the van, jostling it.

Emmett reeled back to swing his whip again, but the invisible super slammed into Emmett, knocking him to the ground.

He rolled over quickly, extending his whip and waving it around in a circle like a deep-sea fish feeling around for prey. It might've felt vaguely ridiculous, except that it succeeded in keeping the invisible super at bay.

"Get up!"

Emmett smirked.

It probably wasn't smart to laugh and provoke an unknown, invisible super, but Emmett needed the bastard to get close enough to grab him... It didn't help that Clara's battle drowned out everything else.

Invisibility was powerful. Honestly, against most other supers, this guy was probably used to winning pretty easily. Even with Emmett's reinforced skeleton and Mutagen-A, he couldn't get pummeled forever. Eventually, this super would wear him down.

Emmett only caught glimpses of Clara's battle on the other side of the alley. Both her and the hair-girl were evenly matched, at least Class 2. With Clara's power limitations, she was using a mix of kinetic blasts and melee fighting, clearly trying to stay out of reach of hair-girl as much as possible.

Hair-girl wasn't phased by any of it. Her black limbs rippled with each impact, but she kept crawling toward Clara.

He couldn't even spare a glimpse up to the roof to see how Athena was doing—Emmett had to do something to even the odds and then end this quickly.

Emmett grabbed another smoke pellet out of his upper arm compartment, broke it on his chest. The smoke quickly enveloped the van, and Emmett pulled a noisemaker out of his utility belt and switched it on—

Now Emmett couldn't see and couldn't hear, *and neither could his opponent.* But he had to act fast.

Emmett rolled to his feet and extended his whip and swung it in a wide, low arc. A second later, he felt his confused opponent and sprung his trap. The whip coiled around his enemy like a python.

Then Emmett wrenched the man off his feet and hauled him in like a fisherman hauling in a catch. The super slid across the ground until he was at Emmett's feet. His opponent stared up at Emmett, completely bound and eyes wide.

Emmett punched him in the face, and the guy went slack. He waited only a moment to make sure the guy was still breathing, then he turned toward the sound of Clara's battle just outside the smoke.

Emmett recalled his whip, and then, with practiced swiftness, disconnected the mod and swapped it for his concealable pistol. He pocketed the noisemaker, then pulled a sonic grenade.

Then Emmett strode out of the smoke and joined the real battle.

Hair-girl was snaking one massive limb around the left arm of Clara's exosuit, while Clara's thrusters pulled and jerked, trying to tear her free. Meanwhile, Clara fired with kinetic blasts with her other hand, forcing hair-girl to shield her body with the rest of the black mass.

Emmett chucked the sonic grenade at hair-girl's feet and a moment later the high-pitch whine of the sonic drowned out everything. Clara claimed the sound was limited, but it still covered the entire alley.

The enemy super recoiled, the mass of hair squirming like it was alive and in pain. Her grip on Clara slackened, and Clara channeled all the power she could to her thrusters to pull away. Hair-girl let down her defenses and spiked her tendrils into the pavement to keep from being pulled by Clara.

Meanwhile, Emmett walked closer and raised his metal arm. As soon as he had a clear line, he shot hair-girl with a sledgehammer round—

And hit her directly in the face. Hair-girl recoiled, almost tumbling over backward.

Emmett winced—he hadn't meant to hit her in the face. He'd just been aiming for center mass.

But before he could feel sorry for her, hair-girl turned toward him, sneering like a crazed marionette. She released Clara, who stumbled backward from her thrusters. Then the angry super scurried toward Emmett.

He emptied the magazine.

Emmett had practiced enough with his pistol mod that he was a pretty good shot, even firing as quickly as he was. Not to mention his mechanical arm was more than able to handle the recoil. Shot after shot, slammed into hair-girl, staggering her and forcing her to half-heartedly cover her main body.

All eight rounds struck her and she kept coming. Kinetic blasts even hit her from the side as Clara rejoined the fight, but it wasn't enough.

Emmett was already reaching back to swap to his sonic blaster when something slammed down on hair-girl—like a giant, invisible hand squashing a spider.

This time, hair-girl didn't get up. She lay crumpled on the ground.

Athena landed beside him and patted him on the shoulder. "You would've gotten her, but we're out of time." She turned toward the loading bay, where guards were tentatively peeking around the corner. "I'll cover you. Take care of the van."

Athena waved a hand and conjured a barrier just as the first shots rang out. Emmett turned his attention toward the prizes in the back of the van.

He tore the lid off one crate, waved away the icy smoke, and quickly scanned the vials.

"Shit."

At least half of them looked like duplicates—colors he'd seen before. Some he'd even taken before.

But not all of them.

To be sure, Emmett grabbed two and three of each vial, stuffing them inside the front pocket of his hoodie. He and Dr. Venture would sort them out when they got back to the lab.

Behind him, the whine of the sonic grenade cut off abruptly as Clara stomped on it with her exosuit. When Emmett stared in shock, all she said was, "We've got plenty at the lab."

"Got everything you came for?" Athena asked. A second later, she slammed a forcefield down on the van, turning it into a pancake.

Emmett winced at the screeching steel and the aftermath. He was glad that Athena was on their side.

Venture's voice came through. "Prepare for extraction. Athena, I trust you can find your own way out?"

She smirked. "Don't worry about me." Then she leapt up to the roof on invisible platforms.

Emmett watched her leap away with superhuman grace until a drone decloaked and opened up beside him.

"Get in, loser," Clara said. "We're going home."

Chapter 30

Venture

While Emmett and Clara were en route, Dr. Venture stood in the hub of section 006, the biomedical wing of the lab. He was watching the wall monitors intently as they replayed drone footage of the mutagen bust. He intended to watch all of it, but right now he was focused on Athena's fight with the gravity warper.

Ever since Emmett had run into her a few weeks ago, Venture had spent considerable time digging up information about the Class 3-3 super. He knew about the many uses of her forcefields, their weaknesses, roughly how much force they could withstand and how much force they could produce.

Not only that, but Athena *supposedly* had increased physical abilities comparable to a Class 2 ranking. On the other hand, her future-sight wasn't documented at all, despite her admissions to Emmett.

But all the archived information and rumors in the world paled in comparison to seeing a super in action. Between this fight, and Athena's fight with the super called Feedback, Venture had more than enough data to form his own opinions.

Clearly, she was gifted with a versatile power, and also extremely proficient in its use. But there were so many nuances one missed without witnessing such a super directly.

First, her physical abilities were likely understated. She might not be a Class 3 super physically, but she was damn close. There was no way anyone less could react to changes in gravity the way she did while also reforming her barriers. Her future-sight could explain some of that... Not only could she see slightly into the future, the power also gifted her with a more immediate 'danger-sense'.

Despite her hand-gestures, she could conjure forcefields at the speed of thought, possibly even faster—some abilities could even react at the speed of unconscious thought. Once again, this lent itself to Athena having a danger-sense.

Those three abilities—barriers, physical prowess, and danger-sense—combined to create a truly formidable super. One worthy of designation 3-3.

Not only did Athena's brief fight install a newfound respect in Venture, it also laid bare the weaknesses of the DSA's power classifications:

Despite the -0-1-2-3 designations after the main ranking, someone with Athena's combination of abilities *could not be accurately classified.* She was given the designation 3-3 because she could likely punch up to Class 4, but even that wasn't accurate enough—

Class levels were about threat level and match-ups against others of their own class. A 3-2 would likely beat a 3-0 or a 3-1. A 3-3 with negation powers would almost always win against 3-2. But where did that leave someone like Athena, who could likely fight *several* Class 3 supers at *the same time?*

She was even good enough to beat Feedback—a super that by all measures was a hard counter to her powers.

Venture watched the playback of Athena's fight one more time with equal parts satisfaction and apprehension. Somehow, Emmett had allied himself with one of the most powerful and experienced Class 3 supers in Belport. It could just be coincidence... but the cynic in him didn't believe that.

For now, Athena would be a valuable mentor and powerful ally, but allegiances could change—Venture would make sure he had countermeasures ready.

Just in case.

When Venture was sure he hadn't missed anything on the tapes, he moved on to examining footage of Clara.

She'd spent most of the time engaged with a single super—one infused with a lesser-known Gnosis mutagen. After watching the replay of Clara's fight with hair-girl, Venture nodded with approval. Clara wouldn't be pleased with the fight or her power limitations, but she'd handled herself adequately.

All Clara's life, she'd been forced to walk a fine line between using her power and maintaining control over its output. Because of those extraordinary demands, Clara had better self-control than most veteran supers. Thanks to her rigorous training they'd only ever experienced mild setbacks.

This fight was likely one of the most difficult of Clara's young life—if only because of the increased limitations she'd been under. Those limitations affected not just output, but also how quickly she could swap between weapon systems, like the sonic blasters. If Clara was at full power, she would've decimated her opponent.

Venture's one complaint about the fight was that during Clara's escape at the end, she'd inadvertently left Emmett open to attack. It was forgivable—this time—because Athena was there as backup.

Venture decided he would commend her for the rest of the fight, and hope she took the praise to heart.

He moved on to Emmett's footage and studied it from every angle. And as he did, a smirk of satisfaction crept across Venture's face.

Emmett had made excellent progress during his training this past month. Between the various mutagens, his prosthetic arm, mods, and hard work, he'd become a considerable threat. Both Clara and Venture pushed Emmett to his limits, but they were still only pushing him *so far*. And so, it was one thing to see Emmett's skills in the relative safety of the Gray Room, but seeing him adapt to new threats on the fly was something else.

Especially the invisible super.

Invisibility was a *very* potent ability, especially when one had super strength or any other abilities to capitalize on the advantage. Low-level supers often didn't have the sensory abilities or otherwise to nullify it—

Emmett didn't either, but he'd found another way.

The smoke and noise maker had rendered both of them deaf and blind, and then Emmett had capitalized on it. Not only that, but he'd used the cover of smoke and noise to get the drop on hair-girl.

In those early weeks, Venture wasn't sure what to make of Emmett's swiss-army knife approach to weaponry. Most supers, including Clara, made do using three or four weapons skillfully, instead of using a hundred different ones. But he couldn't deny the effectiveness.

Emmett's adaptability and versatility would make him formidable.

Most superheroes would be thrilled to have one worthy successor. Venture might have two.

By the time his proteges returned, Venture was almost as excited to see them as Emmett was to see which mutagens he'd found. Emmett emptied the pocket of his hoodie, dumping the vials on the table with almost dangerous gusto.

Emmett said, "I think I've seen some of these before, but not all of them."

From a cursory glance, Venture agreed. "TINA, can you confirm?"

"Yes. The pink vial contains a strength mixture that had diminishing returns when combined with Mutagen-A and other variants. The dark red vial stimulated bone density, but results in protrusions and claws. The bright blue vial increases the body's tolerance to extreme cold. Those other two vials will need to be examined to determine what they will affect."

Emmett sighed, and Venture felt his frustration. Two duds, one with potential, and two unknowns. Now Emmett was looking at the vials intensely, like he *needed* to choose something.

Like a power addict.

Venture had seen them before, usually in a similar position to Emmett. Ever since Gnosis had invented mutagens, they'd become known as one of the few guaranteed ways to get powers.

Clara regarded Emmett worriedly. "You know, you don't have to make a choice right now."

Emmett spared only a quick glance in her direction. "But if I have choices, then I should choose *something*, right?"

Oh, to be young again.

Venture rubbed the stubble of his chin in thought. "What are you leaning toward?"

"Either the cold resistance mutagen or the bioelectric mutagen. Do the nanomachines in my bloodstream help with either of those?"

"If you're leaning toward the bioelectric mutagen, then I'd rather you wait. It's a potent ability, but not without risk. We'll need to reconfigure your prosthetic arm to channel the electricity away from your heart."

Emmett nodded decisively. "Then I'll go with the cold resistance mutagen, and hope the other two will be useful in a few days."

Venture regarded his power hungry protégé. "Well, then what are you waiting for?"

Clara looked at them both with a mix of irritation and disbelief. When Emmett met her eyes, she replied, "Go on, guinea pig."

Emmett didn't waste any more time, and downed the vial in one gulp.

Everyone else watched and waited for the inevitable disgusted reaction... but it never came.

Emmett smiled, no doubt pleasantly surprised. "That actually wasn't too bad. It tasted like raspberries."

Clara groaned and rolled her eyes, and Venture had to admit that he felt a little disappointed as well.

Shouldn't the price of power be bitter and not sweet?

Chapter 31

Data is Compiled

After Friday classes, Emmett found himself back in the Gray Room with Clara—

Well, with Clara's robot.

They were testing the limits of his enhanced night vision against the powerset of a magic-wielding super named *Inkarnate* who used a magic staff to command darkness and forge it into solid objects. It reminded Emmett of Green Mask, who he'd fought twice on the South side of Belport.

Emmett had been right about his vision—it felt magnitudes better than before. Not only had he been able to see the stars above Belport through all the light pollution, now he could still see—even in the near-total darkness of Inkarnate's spells.

Both Clara's robot and Emmett were inside a faux warehouse, slinging furniture at each other in the dark. Gray tables and chairs sailed past the two combatants and shattered on the walls behind them. Even though windows were shattered and daylight should be spilling in, Inkarnate's powers kept the floor of the warehouse almost pitch black.

To Emmett, the strangest part wasn't that he *could* see—it was *what* he could see.

To Emmett, the room was almost completely black, except for the vague outlines of the walls and of Clara's robot.

TINA's voice came through the intercom, confirming Emmett's hypothesis. *"Your enhanced vision is picking up the little ambient light that remains. In addi-*

tion, you're also seeing traces of ultraviolet light from the active portions of the Gray Room and infrared light from the training robot. You can now see slightly outside the visible light spectrum."

Emmett and Clara didn't pause their fight while TINA spoke.

For a moment, Emmett thought he heard a hint of irritation in TINA's voice before she stopped speaking—almost as if she was upset that they hadn't paused to listen to her. But he quickly cast the thought aside.

TINA was a lot of things, but *emotional* wasn't one of them.

So, he ignored it and kept fighting, nearly blind. Only seeing the vague outline of squares that made up the walls and the ghostly image of Clara's robot.

Errant furniture was another problem entirely:

Emmett couldn't see any of the furniture in the room—none of the desks, chairs, or shelves that littered the floor, nor any of them that Clara hurled in his direction. He made up for this by using his whip to feel around the room; he alternated between snaking it across the floor like a blind person's walking stick and waving it in front of him like an insect's antenna to feel incoming furniture projectiles.

"How are you doing that?" Clara shouted as Emmett ducked under another flying desk. He felt the violent rush of air as it passed overhead and heard it slam into the wall behind him.

All the while, Emmett cackled maniacally. "It's like TINA said. Limited UV and IR. Maybe I should lean into it and swap out my eyes so I can see the full spectrum."

"Uh! My helmet can see both of those."

Emmett's cackle turned into a cough. "Maybe I'll make goggles instead."

Across the room, Clara's robot motioned for a timeout. "Seriously, how are you using the whip like that? It's creepy."

Darkness faded, and the Gray Room came back into view. Dividers and inner walls had been blown apart, and mangled white furniture littered the room.

Emmett caught his breath, basking in the scene and in Clara's disbelief.

He explained how he'd been using the whip, then elaborated. "I can't see much, but I can see the robot. Your weight shifts differently depending on if you're throwing something small or throwing a whole desk at me. Then it's just a matter of using the whip to feel where it is in the air."

Clara's robot put its hands on its hips. "I understand that—in theory. But I didn't think you'd be able to use the whip like that. It's like you've got a third arm or something, except that it's, like, twenty feet long and moves like a snake."

"Thanks... I think."

"It's pretty cool," she added, miming out a snake slithering through the air. "Just *weird.*"

The pair of them called on TINA to reset the Gray Room, and while the shattered furniture disappeared into the floors and new pieces rose up to take their place, Emmett dwelled on what Clara had said.

It *was* weird.

Not just how much Emmett had grown into his prosthetic arm and his mods, but how the dichotomy between what he considered real and not-real had changed.

He had a futuristic prosthetic arm and a whip that was so much a part of him it was like having a third arm. Not only could he use his prosthetic hand and whip simultaneously and independently, but Emmett had caught himself almost using the whip in the middle of his apartment on several occasions—it was tempting to use it to grab the remote when it was too far away, or snake over the counter and into the fridge to get a soda.

But then there was the Gray Room and the practice robots that Clara and Dr. Venture used. As much practice and excitement as Emmett got out of sparring against the robots and the hundreds of different powersets the Gray Room could reproduce, there was something mechanical about it. Something cold.

He much preferred when Clara donned her own training suit and flew around the Gray Room with him, or when they both traversed the rooftops of Belport.

It wasn't that he didn't appreciate the training... It was just that he preferred something *real*—

Which was a conundrum for the cyborg who kept thinking about mutagens and upgrades. The more Emmett thought about it, the less he could reconcile the two feelings.

But before Emmett could dwell on his thoughts and before the Gray Room fully reset, Dr. Venture's voice came over the intercom.

"Report to the hub of the mechanical wing. We've finished analyzing the data. We know where the mutagen variants are coming from."

Like most puzzling feelings, Emmett resolved to put it off until some arbitrary time in the future.

Instead, he focused on the task at hand.

They met Venture in the hub of section 002. The entire wall display had been coordinated to display a giant map of Belport overlaid with satellite imaging. Venture was staring at it intently and mumbled a quick greeting. He seemed as eager to get to the explanation as Emmett and Clara were to hear it.

Venture quickly explained the traces they ran on the delivery drivers while TINA added the routes to the map. Emmett and Clara watched with bated breath while several things became clear:

The first was that the distribution of mutagen variants was a massive operation—lines traced chaotically all over Belport. Yet, it was also organized. At first, this was only a gut feeling, but as Venture explained their tracing algorithm, lines began to coalesce into well-worn routes and patterns. This led to TINA circling four points around the Northern side of Belport, just outside the residential areas.

"These are the distribution warehouses. There are four of them. Mutagens are manufactured, stored in these locations, then shipped to their local distribution points—the ones that Athena has been attacking. As capable as Athena is, that strategy is only going to get us so far. It's like cleaning up the mess from a pot boiling over without ever turning off the burner."

Clara crossed her arms. "It's about time we step up our game."

Emmett asked, "Who owns those warehouses?"

Venture sighed and pushed up his glasses. "We're still figuring that out. Two of them are real companies that may or may not know that bootleg mutagens are being run through their warehouses. The other two are shell companies—they exist on paper, but their owners and money are obfuscated. Unfortunately, it will take days, possibly weeks, to figure out who owns those warehouses... The good news is that it doesn't matter who owns the warehouses. They aren't our target. TINA, show them."

New lines appeared, this time running from the distribution centers through the Northern outskirts of Belport. They all coalesced outside the city limits at a single building.

"That's it?" Clara asked, confused.

The warehouse didn't look like anything special. It was one of several unmarked corporate buildings clustered together just outside the interstate. As TINA zoomed in on the warehouse, confusion settled between the two youngest members in the room.

Emmett finally said, "I don't know what I expected, but this isn't it."

Venture chuckled. "Did you expect a supervillain lair with black smoke pouring out over Belport?"

"No, I guess not... Have you scanned the place with drones yet?"

Excitement flashed across Venture's face and was gone just as quickly. "No, I haven't. This is why..."

TINA zoomed in further and showed energy readouts beside the warehouse.

"They are actively scanning in UV and IR ranges," Venture said. "I'm sure you don't want to hear a detailed explanation of the limitations of cloaking technology, but suffice to say that my drones are highly advanced pieces of technology, but they aren't magical. The cloaking systems can hide from the visible light spectrum. Some can hide from UV for a time, and if they're in a low-power mode, then they can hide from infrared... But doing all three while moving... Well, they're not magical. This is the best view I have." Venture shrugged for emphasis.

Clara asked, "What defenses do they have?"

On cue, long distance drone footage appeared on the screens. Venture said, "There's multiple guards and other workers on the premises, along with several supers."

Still frames of the video enlarged to reveal blurry images of four supers along with a small dossier compiled from various sources: The punk-rock looking Feedback, the anti-gravity super and creepy looking hair-girl, both from this previous mutagen bust. The fourth super was one that Emmett hadn't seen before. She seemed completely mundane compared to the others, wearing a plain coat and jeans, except that she was listed as an artifact wielder and in some dossier photos she possessed a sword made out of pure fire.

The last super was clad in a black mask and hoodie, and the sight of him made Emmett's blood run cold—the super that killed Porcelain. The one soaked in Mutagen-X that had trounced Clara at full power.

Venture continued, "Not all of the supers are present at any one time, but we can expect that at least two of them will be on site no matter what time we engage."

Emmett shifted uneasily. He didn't like those odds—not with Clara at half power. Even with Athena on their side, Emmett wasn't sure they could win against the Mutagen-X super, especially if their enemy had backup.

Athena was powerful, but Emmett wasn't sure she could beat the X super on her own. Emmett and Clara would be distractions at best and liabilities at worst.

Emmett and Clara exchanged a glance, and he knew immediately what she was going to ask. There was one organization they could contact for assistance.

Clara asked, "Are we going to tell the Summit of Heroes?"

Venture hung his head in thought before answering. "I know I haven't exactly been forthcoming—with *either of you*... But I don't trust the Summit."

Clara said, "Dad, you can't hold a grudge against them forever."

"It's not... It's not about that. Any of that. This is about the power structure that they've allowed to endure. There's a reason why corporations like Gnosis are untouchable. The world powers have deemed them so. The world is stuck the way it is—in a stalemate of supers, secret cabals, corporations, and govern-ments—because they have all decided to keep their hands off of one another. While the rest of us fight over scraps.

"I don't know who is behind this operation. It could be an inside job or a well-coordinated competitor. Either way, they cannot continue flooding the streets with these products. Evidence would be nice, but either way, the warehouse must be destroyed. I worry that if the Summit gets involved, they will turn everything over to Gnosis. So, we do this on our own."

Emmett stared at the overhead view of their target. Despite the daunting prospect of taking on a well-organized operation and the chance that the Mutagen-X super might be there, he felt a well of resolve in himself.

They needed to do this. Needed to see this through.

But it was more than just that to Emmett. If they could do this and make a difference in Belport, maybe they could eventually do something bigger. Maybe they could make the world a better place.

Even just thinking about it felt both ridiculous and naive but Emmett didn't care.

That was what being a hero was all about. Making the world better. Changing things.

Emmett broke the silence, his words sounding more stoic than he meant them to. "We'll need to prepare."

Venture smirked. "Good. Let's talk preparations."

Chapter 32

Preparation 1

Emmett, Clara, and Dr. Venture settled on three preparations that needed to happen before their mission.

Venture's expression grew stoney as they discussed what was needed. "Emmett, I expect you to complete the first item before you leave the lab this evening."

Emmett nodded, trying to hide his reluctance. "I won't let you guys down."

The first preparation was that Emmett learned how to pull Clara out of her exosuit in case of an emergency.

It wasn't that Emmett didn't want to learn—he knew it was an important protocol, even if he didn't understand Venture's suits or Clara's secret powers. It just felt like a big step...

Like Venture and Clara were trusting him with something *big*. Not to mention potentially trusting him with Clara's life.

Despite that, or maybe because of that, Emmett resolved to finish this preparation tonight. To become as smooth and practiced with the emergency protocol as he was with swapping out his mods. He owed Venture and Clara that much.

Dr. Venture regarded Emmett and Clara before asking her, "Are you ready?"

Clara nodded slightly, for a moment looking like she was putting up as much of a show of confidence as Emmett was.

"Good," Venture said. "Take him to one of the experimental suites of section 003. Tell him everything he needs to know."

Clara turned to Emmett, her normal hard shell faltering. For a moment, she didn't look like the tough engineer or even the badass super that Emmett had come to think of her as.

She looked *normal.*

Like she was just another student at Belport. Like she was about to ask him to study after classes.

"Come on," Clara said with a sigh. "Let's get this over with."

Neither of them said anything as they walked through those first few hallways of the mechanical wing. There was nothing but the hollow echoes of their footsteps on metal—

Which did not help Emmett's slowly building apprehension.

When they got to the main hallway and started toward section 003, Emmett couldn't take it any longer.

"He's talking about your powers, isn't he?"

Emmett winced as soon as he finished. It came out more like an accusation than a question, and immediately he began stammering to add something else.

Clara stopped him with a nod, adding, "Sorry. I just haven't had to explain it to anyone in a while. Give me a minute."

Emmett swallowed dozens of questions, resolving to wait until they got to their destination.

Clara led them past the hub of section 003, past the familiar heat sink testing chambers, and into a small room. It wasn't much bigger than some of the medical suites that Emmett had seen, but this one was the familiar steel gray of the rest of the bunker and lined with exosuit shells. They hung from the walls like old medieval suits of armor and took up most of the room.

As Emmett looked over them, he recognized a progression in design. It was slight, and hard to see, since most of the armor and components were missing, but he was sure it was there.

Clara said, "TINA, please bring up the holographic table and display." A moment later, a holographic table rose out of the center of the floor and lit up with a hologram of Clara's familiar exosuit.

Sure enough, Emmett was even more certain of the progression of the exosuit models. The hologram of Clara's current suit was the newest of the designs.

Clara reached up and spun the hologram, almost whimsically. She watched it as the spin slowed and then turned it so the hologram faced Emmett.

"Here's the deal," she said, her familiar seriousness returning as she crossed her arms over her tank top. "Just because I tell you about my powers doesn't mean I can tell you anything else. Not about where they come from or how exactly they work."

Emmett nodded. "I won't ask."

That didn't mean he wouldn't be curious.

Clara nodded and drew in a deep breath. "So, this is the deal…"

Clara proceeded to draw in several more breaths, starting and stopping before finally groaning in frustration.

"TINA, please explain to Emmett the extent of my powers."

"Dr. Venture said—"

"I know what Dad said, but it will just be easier if you explain it."

"Clara Venture manufactures excess power within her body similar to that of nuclear fusion reactions. Through rigorous training and concentration, she maintains moderate control over her output, staying within nominal levels when in the lab or in public.

"But even with practice, Clara's powers remain too volatile to be used without mechanical guidance. In response, Dr. Venture manufactured special exosuits to channel the energy that Clara generates into flight and kinetic weapons. Even with exosuits and safeguards, there is a nonzero chance of a meltdown."

Emmett listened intently, trying to keep a straight face—it felt like all the questions and all the hints had finally lined up. He was simultaneously mesmerized, blown away, and also felt like a dunce.

He'd spent so much time working on heat sink designs and staring at Clara's armor… None of which had a goddamn generator… And somehow he hadn't put it together that Clara *was the generator.*

As Emmett listened, it felt like both he and Clara were staring at the hologram of her suit. Clara's face was white, like she'd been caught sneaking out of the house or something—

The whole moment felt so ridiculous that Emmett couldn't help but chuckle. "I'm sorry. I just can't believe I missed it."

Clara's momentary surprise turned to a smile. "Dad and I were wondering if you'd ask about it. I thought you were just being polite."

"Secrets are part of being a superhero...but I also knew it was a big deal to both of you, so I tried not to pry." Emmett punctuated the thought with a shrug.

"Thanks."

"...Should I be wearing a radiation suit or something?" Emmett asked.

"No!" Clara replied quickly. "Uh, no. It's *like* fusion, but it's not the same. Unless I'm in the middle of a really bad meltdown, you're fine."

Emmett nodded, and suddenly, the last part of TINA's explanation clicked. "Uh, how bad are your meltdowns?"

Clara's mirth faded quickly. "TINA, show Emmett the surviving footage from my last meltdown in the lab."

They turned toward the one wall of the suite that had monitors. These hummed to life and showed from almost three years ago. Only the year was visible—the rest of the date and timestamp was blurred out. But before Emmett could dwell on it, he became captivated by the video.

The monitors simultaneously showed seven video feeds of Clara sitting in the middle of one of the large heat sink testing chambers. Instead of the familiar fusion apparatus in the center of the floor, the room was completely bare. The only thing in the room was Clara, who wore an earlier model exosuit and knelt in the center of the room.

Even through her thick armor, Emmett could see she was convulsing.

The shoulders of her exosuit glowed orange and then red before beginning to melt and run down her arms. In seconds, the rest of the exosuit was a molten orange. The air in the room grew hazy and Clara was only visible as a bright, glowing mass.

Then arcs of power burst out of her.

They cut through the fog like lasers in a light show, except they arced and curved like they were made of electricity instead of liquid power.

Even watching through a silent video feed, Emmett could imagine the violent crackling sounds rising from his friend. The air was exploding like billions of popcorn kernels. The arcs stretched outward, pulsing in discordant rhythm and the ends whipping like they were possessed.

Video feeds blacked out as arcs of power stretched across the room and vaporized the cameras.

Red lettering flashed across the bottom of the remaining feeds:

CONTAINMENT PROTOCOL ENGAGED

Emmett watched as his friend became a runaway nuclear reaction, his horror slowly building in time with her power. Still, there was beauty there, and something else Emmett couldn't place until only two video feeds were left intact—

He'd seen this phenomenon before; Clara's power looked just like solar flare eruptions.

It felt like it took an eternity for the containment protocol to start, but it couldn't have been more than a second or two. Blocks emerged from the floor around Clara, forming a crude circle. Then more emerged from the ceiling and walls in similar arrangements. Each stuck out about three feet and began to glow with white light.

The arcs of power began to curve around on themselves, tracing molten gashes across the floor. They shrank quickly—in moments their arcs were so tight they were spinning and wrapping around Clara like she was a spinning top.

The last things Emmett saw before the video feeds cut off were the charred and gouged floor and the last of Clara's exosuit melting away. A blinding visage of Clara appeared—a molten, white hot silhouette. She was hunched over, hands clutched to her chest. Screaming.

Even though there hadn't been any sound in the video, when it cut off, the silence in the room became deafening.

"Holy shit," Emmett muttered.

Clara continued staring at the small hologram of her exosuit. She hadn't looked at the video of her meltdown—not once.

"You asked me why I was so good at yoga and meditation. It's because I have to be. It helps me keep control."

Emmett nodded, still staring at where the video had been. "Does it hurt?"

Clara shook her head. "My power doesn't hurt—*not me.* It feels like throwing up and not being able to stop. The containment hurts... All of them hurt."

"There's other ways to stop a runaway reaction?"

"The magnetic field is the best way, but obviously we don't have access to it outside of the lab. There's encasement foam and a drone could always drop me in the bay. They all suck."

Emmett's curiosity got the better of him. "Where does the energy come from?"

It was Clara's turn to shrug. "We don't know. Dad jokes about magic, but for all we know, that's what a lot of superpowers are. Most of them don't follow the laws of the universe. There isn't an equal exchange of matter and energy. There are supers that create and destroy matter... Their powers don't make sense."

Emmett knew this—he'd read the same thing. But it was one thing to read it and another to see it. And another to see how it all affected Clara. To see the turmoil she lived in...

To want to get rid of a part of yourself and not be able to. To barely understand the how or the why, and know that there probably weren't answers to either of those questions.

Emmett said, "The way you guys talked about your powers and how you covered them up made them seem like a burden... But I had no idea."

Clara winced and quickly covered it with a smirk. "I can't change it. I can't change what I am. All I can do is live with it and put it to good use."

"You're doing a good job."

The pair shared a smile.

"I do have a question though... What am I supposed to do if that happens?" Emmett asked.

"Down here in the lab—nothing. Up there, do what Dad and TINA say. Most of the time, the suits have containment and dispersal protocols to stop runaway reactions before they become full meltdowns. There might be a handful of times where you need to pull me out of the suit, which is why Dad wants you to learn. But the general rule is to run."

"Has it ever happened up there?"

The look on Clara's face made Emmett immediately regret asking. It wasn't pain or shock or embarrassment—it was utterly blank and deadpan. Eerily robotic. Like she was reading from a textbook.

"I'm one of the unofficial reasons Dad was forced to retire."

It felt like the rest of the puzzle that was Clara Venture fell into place in front of Emmett. She was always walking on eggshells and afraid of her own power. Hiding not just who she was but tamping down the regret of what her power had already done to people close to her.

"I'm sorry," Emmett said. "And I'm sorry you had to keep it a secret for so long."

The second admission seemed to catch Clara off guard and snapped her out of her stoic trance. She smiled and said, "Don't worry about it. We've talked long enough. You need to learn how to crack open this exosuit."

With a wave of her hand, the hologram of the exosuit expanded and Clara set to explaining how the seams along the head, neck, and back of the suit all came apart.

It was easy—ridiculously easy—for both of them compared to the conversation they'd just had.

In just a few hours, Emmett had successfully completed the procedure for both the hologram and for several of Clara's suits. Which resulted in excited cheers from both of them.

And it felt like their friendship had turned a corner.

Chapter 33

Alias, Pythia

Ash went over the preparations in their head again. And again. And again.

Just because this job wasn't as dangerous, didn't mean that there was any room for error.

The apartment was dark except for the overhead light of the kitchen and the three scattered candles on the table. Ash leaned over their table and examined the documents provided by their employer. The floor plan was mirrored, the names and details written in cipher—these things might obscure the details, but they wouldn't fool anyone in a lettered agency.

It would be immediately apparent that these documents were part of planning an attack.

The obfuscation was to protect Ash's employer—not Ash. They were expendable.

Ash leaned back and rubbed their temples, then their arms.

The apartment was nestled above a laundromat on the edge of downtown Belport. It was cramped and, most of the time, hot from the heat seeping up through the floor. Ash had opened a window in the kitchen, hoping the cold air would help them think.

Ash suppressed a chill, regretting wearing a tank-top and leaving their robe in the bedroom. It would've been a short walk, but then Ash wasn't one to take a break before they were ready.

Or to stop something before they were finished.

Instead, Ash rubbed their upper arms, partly trying to warm up, and partly to practice their power.

Poison gathered in their fingertips, and Ash practiced holding onto it just beneath their skin. It was a delicate art—delicate and dangerous. Hold on too loosely and risk the poison slipping out of their skin and becoming visible and active... Hold on too tightly and risk reabsorbing the poison into their own bloodstream.

It wouldn't kill Ash. At least they didn't think so. But they'd seen first hand what the hallucinogenic compounds in the poison did to someone.

And it was almost time to do it again.

Footsteps in the hallway startled Ash back to the moment. They gathered up the papers in their right hand and held it next to the lit candle. They stared across the kitchen at the front door and waited.

The footsteps stopped in front of Ash's apartment door and then the lock jingled as the key was inserted. Ash relaxed and spread the documents back out as Carter unlocked the door and walked in.

"Lock it behind you," Ash said. Carter usually did, but Ash couldn't help reminding them... Old habits and all that.

The latch turned, and silence followed. Ash could feel their partner staring at them from the doorway.

"Another job?" Carter asked.

Ash nodded.

"Like last time?"

Ash sighed. "Not like last time."

Finally, Carter hung up their jacket and walked over to the table. Carter sidled up beside them, shoulder-to-shoulder, and all hope of Ash concentrating on their work was gone.

All they could focus on was Carter's bare shoulders and their Pirouette perfume.

Ash turned, hoping to meet Carter's eyes, but their partner was looking down at the documents on the table. Ash took in the sight of their partner: Their sharp cheekbones, the tightness of their shoulders, the curve of their breasts that they tried so hard to hide.

In so many ways, the pair were antithesis:

Ash prided themselves in fluidity, at least as appearances went. Though their newfound employment necessitated that personality follow suit. Disguises were necessary in their line of work, after all.

Meanwhile, Carter was rigid in their androgyny, and in who they were... At least they had been.

Ash could feel the stress in their partner increasing. Their jaw was tense, their breathing was getting steadily quicker, and they hadn't blinked. Carter's eyes darted across the documents, unable to read them, and wanting to take Ash at their word.

Ash and Carter had met at a Gnosis work party. Their mutual friend Jessie had introduced them, and they'd hit it off immediately. Both had been wild idealists, who talked a big game about wanting to change the world. Not just the normal liberal-minded talk about workers' rights and the woes of capitalism, but the rightful place of supers, and the dynamics of power across old cabals, nationstates, and rising corporations. Laced through everything was the need for *change*.

Both were activists with disdain for inaction. As fate would have it, they both nearly crossed paths at three separate protests before Jessie introduced them.

'Change might be written into the laws of the universe, but sometimes it needs to be helped along.'

So when the first mutagen variants hit the streets, Ash grabbed a vial for themself and for Carter.

But Carter refused it.

At first, it didn't bother Ash, but then it did.

Soon after, Ash got word of a group of these new supers that wanted to shake things up. That wanted to bring about change a little faster. *Help it along*, so to speak.

Over the better part of the last year, Ash had been involved in six missions—the last of which was the infiltration of the Donjon Club and the poisoning of the super named, Amarque.

For Carter, that mission was a step too far. It was too dangerous, not just for Ash, but for the city of Belport.

They were antithesis:

Carter was inflexible in so many ways, but they bent when it came to the methods. When it came to how far they were willing to go.

Ash was fluid in everything else, except that. They were willing to go as far as was necessary—Belport be damned.

Or so they thought.

At one time, Ash believed they would have stood in front of Paragon and spit in his face. But when Carter saw Amarque lose control because of the poison, Carter pleaded with Ash to stop.

'Too far,' Carter said. *'Too far.'*

When Carter threatened to leave, Ash found how flexible they really were. Ash agreed to take *less drastic* measures and to keep their missions nonviolent.

Carter repeated their partner's words like a reassuring mantra. "Not like last time." A long moment passed before Carter finally looked up. Tears were in their eyes. "Right?"

Ash nodded meekly, wanting the tears to stop. "Not like last time. This is just a little one." The words felt pitiful and stupid, but it was all Ash could get out. They couldn't tell Carter any of the details, and if Ash kept talking, they felt like they would start crying too.

Finally, Carter nodded and wiped their eyes, smudging their mascara. Then they turned and walked off toward the bedroom, leaving Ash standing alone in the lone light of the kitchen.

Ever since that fight, things hadn't been the same between them. Where once their relationship had been unshakable, unflinching, and unapologetic, now it felt...

Broken.

Like building a beautiful house, one you dreamed you'd never ever have. It was a sappy, if not apt, metaphor. Ash and Carter had let each other into such a house, shown each other their heirlooms and memories, furniture marred deeply with sadness and happiness. In a similar sense, they'd begun cleaning out old cobwebs and pulling up rotted floorboards.

Theirs was the kind of relationship built on the ruin of past relationships and hard lessons learned. In school, Ash had learned that stars were built much the same way.

When the universe was first created, there was nothing but hydrogen and helium, so that's what the first stars were made of. As they went through fusion, they produced steadily heavier elements like lithium, beryllium, and boron. These stars eventually went supernova, and after even longer time-spans, their debris coalesced again into new stars. These second generations of stars had slightly heavier elements and metals then the first.

Their sun was a third generation star and the Earth was seeded with elements from those that came before.

It was poetic that the universe was built the same way as the city of Belport—urban sprawl built upon the brick and mortar of the past. And that their relationship was built the same.

But all this, the missions and the fight... It was like a tornado had blown through. Their house was still standing, and at first it seemed like the damage was minimal—nothing that couldn't be rebuilt.

But the damage was much deeper than they feared. Much deeper than either of them wanted to admit. Like finding cracks in the foundation of their beautiful home.

Ash leaned heavily on the table and forced down the lump in their throat.

What else could they do but live a lie? Live like the house wasn't fundamentally broken. Paper over the cracks and hang photos over the water damage. Put the floorboards back down and dance till the candles burned out.

Footsteps.

Ash looked up to find Carter walking back from the bedroom, wearing their mauve robe and bringing the matching one for Ash. The robes were some of the first things they'd bought together when Carter moved in.

Carter handed the robe to their partner and helped Ash slip it over their shoulders. Ash let out a breath they didn't know they'd been holding and leaned into Carter's embrace.

For a moment, time seemed to stop. There was no mission. There was no evening, no night, no tomorrow. No Belport or the packed ruins deep beneath it. The Earth wasn't spinning or hurtling through space toward some. The sun wasn't burning itself out—it wasn't destined to go supernova.

There was just Ash and Carter.

Carter led them away from the light of the kitchen and to the small living room couch. Ash didn't fight it—it would've been like fighting gravity.

For a few hours, the pair orbited one another like twin stars caught in each other's gravity. There was nothing else, and they needed nothing else.

When the hour was late, and they'd already fallen asleep in each other's arms once, Carter pushed themself up off the couch.

Carter shook Ash, whispering, "Come to bed."

In a daze, Ash nodded. Then remembered the next mission.

"I'll be there in a minute."

Carter didn't say anything. Their face was unreadable in the gloom.

A moment later, Ash got up and leaned over the kitchen table. Alone.

It felt like a branch in fate. Like stepping through a threshold and feeling the air change.

It was night now. The world was still spinning, and eventually the sun would rise on Belport. But for a while, it had felt like everything had stopped.

For a while, Ash had chosen Carter.

Chapter 34

Serenity

Serenity and Hunter Nine walked into the downtown headquarters of Aquarius Corp. Their boots echoed on the marble like drumbeats, and everyone in the lobby spared a glance at the capes.

Most people only saw capes when they were passing by on patrol or flying high in the sky.

But then it wasn't often that a company like Aquarius reported a break-in or destruction of property to the Summit of Heroes.

They were greeted in the lobby by the Chief of Security, a neatly trimmed bear of a man, who introduced himself as Clayton and gave them equally strong handshakes. He ushered the heroes to the lobby elevators.

Once the doors closed, Clayton studied the two of them. "Not everything about the break-in was in the briefing. Which one of you is the psychic?"

"That would be me," Serenity said.

Clayton nodded. "Once we get to the scene, I have to ask that your partner stay behind. The board has requested that certain details are only for Summit leadership."

Serenity nodded, ignoring Hunter's grumbling. She was already informed that this investigation would require a debriefing and mind-wipe. "My partner and I understand."

The elevator doors opened to the 34th floor, and Serenity followed Chief Clayton through the halls. Solid walls gave way to glass, and on the other side were rows and rows of computer servers. The mix of metal and colored wires made

Serenity feel like she was walking through a strange aquarium filled with square gravel and strange flora—

Though fish were strangely absent from these rows.

It wasn't until they had walked to the far side of the floor that Serenity saw any workers. Suddenly, there were schools of them, all wearing white shirts and pocket protectors, mulling around charred up blocks of servers like fish on a reef.

Serenity had read the briefing:

Just an hour ago, an unknown super had entered the Aquarius headquarters, gained access to this floor, and poisoned an employee. Said victim was a technopath super under special employment. The poison was a hallucinogen administered via touch.

Serenity had read the official report several times, and each time she was more certain that this was the same team of supers that orchestrated the downtown attack on Amarque and the Donjon club. They were still waiting on forensics to confirm that the poison was the same, but soon they'd have something even better...

Soon, Serenity would scan the victim, and report back to her boss. Then psychic leaders of the Summit would confirm whether the perpetrator was the same super.

It didn't matter how good a super was at disguising themself—there was no fooling a psychic.

Chief Clayton led Serenity to a small room toward the end of the floor. He unlocked the door and opened it to reveal a small meeting room. Several security guards leaned against the walls and stared intently at the man sitting alone at the center table.

He was a pudgy, middle-aged man. His eyes were bright, despite the bruise under one of them, and he looked up at Serenity with a hopefulness that pained her. Like a lost puppy hoping to be taken home.

Aquarius's security had clearly worked him over—

And conveniently left it out in the official report.

Serenity tried to keep a straight face, but it must've looked more intimidating than she meant because the man quickly looked back down at the table.

"He's safe?" Serenity asked.

Beside her, Clayton's face was truly unreadable. "He's no danger to you or your phone. Isn't that right, Mr. Jensen?"

Jensen nodded meekly.

Serenity walked over and took a seat beside him. Jensen seemed surprised at first, but the close proximity forced him to turn and focus on her.

"My name is Serenity, and I'm a psychic from the Summit of Heroes. I know this has been a difficult day, Mr. Jensen, but I need your cooperation for a little while longer. Instead of recounting what happened, I need your permission to read your mind. I would like to see the events through your eyes. Do you understand what I'm asking?"

Jensen nodded, glancing up only briefly. "They—they explained it to me."

"Good. It's not painful, but it can be disconcerting. It should only take a minute or two. Do you consent?"

"...Yes."

Serenity sat back in her chair and tried to relax. The more at ease she was, the less residual transference that Mr. Jensen would feel.

Then she closed her eyes and began.

For a psychic, reading someone's mind was like turning on the television. Most people appeared only as blank screens until Serenity decided to peer inside someone's mind.

The real world fell away—

And revealed the digital mindscape beneath.

From there, it was a matter of turning the feed to the correct channel.

Surface level thoughts came easily, like the static that filled all the space between channels and memories. Serenity could've sat at this surface level connection and let Mr. Jensen's immediate thoughts bubble to the surface:

Scared of the super sitting across from him. Worry about his job and whether he'll get fired from Aquarius. Worry about his family. Sweating. Feeling Awkward. Shame. Regret. Feeling small and powerless. Cog in the machine. Sand beneath the boot.

Some psychics trained themselves to listen to those surface thoughts in a fight—seeing their opponent's moves before they happened and hearing their plans before they could come to fruition. It was a powerful ability—one that Serenity was still working to master.

But today she pushed past the static.

Surfed the channels. Dove deeper.

In a case like this, searching for the correct channel, the correct memory, was easy. Mr. Jensen was cooperative and the event was fresh in his mind. As soon as Serenity pushed past his surface level thoughts, Jensen's memory of the incident came to the forefront.

Serenity whispered, "Take me back to when you first saw the suspect. Try to picture them as clearly *as you can. Relive your conversation. Show me what happened."* As she spoke, the audible sound of her voice faded away until Serenity was using her telepathy to speak through their connection.

Having been on the receiving end of such a trick, it felt like falling asleep—impossible to know when reality ended and when the dream began.

Serenity saw the Aquarius offices through Mr. Jensen's eyes…

It was a bit more intricate than merely watching though: Serenity sensed everything just as he did and felt everything just as he did that morning.

Mr. Jensen walked through the server room, greeting Childs and McCleary, who retorted with the same tired jokes about getting close to retirement. Jensen paused just outside the door to pick up his travel mug of coffee. He'd left it there, as per company policy: No liquids in the server room.

He took a sip and lingered in the hall. Jensen wasn't a praying man, but he muttered aloud his hope for a slow day.

A day he wouldn't get.

A ping on his work phone brought Jensen back to the moment and summoned him to the front desk of the floor. Jensen swallowed his groan like the twenty-year veteran that he was and walked to the front desk of the 34th floor.

The woman waiting at the front desk made both the attendant and Jensen tense up. She wore a well-tailored pantsuit, and her sharp expression and purposeful gaze combined into the look of someone in upper management.

She didn't wait for the intern at the front desk to introduce her.

"Are you Jensen?"

Indeed, he was.

She nodded approvingly and cast her gaze down the hall toward the servers. "I'm VP Ramsy. Show me the servers."

While Jensen quickly examined the badge on the VP's chest, Serenity examined the suspect's face and build, trying to take in as many details as possible. The suspect was given only the vaguest of descriptions in the official report, but this had to be them.

Jensen had received a last minute Email giving him the briefest-of-warnings to expect her, and though she looked much younger than Jensen expected, her badge was in order. So Jensen led her to the servers.

While Jensen tried to hide his nerves, Serenity memorized everything she could about the suspect—even though it would be wiped from her memory later.

The suspect's no-nonsense gaze. The cadence of her walk, and breadth of her shoulders. Her accent that Serenity couldn't quite place...

By the time they got to the server room, the memory had begun to degrade, like a skipping song or bad data connection.

Now, Serenity worked by feel more than by sight. She waited for the touch that she knew was coming.

It was hidden among the last things that Jensen remembered. *The surprising touch of the VP's fingers on the back of his neck.*

And a coy flash of a smile.

By the time Serenity came out of her trance, beads of sweat were on both her and Mr. Jensen's foreheads. Jensen reached up and tentatively wiped his brow, seeming surprised to find the sweat there.

"Is that it?" Jensen asked. "Is it over?"

Serenity nodded, adding, "If done right, you shouldn't feel anything amiss."

It was a delicate process for a psychic to delve into the mind or memories of another. Even more so to manipulate those memories.

Altering small details of a memory was difficult enough. Creating a false one was a skill few psychics could claim.

Deleting a memory depended on how willing the subject was. In Mr. Jensen's case, the hallucinogen had already done much of Serenity's work for her. Now it was as easy as dusting off a shelf.

Uploading a memory to the resonance crystal back at base was much more painful. As painful as having something torn out of you.

"Thank you for your cooperation, Mr. Jensen," Serenity said. She stood and left the witness wondering to himself about what he really had seen today and how exactly he'd lost control before his technopathy had obliterated half the servers on the floor.

Chief Clayton was waiting at the door.

"He's clean and ready for release," Serenity said.

Clayton nodded thanks—the sliver of a gesture was the most that she'd seen his face crack since she'd been there.

"We have the camera footage of the suspect, if you want to see it."

"We don't need it," Serenity said, walking out the door and into the hallway. She already knew how the rest of the story went.

Chapter 35

Preparation 2

It was already late Friday night when Clara declared Emmett proficient with the emergency extraction protocol.

Venture had called over the intercom for them to come back to the hub of sector 002. The pair walked quickly, both joking and eager about hearing what the other two preparations were for the mission.

Despite the cool air and metal confines of the halls, the air between them felt a little lighter. The air between them felt a little lighter, and the prospect of carrying out their mission and taking out the distribution hub felt *real*.

Like they had a chance of pulling it off.

And even though Emmett still couldn't get over the revelation about Clara's powers, or get the footage of her meltdown out of his head, he was glad to know. Glad that Clara and Dr. Venture had confided in him, even though it felt like it had taken forever.

Dr. Venture was waiting for them, and as soon as they walked in, the screen flickered and changed back to the view of the distribution warehouse. He didn't bother with a greeting and launched into an explanation as soon as they entered.

"Now that all that's out of the way, we can focus on the second preparation—finding additional team members. The drones won't be close enough to provide support, not unless things truly hit the fan. So you'll need to compensate with backup."

Both Emmett and Clara shared a surprised look, but it was Clara who asked, "You think we should bring someone in that quickly?"

Venture's face was stern, like a professor delivering a dry lecture. "Working with someone isn't the same as bringing someone in. I'm not saying you need to find someone to trust with your secrets, but someone you trust enough to watch your back. Someone who is smart, capable, and *trustworthy-enough*. With those considerations in mind... Emmett, do you have any ideas?"

The suddenness of the question caught Emmett off guard. Not to mention the gleam in Venture's eyes as his attention fell on Emmett.

Emmett rubbed the back of his neck awkwardly. "Well, Athena said she's been working with other supers that she presumably trusts. That's a start. Then there's McGuire..."

Emmett trailed off, waiting to see their reactions. Both of them knew about McGuire. But Emmett wasn't sure how much more Dr. Venture knew about the eccentric super, or how much of that Venture would've shared with Clara.

But neither dismissed Emmett's suggestions.

Venture's face was still unreadable. "Athena's team is a good start, and she'll likely want them involved. As for McGuire, figure out if he would be useful and if you can trust him enough for the mission. Decide if you want him on your team."

He had only spoken to Emmett, and Emmett glanced at Clara uncertainly. "Shouldn't we all be making this decision?"

Venture shook his head. "McGuire is your connection. Your decision. Besides, we don't have many options. I've tried looking into Athena's team, but she's rather good at covering her tracks... We don't know how many allies she has or what their capabilities are."

Clara nudged Emmett. "Dad's trying to say that you should ask Athena about her team."

Emmett smirked, then sighed. "Yeah. Yeah. I'll contact McGuire tonight for sure. Then I'll contact Athena."

Venture nodded approvingly. "Part of being a super is figuring out—*quickly*—who you can trust, and then deciding how far to trust them."

Venture's words hung heavy in the room. He didn't need to state the obvious.

This was a big step. And Venture was trusting Emmett to make the right choice.

Emmett nodded resolutely. "I won't let you guys down."

Venture smiled.

Clara nudged Emmett again. "You better not."

M 11:51 PM: *Hey are you free?*

MG 11: 51 PM: *YES. On the corner of 17 and Blake*

Emmett sighed. He wasn't exactly keen on meeting on the edge of the slums, but who knew what McGuire was up to.

M 11:52 PM: *On my way*

Half an hour later, Emmett was racing across the rooftops parallel to the L train rails. Emmett scanned the rooftops as he went. It took a few more minutes of searching, but Emmett spotted McGuire crouched on one of the support struts of the L train.

He was peering through a crude device, which Emmett assumed were night vision goggles. Emmett and McGuire locked gazes, and the gadgeteer frowned and waved for Emmett to come over.

Emmett jogged and then used his whip to swing up to the graffiti-covered support strut.

McGuire let the cobbled together night vision goggles hang from the strap around his neck.

"Don't tell me you can see in the dark too..."

Emmett shrugged.

"Man! I was excited about this spot too—was going to give you riddles and everything to help you find me. But *no*, someone's gone full cyborg and can see in the dark." Despite the haphazardly stitched mask covering his face, McGuire's complaints were in good spirits, and the pair shared a laugh.

Then the gadgeteer asked, "So what's up? Are you ready to go another round?"

Thoughts of that sparring session on the roof flashed back to Emmett. "As tempted as I am to see more of your gadgets, I have to pass tonight. How would you feel about teaming up for a mission?"

McGuire's eyes widened. Then he suddenly cleared his throat and cleared the surprise from his face, like he was trying to look more professional. He leaned against the metal pillar, his backpack making a dozen different *clanks* and *shuffling* sounds.

"I'm listening."

"What do you know about knock-off mutagens?"

"Enough to know that someone's up to no good. I've fought a couple supers with weird powers—acid spit, weirdly long tongues." McGuire quickly mimed out the powers as he said them, then crossed his arms over his chest like he was attempting to be serious again. "Past that, I don't really know much. Most of it I've heard through the grapevine; masks love to gossip."

Emmett whispered, "What if I told you that we know where they're being made?"

McGuire scoffed. "I'd ask why you haven't done something about it yet."

"...Well, we just found out."

"Oh. That makes sense..." McGuire's eyes widened again. "Are you asking me—are you asking me to come with you guys?"

Emmett stifled a laugh. "Well, yeah. I'm not just meeting up with you to tell you about our plan and then say bye."

"Okay, point taken. So what's the plan?"

Quietly, Emmett summarized the meeting he'd had with Dr. Venture and Clara. Even though they were hidden beneath the L train and high above the streets, Emmett didn't want to chance someone listening in.

McGuire nodded thoughtfully as he listened. For the first time, he looked truly serious—not like the super was just putting on a face for Emmett's benefit.

When Emmett finished, McGuire leaned back against the metal and stared off across the bay in thought. The waves were barely there, and the lights of Belport looked promisingly beautiful.

Finally, McGuire's stoic demeanor subsided. "I don't know, man."

Emmett did a double-take. "What do you mean?"

"I just don't know, alright," McGuire replied, lowering his voice again. "Can you go over it again?"

Emmett took a deep breath and went back through his summary again—

But he could already tell something had changed in McGuire. The super wasn't jovial or serious... McGuire looked sad.

It caught Emmett so off guard that he stopped half-way through his summary. "What's going on?"

McGuire shrugged. "I can't help you."

"Why not?"

"I just can't."

Emmett sighed heavily and looked out over the city. "Fine. We'll manage, I guess."

McGuire didn't say anything else.

Emmett shook his head. Now he was just irritated. Something was clearly up, but Emmett could tell he wasn't going to get an explanation—

There was a *pop*, and suddenly Emmett and McGuire were set flying sideways in opposite directions. Something had exploded.

Emmett tumbled through the air and slung his whip to try to grab something. Anything.

He managed to latch onto the edge of a nearby roof and swung himself around to land on top of it. He looked back at the L train strut, where he'd been standing, and found it untouched. But Emmett didn't have time to dwell on just how strange that was.

McGuire was hanging from a fire escape two buildings over and managed to pull himself up and over it to safety.

Emmett scanned the rooftops, looking for threats, and found two supers standing on the edge of a third story roof—looking down on Emmett and McGuire.

"There you are!" One of them shouted.

Two more silhouettes came into view behind the enemy supers—a giant black crow twice as tall as a person, and a slightly smaller walking tree.

Emmett sighed and got ready to fight. "Why does it always happen on the South side?"

Chapter 36

Why is it Always South Side?

The two enemy supers peered down from the rooftop. The woman at the front stood with her hands on her hips like she'd just stepped out of a comic book—clad in leather with her long, bright pink hair waving in the wind.

Two summoned creatures stood just behind her. Both the giant crow and the walking tree looked like they were made of pure shadow. Even in the bright lights of Belport, the two creatures looked more like black ink than anything real. The illusion was particularly striking on the crow. It was absolutely void black, save for its yellow eyes.

The second super was crouched next to the tree, wearing a bodysuit that shimmered like dark green snakeskin. Their hands were held close together and their fingers moving in a spellcasting pattern that Emmett didn't recognize.

Before Emmett could look too closely, several things happened at once:

The giant crow beat its wings once and it erupted into the air. The gust of wind was so powerful that Emmett had to brace himself so he wasn't pushed back. On the fire escape across the way, McGuire scrounged in his backpack for something. And the pink-haired super made a finger-gun with one hand and pointed it in Emmett's direction—

Neither of the supers looked like they were carrying weapons, or wearing backpacks or utility belts. The explosion that knocked Emmett and McGuire apart had to come from *somewhere*.

Now he knew.

Emmett sprinted forward as fast as his enhanced legs would take him, ready to leap off the roof and swing to safety. He'd flank the two supers, opposite McGuire, and use his whip to get up to their roof.

He didn't get the chance.

Pop.

The almost-comical noise behind him didn't do justice to how violently Emmett was thrown through the air. He hadn't even made it off the roof, but now he was flying clear over the next building.

Thankfully, he wasn't tumbling through the air, and with his enhanced coordination from the Mutagen-A in his system, Emmett used those air-borne seconds to counterattack. He pulled a smoke bomb out of his upper arm compartment and tossed it at the enemies' rooftop, covering it in smoke.

By the time Emmett was descending through the air, he lashed out with his whip, grabbed a nearby light pole, and was swinging in a wide arc toward his targets.

Past the smoke and on the opposite side of the building, Emmett heard shouts, clangs of metal, and something like the whirring of an electric drill.

Pop. Pop.

The air shuddered behind him as the explosive super used her power. She was firing blindly through the smoke, but Emmett flinched and he still felt the edge of the shockwaves.

Emmett didn't have enough momentum to land on the roof, so he settled for landing on top of a sign on the outside of the building. From there, he could climb up to the roof and ambush them before the smoke cleared.

However, the explosive-super's power worked, she wasn't making normal explosions. The force produced should've been shattering windows, but Emmett didn't see any damage to the other buildings. Her power must disproportionately affect living things...

Emmett hesitated only a moment before swapping his whip out for his concealable pistol. It was a hunch, but if her abilities were closer to that of a psychic, then she wouldn't be able to stop a bullet.

Emmett hauled himself up the last two stories, grabbing window ledges and cracks and being eternally grateful for his super strength. He was just about to peek over the edge of the roof when the giant crow flew by—

Holding McGuire in its claws.

Shit.

There was no telling if a well-placed shot would be powerful enough to hurt a summoned creature, or if an attack like that would affect the bird at all. And that was assuming Emmett could hit a moving target without hitting his ally. He'd have to attack the caster and break his concentration on the spell.

Emmett grit his teeth and hauled himself onto the roof.

By now, the smoke was mostly cleared—aided by the tree that swung its bare limbs around in an eerily human gesture. The creature's body was night black, except for faint shimmers of brown and green.

For a moment, Emmett could just make out the silhouettes of the two supers in the fading smoke, and he raised his prosthetic arm in anticipation.

Until the damn bird came back.

McGuire was shouting something incoherent, and punching the bird with his brass knuckles, causing sparks to fly off of the bird. As they passed overhead, the crow beat its wings and blasted away the rest of the smoke.

Suddenly, Emmett was in a standoff on the roof with both supers and the summoned tree.

The pink-haired super raised her hand—

Emmett was faster. And his hand was already raised.

The pistol emerged from his prosthetic and fired, the blasting mechanism making a subsonic *thunk*. The sledgehammer round hit the super square in the chest and she doubled over. Emmett heard a *pop* somewhere far behind him as her shot missed.

Quickly, Emmett aimed for the second super and fired, but the dark tree stepped in front of the shot. Just like Emmett feared, the bullet bounced off and rolled across the rooftop.

Emmett weighed his options, but ultimately didn't have much time.

Pink-haired girl tried to push herself up, and Emmett shot her again. This time, the tree didn't bother to block the shot, and it hit her square in the side. She rolled over and stayed down.

Emmett muttered, "Should've stayed down."

The summoner didn't appreciate the cheap shot, though. He whispered something, and the shadow tree lumbered forward.

Emmett erred on keeping his pistol equipped—he'd gotten a lot quicker at changing mods, and so he might have been able to swap it out for something else. But Emmett was glad he didn't chance it when he saw just how fast the tree could move.

There might've been thirty feet between them, and the tree covered the distance in four huge steps. Its two thick legs split into four, five, and six, giving it spider-like speed. Simultaneously, its limbs stretched out in every direction, making it even taller and wide enough to cover the roof—

The whole sight happened so quickly, it gave the illusion that the tree was falling on him.

Emmett crouched and feinted left before diving right, his enhanced strength taking him clear across the roof. He rolled to his feet, gun leveled to take a shot at the summoner. But his enemy was just as swift. Both the summoner and the tree moved in perfect unison, only giving Emmett slivers of a shot.

Emmett saved his ammo and pulled out a sonic grenade, hoping it would affect both the tree and the caster. Maybe the grenade alone would be powerful enough to get the caster to drop the spell. He pressed the button and chucked it at the base of the tree, and the high-pitched whine of the sonic covered the roof.

Immediately, the bark of the tree rippled like wind blowing across water. Limbs recoiled and its roots shuffled.

Emmett dashed as quickly as he could to the right, trying to flank the tree. He grit his teeth and passed as close to the sonic as he dared. The summoner came into view—he was reeling backward from the sound, hands clasped over his ears.

Just as Emmett raised his arm to fire, the tree stomped on the grenade and flailed a massive branch in his direction. Black leaves sprouted all across it, blocking the summoner. Emmett's two shots slammed harmlessly into the branches.

Emmett groaned in frustration—ready to toss his whole compartment's worth of bombs just to end it.

McGuire's scream brought him back to the moment. Emmett whirled around, trying to keep one eye on the tree and find his ally.

The giant crow was soaring toward the roof and McGuire had managed to wriggle an arm loose. It took Emmett longer than he would admit to realize that his ally wasn't shouting for help—

"Jump! Jump off the roof!"

McGuire had something in his free hand and was chucking it at the roof as the bird passed.

Emmett ran for the edge, swapping his gun for his whip, and jumped.

Behind him, there was a *poof* sound, followed by what Emmett could only imagine was a long, wet fart.

He lashed out and grabbed the edge of a windowsill to stop his fall, then swung up to the next building over. From the opposite roof, Emmett looked over and saw a faint green cloud covering where he'd been moments ago. The tree was flickering out of existence.

And both the summoner and the pink-haired super were doubled over, coughing and gagging.

McGuire jogged up behind Emmett. "You really like those smoke bombs, don't you?"

Emmett chuckled. "Yeah. Jealous?"

McGuire shook his head. "I've got my own. You want a battle over quickly? Use a stink bomb."

The pair watched silently as their enemies gagged for a solid minute on the putrid fumes. Emmett caught a quick whiff and nearly gagged on it himself.

"I'm glad you didn't use one of those on me," he muttered.

McGuire laughed, then squinted seriously. "Don't go mad with power, and I promise never to use one on you."

"Deal."

Finally, the wind picked up enough to clear the roof, taking their enemies' coughing fits with it. As the wind picked up, Emmett swore he heard a cough or two downwind.

Emmett focused on the two enemy supers, who were still recovering from the stink bomb. "What did they want, anyway?"

It was a rhetorical question, and Emmett was already swinging over to their rooftop. McGuire hollered after him and used a grappling hook to follow.

Containing his irritation, Emmett swapped out his whip for his pistol again and checked how many shots he had left.

"What's the big idea?" Emmett asked, training his pistol on the supers.

Both the summoner and pink-haired girl were taking their time standing. Neither answered until McGuire was standing beside Emmett.

"What's the big idea, McGuire?" the girl asked. She sat up on her knees and pushed a clump of pink hair out of her face.

The summoner was still laying on the ground. "You said you wouldn't use those anymore. God, that's the most awful thing I've ever smelled. It's even worse than last time. How is it worse?"

Emmett's mouth was open in a dumb stare, which he finally aimed at McGuire.

McGuire shrugged. "What? It's a new recipe?"

"You know these guys?!"

The girl snorted a laugh and helped her partner stand. "Yes, he knows us."

McGuire fixed his mask. "Oh yeah. This is Cherry and Larian. Guys, this is Mod."

"Hey," they both said in unison.

Emmett glanced between McGuire and the pair. "But they attacked us?"

"It's just sparring," McGuire said. "Same as we did."

Emmett sighed, unsure of what to think. He put his hands on top of his head and turned to look out over the city. Just *sparring?*

Really?

McGuire, Cherry, and Larian talked quietly behind him while Emmett tried to process what had just happened. At first, Emmett had thought about both times he'd been ambushed by Zanté and Green Mask, but this was clearly different.

Zanté had fought brutally, but now Emmett didn't have a scratch on him. Neither did McGuire, for that matter. If anything, Cherry and Larian had fared far worse.

It just seemed... weird. How often did McGuire spar with random supers? But maybe that was just how things were. After all, how many supers had a Gray Room to train in? How else were supers supposed to get better at using their powers?

Emmett took a deep breath and turned around to join the group. All three turned mid-conversation.

Emmett muttered, "I, uh... Nice to meet you guys." Then to Cherry, he added, "Sorry about shooting you while you were down."

She nodded. "So long as you remember it next time."

Emmett chuckled. *Next time*—there was a thought. Was he just going to make friends with every mask in Belport?

Cherry and Larian said their goodbyes. Then Larian summoned the giant crow again. It coalesced out of the air, its feathers coating it like dark icicles until it was fully formed. It carried the pair off across the skyline. Emmett and McGuire watched them go.

"They're good guys," McGuire said. "It's been like three years, I think."

Emmett suddenly remembered the disappointment of the super's answer. He'd come out here hoping McGuire would come join them in taking down the distribution plant... As cool as it was to train out here in the actual city, the whole thing just felt like a waste.

Emmett almost walked away right then.

"Hey Mod..."

McGuire's face might've been covered in a shoddy mask, but his voice sounded shaky.

"...Look, I changed my mind. I want to come with you guys. I'm tired of doing this—no matter how much I practice, ultimately it means nothing. And I'm tired of doing nothing. Even taking on street-level criminals doesn't *solve* anything.

"But what you're talking about—taking on whoever's peddling these mutagen knock-offs? That just might solve *something*. So count me in."

McGuire stuck out his hand for emphasis. Emmett didn't waste any time shaking it or smirking behind his mask.

Emmett's team, and his plan, were slowly coalescing.

Chapter 37

Preparation 3

Venture insisted that Emmett get his schoolwork in order before working on Preparation 3.

Emmett worked through most of Saturday morning, wondering if his room-mate would ever wake up and come out to the common area. It was 2 o'clock when Emmett finally left for the lab.

Lock wasn't awake yet. His door was still shut.

By the time Emmett met up with Clara and Dr. Venture in the lab, he was jittery with anticipation. Emmett told himself that it didn't matter what the final preparation was—it felt like he was ready for anything.

Venture pushed up his glasses and crossed his arms sternly. "This final preparation is the most important and, in all likelihood, the most difficult. We need to neutralize their trump card... We need to deal with the Mutagen-X super."

Both Clara and Emmett shared an uncertain glance.

Emmett asked, "Do you mean going after them before the mission?"

A dark smile crossed Venture's face and was gone just as quickly. "The possibility crossed my mind, but even alone, that super would be far too dangerous to take on. Clara can't use her full power without being tracked by the Summit. Even with McGuire and Athena... No. We need to find another way."

Venture locked eyes with Emmett. *"You* need to find another way. You need to find a countermeasure for Mutagen-X."

Emmett chuckled awkwardly. "You want *me* to find a weakness in the most prized black ops super serum on the planet?"

"Yes."

Emmett glanced from Venture to Clara, but she was staring straight ahead, like she was a student in class, afraid to draw attention to herself.

So he was on his own...

"Shit," Emmett muttered.

Venture smirked. "TINA will provide you with the specs for Mutagen-X. You come up with your own ideas *first*, then—and only then—TINA will match them against the ideas we have saved. This is an opportunity, Emmett. Seize it. One day, we won't be there to guide you. So, start acting like the Tech-Super you are."

Emmett nodded solemnly.

Of all the things he'd come up against so far, this was... Well, to call it 'daunting' was the understatement of the century. 'Hopeless', maybe?

Shit.

Emmett tried to salvage what motivation he could. He had a job to do, and if he couldn't solve this, then the mission was a lost cause.

"Alright," Emmett said. "Which lab can I use?"

"It's just another problem to solve," Clara said. She walked with Emmett to the hub of the biolab. "It's just like engineering. And you're good at that."

Emmett managed a chuckle. "Thanks, but there's building an antenna and then there's taking down a world-class bioweapon... One of those things is not like the other."

Clara led the way into the hub and asked TINA to bring up all the data they had on Mutagen-X. The wall of monitors and the holographic table whirred to life.

Emmett stared at her. "Don't you have your own training to do?"

Clara put her hands on her hips, causing her oversized hoodie to bunch up. "Oh, so you don't want the help?"

"I didn't say that." Emmett backtracked without really knowing why.

It wasn't that he didn't want Clara there. She'd sworn to her dad not to help Emmett directly, but every bit of encouragement was welcome.

If Emmett was being honest with himself, he was self-conscious about Clara being there. Which was weird because Emmett wouldn't feel that way if they were training in the Gray Room...

What was so different about this?

Emmett stood next to Clara and looked over the spec displays on the wall, but he wasn't really looking. He was still stuck. Still self-conscious.

Clara asked, "What do you think?"

Emmett hummed noncommittally, trying to stall for time.

Maybe he felt fine in the Gray Room because Emmett knew that he had a lot to learn. He was always the one on the ropes, or playing catch-up. It was alright if he messed up or hadn't learned something yet. No one expected Emmett to be an expert at fighting, at least not yet—he knew that. Clara knew that.

But Emmett *was* supposed to be good at engineering. He was supposed to take the lead.

Emmett rubbed his face and eyes, and forced himself back to the moment, muttering, "Give me a sec."

He needed more than a second.

There was *a lot* of data. Diagrams and charts covered the screens, showing everything from bodily systems affected, to rates of growth, projectile calibers withstood, healing factors, possible side effects, and even recommended psychotherapy treatments.

"...How did your dad get all this data?"

Clara shrugged. "Some of it's speculation. Part of its data from combat zones around the world. Some of it probably came from Gnosis."

"It looks like he hacked their systems to get all this."

"He probably has, but that's not saying much. Dad hacks a lot of people... *Bad* people." Clara muttered.

The pair settled into silence as they looked over the data. At first, Emmett just wanted to get a sense of what Mutagen-X actually did to someone.

In a lot of ways, it was similar to Mutagen-A, in that it caused a broad spectrum of changes to the subject. But if Mutagen-A took a normal person from a 1 to a 2, Mutagen-X cranked them up to 11.

Or, more accurately, to Class 3.

Solid Class 3.

Bones stronger than steel. Skin that shrugged off anything less than high caliber armor-piercing rounds. Veins and arteries that were made to seal off lost limbs. Platelets that instantly coagulated to stop blood loss.

Virtually unkillable—not that most of their enemies would get the chance to fight back.

They also had heightened senses—a sense of smell better than most hunting dogs, hearing better than a cat, and eyes that could see in UV. They were strong enough to tear through steel...

Emmett could remember the rest. He'd seen the Mutagen-X super that night. The super had broken through a steel door, torn apart Venture's drones, and mangled Clara's high-tech exosuit... Porcelain had been a formidable Class 2, and that super had snapped her neck as easy as breaking an egg.

For every chart or diagram that Emmett looked over, there were more details, but that was the jist of it. They were hopelessly outmatched.

Emmett desperately wanted to skip this part—Venture said they'd already brainstormed a couple of solutions. Did Emmett really have to bang his head against the wall to come up with another?

TINA had helped him out before. Maybe TINA would help him out again... Just this once.

Emmett smirked to himself and pushed the thought from his head. This was a test. Venture had given him a task, and Emmett needed to try despite how hopeless it felt.

So he and Clara started bouncing ideas off of each other.

Guns were an obvious place to start. A .50 caliber rifle or armor-piercing rounds would be enough to pierce the skin, but they were big and there was no guaranteeing the super would stay still enough to hit. Even if they did land a shot, one wouldn't be enough before the wound healed. Drones were out—they couldn't get close to the warehouse without getting detected. Besides, once gunfire started, they would attract attention.

Emmett asked, "What about scaling up your kinetic blasts?"

Clara shook her head. "It's a bad weapon against someone with high defense. The explosion doesn't have enough *punch*." She slammed her hand into her first for emphasis. "At that point, you might as well just use a regular laser, and well, a battery large enough to run a laser that powerful isn't something we can just lug around."

Emmett rubbed his chin in thought, but immediately stopped when he saw Clara raising an eyebrow. He wasn't trying to look like her dad right now.

"What about fire?"

Clara sighed. "Mutagen-X makes the subject tolerant to extreme cold and extreme heat. Unless we can trap the guy and cook him alive, it's a bad choice."

Emmett suppressed a shudder. That would be a horrible way to go.

He mentally checked off several other options: Bombs were out for the same reason as Clara's kinetic blasts. Knives had a slightly easier time piercing the skin, but with their healing factor even puncturing an organ wouldn't stop the guy. Sonic weapons had potential, but Mutagen-X also gifted the super with a pain tolerance that was through the roof. There was a similar problem with trying to stun them with electricity—their muscles could reset within milliseconds of impedance...

Emmett laughed bitterly. "Maybe we could just bring the building down on him."

"Dad made that joke yesterday," Clara replied, deadpan.

"I mean, we were going to destroy the place, right?"

"Probably."

Even poisons weren't much of an option. Mutagen-X allowed the body to operate in an extended anaerobic state—allowing the super to function without oxygen for hours at a time. Even if they managed to get a poison into their bloodstream, bio-engineered white blood cells could fight off or quarantine any infection, and then expel other toxins like heavy metals through sweat.

Emmett sat down at the holographic table and rubbed his temples.

Clara clapped a hand on his shoulder. "You've got all weekend. I'm going to get a snack. Want anything?"

Emmett shook his head.

"Suit yourself."

As soon as Clara left, Emmett asked TINA for the answers, reasoning that he should use all the tools at his disposal.

"It's just like hacking a database."

TINA didn't give Emmett the answers, much to his dismay. At least he tried.

Emmett kept examining solutions, eventually superimposing a list of ideas and failed ideas on the left side of the monitors.

After several hours, Emmett concluded several things:

Overpowering the super was out of the question. Any weapon powerful enough to hurt them wouldn't be viable in their current mission.

Tricking or trapping the super *might* be viable, but even that had limitations. The heightened senses meant that Emmett's normal smoke pellet-tricks wouldn't work. And those same senses made them resistant to most telepathic attacks from all but the most skilled psychics. Emmett and the others also didn't know the layout of the building, so laying a trap would be difficult at best.

Sadly, the best option was to schedule the mission on a night the Mutagen-X super wasn't there...

The longer Emmett thought about it, the more it seemed like the best option.

But Emmett couldn't stop thinking about it—there had to be *something*. Venture wouldn't have tasked him with this if he didn't think Emmett could come up with an answer.

At least one answer. The stark reminder came back to Emmett that Venture and TINA had multiple potential ones.

For some reason, Emmett kept coming back to the super's healing factor: No matter what method of attack they used against the super, their healing factor and disease resistance were the final barriers to overcome.

Clara had come and gone several times over the last two hours, but Emmett had continued working. Now he was alone in the biolab hub.

"TINA, show all the information you have on the healing factor and disease resistances of Mutagen-X." The wall of information changed to reflect his request and Emmett searched the rest of the data.

Maybe he'd been going about this all wrong. Maybe instead of worrying about beating this super in a fight, he should figure out a way to take them down from the inside—

Fighting smarter instead of just fighting harder.

"TINA, what nanomachines do I have access to?"

There was a delay before TINA answered. *"I'll send for Dr. Venture."*

Chapter 38

Lock

Lachlan sat on his bed and stared at the missed messages on his personal phone:

Carter 8:29 PM: *Hey can we talk?*
Carter 8:33 PM: *It's probably nothing*
Carter 9:32 PM: *Worried about Ash*
Carter 10:03 PM: *Just call when you can*
Carter 10:29 PM: *It's probably nothing*

Lock shook his head, trying not to worry that he'd managed to sleep through all Carter's messages. He'd been a bad friend. Maybe he'd just been… busy. That was what Lock told himself, anyway.

Whatever was going on between his friend and their significant other had to wait till morning. Lock left his personal phone behind and took his burner phone with him.

He had a job to do.

Lock let the night air of Belport wash away his worries and bring him back to the moment. Back to the hunt.

He walked the side streets and back alleys of the South side of Belport, wearing a black mask and black hoodie. Hidden in plain sight.

There was the Code for heroes, and then there was the Code for the *other side* of Belport. The slums, as it was called by those that didn't live there, the underside, by supers that worked there. For Lock, it was a home he couldn't get away from.

If you were a super, then you were expected to wear your mask when you were working. If you belonged to a gang, then you wore your colors too. That way, people knew who you were.

And you stayed on your side of town.

Lock broke the rules every time he came to the underside.

Supers weren't supposed to wear all black here. It meant you were trying to hide who you were.

Though Lock walked with his hood up and hands tucked in his hoodie, he walked with confidence that only a powerful super had. And people on the street moved out of his way—didn't matter if they were civilians, delinquents, or fellow supers. All of them gave him a wide berth. The only thing Lock watched his step for was the occasional bag of trash that had split or been rifled through. Even if nearby supers were suspicious, no one said anything to him as he passed.

Supers that knew the rules of the underside and still had the balls to wear all black were dangerous. Hiding their identity wasn't protection for them so much as it was protection for any bystanders that might lay eyes on them.

But Lock suspected it was something else that kept the people of the underside away from him. That primal, gut feeling of danger—something like the hair standing up on the back of their neck when a predator was close.

It was like they knew what he was. Even if they couldn't see his muscles flexing beneath his hoodie. Even if they couldn't smell the mutagens suffusing his every cell, or read his mind.

Lock felt like a shark swimming through a school of fish, paying no mind to all the people that got out of his way.

No one said shit to him.

The fish knew better.

Lock double-checked the address in the encrypted window on his phone. He was in the right place.

He tucked the burner phone in his pocket and began to climb the brick wall of the slum apartment, fingertips growing into a bastardized mix of sharpened nails and bone spurs. They hooked into the bricks and mortar as easily as a cat's claws, and the only sound was the quiet scratch as he gripped a new handhold.

He kept his shoes on, not bothering to change his feet. Lock merely used his legs to steady himself as he climbed up the side of the building to the third floor, slowly and methodically.

His target lived in one of the small, one-room apartments. The windows all had bars around them—the kind that were like a cage door that opened from a latch on the inside. Lock peered through the first window and saw the bedroom beyond.

Saw the man named Peter Wendell, sleeping still in his bed. An old blanket was tucked, pulled up taut under his chin. Most of the room was bare.

Lock crawled across the bricks to the next window that looked into the kitchen. If he entered here, Lock would be between his target and the front door—

Not that Mr. Wendell could get past him, anyway.

Lock grabbed the cage of the window and, with just enough pressure, pulled the bars until the latch gave way with a snap. In another smooth motion, he did the same with the window itself, and the latch gave way with another snap.

Then Lock crawled through the window.

All the times that Lock had entered through an upper window, the only way he could describe how he felt was like a spider. Climbing, contorting, and pulling himself through a window—it was effortless and completely quiet.

It was dark in Mr. Wendell's kitchen, but Lock could see well enough. Old takeout cardboard and plastic ware were on the counter. There weren't any normal dishes. No decorations on the walls. No furniture, save for two folding chairs in the adjoining living room.

Wendell wasn't staying here for long. He was on the run from Gnosis.

Was.

Lock stood there in the darkness of the kitchen, waiting.

In the other room, Wendell was getting out of bed. No doubt he'd heard the snaps of the latches. The former school teacher crept to the bedroom door, floorboards creaking with every step.

Lock waited.

The bedroom door groaned open, and Wendell peeked through the crack. A moment later, Wendell stepped out from behind the door.

In the darkness, Lock could see him perfectly, could see the day-old stubble on his face and the few graying hairs on his head. He shuffled forward, wearing ragged pajamas and an equally old shirt, and clutching a long screwdriver like a junkie clutching a fix.

Even from across the room, Wendell reeked of Mutagen-A, and... something else—another mutagen, maybe.

Something else that didn't matter.

Lock saw the slowly dawning fear as Wendell's eyes searched the gloom of the kitchen and found a silhouette staring back at him.

Lock waited. Waited to see what Wendell would do.

He shouldn't have. Depending on the next second, he could make Lock's job slightly harder and the cleanup more cumbersome.

But truthfully... He liked seeing the fear in their eyes. Liked watching as that slowly dawning fear turned to sadness and terror.

Sometimes they tried to bargain. Others tried to run. But it always ended in terror. Like garnish on a well-prepared meal.

The second dragged on and in the dark, Wendell's eyes widened as his brain finally realized that he was looking at a person in his kitchen. Lock could hear the thumping of his heart growing fast and loud, even from across the apartment.

"Are you... Are you from Gnosis?"

Lock waited.

Wendell swallowed and his knuckles turned white as he gripped the screwdriver desperately.

"I can explain," Wendell muttered. "Really. I... Oh god. I... I have a son and a daughter. Please."

Lock waited. Savoring the fear.

"...I'll scream."

"No, you won't," Lock finally said. "Because if you do, they won't hurt just you."

The implication of his kids' lives hanging in the balance snuffed any remaining hope in the man. Mr. Wendell fell to his knees, still clutching the screwdriver, and sobbed.

Lock strode forward, so quickly and suddenly, that Wendell almost didn't have time to look up. He seized Wendell by the throat with both hands. Wendell's eyes bulged as Lock squeezed.

He could've broken the man's neck, but he didn't.

It wasn't because Wendell's body was half-suffused with Mutagen-A. Wendell was a failed experiment, but he was still stronger than a normal human. No—

That wasn't it at all.

Wendell struggled, pawing desperately at Lock's hands. He was still holding the screwdriver. Spit dripped down Wendell's mouth and onto Lock's hands.

Then Wendell stabbed him in the stomach with the screwdriver.

Lock let him—

Kept his grip on the man's neck as he stabbed Lock over and over again.

Felt the metal pierce his skin and plunge into whatever strange organs now filled his abdomen. Felt as the blood coagulated almost instantaneously, as membranes stretched and reformed a hundredth of a second later.

Watched as Wendell realized that there was nothing, absolutely nothing, he could do. Savored the moment that realization was distilled into fear in the man's eyes.

Then Lock squeezed in earnest—

Wendell's neck snapped. His arms dropped and his body hung limp in Lock's hands.

Lock could smell the blood—could taste the iron.

Wendell's lifeless face stared up at him, eyes frozen in pure terror.

Lock stared.

A minute or two later, there was a knock at Mr. Wendell's front door.

It startled Lachlan, even though he was expecting it. Even though the knock always came after a job.

He finally let go of Wendell's neck and the body fell over on the floor.

Then he went over and opened the door to find a maskless, hunched old woman waiting for him. Her hair was completely gray, frizzy, and she was fond of wearing dresses with flowers on them.

Granny Gap.

Today her dress had bluebirds and what looked like yellow roses—Lock wasn't sure. He didn't know much about flowers.

She hummed an old song and pulled a stretcher in behind her. Neither her shoes or the stretcher made a sound.

"Evening, Lachlan," she said. "Nice night to work."

Lock nodded, half-listening. He was focused on his breathing and trying to relax.

A moment later, he realized Granny Gap was staring at him expectantly, hands on her hips.

"Don't just stand there," she exclaimed. "Put the bastard on the stretcher."

Lock tried not to wince. He still wasn't used to how carefree the old woman was about her job. Apparently, it was a trait that reality warpers had in common.

He walked over and picked up Mr. Wendell's lifeless body and laid him on the stretcher, taking care to place his arms and legs respectfully in line. She'd chastised him for that before.

"Thank you," she said as she pulled a handful of cleaning wipes from her pocket. The rubbing alcohol made Lock's nose wrinkle. She added, "Clean up that blood, and don't dally, young man."

Lock looked down at his hands and saw specks of dried blood under the bone spurs of his fingers. Some of it was caked in the creases of his skin too.

"I'm good, thanks," Lock replied. He didn't wash his hands until he got home. It was practically a ritual for him now.

"Not *that*," she said, then pointed to the floor where the body had been. "That."

He hadn't noticed the few drops of Wendell's blood on the floor. Lock must've squeezed harder than he thought.

"Yes, ma'am," Lock muttered as she wheeled the stretcher and the body out the door. He shut it behind her and locked it.

Granny Gap would wheel the stretcher right out the front door and down the street, humming as she went. And no one would see, hear, or smell a goddamn thing.

Lock used the wipes to clean up the specks of blood on the floor then pocketed them. He'd throw them out later, in a random trash can.

Lock left through the window and crawled back down to the alley, and started the long walk back home. He chewed the bone spurs off his fingers as he walked, then concentrated on regrowing the skin over his fingertips.

A few months ago, the process had been painful. Now he simply turned off those receptors.

Lock felt nothing—not pain or disgust. Not regret.

He turned off most of his emotional receptors too.

Chapter 39

The Nonlethal Window

"Explain."

Dr. Venture stood beside Emmett, staring at the wall monitors of the biolab expectantly. Clara stood just behind Emmett, peering over his shoulder. Both were waiting to hear his idea for taking down the Mutagen-X super.

Emmett said, "Unless we can bring military-grade hardware with us, we won't be able to overpower this guy. Even if we could somehow harm him, his healing factor can keep him alive, even with catastrophic damage. He's also immune to most poisons—again, unless we start breaking international war treaties, those are out too."

Emmett held up a metal finger for emphasis. "But what about nanomachines? They're small enough to attack his body from the inside, but they're also able to fight off his white blood cells."

Venture rubbed the stubble on his chin. "What's the end goal?"

"This is where I need your help. The data says that the subject can heal from most injuries within two days, including deep tissue injuries... But it doesn't say anything about nerve damage."

TINA's voice came over the intercom. *"Nerve damage is notoriously difficult for the body to heal, even one suffused with Gnosis Mutagens."*

Venture grunted noncommittally. "That's a solid start, in theory, and I do have nanomachines that can be repurposed to do just that. However, they would require close application to deploy. A single injection in the torso won't be enough. You would need to target specific limbs to disrupt them. The spinal column would be ideal, but good luck getting through the bone." Venture looked to Emmett expectantly, as if he already knew Emmett had one more option prepared.

Emmett took a deep breath. "Then we target the bloodstream... TINA, can you run a simulation for us?"

"Yes."

As Emmett described his theory, TINA brought up a simulated view of the super's circulatory system.

"We deliver nanomachines close to the heart or major arteries. They cause damage inside the main arteries, causing clotting and slowing the flow of blood around the body. The nanites spread throughout the body, causing roadblocks behind them—preventing white blood cells from following and cleaning up the mess."

From behind him, Clara said, "But they can keep fighting in an anaerobic state, right?"

Emmett added, "Yeah, this probably wouldn't kill the guy, but it will take him out of the fight. His body will go into something like rigor mortis, making it harder and harder to move. If he struggles enough, he'll become completely immobile until his white blood cells can completely clear the blockage."

Dr. Venture nodded, a hint of a smile creeping onto his face. "Now that is a strategy. We'll need to make some modifications, but I have nanites that will work. Good job, Emmett."

Emmett sighed. It felt like a weight had been lifted off his shoulders.

This meant they had a chance at pulling this off. They could do it.

Clara clapped a hand on his shoulder, then did a fist pump in celebration.

Emmett turned back to the doctor. "Now, will you tell me about the solutions you and TINA already had?"

Venture let out a hoarse laugh. "Our solutions were more for emergencies or for open warfare. Armor-piercing rounds, satellite drone strikes, high-heat phosphorus rounds—that sort of thing. Although we also worked on Grey Goo nanites. Those were promising, but troublesome. They're similar to your idea in the bloodstream, except that the chain reaction turns all organic matter into more nanites or something inert. In tests, we had to default to inert-matter-conversion because it was hard to stop the reaction… But I digress."

It felt like the air in the room had gotten heavier while Venture spoke. Emmett felt like he knew the doctor well enough, even if the man still had secrets. But listening to him know—how cavalier he was about that kind of violence—it was clear that Venture still had some hidden depths to him.

Emmett swallowed dryly. "What about international arms treaties and rules of engagement?"

Venture's smile went cold. "Emmett, if it gets to the point where I am in open war with Gnosis and their soldiers, something has gone terribly wrong with the world, and there are either few people that will care or few that will stop me."

He couldn't disagree with that. Instead, Emmett glanced at Clara and almost laughed.

She was staring at both of them like they were crazy.

"What?" Emmett asked.

"Oh, nothing. I'm just trying to ignore you both talking about murdering this guy with tiny robots."

They settled on using a knife with a hollow titanium blade instead of a syringe for delivering the nanites. A knife would be slightly more durable and hopefully disarming—the super might be wary of an unknown variable, but might not bother defending against a knife.

Either way it was a gamble to get that close.

The three wrapped up work for the rest of the night. Dr. Venture went off to another part of the lab to work alone, while Clara and Emmett watched an episode of *Full Throttle Heart* in the living room of section 001—

While also trying to explain how they totally weren't going to murder their enemy with tiny robots. They sat across from each other on the couch, talking over the show. Both barely staying awake.

"It's not going to kill him," Emmett muttered, rubbing his temples.

"How do you know?" Clara asked. She'd taken off her hoodie and had it draped across her chest like a blanket.

Which Emmett thought was silly and defeated the purpose.

"The guy can survive anything, except for a, like, a headshot."

Clara added, "Maybe not even that. I saw the readouts. Mutagen-X turns people into zombies. They're horror movie antagonist-level resilient."

"See," Emmett said. "That guy will be perfectly fine."

Clara stared at him for a moment, like she wanted to say something, but didn't.

"What?" Emmett asked.

"Nothing." Then a moment later, she added, "You know it could happen though, right?"

Emmett shook his head, not following her. "What are you saying? You just said this guy is horror-movie resilient."

"That's the problem." Clara sat forward on the couch, like she was drawing herself up to say something important. Emmett tried to focus, except that her hoodie-blanket also slipped down, revealing her shoulders and arms.

Emmett cleared his throat and met her eyes.

"That's the problem with supers," Clara said. "Sometimes growing too power-ful *is* the problem. If someone normal breaks a leg or gets punched hard enough, they go down for the fight. But that doesn't work with someone like... Well, like this guy. He's got super strength and resilience and healing, and that window of damage that can take him out of the fight is way smaller than for someone else.

"You have to hit someone like him *really* fucking hard to knock them down. The problem is, that nonlethal window starts getting really close to becoming lethal."

Emmett saw that same darkness in Clara that he'd seen in Dr. Venture, except that Clara didn't have the years of superheroics to deaden her senses.

As new as he was to this life, Emmett thought he understood.

"You're saying that we might kill this guy. You're saying that I will probably kill someone eventually."

Clara sighed. "Yeah."

Emmett understood that fact as much as anyone could. It felt like one of those intangible truths, like knowing he would die someday. He *knew* it—even if he couldn't fully comprehend the weight of it.

He thought back to Clara's accident on the surface. Emmett's throat felt hoarse, and he almost couldn't get the question out.

"Have you ever killed someone?"

Clara nodded. "I was outside Belport, in a warehouse that was supposed to be abandoned. When I lost control, the fire collapsed the building and the old tunnels beneath it. There were people down there that we didn't know about. Just homeless people down on their luck, you know?

"I didn't even find out until later. Until the Summit came to investigate. Dad didn't want to tell me, at first. I made him.

"Officially: Five people. But it's not like we check on every super or hench-man that winds up in the hospital."

As Clara spoke, her expression changed. At first, it was solemn or regretful. Then it was just flat. Like part of her had grown numb to what had happened.

Or maybe it was just too hard to talk about.

Emmett wished there was something he could say, but it all felt pitifully insufficient or contrived. Clara had been working on controlling her powers and processing everything that had happened. She'd probably heard it all and tried it all.

Still, Emmett didn't need enhanced vision to see that it still hurt for Clara to bring it up.

Maybe it always would...

But Emmett wanted to help, even if he didn't know how. Or at least let Clara know that he was there if she needed it. His mom had always been good at that, and Emmett heard his mother's words coming out of his mouth.

"I'm here if you ever want to talk about it," he said. "I might not know what to say, but I can listen."

Clara smiled. It felt like the warmth of it cut through the room, like ice between them had cracked.

"I know," she replied. "Thanks."

Full Throttle Heart

A Great Adventure

[Truck-kun's headlights cut through the gloom of the ancient forest, and the two heroes emerge a moment later.]

Truck-kun and the bluebird, Al, drove through the forest, leaving Lilith and the ruins behind them. As eager as the demon was to help, Truck-kun knew that there was nothing she could do to help them.

All the while, the package inside Truck-kun's cargo container hummed with a mysterious power. A power that it needed to decipher if it had any hope of returning home to Joe.

There was one soul in all the land that could help—a powerful wizard, whose identity remained shrouded in mystery.

[Cue montage of Truck-kun and Al traveling through the forest and camping at night. Truck-kun's headlights flicker as it winces each time Al tries to sing.]

Two more days passed as Truck-kun and Al searched the forest. Al swore he knew the way out, but with each passing day, Truck-kun's doubt grew.

"Are you sure you know where we're going?"

Al coughed, the gruff sound causing leaves to wilt and small rodents to scurry away in fright. "Of course, Truck-dude. You just stick to driving. I'll do the navigating."

Truck-kun grumbled in defeat, driving on through the ancient forest.

[Montage interrupted by distant Human Screams.]

Al ruffled its feather like he was fending off a chill. "What—what was that?"

"Someone needs help!" Truck-kun replied fearlessly.

Its mighty engine rumbled and its tires kicked up dirt. Moments later, Truck-kun was racing through the forest, passing dangerously close to the giant tree trunks while Al, the bluebird, held on tight.

They emerged into a giant meadow, and the heroes took in the frenzied scene:

Two people stood defiantly in the middle of the clearing—a heavily armored knight and a scholar clad in robes of gray and white. They were surrounded by a hundred plant-men. The green-leafed horde stalked closer, branches cracking as the knight fended off their attacks.

The knight fought valiantly. Their slashes were quick and decisive, but their guard was faltering—a skilled knight on the last legs of their endurance. Meanwhile, the scholar struggled to stay at the knight's back and out of the plant-men's reach.

"Dryads!" Al croaked, flying up toward the safety of the high branches. "You have to help them Truck-dude—those things aren't vegetarian!"

Truck-kun had seen the aftermath of vehicles hitting trees before, and it was fully prepared to give its life for these strangers. Doubt never crossed its mind.

[Quick Cuts between Truck-dude and the horde of plant-men. Truck-kun's engine revs and the roar grows deafening.]

It was a simple, yet effective, battle-cry.

The heroic box truck sped into the fray, not bothering to transform for battle. Truck-kun floored the pedal, its revometer redlining. Five hundred horsepower and four tons of steel plowed through the meadow.

Truck-kun expected resistance as it plowed through the first dryad, but the creature had the density of dry kindling and exploded on Truck-kun's bumper, sending a hail of wooden shrapnel flying through the air.

Truck-kun's chassis cut a swathe through the horde, leaving a haze of dust and destruction in its wake.

It swung around, cutting a tight circle around the two strangers, slowing only enough not to tip over. As it turned, its back wheels slipped and drifted through the dirt, causing its box compartment to swing like a wild haymaker.

In one chaotic minute, Truck-kun cut down the field of dryads like an industrial mower. The strangers finished off the few enemies that remained.

When it was over, the truck and the strangers faced each other in the clearing.

"Stay behind me, Morden," the knight said in a gruff voice. Though most of him was covered in armor, piercing green eyes and a clean-shaved chin peered out from behind his helmet.

Their partner, Morden, crouched behind the knight's tower shield, and peered at Truck-kun hesitantly. "I don't think it means to harm us, Gabriel. You don't mean to, do you?"

Truck-kun engaged its windshield wipers to clean some of the wooden gore from its front, then concentrated on slowing its engine—the thrill of battle was not easily forgotten.

"I'm just another traveler," Truck-kun said, reassuringly. "I—we—saw you were in danger."

That seemed to put the knight, Gabriel, at ease. He lowered his sword and shield, and his shoulders sagged with the weight of fatigue.

"That we were," the knight said, taking a step back so that Morden could step forward. The young man bowed graciously. "Thank you for your assistance, strange sir, but—"

"Woo wee!" The bluebird's grating voice drifted down from the treetops, making Gabriel and Morden flinch.

Al glided down from the treetops and landed on Truck-kun's cab. The bluebird's chest heaved as it struggled to speak. "You two... You two were lucky... That we came along... when we did!"

Both raised an eyebrow at the bird.

Morden asked, "This is your companion?"

Truck-kun's engine rumbled in agreement. "I am Truck-kun, and this is Al."

Al sighed. "Woo! Retreating is hard work." Then added, "Pleased to meet'cha."

The box truck asked, "What are you doing out here alone in such a dangerous place?"

The knight's eyes narrowed. "I might ask you the same question."

Truck-kun rumbled. "I asked you first."

Now Gabriel looked to his compatriot. But Morden reassured him, "It's alright. I trust them. I was sent out here to the ancient forest to gather herbs for my maester."

Al ruffled his feathers. "Kid, do you mean *master?*"

"No. My *maester.*"

"Tomato, tom*ato*, kid."

"He's my teacher and I'm his apprentice. He's a mighty wizard. Well, he *was* a mighty wizard. Now, he's mostly just a professor."

Truck-kun's engine revved eagerly. "Your teacher is a wizard?" When Morden nodded, Truck-kun added, "We need to speak with a wizard. Maybe we can help each other."

Morden looked to the knight, deferring to his protector. Gabriel looked over both Truck-kun and Al thoughtfully.

"I think that can be arranged," Gabriel finally said. "It is safer to travel in numbers, and I cannot help but notice that you are carriage shaped."

Truck-kun glanced through the treeline apprehensively. "I don't know the way out."

"That's alright," Gabriel said. "We will show you the way."

[Cut to Truck-kun driving through the ancient forest, while Al, Gabriel, and Morden riding atop its box compartment.]

Al had just finished regaling them with their recent run-in with the demon, Lilith.

Gabriel spat off the top of the truck. "Demons... They're horrible, evil creatures. They defile the innocent and corrupt the hearts of men."

Al groaned. "I know! I tried to get defiled, but Lilith only had eyes for Truck-kun's package."

Truck-kun grumbled apprehensively. "Al, they do not need to hear about my package."

"But you need to show it to this wizard guy, don't 'cha?"

Morden asked, "What's the bluebird talking about, Truck-kun?"

[While Truck-kun narrates, Cut to Montage of Truck-kun's Accident and Arrival in the Ancient Forest.]

"...And that's how I wound up here," it explained.

Morden said, "Wow! That's quite the story... And that does sound like something my maester or his brethren could decipher."

Gabriel added with a smile, "Then we shall journey back to the city and to the mage's college. Together."

Al jumped around on the roof excitedly. "We're just like one of those adventuring groups from the days of old! A knight... a priest... a Truck... AND A BARD!"

Morden muttered, "But I'm not a priest."

Al croaked excitedly, "I'll sing our praises!"

All together, the others answered, "No, no. That's alright, Al."

[Outtro — Slow, Instrumental version of Theme Song — "Hātofurusurottoru" by Gunpowder Audition]

[Outtro Still Shot of Joe driving Truck-kun on the highway. Al is sitting on Joe's shoulder with tape over his beak. Gabriel and Morden are waving to be picked up on the side of the road.]

[Local Commercial Break]

[Camera view of the Belport Bulletin anchor desk. Bethany Wonder sits alone at the desk with deep blue hair and a brilliant purple dress. Bethany looks up from her papers and flashes a smile for the audience.]

"It's been almost a month since the frightening attack on downtown Belport that left the city in shock and the Summit of Heroes scrambling for answers. Tonight we finally have them.

"A rogue super, acting alone, used stolen technology to cause the blast. The device is said to mimic the abilities of reality warping supers. This was how Paragon was able to quickly intervene and stop the device before any permanent damage was caused to the city.

"I think we can all agree that Paragon and the Summit of Heroes are looking out for us.

"Tonight at ten, we'll go live to Johnny Armour, who's got an exclusive interview with Paragon—the savior of Belport. Here from the hero himself, in his own words.

"Remember, the Bulletin is on your side."

[Camera view of Belport Bay pier. Reporter Johnny Armour pulls down a thick red scarf as he talks. The end of it billows in the wind.]

"Good evening, Belport. I'm standing here tonight on our beautiful bay with none other than our savior, the leader of the Summit of Heroes, Paragon."

[Camera pans to the most iconic cape in the world. Paragon stands head and shoulders above the reporter—his height and physique cutting a silhouette that would shame ancient marble statues. His skin is albino white, and his long, pale hair hangs lifeless across his shoulders, completely unaffected by the wind of the bay. Despite his status, he wears a plain silver bodysuit.

[Tonight, his eyes are tinged with red, not from his powerful heat vision, but from weariness. Still, as he talks, he manages faint smiles, as if he's reassuring not just the audience, but himself as well. Together, these things make the pinnacle of supers seem human.]

"I'm glad to be enjoying a quiet evening with you, Johnny," Paragon said. His voice is measured, his tone sincere.

"Quiet evenings must be rare for a super like you."

"Yes. Yes, they are."

Johnny cleared his throat. "I'll get right to it then. Everyone in Belport is grateful for what you did for us that day."

Paragon nodded. "Just doing my job."

"Still, can you tell us what you were thinking during the attack?"

Paragon stared over Johnny's shoulder, off across the bay as if searching for the words. When he finally spoke, the words were heavy.

"I wasn't thinking. I just did what needed to be done." A moment later, Paragon smiled playfully. "Truthfully, my job is easier than people think, Johnny. The Summit tells me what to do, and I do it. It's easy to fight a natural disaster—even if it hurts.

"I'd rather go up against a meteor than try to solve our current geopolitical conflicts, or try to solve world hunger. Those things are hard. They require much more than one person—no matter how powerful.

"I wish I could do those things, but there are better people than me working on them... At least I hope there are. I'm just fine—"

Concern flashed across Paragon's face. "I've got to go."

A moment later, Paragon erupted into the sky and streaked out over the bay. A few seconds later, a sonic boom was heard over the water as he sped up faster than the speed of sound.

The stunned reporter turned to the camera and pulled his scarf down to speak. "A short conversation with the leader of the Summit of Heroes, but I'm sure wherever Paragon is heading needs him much more than we do. This is Johnny Armour signing off. Remember, just like the Summit, the Bulletin is on your side."

Chapter 40

[Title Removed]

Emmett woke up on the couch Sunday morning and rubbed his eyes. Every other time he'd crashed on the couch in the lab, Dr. Venture had been sitting nearby, enjoying his morning coffee.

Emmett sat up and glanced around the living room, but today the doctor was nowhere to be found. Clara was presumably still sleeping.

That was fine by him. He still had work to do.

"TINA, is the biolab available?"

"Yes. Will you be continuing your work on the countermeasures for Mutagen-X?"

"Yes... But coffee first."

Together, Emmett and TINA made solid progress on the Mutagen-X countermeasure.

They started with three different batches of nanites. All were similar in that they were mildly self-propagating—once injected into the bloodstream, they would cascade through the target's veins, causing clots in their wake while making more of themselves and fending off the few white blood cells in their path. Like a surfer riding the crest of a wave.

They alternated between simulations and molecular testing—which Emmett watched via monitor. After each test, TINA would refine her models, adjusting dosages, nanite replication speeds, or making refinements at the molecular level.

Though TINA tried to walk Emmett through the process, it was admittedly hard for him to follow the more minute details.

At several points, TINA showed Emmett walls of chemical formulas, updating them in real time. Each time, Emmett's eyes glazed over.

"TINA, I'm an engineer, not a chemist."

"Just keeping you informed."

Emmett rubbed his temples and tried in earnest to understand what looked like a foreign language on the screen.

"Dr. Venture would probably understand all this, wouldn't he?"

"He would understand most of it, but even Dr. Venture needs assistance. Why do you think he made me?"

Emmett nodded. "Fair enough."

Even with TINA's immense processing power, it took time to run simulations and make updates. Dr. Venture stopped by once for a quick update, and Clara stopped by twice, but she seemed almost as preoccupied as her dad did.

Were they as worried about this mission as he was? Emmett hadn't really thought about it, but this must be a big deal for Venture and Clara, too.

Emmett had assumed that Clara had done all kinds of missions as a super, but that was before her confession about her powers. He'd had her figured all wrong. This might be her first big mission in years. Venture was probably worried for the same reason.

Emmett pushed the thought from his head. He couldn't think about that now. Sure, a lot was riding on the mission, but dwelling on it would just make him even more nervous.

Instead, Emmett looked over the information on Mutagen-X again—mostly to make sure he hadn't missed some other angle that they could exploit. Emmett checked it twice before he was satisfied.

During an afternoon calibration, he opened up the psychology profile for Mutagen-X subjects—

His jaw fell open.

Emmett hadn't really known what to expect. For one, he'd never read a psychology profile or report before. And two, he hadn't expected it to be *even longer* than the biology and combat data. There were brainwave scans, reports from psychologists, clips from test subject interviews, psychological comparisons with other mutagen subjects—Emmett spent twenty minutes just skimming over the reports.

He spent the rest of his idle time that afternoon reading the reports in more detail:

In addition to all the physical abilities that Mutagen-X gave the subject, it also allowed them greater control over what they felt and experienced. Test subjects could dampen and experienced subjects could completely turn off their pain receptors. This was partially responsible for the ability of X-subjects to fight through grievous injuries like losing limbs.

"During development of Mutagen-X, it was necessitated that subjects should have greater control over their bodies. These subjects are often chosen from the pinnacle of human soldiers, and so should be afforded autonomy, not just in accomplishing their mission, but in dominion over their own feelings and sensations." – [Citation Removed]

Most of the quotes and excerpts had their citations blacked out.

"TINA, is there a way to recover the citations for these sources?"

"No. The information was already expunged on Gnosis's servers before this copy was made."

Emmett's ears perked up. "Gnosis's records were corrupted?"

"Not likely. Citations were selectively scraped from this particular server. It is likely that their central server would have the unaltered records."

That sounded... odd. Emmett's face wrinkled as he struggled to word his question. "TINA, do you know how Dr. Venture got these records?"

"I do, but don't bother asking."

He chuckled. So that explained it. "For a second, it sounded like Dr. Venture was keeping their source from you."

"*I know everything that Dr. Venture knows.*" It sounded like there was a hint of uncertainty in TINA's voice, but Emmett decided he must have been imagining it.

Emmett turned his attention back to the data on Mutagen-X subjects. As it turned out, turning off pain receptors was just the start.

"Psychological decline was a significant hurdle in first generation Mutagen-X subjects. The sheer number of changes to the body, demands of training, and... subject matter... of the missions, were ultimately too much for 76% of test subjects. An unacceptable rate of asset depletion.

"However, those 24% of acceptable test-subjects were discovered to have a mutation that would lead to the final formulation of Mutagen-X... The ability to turn off psychological pain, as well as physical pain." — [Citation Removed]

Emmett continued reading, equal parts scientifically, tactically, and morbidly curious. Though the longer he read, the heavier the pit in his stomach.

"Psychological trauma... Post-Traumatic Stress... Flashbacks... Night terrors... functionally non-existent in the final generation of test subjects.

"Rates of satisfaction with mutagen testing increased sharply before leveling off." — [Citation Removed]

"However, problems began 3-4 months after final dosage...

"Emotional satisfaction in non-mission critical aspects, including subject's personal lives, take a sharp decline... Subjects begin to regulate emotions during non-mission activities. Emotional control degrades, creating a negative feedback loop...

"Emotional regulation degrades until subjects are forced to dampen ALL emotional responses, not just trauma responses." — [Citation Removed]

"43% of Mutagen-X subjects continue to function satisfactorily up to 1 year after final dosage... 21% of subjects function after 2 years... Complete cohort loss before 3 years due to psychological degradation...

"Acceptable rate of asset depletion." — [Citation Removed]

"Once subjects show signs of emotional degradation, active monitoring should start and disposal protocols are readied." — [Citation Removed]

"Emotional degradation deemed non-salvageable. Once lack of emotional connection begins, subjects begin to experience psychopathy, psychosis, and disconnect... psychotic breaks... resulting in a complete break from reality. Imminent violence.

"It is in [Name Removed]'s professional opinion that Mutagen-X subjects be terminated once the first signs of emotional degradation begin." — [Citation Removed]

Emmett slumped down in a nearby chair and leaned on the holographic table. He couldn't decide whether he felt more disgusted or hollow.

A part of him knew that he was reading scientific papers and that they were written to be sterile and unemotional—ironically, like the test subjects they were recommending for termination.

These were people. Every one of those statistics was someone's sibling or child.

A part of him couldn't fathom how a corporation, even one like Gnosis, could have such a casual disregard for human life. But that was just the smallest sliver of their crimes—Gnosis was a bioweapons company that supplied most of the world's armies.

It was like a giant machine digging through the earth, each bucket tearing hundreds of tons out of the ground, then pulverizing boulders bigger than houses like they were styrofoam. Except Gnosis wasn't some industrial digging machine...

They were mining people. Destroying people. Throwing the chunked up remains of them away once they were broken.

It was almost too much to comprehend.

It was too much.

Emmett knew that he could look through the data and find out exactly how many, but putting a number to the suffering wouldn't change a thing.

No. Gnosis was too big.

Gnosis was so big that they continued to operate unimpeded by the likes of world powers or even the Summit of Heroes.

Gnosis was too big...

Instead of the incomprehensible scale of tragedy, Emmett focused on the mission at hand.

Taking out this manufacturing plant might not change the world and it probably wouldn't hurt Gnosis, but it was a start. It would get rid of the knock-off mutagens, and maybe even make the streets of Belport a little safer.

It was a start.

There was a bigger thought weighing on Emmett though, even with his new-found resolve:

It had been almost a month since the last confrontation with the Mutagen-X super. They'd sounded sane enough that night, but who knew how long they'd been in the program and how much sanity they had left.

"I'm not your enemy..."

A part of Emmett had hoped that he could go through with the mission without accidentally killing this super... But now, Emmett might have to kill him.

There might not be any other way.

Chapter 41

Approach

When Emmett was young, he'd read a memoir written by the super, *Wave Warrior*. It was one of hundreds of memoirs written by capes, masks, and villains, but it was the first one Emmett read and so it held a special place in his memory. It was somewhat dated, being almost thirty years old now, embellished, and edited. That last part was something Emmett only came to realize in the last month and a half after becoming a super.

There was nothing about the Code or about the stalemate that existed between powerful heroes, villains, and organizations. To Emmett, those two things were perhaps the most important aspects of this new world that he half-existed in. For them to be hidden from public knowledge was unacceptable.

But all through Monday, there was one thing from that memoir that was constantly on Emmett's mind:

"People always underestimate how heroes spend their time. Sure, there's the throwdowns and they are totally righteous when they happen, but most of being a hero is waiting. Waiting for work to be done, waiting for a brawl, waiting for someone who needs saving. Sure, if you're one of those rich supes then you can wait in style, but it's still waiting.

"It's like surfing. A lot of time is spent sitting out past the breakers, waiting for a primo swell. After the violence, that's probably the second biggest thing that heroes have a problem with.

"So, yeah, it's a lot like surfing. Or working in IT." — Wave Warrior; *Catching Waves, Chasing Bad Guys*

They'd decided on hitting the mutagen manufacturing building on Wednesday night. Emmett tried to tell himself that it was only two days until then, but that didn't help the week go by any faster.

Wave Warrior's words came back to him, and Emmett realized just how difficult waiting would be.

So he spent those two days burying himself in schoolwork and double checking his preparations. He made sure his utility belt was stocked, and his mods and connectors were in perfect shape.

Emmett went to the lab Tuesday night just to get out of the apartment, but Dr. Venture and Clara were preoccupied with their own preparations.

Lock was busy, too. It felt like Emmett hadn't seen him at all this past week.

By the time Wednesday night finally arrived, Emmett debated leaving a note for his roommate, saying that he was at Marianne's… Just on the off chance that he didn't make it back. It was a morbid thought, and Emmett immediately pushed it from his mind.

They were going to succeed. They were going to bring down the factory and put a stop to the knock-off mutagens—

And no hired supers were going to stand in their way.

It was 10:51 PM Wednesday night—nine minutes until a Fast-Response Drone would pick up Emmett on the roof of his apartment.

Emmett killed the music and stared at Lock's empty room. He was hoping to see Lock on the way out, but his roommate hadn't come home yet. Even though Emmett kept thinking positive, he had at least wanted to see Lock. Just in case.

He contemplated leaving a note on the kitchen counter—seeing Marianne—or something like that. But he didn't.

Emmett had to keep thinking that he would make it back without an issue.

And if there was an issue, if things went sideways, it likely wouldn't be his problem anymore.

Emmett sighed and walked away without leaving a note. He climbed out to the fire escape and shut the window behind him. Then he went up to the roof and waited for the Fast-Response Drone.

He didn't have to wait long.

A moment later, Emmett heard the telltale hum of the drone as it approached. It decloaked, appearing as a sleek, dark metal box some ten feet tall and six feet wide. It split open, and Emmett climbed inside, settling into the cool mesh as it enveloped around him. The whole process took only a few seconds, and then Emmett was completely encased in the protective matrix.

It didn't matter how many times Emmett had been inside one of the drones, it still took him a minute to get over the claustrophobia.

There was a quiet rumble and a soft lurch as the drone took off toward the outskirts of the city.

TINA's voice came through the intercom. *"Mod is en route."*

Then there was nothing to do but settle in for the ride. And wait.

Thankfully, Emmett wasn't alone with his own thoughts for too long before the doctor's voice came through.

"Mod, we're dropping you at the rendezvous point outside the city limits, just East of the highway. Arsenal, McGuire, and Athena's group are a few minutes away. From there, cloaked drones will scout your approach on foot over those last two miles.

"After that, you're on your own. Even staying low, the drones can only take you so far without risking being discovered."

"Yeah, but the drones can still pull us out if things go sideways, right?" Emmett asked.

"Yes. But you won't need them."

"Thanks for the vote of confidence."

By the time the drone finally split open and dumped Emmett out onto the grass, he was getting antsy.

He was in the middle of a sparse cluster of trees—what passed for a forest this close to the city. The highway drifted over from the East, and the lights of Belport were surprisingly bright to the South. But then Emmett's eyes adjusted to the darkness than they used to.

Emmett waited in the cover of the trees for the rest of the group to arrive.

McGuire was the first to arrive, and Emmett heard the super breathing heavily long before he saw him. McGuire came trudging through the brush with his cobble-together night vision goggles, scarf and long coat, and sounding like he was going to keel over at any moment.

"Did you run the whole way here?" Emmett asked.

"Yeah," McGuire wheezed, leaning over with his hands on his knees. "How—how did you get here?"

"I flew."

"You suck."

Both Emmett and McGuire shared a laugh before Clara arrived. She flew in low and fast, setting down smoothly beside Emmett.

Emmett and Clara said a quick greeting before Clara turned to McGuire. "Are you alright?"

The gadgeteer was just starting to catch his breath. "Arsenal. I see you suck as well."

Arsenal scoffed in confusion. "What did I do?"

"You flew," Emmett replied.

"Yeah... That's what I do..."

McGuire replied, "Don't rub it in."

Athena arrived with two teammates. All three jogged over the slope and into the cluster of trees—none of which were out of breath. She introduced her teammates quickly and Emmett did the same.

Luna looked like she could've been Athena's twin sister, except that her hair was jet black instead of white and she seemed even more no-nonsense than Athena. She wore a thin cloak over leather armor and pulled out a folding compound bow, which she unfurled as they spoke... She didn't seem to have a quiver with her, but Emmett didn't get a chance to ask before Athena introduced her other ally.

Borealis was short and stocky, sporting a thick beard and heavy furs that at first looked weirdly out of place for a springtime mission, even if it was at night. His cryokinesis both kept him comfortably cool now and allowed him to run long distances without overheating.

"Wait a second," McGuire said. "Do you guys all have special running powers?"

Borealis laughed heartily. "I keep myself cool. Athena uses her forcefields for a longer stride, and Luna used to run marathons *for fun*—who does that?"

Luna shrugged.

McGuire sighed. "Note to self, make spring shoes—no... Make pop-up, all-terrain rollerskates..."

Arsenal interrupted, "You should just make a hoverboard *after* we're done with the mission." She'd clearly meant it as a joke, but McGuire's eyes lit up.

"Yes. All the yes."

Emmett thought he could hear Arsenal's eyes roll behind her helmet.

This time Luna interrupted. "If this is everyone, we should go. Every minute we delay, we risk detection."

Athena turned to Emmett and a moment later, everyone else's eyes settled on him.

"Oh, right..." Emmett reached into his utility belt and pulled out two intercom earpieces—one for Borealis and one for Luna.

But even after that, everyone continued staring at Emmett expectantly.

Emmett held up his hands and muttered, "Oh no. I'm not that guy." Then he cleared his throat and in a more even voice, he said, "Doctor, we're ready. Lead the way."

Venture's voice came through to everyone. "The drones will find you a clear approach to the warehouse, but you'll be on your own for the last half a mile. From then on, the drones will stay just outside the perimeter and will only engage in case of an emergency. I'll stay on the line."

With that, Emmett watched as several drones emerged from the skyline of Belport. Each shimmered, their cloaking barely visible in the UV parts of his vision. From there, Emmett and Arsenal followed the drones on foot, while their teammates followed just behind them.

Chapter 42

Infiltration

The cloaked drones led them through the sparse trees that ran alongside the highway. Emmett couldn't imagine running into anyone out here. He supposed there was always the chance of running into a guard as they got closer or maybe even a migrant camp, but they didn't see anyone at all. As they traversed hills and gullies in the cover of night, it almost felt like they were deep in the woods—except for sounds of distant cars.

Still, he was grateful to have Venture's drones scouting ahead for them.

By the time they reached their next checkpoint—a half-mile out and where the drones could go no further—Emmett was getting antsy. This was the edge of tree cover and they'd have to make their way through the last half-mile, using buildings and parking lots as cover.

Venture had managed to pinpoint most of the security cameras so the group could avoid them, but there were two points in their approach where they couldn't avoid the cameras. Venture assured them that if they were quick enough, the likelihood of any night guards seeing them on camera would be low, and after the mission any footage would only be moderately useful to the Summit of Heroes—

They were wearing disguises, after all.

Arsenal led the way through this final approach, using the HUD inside her helmet for guidance. Her exosuit looked almost comical as she snuck between cars and alongside buildings, moving with eerie silence.

Emmett and the others followed close behind—so close that, twice, McGuire stepped on the back of Emmett's shoe.

"Sorry," he muttered. Emmett stifled a groan.

They only paused two times—once for a car passing by in the parking lot, and a second time for a night guard who'd chosen to walk his beat instead of just watching the cameras.

They snuck through the dim lights of the final loading bay and paused at the corner.

Their target warehouse didn't look any different from the other unmarked warehouses in the cluster. If not for tracking cellphone signals the past few weeks, they would've had to scout each of the buildings. Considering the lack of guards so far, it wouldn't have been too difficult, but it would still take more time and be far riskier than simply hacking their way to the information.

Dr. Venture's voice came through their earpieces. *"Does everyone remember their part of the plan?"*

Each hero met Emmett's and Arsenal's helmet and nodded. Emmett was glad to be wearing a mask, so no one could see how nervous he was. His heart felt like it was beating in his throat.

"No supers visible outside. Proceed to the loading bay."

Arsenal led them around the perimeter of the building. They still tried to move quietly, but now they were practically jogging across the pavement. Even if everything went according to plan, TINA's simulations still showed a 64% chance of them getting discovered by security at some point during the mission. In Emmett's eyes, it wasn't a matter of *if* they would get discovered but a matter of *when*.

They stopped at the first loading bay door, which would put them nearest to the stairs.

Emmett swapped for his concealable pistol and the weapon slid in with a click. Since the rounds were subsonic, he didn't have to worry about the sound traveling throughout the entire warehouse—just the immediate room.

TINA had simulated methods for opening the roll-up bay doors—some quiet, others not so quiet.

Arsenal pressed a gauntlet up to the metal door and sent out a jolt of electricity to interrupt the door controller, causing an audible pop on the other side. Then, with a flick of her controls, Arsenal switched to a powerful magnetic and used it to release the latches manually. These gave way with a metallic screech.

Emmett's mechanical fingers twitched with anticipation.

Arsenal gripped the bottom of the door and pulled it open just enough.

Emmett and Athena were first, rolling under the door before it was even waist high. A breath later, they were on their feet inside the warehouse.

Immediately, Emmett noticed things:

The loading bay was enormous—at least thirty feet high and easily several hundred feet across. Rows of tall shelves lined the back of the room. For a moment, it almost felt like he was back in the Gray Room, except that the floor and walls weren't pristine white so much as caked with grime.

And that a lone guard was staring at them, dumbfounded.

Before the man could reach for his sidearm, Emmett had already raised his prosthetic arm and fired. The sledgehammer round slammed into his chest, and the guard dropped to the ground.

Emmett waited, pistol still trained on his target, but the guard didn't stir.

"Good shot," Athena whispered, patting Emmett on the back.

The pair jogged across the loading bay, sweeping the rows of shelves and then turning to start on the offices along the far wall. The rest of the squad was through the door and right behind them.

Borealis knelt over the unconscious guard and pressed a hand to his chest, using his cryokinesis to chill the guard and put him into something akin to hibernation. It would keep any of their targets from waking up too soon, then sounding the alarm or rejoining the fight. Then Borealis deposited him in one of the empty side offices.

The plan was to keep the incapacitated guards together. In case of the building coming down, Athena claimed she could use her forcefields to either quickly transport them out of the building or to keep the building from crushing them.

Hopefully, it wouldn't come to that.

The group confirmed that the rest of the loading bay was clear, then Arsenal and Athena led the way to the other side of the warehouse. A long wall ran down the center of the building, bisecting the ground floor into the loading bay and a manufacturing section.

They could've gone through a massive set of central doors, but opted for the quiet route, sneaking through the office halls.

Borealis took out a second patrolling guard. He snuck up behind the man, grasped his shoulders, then the man collapsed. Borealis caught him under the arms. The guard's lips were blue and his eyes open and blank.

As Borealis dragged the guard down the hall, McGuire whispered, "That wasn't freaky at all."

Athena chuckled and quietly replied, "Borealis's powers can slow someone's heart rate. It's like fainting."

McGuire shivered, and Emmett couldn't deny that it was an eerie sight. Still, he turned away from the guard and focused on the task at hand.

The group prowled the hall like a pack of wolves, moving with ghostly silence. After another bend in the hall, they came upon a third guard and almost hit their first snag.

The guard saw Athena and Emmett a split second before they registered him. He reached for the office telephone, but his hand slammed into an invisible barrier. It took Emmett only a moment to slip past Athena and inside the office door, meanwhile, the guard pawed at the barrier like a panicked mime.

He barely turned before a sledgehammer round dropped him. Borealis rejoined the group only to haul the new guard away a moment later.

Arsenal whispered, "The entrance to the manufacturing section is up ahead." She stopped in front of a single heavy-duty door. "Is everyone ready?"

Athena added, "Our secrecy won't last much longer." She tapped the side of her head, indicating she'd seen something in her future-sight.

"We were never going to get that lucky," Emmett said. Despite his sweating and his racing heart, he'd never been more ready for anything in his life. "Let's do this."

Arsenal pushed open the door and the slight creak was immediately overshadowed by the sounds of bubbling vats and whirring machinery. A noxious mix of smells wafted through the door, causing Emmett's eyes to water.

This half of the warehouse was filled with what looked like a mad scientist's laboratory—except made for a giant. Three enormous vats took up the majority of the room. Tubes sprouted off these and flowed to a dozen smaller vats, each dotted with pressure valves and indicator lights. It looked like the facility had been retrofitted—old conveyor belts hung lifeless and ended abruptly in the middle of the air, like sections had been cut away to make room for the mutagen processing equipment.

Emmett's group was supposed to plant explosive charges on the equipment, but they had another problem:

Three workers milled about the center of the room. They held clipboards and stared at gauges on the piping like they were doing their evening rounds.

Athena whispered, "Sneak around the outside and plant the charges. Luna, Borealis... See if you can get the workers out without making a racket—"

Athena was cut off as a bright light flashed from an upper catwalk.

Everyone ducked back inside, pulling the metal door shut, just as a wave of orange power crashed into it. The door rattled on its hinges but held.

"New plan," Athena said. "Get the workers out, and trash this place."

With that, Athena shoved the door open and made a forcefield above them, shielding them from another wave of energy. Gunfire erupted from the catwalk a second later as guards joined the enemy super.

"Go!" Athena shouted.

Borealis and Luna ran left. The ice super conjured a haze in the air while Luna returned fire with gleaming silver arrows. McGuire stayed back with Athena. Emmett and Arsenal ran right, adding to the barrage with pistol fire and kinetic shots.

The guards on the catwalk quickly ducked back inside the door while the lone super leapt over the railing. Emmett hadn't been sure at first which super they were facing, not through the cold haze in the air—

Not until her fire sword sprang to life. She slid down the wall, digging the blade into the metal and using it to slow her fall.

Emmett ignored his pang of jealousy at her flaming sword. Then he smirked, realizing that McGuire probably felt the same way.

Emmett reached into his pack—instead of swapping weapons, he grabbed the first explosive charge and stuck it under a medium-sized vat.

Dr. Venture said, *"They've officially tried to call out. I've blocked them, but it's only a matter of time before one of them wises up and trips the hardline."*

Across the room, metal screeched, and Emmett could just make out the long, thin arms of hair-girl as she climbed through the wreckage of the door—over by Borealis and Luna. Then there were cracks that could've been anything from ice breaking to concrete shattering.

"Your timeline is officially measured in minutes. Good luck."

Chapter 43

Athena / Engagement

Athena quickly took stock of the scene as it unfolded across the warehouse:

Across the warehouse, Luna and Borealis engaged the new super—the one Emmett had dubbed hair-girl. The super had torn through one of the steel doors easily enough, but Athena's teammates should be a good counter. Borealis ran interference, using his haze ability to chill the room and slow their enemy. Then he pushed even harder, conjuring icy pillars to slow her and hurling javelins as he dodged her tendrils. Throughout the battle, Luna stayed just behind her teammate, firing over his shoulder with a veteran's accuracy. Hair-girl was forced to armor herself with most of her tendrils instead of attacking with them, severely hampering her offense.

Meanwhile, Athena readied herself to block another wave of fiery energy from their sword-wielding enemy—she slid down the far right wall, kicking off at the last second, and hurled a blast of power at Athena before dropping the rest of the way.

Athena conjured a forcefield, but the wave of power crashed through it, barely slowing. At the speed of thought, she conjured two more barriers. The wave broke through the second, but lost enough strength that it dissipated against the third.

It had been a gamble, and if Athena hadn't seen similar powers in her long career, she would've leapt out of the way. At least there wasn't any pain this time—not like when she'd fought Feedback.

But now the sword-super was hidden by the twisted jungle of equipment, and Athena would be of minimal help to Emmett and Arsenal.

Athena yelled back to McGuire, "Hurry up and plant the—" She was cut off by gunfire from four more guards on the catwalk.

Though McGuire was safely under her wing, so to speak, she needed to protect her other teammates. Athena quickly expanded the barrier, completely cutting off the catwalk from the lower levels.

"Already ahead of you!" McGuire yelled.

The gadgeteer ducked under one of the nearby vats and glued an explosive to the bottom. They were custom-made by the Doctor. Despite his assurances that the charges were stable, each set explosive made Athena sweat a little more.

McGuire popped up and fired his slingshot at the guards. With barely a thought, Athena's shield flickered and let the shot through. A moment later, green noxious-looking smoke emerged on the catwalk. The guards began doubling over, retching violently, and staggering back through the upper door.

McGuire followed with a second shot which looked weirdly like a bolas snare. The tiny rockets on either end ignited, spinning the projectile so fast it looked like a flying halo. It slammed into the door on the catwalk, pinning it shut.

Athena smiled quickly. "Not bad."

McGuire replied with a modest shrug, the rest of his expression hidden behind his home-made mask.

The pair ran into the jungle of equipment, cutting diagonally through the cavernous room. *Cutting* was more literal than Athena realized, as she used her powers to bisect piping and hurl metal to either side like she was throwing open sliding double doors.

While they bushwhacked through to the center of the room, battles continued on either side. Athena kept a lookout as they pushed forward, ready to throw a shield up in either direction. McGuire followed close behind her, the snaps of his slingshot barely audible against the screeching metal.

She had no idea what McGuire was shooting, only that each shot seemed different than the last—a noisemaker that sounded like a cackling witch sailed toward hair-girl then exploded into pink silly string. Something like a signal flare went in the opposite direction toward the sword-super.

McGuire managed to get the latter's attention when he flung a cluster of caltrops. They shimmered in the air as they flew into sword-girl's path—

"Goddamnit!" the enemy super screamed.

Two erratic waves of power rushed across the room. The first missed completely, flying wide to Athena's right—cutting clean through the mixing equipment and sending sprays of mutagen into the air.

The second wave came directly at them.

"Oh, sh—" McGuire's voice was drowned out by screaming metal.

Athena stopped running and put an arm out to stop McGuire behind her. Instantly, she conjured five forcefields, each butted up against one another and angled just slightly.

The blastwave careened into Athena's barriers. Instead of impacting directly, the energy skimmed over the top layers like a surfer over a wave. Power flared as it banked to the left—

Directly into the main holding tank. Through it.

Dark purple liquid burst from the tank. Support beams twisted and sheared free. Tons of metal and liquid fell like a meteor.

Athena immediately conjured a wedge of barriers in front of her and McGuire from the immediate impact—then two more to shield the others as best as she could.

For a moment, it felt like she was watching the impact in slow motion. The support struts folded like cardboard. When the tank hit the floor and burst like a ripe watermelon. The subsequent crash and squeal of metal drowned out everything else. Then the entire building rattled with impact, knocking Athena off-balance—for a moment, it felt like she was standing on a surfboard. Purple mutagen slammed into her barriers, splashing so high it nearly blotted out the overhead lights.

Emmett and Arsenal flanked the far right side of the warehouse, firing back at the guards with pistol shots and kinetic blasts. Their troubles were compounded as the flamesword-wielding super directly in their path. Emmett and Arsenal dodged behind a mixing station to their left just in time for a blast of sword energy to sail by.

A cacophony of battle erupted all across the warehouse. Emmett could only guess how Borealis and Luna were fairing on the other side of the giant room.

From his cover behind the mixing station, Emmett fired two more shots up toward the catwalk and then another two at sword-girl. He was almost out of ammo. They couldn't stay hunkered down—not in view of both the upper guards and the enemy super. She would shred their cover in seconds.

Contrary to all of Emmett's training, the safest place to be was right in front of sword-girl. They'd be beneath the catwalk and could see all of her attacks coming. Granted, it wasn't much safer, but Emmett didn't see any other choice.

"We need to close the gap," he muttered between Arsenal's shots.

"Let's do it—" Arsenal was cut off by a cackling noisemaker across the warehouse, which had to be from McGuire. A flare followed soon after, casting the entire warehouse in a blinding glow.

Then the gunshots from the catwalk stopped. Athena's and McGuire's covering fire had worked.

Emmett swapped his pistol for his impact shield, then flicked it open. Expanded, it was about the size of a medieval buckler shield and it was made to withstand bullets, knives, and even elemental attacks.

Emmett wasn't sure if it would stand up to a magical flaming sword, but he didn't have time to second guess it.

"Go!" Arsenal shouted. She ran out from cover, firing kinetic blasts at the enemy super. Emmett followed directly behind her.

Sword-girl blocked the first few of Arsenal's shots with her blade, the kinetic blasts deflecting harmlessly to either side.

They'd practiced this once before in the Gray Room—at the last second, Arsenal leapt to the side, blasting the enemy super with her sonic weapons. Even with her weakened power output, the sonic was still a formidable weapon.

Sword-girl winced, clearly torn between covering her ears and keeping her guard stance. Her blade shimmered—

And Emmett barreled into her, shield-first.

Metal alloy connected against the magic blade, erupting in a shower of sparks. Then bodies collided.

Emmett got the wind knocked out of him, but sword-girl went tumbling backward, eventually digging her fiery sword into the concrete to stop herself.

Emmett's heart sank—sword-girl took the hit. So much for her just having a magic weapon. She rose defiantly, ready to fight, but then lost her footing as a rain of caltrops fell from above.

"Goddamnit!" With a frenzied gleam in her eye, sword-girl slashed twice in retaliation, sending beams of power through the center of the room. Machinery screeched in protest, but moments later, sword-girl turned to meet Emmett and Arsenal head on.

For once, Emmett led, while Arsenal stayed behind. Emmett met the flaming sword with his shield, sending more sparks flying, while Arsenal fired kinetic blasts over his shoulder. If not for the Mutagen-A and his training the last month, Emmett would never have been able to parry sword-girl's attacks. Now, he matched her strike for strike.

Emmett had Arsenal helping him, but he still felt a swell of pride.

Which was almost undone when he heard the ear-piercing screech of metal and thud of impact when the center holding tank fell. Emmett, Arsenal, and their enemy lost their footing for a moment. Emmett prepared for a wall of water, but it splashed against an invisible barrier—only a few drops sloshing over the side and raining down on them.

Emmett just managed to raise his arm to guard against sword-girl's next strike.

Holding their own wasn't good enough. Emmett and Arsenal needed to plant two more bombs. And the longer they fought, the more certain Emmett was that Arsenal's kinetic blasts weren't that effective against their enemy—

Which made sense: Both her sword and the lasers that powered Arsenal's kinetic blasts were based on heat.

"Stick with the sonic!" Emmett shouted.

A millisecond later, the familiar high-pitch whine returned. Sword-girl winced and fought to keep her composure. The next breath, Emmett had her backpedaling.

Then a *crunch* sounded from the catwalk above, followed by a metal door slamming into the ruined equipment below—the signal that another super had joined the fight. A thin man dressed like a punk rocker leapt down to the floor, landing inches away from Emmett and sword-girl.

Feedback smirked at the sight of Emmett, clearly remembering him from their last encounter during the mutagen bust with Athena.

The direction of the sonic changed as Arsenal turned it on Feedback. Emmett didn't have a chance to stop her.

Feedback winced and then his entire body rippled with power, like his skin had turned to liquid. Then Arsenal's sonic weapons shattered. It happened so fast that Emmett barely managed to defend himself as Feedback threw a follow-up punch.

The punch connected, clanging against Emmett's shield and sending him skidding backward across the floor. The last time Emmett had been on the receiving end of a punch from the rocker, energy had fried the last few links of his whip—thankfully, the shield seemed partially insulated. Instead of pain traveling up his prosthetic arm, steam rose off of the shield.

"A little help!" Emmett muttered, hoping Athena or McGuire were listening. Across the room, it sounded like Borealis and Luna weren't fairing any better.

So much for everything going smoothly.

Chapter 44

Onslaught

Feedback and sword-girl pressed forward, their attacks keeping Emmett and Arsenal backpedaling. He managed to block both, sometimes haphazardly rolling out of the way when needed, but they were still holding their own.

But blocking their attacks was beginning to take a toll on Emmett. His shield was steaming, his prosthetic arm rattled with each impact, and the bones of his shoulder ached where metal anchored to bone.

Arsenal stayed behind Emmett, firing kinetic blasts over his shoulder, but Emmett could hear her frustration. Arsenal's weapons weren't effective against either of their enemies, and they were hard counters to her. Getting close risked a breach in her exosuit.

Emmett almost risked switching out his shield for something else or giving it to Arsenal, but he didn't have a moment's respite—

Feedback punched and Emmett caught it clean on his shield. Even though he was ready for it, the force hurled him backward. Emmett slammed into the side wall, his back and head cracking against the concrete.

Emmett caught himself on his knees, gasping for breath and vision swimming. He struggled and pushed himself up in time to see Feedback closing in on him.

Even with his hardened skeleton, Emmett knew he wouldn't survive trading punches with Feedback.

Out of the corner of his eye, he saw a flash of fire and Arsenal narrowly avoiding it.

"Anybody?" Emmett muttered, putting his hands up to fight.

An answer came in the form of gunfire from the catwalk above. The guards were back, and Emmett could only hope that Athena kept up her protective shields... but that meant she wasn't coming to help.

The second answer came from McGuire. Emmett just saw him out of the corner of his vision; McGuire was running toward them. Then he raised his slingshot and fired.

Black fabric wrapped around Feedback's face, enveloping it completely. He pawed at the trap in confusion—then a second shot, a rocket-powered snare, wrapped around Feedback's arms, trapping him.

Emmett didn't waste another moment, punching Feedback as hard as he could in the stomach *with his left hand*. Feedback doubled over and collapsed. Emmett wasn't sure how the super's power worked, but hopefully that would keep him down long enough.

A gasp from Arsenal brought Emmett back to the moment, and both he and McGuire turned to help her. McGuire fired his slingshot again, this time at sword-girl, but she sliced the shot out of the air. Arsenal backpedaled away from her attacker while Emmett sprinted after them.

But he was too late—

There was a deep molten gash in Arsenal's shoulder where the flame sword had cut through her exosuit. The wound glowed, and not from the flame sword's magic. Spurts of molten liquid bubbled out of the crevice, the air around the battle immediately turning to steam. Emmett barely heard TINA's voice in his ear.

"Exosuit breached."

Emmett leapt at sword-girl, tackling her shield-first, and sent her skidding away.

For a moment, Emmett glared at the enemy super, ready to take her on himself. His hands shook with rage. Until then, everything had been just another battle—now Clara's suit was breached and they were all in imminent danger.

Sword-girl must've sensed the change too, because she looked apprehensively at both Arsenal and Emmett.

Before either could react, three glowing arrows slammed into sword-girl's back. She screamed and fell to the ground. Her sword vanished as she writhed in pain.

A second later, Luna and Borealis emerged from the twisted wreckage—having finished their own fight.

Borealis ran to the sword-girl and conjured a sheet of ice over her back that seemed to both keep her pinned and from bleeding too much. Luna's arrows vanished as he did.

Dr. Venture's voice came through their earpieces, bringing Emmett back to the moment. *"Borealis, can you slow* Arsenal's *energy leak?"*

The stocky super reached out his hands to Arsenal, careful to avoid the spurts of molten liquid. Frost coalesced in the air, swirling and condensing around the breach in Arsenal's suit.

Emmett watched the scene, heart pounding in his chest, unable to ignore Clara's labored breathing.

Athena jogged over and shouted orders. "Mod, McGuire, hurry up with those charges! Go!"

Athena shoved Emmett, knocking him out of his stupor. He ran to catch up with McGuire, then sprinted past him, swapping out the impact shield for his whip in the process.

Emmett ran to the far side, slapping two more explosive charges under the vats and trusting McGuire to do the same.

The sounds of gunfire stopped above them as the guards presumably realized that they couldn't shoot through Athena's barriers. Emmett hoped they'd come to their senses and began evacuating, but those hopes came crashing down as the first guards came spilling out of the door in front of him.

Borealis said, *"I don't know if this will hold it."* Even though he whispered it, Borealis's words sounded deafening.

Emmett's anger redoubled and he leapt at the guards with reckless abandon. He met the first four with his whip extended in a massive haymaker and they were knocked off their feet and flung back into the wall. Emmett barreled through the next two guards, shoving them back through the door and into the hallway.

Emmett crashed into the wall and kept fighting. He slung his whip like a wrecking ball, dropping three guards at a time with a strike. In seconds, he'd dropped twelve men, and the hallway was silent except for whimpering.

He probably wouldn't admit it out loud, but thrashing them felt *good*. Not in a sadistic way, but in a *letting off steam* sort of way.

Emmett resisted the urge to hit them while they were down. He didn't need to. None of the guards were moving to get back up—they were only human.

He did, however, grab every gun and chuck them into the wreckage in the middle of the room. Then Emmett snapped the door handle off with his prosthetic arm. He would close it behind him and keep anyone else normal from following.

As Emmett turned to leave, he said coldly, "Don't get back up."

Emmett ran back to the group.

Everyone was gathered around Arsenal and Borealis as he struggled to contain her leaking exosuit. His hands were coated in blue ice and gusts of frost emanated from them. But even with his power, heat radiated off of her and steam clouded the air.

Emmett could feel the struggle in the air, like winter winds trying to hold back a volcano.

McGuire had finished planting the rest of the bombs and jogged back over, panting through his mask. "That's not good, is it?"

Borealis muttered, "No, it's not."

Clara's breath was ragged and her arm was trembling, even in her exosuit. It seemed like each time she moved, it widened the crack in her suit.

"Please keep still," Borealis added.

Athena stood apart from the rest, her eyes sweeping the room and the exits. "What do we do with her, Doctor?"

The comms were silent, and Emmett imagined Venture was weighing their options. There were always the drones, but then Gnosis and the Summit might find out about Venture's involvement. Of course, there was the possibility that they waited too long and the drones couldn't contain a meltdown.

"Drones inbound. Emmett, Luna, pull a fire alarm and evacuate as many of the guards as possible."

TINA added, *"Containment protocol engaged."*

"I'll help too," McGuire said, running over toward the still-downed sword-girl.

Before Emmett could protest, the gadgeteer pulled a contraption out of his backpack. It unfolded into a thin frame—a mix between a stretcher, a luggage cart, and the skeleton of a wagon. McGuire slid the downed super so that her hips were held up by two wheels and the third wheel was under her shoulders. He pulled the contraption, half-rolling, half-dragging her across the ground.

It was almost comical, but it worked.

Luna picked Feedback up onto her shoulders in a fireman's carry. The bound super kicked at first, but then Luna whispered something to him and he quickly stopped.

Emmett sprinted across the warehouse, back to the offices where they'd left the unconscious security guards. He pulled a fire alarm on the way. Then he grabbed them two at a time—one over his shoulder and dragging the second with his whip—and hauled them outside and deposited them against a nearby building.

As he ran back in for the second bunch of guards, drones crashed through the upper windows of the warehouse.

Emmett grabbed the rest of the guards and tried to ignore Clara's distress. Tried not to think about her boiling inside her suit... There were still a bunch of other guards that he'd dispatched on the other side of the warehouse. They had to get everyone out in case Arsenal melted down.

The world felt like a haze as Emmett hauled the men outside, then ran back into the warehouse. Two drones hovered above Arsenal while a third hovered over the breach in her suit. The drone was attempted to weld the breach shut. Meanwhile Borealis had turned his power toward the drone, trying to keep it from melting.

"It's not going to hold," Venture said. *"Switching to containment foam."*

All three drones surrounded Arsenal, turning into futuristic fire extinguishers. Clouds of black foam sprayed out and enveloped her exosuit. In seconds, she was gone—encased like a statue in a block of dark marble.

Emmett ran past them to get the other guards, the whole time trying and failing to forget what Clara said about the containment protocols:

They hurt. All of them hurt.

"Hang on, Arsenal," Venture said. *"We'll fly you out and drop you in the bay."*

Emmet made it to the other side of the warehouse and tore the broken door off the hinges. The guards were still strewn about, some conscious and groaning. Emmett would have to make three trips to get everyone out.

"I'll help you," Athena said, patting him on the shoulder. "Don't worry. It's almost over."

He hadn't even realized Athena had come to help him. She raised up a barrier beneath three guards, then used it to drag them down the hall.

Emmett looked back, watching in silence as the drones lassoed the block of foam and lifted Arsenal up into the air.

"Goddamnit," he muttered. Everything had gone to shit.

Emmett grabbed three guards and began to drag them, when Venture came back over the comm. His words sent a chill through Emmett's body.

"Mutagen-X Super inbound!"

Emmett barely had time to react.

Something crashed through the roof. He spun around in time to see an unknown super slam into the drones, grabbing one and tossing it like a toy into another, then tearing the third apart with his bare hands—all as he fell through the air.

Clara and the new super plummeted to the ground. The crash sent McGuire, Borealis, and Luna scattering backward.

The containment foam cracked and began bleeding molten liquid.

A familiar enemy, clad in a black mask and hoodie, stood in the wreckage, completely unperturbed by the heat. His body was suffused with Mutagen-X.

"None of you are getting out!"

The man's voice was a mutagen-enhanced bellow. But Emmett almost didn't hear him—

Clara was screaming.

Chapter 45

ATTENTION

Borealis, Luna, and McGuire stared down the Mutagen-X super amongst the twisted, flaming wreckage of the drones and piping.

Luna raised her bow and fired two gleaming arrows. McGuire fired a rocket bola from his slingshot, and immediately after, Borealis leapt in front to protect them.

The new super stood in the middle of the wreckage and let the projectiles hit him. The arrows slammed into him, their magic dispersing in a harmless flash of light. Even though the bolas wrapped around his arms, the super casually snapped the line.

Then he attacked, leaping forward in a blur.

Borealis roared and conjured a wedge of ice, like the plow on the front of a train and so thick it completely obscured the three of them—

And the super crashed through it like it was made of paper, completely obliterating one side of it.

Luna, Borealis, and McGuire were thrown backward and scrambled to their feet, desperately trying to avoid being maimed by chunks of ice. They dodged in Emmett's direction.

Meanwhile, Emmett swapped out his weapons. He equipped his sonic blaster and pulled a knife out of his upper arm compartment. It was hollow titanium and contained a dose of clotting nanomachines.

"Athena, Doctor, we need you guys!"

Emmett sprinted toward the fray, readying the sonic and holding the knife tight in his other hand.

Borealis formed wall after wall of ice, each wedge springing up in a flash of blue—each smaller than the last. At first, Emmett worried his power was fading already, but in his right hand he seemed to be conjuring a weapon.

The Mutagen-X super broke through each, stalking forward like the monster out of a slasher film and sending chunks of ice across the warehouse.

Luna and McGuire dodged backward, weary of the fight and the debris. Luna sent progressively larger arrows at their enemy. Each time, it took her a moment longer to instill her magic, but now the arrows lodged in the super. McGuire fumbled desperately in his pack and hurled two handfuls of marbles at the oncoming super.

For once, the Mutagen-X super staggered—nearly falling into the splits.

In that much-needed second, Borealis conjured one last ice wall, then finished summoning a jagged sword of deep black ice. Luna notched an arrow so powerful her bow crackled with electricity. McGuire ran further back—

Right past an oncoming Emmett.

The super burst through the ice wall, his yell so loud it sounded like a roar. Luna's shot speared him through the shoulder—completely through. Both ends of the arrow cast him in a grotesque light.

At the same time, Borealis swung his sword down like an executioner's axe, meaning to cleave his enemy in two.

The super batted away the sword like a child's toy. The crack of ice echoing through the warehouse. Borealis didn't have time to swing again, and instead brought the flat of the blade around to block the super's next attack. Borealis stayed standing but he slid back ten feet from the attack.

Leaving Emmett face-to-face with his enemy.

Emmett cranked the power up to the max, leveled the sonic, and fired. The whine cut through the room like a knife, drowning out everything else. Even on the other end of the blast, Emmett's teeth were rattling so hard that they felt like they would fall out of his skull.

He saw the Mutagen-X super wince—

Then he only saw a blur.

Instinctively, Emmett sidestepped and braced to protect his head. Instead of punching, the super merely slammed shoulder-first into him.

Emmett gasped and went hurtling backward, crashing through piping and knocking over a vat.

Stupid, he thought. He'd hoped to catch the super off guard—stabbing him with the hollow knife while he attacked... It was a miracle he was still holding it.

Emmett's arms shook as he pushed himself up out of the twisted metal. He fought for air. It felt like he'd been hit by a truck—again. Even with his reinforced skeleton, Emmett couldn't trade blows with this guy. Maybe it had been stupid to even try to get close, but he had to do something.

Emmett readied himself to run back into the fray. Borealis was fighting to stay between the enemy super and Luna—barely keeping him at bay with his walls and sword.

"More drones are inbound," Venture said, his voice wavering. *"Hold him off until we can get* Arsenal *out of there."*

"Copy that," Athena said, adding, "Sorry. Had to get the rest of the civilians out."

Emmett turned to see his last teammate standing stoically beside him. Until then, Emmett had worried how a fight between Athena and the Mutagen-X super would turn out. But seeing her now, Athena looked larger than life. Light danced on the woven shards of her jacket.

She *looked* like a superhero. And Emmett felt a swell of pride to be standing beside her.

In that moment, there was no question of if they could beat this guy. Emmett was going to fight.

Athena sprinted forward, moving at a speed that Emmett could barely keep up with.

The enemy super punched through an ice wall, but ran up against an invisible barrier. He swung again and this time Emmett could *feel* the shockwave from the impact—

But he couldn't break through.

The super glared at Athena and it felt like the room stood still.

Then chaos erupted.

Everyone lobbed attacks at the Mutagen-X super. Arrows, icicles, bolas, and the sonic slammed into him one after another—Athena flickered her barrier just long enough to let each pass through and keep their enemy from advancing. Glowing arrows pierced his chest and a single spear of ice pierced his stomach, but the super didn't even stagger.

He swung again and again at Athena's barrier. Shockwaves rattled the floor.

Emmett spared a glance over his shoulder and saw Athena's nose was bleeding, just like her original battle with Feedback—except that Feedback's power was a hard counter to her own. The Mutagen-X super was doing this on strength alone. Even Athena couldn't keep this up forever.

Beside them, Arsenal's exosuit lay in a cracked pile of containment foam. The seal had burst open after her fall and molten power was leaking out again.

As if on cue, Borealis conjured a pillar of ice beneath the super's feet, lifting him up into the air, and Athena shoved the whole thing backward with a forcefield—

Sending their enemy hurtling backward. He flew across the length of the warehouse, disappearing behind the wreckage.

In between ragged breaths, Luna said, "We need to get out of here and blow the place!"

Three more drones buzzed through the broken windows and quickly surrounded Arsenal—two lassoing her exosuit and the other dousing her with containment foam.

Emmett held his breath and scanned the wreckage. His sonic was spent and he quickly swapped to his whip. If they could just get Clara out, then the rest of them could run. Dragging her suit wasn't an option; any jostling could break the containment foam, and being that close to her during a meltdown was a death sentence.

A roar came from the wreckage—something that sounded barely human—followed by a steel beam. It hurtled through the air toward Clara like a javelin, far too fast for Emmett to intercept. He had barely even registered it. The steel beam slammed into one of Athena's invisible barriers and sailed overtop of the group.

A dozen more steel projectiles flew toward them so fast they felt like a burst of machine gun fire. They screeched across Athena's barriers and stuck in the wall behind them.

The Mutagen-X super must have realized that an up close fight with Athena wouldn't go in his favor. So he'd switched tactics to a distant hit-and-run.

Emmett spared a glance toward Athena, but she was weathering the assault. Venture asked, *"Athena, can you cover the drones?"*

"Yes," Athena replied coldly.

The three drones resumed lifting Clara's sealed exosuit into the air, and the enemy super redoubled his assault. But no matter how many spears he threw, Athena blocked all of them.

Luna shot arrows in response, but it seemed like an impossible task to hit a target like that amidst all the debris. Borealis also tried conjuring another ice wall to the far left and throwing his own ice lances, but his wall was demolished as quickly as he made it. Athena was the only one that could withstand the assault.

All the while, Emmett didn't dare take his eyes off the wreckage. He could barely keep up with the fight, and one errant projectile would probably kill him.

Soon Arsenal and the drones were twenty feet in the air—nearly half-way up to the windows and to their escape.

When the next barrage came, it wasn't aimed at Clara—

Sparks exploded and metal screamed right in front of Emmett. Athena had managed to make a wedge barrier to shield her and her teammates, but just barely. Previously, she'd created barriers at least ten feet away, but this one was close enough to touch.

Athena screamed and pushed out a barrier. It moved like an invisible wave across the room, taking a ten-foot swathe of debris with it. But the barrage of metal didn't stop.

Emmett's heart was in his throat, but he barely noticed. He'd witnessed the power and durability of their enemy before, but somehow this was even more terrifying. Not only was he tearing off steel beams and hurling them with deadly force, but he was also weaving through the wreckage so quickly that the barrage seemed to come from everywhere at once.

Clara and the drones were nearly at the windows when one of the drones exploded—speared by one of the Mutagen-X super's throws.

Borealis's ice wall exploded. Luna was knocked off her feet, but McGuire was thrown backward. He tumbled across the ground, and for a moment, Emmett thought the gadgeteer wouldn't get back up. But McGuire quickly rolled to his feet, looking puffier than before...

It took Emmett a moment to realize that McGuire had rigged an airbag in his coat.

The gadgeteer quickly moved behind Athena, then tugged a string on his coat. The jacket deflated back to its normal size. If Emmett had a moment, he would've given McGuire props for his ingenuity.

The barrage didn't let up, and soon Athena's screams were drowned out by the screech of metal. The next throws came so fast that Emmett couldn't place what happened—

Only that all three drones and Clara were falling.

Emmett felt like he was watching the scene unfold in slow motion. Severed parts of the drones fell like firework sparks. Clara drifted downward like she was a stone sinking underwater.

Then she hit the ground. Containment foam cracked. The wound in her exosuit reopened. Molten fire gushed out like a dam burst. It cascaded through the air, turning the world to steam, and instantly melting any metal that it touched. Even though Emmett was behind one of Athena's barriers, it did nothing to stop the heat from reaching him.

Clara's breath was ragged. Despite all her destructive potential, she was still trying her hardest to hold it back.

"Mod, listen to me," Venture said, the slightest shake in his voice. *"You need to manually disengage Arsenal's exosuit. Release the helmet and her power will take care of the rest."*

"But that will cause a meltdown!" Emmett said, wincing as a steel beam crashed in front of him. Judging by the confused glances of his team, Venture was speaking to all of them.

"I know. She'll melt through to the tunnels below the building. There's a maintenance entrance in the stairwell behind you. The concrete will cool her down and stabilize her, then you can dig her out. Use the tunnels to escape—"

"Go! I'll cover you," Athena shouted, blood trickling from her nose.

Emmett pocketed the knife. Another beam struck the shield in front of Emmett, but he ran directly at it—toward Clara. The heat was blistering even before Emmett was close, and when he knelt down beside her, it felt like his skin was burning. A wave of cold swept over Emmett's back, but it barely dampened the heat.

It was nothing compared to when Emmett touched her helmet.

It felt like he stuck his hand in a grill. Emmett grit his teeth at the pain and ignored the sizzling of his skin. He fumbled for the release mechanism on Clara's helmet, forced to go by feel because he couldn't open his eyes.

"Emmett..." Clara's voice was a broken whisper, and hearing it scared him almost as much as the heat. It sounded like she was about to pass out.

"I'm hurrying," Emmett said, hoping it would reassure her.

"No... Get away..."

Chapter 46

Collapse

Emmett fumbled for the release mechanism on the back of Clara's suit, hands sizzling on the scorching metal. Somehow, the surrounding air felt even hotter from the molten power leaking out of her shoulder. Like he was standing on the edge of an active volcano.

Somewhere beyond the heat, there was still a battle ongoing between Athena and the Mutagen-X super. Clara was whispering something. But Emmett could barely focus on opening her suit, let alone on everything else going on.

Clara writhed in his grip, probably delirious from pain, like she was trying to get away from him. As she turned, the release gave way suddenly, and the back of Clara's suit exploded.

Thankfully, she'd rolled so her back was facing away from her allies.

Molten slag gushed out like a firehose turned on, spraying across the wreckage of the warehouse. As the arcs fell, they became jagged, behaving more like electricity than liquid. Mutagen equipment melted like butter.

The concrete floor beneath her was already turning into a molten puddle.

The heat around Clara became blinding and Emmett rolled away instinctively. Even twenty feet away, Emmett had to shield his eyes. The rest of his allies were quickly backing away. If not for Borealis's cryokinesis blanketing the area, Emmett might've been seriously injured.

Even the Mutagen-X super had ceased his onslaught in the presence of overwhelming power.

"We need to get out of here!" Athena shouted. Blood streamed freely from her nose now as she struggled to keep her barriers up.

For the first time, Emmett heard panic in Athena's voice, and it was even more unsettling than the rest of the scene.

An explosion shook the warehouse, knocking Emmett and the others to their knees—Clara's power had set off one of their charges.

"Drones inbound," Venture said. *"Run. Once everyone's underground, I'll bring down the building."*

"Go!" Athena shouted.

Everyone turned and ran across the warehouse. This time, no one bothered shooting arrows or throwing ice at their enemy. Emmett didn't even hear the Mutagen-X super throwing anything in retaliation.

They reached the maintenance doors and paused to take stock of the situation. They were ragged, and Borealis and Luna were bleeding, but everyone was in one piece—if anything, Emmett was the most injured. He clutched both hands to his chest, not wanting to look at them. They were charred and *throbbed* with pain.

Athena was still out there. She was backing toward the door, but was shuffling instead of running, like she still expected an attack.

It didn't come until Athena was almost at the door.

Three spears flew out of the wreckage and slammed into Athena's barrier—

Then another slammed into Clara.

"No!" Emmett yelled.

Clara was sent sprawling across the ground, but instead of being impaled by the spear, it had liquified when it touched her and burst like a water balloon. The rest of her exosuit fell away like orange petals.

Clara struggled to her feet. Her entire body blazed like the sun. She swept her arm out and sent a spray of molten slag across the warehouse. Steam and fumes clouded the room, like they were in an active volcano.

Athena started running now, covering her mouth as she did. Emmett felt an invisible barrier pushing him back into the hallway. "Get out, now!"

Despite the danger, Emmett struggled to watch as Clara's glowing form melted into the floor and disappeared from view.

Just as Emmett was about to turn and run, steel spears slammed into the nearby wall and Athena's barriers. The Mutagen-X super streaked toward them, his clothes and skin charred.

By now, everyone was inside the doorway, and Athena reinforced her barrier. Their enemy slammed into the invisible wall shoulder first, then reared back and tackled it again.

The super's mask was burned so that Emmett could see his lips wrinkled into a sneer.

"Bring it down," Athena said, her face hard set. She grunted with effort, and a second later, the super was hurled clear across the room.

Then they turned and ran down the hall toward the underground access. Venture guided them using floor plans of the warehouse. They were down the first flight of stairs when the structure above rumbled from explosions.

Somewhere above, the Mutagen-X super roared.

Moments later, they came to the third level of the basement and a set of imposing double doors marked *'Maintenance Tunnels.'*

Athena used a barrier to force open one of the doors, which screeched in protest. Once everyone was through, she used her power to wedge the doors shut. Borealis quickly conjured a wall of ice to reinforce it and didn't stop until it was four feet thick.

Explosions shook the building, rattling the piping along the walls and shaking dust loose. No one moved, and Emmett didn't even breathe. There was one final crash as the building collapsed, and then it was silent.

The lights in the maintenance tunnel cut off a second later, leaving Emmett and the others in darkness.

Emmett pulled out a flashlight and fumbled for the switch. It took a few tries before he was able to turn it on—not only did his hands hurt like shit, his left one felt like he could barely move. He clutched both hands to his chest to keep the flashlight from trembling.

McGuire pulled out three more and handed them out to everyone. Then beams of light illuminated the dusty maintenance hall.

"We need to find Cl—Arsenal," Emmett said. He was stating the obvious, but needed something to take his mind off the pain and the nausea.

Athena led them. She jogged through the tunnel, ushering them to keep moving.

"She should be on this side," Athena said, turning right at the first junction.

As they ran, Borealis came up beside Emmett. "Let me see your hands." Emmett handed Borealis his flashlight, then held out his hands and tried not to throw up.

Emmett's hands were charred and bleeding. Blackened flakes fell off as he tried moving his fingers. His prosthetic hand had gotten the worst of it—bits of silver shone through in slivers where the skin and other synthetic tissue had been completely burned away, leaving only the frame beneath.

Borealis loosely wrapped Emmett's hands in gauze, then chilled the dressings with his power. The cooling effect was almost too much and Emmett both winced at the sensation and wept tears of relief.

"You need a doctor," McGuire said. The gadgeteer walked on the other side of Emmett, eyeing his wounds reluctantly.

Borealis added solemnly, "He's right. You'll be lucky if you don't have nerve damage."

Emmett grit his teeth. "Could be worse."

Luna was walking ahead of them and apparently listening in. "It could *always* be worse," she added.

Athena led them through another junction and then stopped suddenly. She carefully touched the wall and then nodded. "Arsenal's here. We need to dig her out."

Borealis said, "You might want to back up." Then he pressed his own hands against the wall. Ice formed, branching out in fractals before seeping into the pores of the concrete. Pits formed in the wall and chunks began to crumble and fall to the floor. Athena used her power to sweep rubble away, so that Borealis wasn't overwhelmed.

In minutes, Borealis had excavated a hole as tall as himself and five feet deep. It felt like everyone except Athena was holding their breath. Meanwhile, she was watching the hallway.

Clara emerged from the wall and fell to her knees, coughing. Steam was still coming off her skin, but she was no longer violently hot. Her exosuit was completely disintegrated and only her bodysuit survived by virtue of being skintight.

Luna and Borealis helped Arsenal to her feet. She looked around like she'd just woken up from a dream. Luna pulled out a spare mask and helped Clara put it on before she stood.

"Is everyone alright?" she asked.

Most answered with nods, but there was an uncertainty in the air, one that fit the otherworldly display of power they'd all witnessed. Even Emmett was hesitant, despite knowing what Clara was capable of. It felt like everyone was afraid to speak.

Everyone except Athena. "We'll manage. Can you walk?"

Clara mustered her strength and stood on her own. "Yeah. I'll be fine."

Athena replied, "Good, because we need to leave. The Summit will be arriving shortly, and we need to get as far from here as possible."

The group started running through the tunnels, this time following Luna. In addition to being a deadshot archer, she was also an empowered tracker and navigator.

Luna explained that if they could get to the tunnels beneath the highway, then it was a straight shot back to Belport. Then they could emerge somewhere in the city and go their separate ways.

Getting to the highway was the most important thing. It was the only nearby passage beneath Belport. If Emmett and the others were too slow, it was likely that the Summit would intercept them.

Clara wound up running alongside Emmett for support, occasionally leaning on his shoulders. Thankfully, it wasn't that far to the highway, or someone would've needed to carry her and McGuire. If Emmett was being honest with himself, he wasn't feeling too hot either—Clara had mentioned that a meltdown might release radiation, but right now he had to trust that his body could handle it. At least until he got back to the lab.

The tunnels changed as they ran. Beneath the warehouses, they'd been made of concrete and lined with piping and lights. But soon the tunnels were brick and mortar, and looked far older than anything else Emmett had seen in the city.

They finally reached the highway. The tunnel widened until it was twenty feet across and ten feet high. A series of red emergency lights illuminated the gloom and extended out as far as Emmett could see.

Athena explained, "These tunnels run all throughout Belport. Most were dug during the second civil war, but some predate even that. Now that we're here, we'll make faster progress."

She waved for them to stand close to her. Then Emmett lurched slightly as Athena conjured a forcefield beneath their feet.

"Hang on."

There was another lurch as they started down the corridor. Athena slowly accelerated, using her barrier as a mobile platform. Soon, they were speeding through the tunnel far faster than most of them could run. Athena must've been using barriers to break the wind in front of them as well, but even so the rushing sound grew to a roar, and the group held onto each other for support.

Clara leaned close to Emmett and spoke just loud enough for him to hear her. "Are your hands okay?"

Emmett pulled them a little close to his chest, not wanting her to see his injuries. "I'm fine."

"We'll go to the lab as soon as we can... I'm sorry—"

"No," Emmett said quickly. "It's okay. You helped us get out of there."

Clara seemed to relax a little and didn't say anything else. She looked as tired as Emmett felt, and he knew that both of them would need medical attention when they made it back to the lab.

But despite her ordeal, Clara seemed well enough.

Emmett tried not to worry about her. There was nothing to do now but try to relax and conserve his strength as they raced through the tunnels beneath the highway. Clara rested her head on his shoulder and Emmett found the process a little easier. He let out a deep sigh.

Meanwhile, the stale underground air roared past them.

Chapter 47

Aftermath

The group raced through the underground tunnels toward Belport, using Athena's forcefield as a makeshift train car. Emmett couldn't determine how fast they were moving—he'd lost track of time now and on the way to the mission. But Athena assured them they'd be safe beneath Belport in another few minutes.

Athena stood at the back, silently concentrating, while the rest of the group licked their wounds. Luna and Borealis whispered between themselves, and Emmett got the sense that they were extremely close or maybe even romantically involved. He tried not to listen in—

Which was helped by McGuire talking over everyone.

"That. Was. *Crazy*—I mean, it didn't go anything like we planned, but I think we did alright. Don't you?"

Emmett nodded. He didn't want to move too much and wake up Clara, who was still resting her head on his shoulder.

Emmett asked McGuire, "Better than sparring on the rooftops?"

McGuire let out a long sigh. "Yes, but I think I need a few days before we fight another Class three super and destroy another warehouse."

Emmett chuckled. "Deal."

The tunnel beneath the highway was straight, and it wasn't until other tunnels and junctions appeared that Athena announced they had made it to Belport.

"Doctor?" Emmett wasn't sure if they could receive transmissions beneath the city, but he stayed hopeful.

Some minutes later, Emmett heard static.

"Mod... Arsenal... thena... Does...one copy?"

"We hear you," Emmett replied. Clara sat up and both exchanged a smile.

"It's damn good to hear your voice, Mod. Is everyone accounted for?"

"Yes. We're beneath the city."

Athena asked, "Do we have a tail?"

"No. The Summit is on the scene. They've established a perimeter around the block, but they're not checking the underground yet. By the time they sift through the rubble, you'll be home free."

Clara stirred off of Emmett's shoulder. "What about that super?"

"They fled the scene... but a drone did manage to tag him with a tracking beacon. It's active. He's in an apartment block on the Southside—probably a safehouse. He doesn't appear to be tracking you, but I'll keep an eye on him."

Emmett stayed silent. Despite the hectic ending, it seemed like they had succeeded—that they were out of the woods, so to speak. But Emmett knew better...

"Doctor, how much do I have to worry about radiation from Arsenal's meltdown?" Everyone else perked up a little, waiting for the Doctor's response.

"The radiation from a meltdown is short-lived. You've been exposed because you were so close when it happened, but the particles are inert within a few seconds of exposure. No one else needs to worry, but we won't know what the full extent of your damage is until we get you to the lab. The good news is that if you're still talking, then your body has done a good enough job with the damage."

Emmett might've been imagining things, but it felt like the nausea subsided a little. He almost asked Dr. Venture what their next steps were. Clara had melted down in the warehouse. If the Summit had cracked her energy signature, then they would figure out that Clara was involved. They'd be coming after Venture next, wouldn't they?

Silence dragged on between the group, and Emmett realized that Venture wasn't going to mention it. Maybe he didn't want to put out that information to the rest of the group.

Emmett added it to the list of things to talk to Dr. Venture about as soon as they got back.

Even though Venture assured the group that they weren't followed, Athena still took them down several other tunnels. She, Borealis, and Luna were surprisingly familiar with the layout of the tunnels, and had even used them as hideouts and staging areas in the past.

They didn't return to the surface until they were at the edge of Eastside—almost three in the morning. Athena led them to a maintenance hatch on the edge of a parking lot and the team emerged into the cool night air and soft glow of streetlights.

Each took a minute to alter or cover their disguises, leaving only their faces covered until they went their separate ways. Soon they were standing around quietly in a circle.

"Let's not make this any bigger of a thing than it is," Luna said, breaking the silence. To Emmett, Clara, and McGuire, she added, "Not bad today."

"She means it," Borealis added with a chuckle. "And that means a lot, coming from her."

Luna punched Borealis in the shoulder before turning and walking away. He followed, waved over his shoulder, and called back, "Don't get into too much trouble without us!"

Venture cleared his throat. *"Needless to say, we should all lie low for a few days."*

Athena crossed her arms and looked over the three junior supers. "Are you going to be alright getting where you need to go?"

Emmett and Clara nodded. Though Clara was standing on her own, it felt like she was standing closer than usual.

Meanwhile, McGuire waved dismissively. "Don't you worry about me. I'm going to go home and go straight to sleep."

Athena chuckled and gave a quick nod. "Call me next time you want to blow something up." Then she stuffed her hands in her jacket pockets and walked quickly after her friends.

McGuire added, "That goes for me, too. You know, after a few days of recuperation." Then he ran off, leaving Emmett and Clara alone in the parking lot.

"How are you feeling?" Emmett asked.

Clara shrugged. "As good as can be expected."

"I meant, are you feeling up for the walk back to the lab?"

"Walk?" Clara scoffed. "Doctor, are there any drones nearby?"

Emmett and Clara flew back to base and went straight to the biolab in section 006.

Venture spared a nod for Emmett and a hug for Clara, but then he escorted Clara through the halls and back to a holding tank. Emmett insisted on following.

As they walked, Venture kept mentioning a *holding tank*, and so Emmett pictured something like the tank he'd been submerged in for surgery—

Clara's tank was markedly different.

The sphere took up almost the entirety of the room it was in—rising over twenty feet tall and towering over them. Pipes and wires crisscrossed the surface, which Emmett immediately recognized as modified versions of the heat sinks that he and Clara had spent so much time working on.

A hatch opened as they approached, small enough that Clara had to crouch to get inside. Seeing the hatch open also showed the true scale of the structure—the walls were nearly a foot thick.

They had to be to withstand Clara's power.

Clara ducked inside and turned around to face Emmett. For the first time in a while, she struggled for words. In the end, all she said was, "See you in a few days." Then the hatch shut behind her, sealing her in.

Then Dr. Venture and Emmett walked down the hall to a surgical suite and pointed him toward the center table.

"TINA, I'll need some assistance." Then to Emmett, he added, "Put your arms out on the table."

Emmett sat down and tried to lay his arms flat. He'd been clutching them tight to his chest since they'd fled the warehouse. He was able to stretch out his arms so that his forearms were flat, but his hands... His hands were charred and fresh blood seeped out of the crevices when he tried to uncurl his fingers. The muscles felt impossibly tight—almost as if they'd frozen in place.

Each time Emmett tried to move his fingers, the pain made tears well up in his eyes.

While Emmett struggled, Venture pulled up a chair beside him and mechanical arms descended from the ceiling. One arm looked like a microphone and deftly moved around Emmett's injured arms, scanning them.

A second later, a holographic display appeared above the table.

"The damage is better than I hoped.," Venture said, expanding the hologram.

Emmett laughed bitterly. "Better? Really? It seems pretty bad to me."

Venture pointed to the image of his prosthetic arm first. "The important parts held up rather well. The damage is mostly superficial, though there is some ligament damage. But it's nothing that we can't remedy. You have latent nanites in your system monitoring your prosthetic arm, and these have already started repairs. We'll give you a booster shot of nanites to help..."

He spun the image around to show Emmett's regular hand. "I told you before that your body bonded surprisingly well to Mutagen-A... If not for that, you'd be looking at another prosthetic hand. Between the mutagen and the additional healing nanites you're infused with, you're looking at 2-3 days of recovery. As for your radiation exposure, the nausea should subside by the end of the day... You were lucky, Emmett—on several counts."

Emmett let out a sigh of relief. He wasn't sure whether it was the good news or his body's healing factor, but his hands were already feeling better.

They still *hurt*, but better was good enough for Emmett. He could take a few days off.

While Emmett sat in silence, the mechanical arms began working on him—cleaning his wounds and injecting him with additional healing nanites. Emmett's stomach turned and he looked away while the arms worked.

"Is Clara going to be okay?" The question came out so suddenly it surprised both of them.

Venture leaned back in his chair and nodded, then seemed to choose his words carefully. "Clara's *condition* comes and goes, and particularly bad dips are marked by meltdowns. Now you know how dangerous her condition is, and why I've gone to the lengths that I have to protect her and others."

Venture eyed Emmett to make sure he understood the gravity of the situation. "For all the difficulty, she's gained remarkable control over her power. I'm inclined to think that tonight's flare up was due to the restrictions of her exosuit, as much as from the difficulty of the fight. Containment would've likely been possible... I don't think her condition is worsening."

Emmett nodded and thought about Clara trapped inside the containment sphere.

See you in a few days, she had said. Emmett hoped it was true.

By now, the mechanical arms were finishing up on Emmett, coating his wounds in a spray-on bandage.

Now there was just one more loose end:

"Where is that super?"

Venture's face wrinkled in question. "Why?"

Emmett didn't answer right away. "I... I just want to know."

"I find that hard to believe."

"You're still tracking him, right?"

"Of course. TINA, please bring up the location of our Mutagen-X super."

The holographic display changed from Emmett's mangled arms to a 3D view of Belport. The super was still on the Southside, but now he was walking steadily West across the boardwalk.

Emmett stared at the display. Not only had they possibly found a Gnosis saferoom, but now they might even know where their enemy lived.

That was a dangerous prospect, Emmett realized. How many times had Venture tracked a rival super to their home?

"Just what are you thinking about doing?" Venture asked. His voice and his expression were hard.

Emmett studied the map and the super's direction. "I want to follow him."

"Don't."

"I'm not going to do anything. We need more information about him.... He almost killed us."

Venture didn't relent. "That's not why you want to follow him."

"Fine," Emmett retorted, frustration getting the better of him. "He's our last lead with Porcelain and the accident on Champion street. I need to know what happened."

Emmett stood and flexed his hands despite the pain. A bit of blood sneaked through the cracks in his wounds, but the bandages held. He turned to leave.

TINA's voice came through the intercom. *"I agree with Dr. Venture."*

That made Emmett pause at the door. It didn't dissuade him though—not in the slightest. Before Emmett could think of something to say, Dr. Venture answered somberly.

"No, it's okay, TINA. Emmett needs to know."

Emmett left and didn't look back.

Chapter 48

Last Lead / Lock

Emmett stormed out of the lab and into the night air. He started jogging down the streets so fast it bordered on a run. He arced down toward Southside, not wanting to call attention to himself by sprinting through the streets like a madman or a criminal. It was a little after three in the morning, after all.

As soon as the roofs were close enough together, he climbed a fire escape. Then he broke into a sprint and raced across the rooftops of Belport.

"TINA, let me know if he deviates from his course."

"I will."

TINA's sounded almost reluctant, but Emmett had to be imagining things. He didn't pay the thought anymore mind as he ran—

Mostly because he was going so fast that one misstep could send him crashing down into an alley.

TINA guided Emmett across Southside and toward the West End, then North. Emmett lost track of time as he ran.

"I'll align your path so you have a visual, but you can't get within three blocks of your target. Any closer and he might hear you."

"Understood," Emmett said between breaths.

He'd slowed to jog by now and was within ten blocks of his target. Even though his endurance was inhuman, apparently sprinting full speed across the city was close to his limit. His chest heaved and his legs felt like they were on fire.

"Don't engage him," TINA added.

Emmett would have scoffed if he had the extra breath. He wasn't blind with rage and he wasn't dumb. He knew better than to attack a Class 3 super that fought his entire team to a standstill.

"You should have a visual now. Moving North by the corner of Lomax and Charles."

Emmett reached the end of the roof and skidded to a halt. The Mutagen-X super was a little over three blocks away and walking on the left side of the street. He wore a black hoodie with the hood pulled up—even from three blocks away, Emmett could see how tattered it was.

Emmett crouched down and watched as the super turned and disappeared around the corner. The wind had picked up and Emmett suppressed a chill. After a moment, he took a parallel path across the rooftops so that he could maintain a visual.

The entire time, Emmett's heart felt like it was in his throat. He was exhausted from the fight, from running, from constant adrenaline, but he couldn't stop.

Not when he was so close to answers.

Even if Emmett wasn't going to fight this guy, he could stake out his place. Maybe even break in later and see if he could find any information.

It wasn't for some minutes later that Emmett realized how far into the West End they were—right about when the rooftops grew further apart and Emmett had to climb down to street level to continue his pursuit.

They were only a few blocks away from the Woods apartments.

Emmett slowed and put a little more space between him and the enemy super. The buildings were further apart and Emmett didn't have as much cover to hide his pursuit.

And he wouldn't admit it, but he was getting worried.

Just how close did this guy live to the Woods? Had Emmett been living a few streets away from a powerful rival this time?

Emmett's head was practically swimming as he followed the super all the way to the Woods apartments...

Was the super a fellow student? Had Emmett been going to school with a murderer?

Emmett skulked through the treeline now, watching as the super walked across the lawn of the Woods—

And walked into Emmett's apartment block.

If apprehension and dread had been building inside of Emmett like a pit in his stomach, now it felt like horror had grabbed him by the shoulders and was forcing him to keep walking.

"Where is he going now?" Emmett's voice was barely a whisper.

"You know where he's going."

Emmett couldn't look away from his building.

He didn't pull out of his phone to text his roommate. Emmett already knew that he didn't need to warn Lock.

Lock had barely been coming home the last two months. He'd been working late at night. Getting into fights. He'd hurt people.

All this time Emmett thought Lock had been roughing people up at the bar.

Emmett barely realized that he too was walking toward the apartments. He walked up the stairs, following the path to his front door blindly like he was in a dream.

All the way up to the top.

Emmett stopped in front of door 449 and stared.

How had he missed it?

Emmett admitted that he hadn't been looking that closely... Who expected their roommate to be a supervillain? It already felt ridiculous that Clara and his boss were supers too...

But how had he missed Lock?

The fights... the hoodies... It was all him.

Desperately, Emmett thought back to the night Porcelain died.

I'm not your enemy.

...Did Lock know about him?

Emmett's throat was bone dry. He was afraid to breathe.

I'm not your enemy.

Was that even true? Even if it had been true once... was it still true?

Instinctively, Emmett reached for his keys, ready to let himself into the apartment like it was any other night. Like Lock hadn't just tried to kill or maim him and his friends. He stopped short, hand frozen in his pocket. Emmett stayed absolutely still and listened for any sound of movement from inside the apartment.

He didn't hear anything.

Emmett shivered as that same paralyzing fear crept over his shoulders and over his neck.

Lock waited.

Lock had smelled him following. Emmett had probably followed him from the rooftops, staying just far enough away so that Lock couldn't see him. But Emmett hadn't accounted for Lock's heightened sense of smell...

Emmett hadn't accounted for a lot.

But that didn't explain how Emmett had managed to follow him home. Lock had been careful—scanning the skies to make sure Dr. Venture's drones weren't following him. Making sure that Venture wouldn't retaliate for slighting his daughter. The old man was smart—he'd know that attacking Lock in the middle of the city would only violate the code and paint a target on his back. He wouldn't cross Gnosis.

The old man was smart. Emmett... not so much.

For the last few weeks, Lock had contemplated confessing everything to Emmett. Dropping out of school, his real job at Gnosis, his *new* job at Gnosis... Even contemplated confessing the murders. Then Lock had envisioned having a heart-to-heart with Emmett—his roommate confessing his real job with Dr. Venture and moonlighting as a superhero.

They would've had so much to talk about...

Tonight, Lock had went back to their apartment and waited. He stood just inside the door. Emmett would open up the door and see Lock standing there—

Then Lock would end it.

He'd have to be quick so Emmett wouldn't make any noise. Snapping his neck would be easiest. Quickest. Maybe he owed Emmett that.

Lock stood just inside the door in darkness, waiting for his roommate to come home.

By the time he heard Emmett's footsteps in the hall, Lock had to smother his excitement. Was it wrong that Lock was ready to kill his roommate? Was it wrong that he wanted to?

Lock waited.

Emmett's footsteps stopped just outside the door.

A smile crept across Lock's face.

But Emmett didn't come in. He stood outside the door, while Lock's impatience grew. His smile slowly twisted into a sneer.

The footsteps receded quietly, like Emmett was backing away from the door.

Lock nearly ran out after him. Nearly ran out the door and strangled him in the hallway—only the shock of the realization kept him there. He listened while Emmett carefully backed away. Lock's disbelief grew and it felt like a knot in his stomach had finally fallen away and left him hollow. Emmett ran down the stairs, and his footsteps completely faded away.

Anger boiled up in Lock—somehow making it past his emotional blocking. It took him a minute of concentration to snuff it out.

Finally, Lock turned and went to the kitchen. He relaxed his hands, grabbed a kitchen knife, and went to the bathroom. He undressed and sat in the tub. Then he concentrated.

Lock thought back to the battle in the warehouse, to his already closed wounds where metal had cut him and drones had shot him. Some had grazed off his skin. Others had barely penetrated and his skin had already pushed those out. But he probably still had a few bullets left inside him.

He thought back to Emmett tracking him across the rooftops... Then he smirked in annoyance.

Lock's muscles writhed like they had minds of their own. They contorted, the fibers pulling and separating—moving the bullet fragments closer to the surface of the skin. It would've been a painful process if Lock cared to feel it.

Lock felt the lump in his thigh grow, then cut it out with surgical precision. A second and third appeared between his ribs.

He held the third bloody bullet and rolled it in his fingers, feeling the faint energy coming off of it.

A tracker explained it. Emmett couldn't have followed him otherwise.

That was fine. The game was up.

Emmett had come a long way with the old man's help.

Lock tossed it in the trash, not bothering to crush it or clean up the mess.

Chapter 49

Confession / Venture

Emmett sprinted down the street, all his thoughts on getting as far away as possible from Lock. When he was back in the city proper, he weaved through the streets, taking back alleys, climbing up to the rooftops and back down again on a different block. Emmett covered his tracks as best as he could, but knew deep down that if Lock was following him, he wouldn't really have a chance.

He'd have to hope that Lock would talk to him.

Emmett was so distraught he actually got turned around and had to reorient himself before he wandered too far into South Side.

Disbelief.

Dread.

Confusion.

Anger.

Dread...

Dread never left him, even as all the other emotions bubbled up, poured out, or burned inside him. Not even when he made it back to the lab and the heavy blast doors shut behind him.

Emmett stayed there in the entryway, leaning against the cold steel and trying to catch his breath. His chest and lungs burned. His legs ached so badly that they wouldn't stop shaking, even as he leaned against the wall for support. He could've slumped down and gone to sleep right there.

Running all the way across the city will do that to a person. Being betrayed by a mentor and best friend will do that to a person.

Emmett focused on his breathing, trusting the mutagens and nanomachines in his body to help him out. He still had one more thing to do before he went to sleep.

"TINA..."

"Yes, Emmett?"

"Please wake Dr. Venture. I need to talk to him."

"He's already awake and expecting you in section 001."

Emmett walked on tired legs down to section 001, all the while trying to think of what to say to Dr. Venture. In the end, he realized the question was a simple one...

He walked into the living room and found Dr. Venture standing in front of the wall display. His hands were clasped behind his back and he stared thoughtfully at the lights of the city skyline. He didn't bother to turn to greet Emmett as he came in, despite the mechanical hiss of the doors.

Emmett waited, but not for long. "Why didn't you tell me?"

"I thought I was doing you a favor."

"How do you figure that?"

Venture turned and sighed. "At first, I thought you and Lachlan might confide in each other. But he never told you."

"...What do you mean? How long have you known? ...How long did Lock know?"

Venture's face was hard as he answered. "I knew the first time I saw him. Clara and I passed him in the hallway of your apartment when we took you home. Mutagen-X has a unique signature.

"As for Lachlan...I suspect he knew back when we were looking for Porcelain. Mutagen-X grants enhanced senses—one of which being a heightened sense of smell. He would've been able to smell the Mutagen-A in your system."

Emmett's skin felt cold. "This entire time, I've been living with a murderer—with someone on Mutagen-X, whose sanity was slipping, and you didn't tell me?"

Venture nodded, and for the first time, his steadfast gaze faltered. "I had no reason to believe that Lock was a threat to you. Despite his working against us, he still maintained a ceasefire."

"What if I would've killed him?"

Venture considered his words before answering. "If you stay in this business, the odds are almost certain that you will kill someone. Lachlan would've been an unfortunate start."

"Goddamnit. So it's better to kill someone that I don't know..." Emmett shook his head. "It doesn't matter how you justify it. I've tried to be patient with all the secrets—I get it. But this..."

Venture said, "Knowing the truth would've made things more complicated for all of us, but ultimately, things would've worked out the same—"

"You don't get it," Emmett interjected, jabbing a finger at his mentor. "This was *my* life. Not yours. You don't get to make that call."

Venture nodded slightly, his hard look returning. "You're right. I made a call, and it was the wrong one. I'm sorry for that. But I need you to understand something, Emmett: Our decisions don't just affect one person. I'm not just responsible for myself or for you, but for Clara, for my contacts and allies, and for the city. Any decision I make is weighed with all those things in mind, and *not all of them are equally important.* Do I make myself clear?"

Emmett stared back, fully understanding and not faltering under the weight of it.

He was at the bottom of that list.

Emmett nodded coldly. He understood.

For the first time, Emmett felt like he saw the real Venture. The man who was capable of living a secret life, fighting life and death battles against Class 4—maybe even Class 5 supers. Someone who lied as easily as they put on a mask.

"Did Clara know?"

Surprisingly, Venture's face softened. "Yes, she did. She wanted to tell you, but I ordered her not to."

Despite his reassurances, Emmett still felt like he'd been punched. Clara knew too. Everyone knew…

"Everyone knew *except me.*" The words were so quiet and hollow that Emmett wasn't sure he'd even spoken them aloud.

Venture added, "I know you're upset with me, but don't be upset with Clara."

Emmett wanted to scream. Wanted to punch something. If he wasn't so fucking exhausted… Now he just felt numb. He needed sleep.

"I'm going to go lie down in a guest room, since I can't go back to my apartment."

"We can talk tomorrow."

Emmett had already started walking away, but now he turned back to Dr. Venture. "I don't want to talk. I need some time to think."

Emmett went into the guest room and shut the door behind him. Then he collapsed onto the bed. The lights dimmed automatically.

TINA's voice came quietly from a speaker on the bedside table. *"Emmett, is there anything I can do to help?"*

"No, TINA." Before drifting off to sleep, Emmett muttered, "Thanks."

Emmett woke up in the guest room and lay in bed, staring at the ceiling. It was already ten—he'd slept through Thursday morning classes—so there was no point in rushing to get up. Or to go anywhere.

He couldn't stop thinking through the events of the last two months.

Emmett had been so ready to be a superhero, and he'd had no idea what he was getting into. It felt cliché to even think, but being a hero was a whole lot different from what he'd expected. The Code and violence, the secrets and the lying.

He'd grown up idolizing superheroes, all the while not realizing what kind of sacrifice it took and the lengths they had to go.

In a nauseating way, facing down Venture had felt like looking in the mirror. Emmett had already lied to Lock and to his family. It hadn't even been that hard.

If Emmett wanted to be a mask or a cape, he'd have to live his entire life like this. Venture was the type of person Emmett would become if he kept going.

Keep wearing a mask and playing at being a hero, and eventually you become that mask.

Emmett laid in bed another few minutes, staring at the ceiling, before he finally got up. He made sure he had all his things and his backpack, and then he left. Thankfully, Dr. Venture wasn't in the living room, so there wasn't an awkward goodbye.

He walked out of the lab and out onto Eastside. He shielded his eyes until they adjusted and welcomed the dull burn in his legs.

It felt good to leave. Now that the manufacturing warehouse was destroyed and the knock-off mutagens would be off the street, Emmett could focus on finals and graduating.

He wasn't looking forward to schoolwork, but it would take his mind off of things.

"TINA, is he still at the apartment?"

"Yes."

Emmett tried to enjoy the long walk back to the West End, but he still had one more thing to take care of. All the while, he couldn't stop thinking about the hollow knife in his arm compartment.

Venture had hoped Emmett was going to campus, but that hope had died when he walked past the entrance.

Emmett was going back to the apartment.

Venture went over to the kitchenette of the living room and made a gin and tonic. It was only ten in the morning, but between his conversation with Emmett and what the young man was about to do, Venture needed it. He mentally tuned down the nanomachines in his system and made an exception for the alcohol.

Nothing had gone like it was supposed to, least of all his conversation with Emmett. Venture had always been a direct parent with Clara and he felt an echo of that in his relationship with Emmett. He wasn't any good at sugar-coating things… And he wasn't good at admitting when he'd made a mistake—that was something he resolved to change. Frankly, the idea terrified him…

But It didn't matter now. What was said was said. But that didn't mean Venture would leave the next events up to chance.

He went back to the couch and sat down to enjoy his drink while he waited.

Even if Emmett was set on doing this alone, Venture had his back. He owed Emmett that much.

"TINA, keep five drones on standby. Move them into a stationary position around the apartment and engage their cloaking so that Lachlan won't see them coming."

"Five drones won't be enough—"

"Heavy drones."

"The Summit will see this as a clear escalation. Expect a visit from Mr. Wight."

Venture waved dismissively. "Wight will thank us for removing one of Gnosis's military-grade bioweapons from the city."

"They won't be able to hide completely. Lachlan will smell the drones."

"...Shit," Venture muttered. TINA was right—even in a low-power standby mode, the drones still produced exhaust gasses. "Position them as high as possible while still allowing for optimized response time. Reroute exhaust gasses into the air."

It wasn't a perfect solution; there was still a chance that changing wind patterns could give away their plan. Still, Venture wasn't about to leave Emmett completely at the mercy of Lachlan, and a part of him was tired of playing nice.

Venture might have been imagining it, but he thought he could feel the lab rumble as the heavy drones booted up. Mutagen-X was made for war; so were these.

Venture leaned back and took a long sip of his drink. "Let's see Lachlan stand up to those."

CHAPTER 50

Goodbye

Emmett walked home Thursday morning, taking his time as he crossed Belport.

There was no point in rushing what came next.

He focused on the knife hidden in his upper arm compartment, focused on the rhythm of his feet on the pavement, on the growing bustle of the streets and the noise of the crowds. Felt as it rose to a crescendo in the heart of Belport and as it faded the further he got from downtown.

The deeper he got into the West End. The closer he got to his apartment.

Emmett didn't think about what he was going to do once he got there—just the few steps in front of him. Just the next block.

He didn't even think about what might happen afterward, or what might happen to him.

The sun was high in the sky when Emmett got to the Woods. He'd almost forgotten it was Thursday until he saw the crowds of students on the lawn.

Emmett slowed and scanned the crowds, wondering if Lock would be bold enough or crazy enough to attack him out in the open. But Lock wasn't there, and Emmett crossed the lawn to his apartment block unscathed.

His heart raced as he climbed the stairs and scanned each floor.

By the time Emmett got to his floor, each step felt like he was turning a ratchet—slowly cranking up the tension until something finally snapped. Except, in this case, it wasn't that Emmett would break. The closer Emmett got to his room, the closer he got to Lock. With each step, the chances grew that his murderous roommate might be around the corner.

Ready to grab him.

Emmett still had his earpiece in. He whispered, "TINA, where is he?"

"The tracker is still in your apartment."

Emmett was halfway to his apartment door when he could no longer resist the urge to pull out the hollow knife. He reached up his sleeve, then hid the blade against his side while he crossed the last few steps. Emmett's hand ached, but he held the weapon tightly.

Emmett unlocked the door and pushed it open.

No one was in the kitchen or living room. There was no sound.

Emmett slowly shut the door behind him. He held the knife in front of him, not bothering to hide it anymore. He inched forward until he could see the door to Lock's room in front of him.

It was open—which would normally mean that Lock wasn't there.

"Lock? ...Hey man... You home?"

No one answered.

Emmett groaned. If Lock was going to kill him, why would he answer?

Emmett inched around the corner until he could peek in both rooms. When he didn't see anyone, he checked his room and then Lock's room—checking all the normal hiding spots like closets and under the bed. It didn't look like Lock was home...

His suspicions were all but confirmed when he saw the remnants of bloody bullets and cloth in the bathroom trash can. One of them had bits of wiring hanging out. Lock must know that someone was tracking him now...

Which meant Lock might have fled.

For a moment, Emmett considered the repercussions of that. If Lock skipped town, then neither of them had to die...

But there was still one more place to check.

Emmett wedged a chair under the front door handle. It wouldn't keep Lock out, but it might make enough noise to alert Emmett.

Then Emmett carefully climbed the fire escape up to the roof and felt his dread returning. Checking around each of the rows of air condenser units was a nightmare, and Lock could have been behind any one of them—not to mention the noise drowned out any chance of hearing footsteps.

Painstakingly, Emmett checked the entire roof until he was satisfied that Lock wasn't home.

Then he went back into the apartment and checked everything one more time. Emmett muttered to TINA, "He took the tracker out."

"Dr. Venture and I are maintaining a visual on the block. I'll alert you if we see him."

Lock not being home wasn't much of a comfort, but it gave Emmett some time to prepare.

In the end, there wasn't much Emmett could do.

He could have all the time in the world, but Lock would still have Mutagen-X. His most reliable weapon—the hollow knife and the nanites it contained—meant that Emmett would have to get up close to use it.

Not only that, but one wound likely wouldn't be enough.

Emmett took the chair away from the door and rigged a simple pressure sensor to the bottom of their welcome mat. It wouldn't stop Lock from entering, but it would alert Emmett's phone if he did. If Emmett nodded off, it would keep him from getting killed in his sleep.

Then Emmet resolved to hang out in his room. He grabbed some snacks and locked the door, then spent the day doing what work he could and watching TV when he couldn't bring himself to work.

All the while, the hollow knife was in his arm compartment and never far from his thoughts.

Emmett fell asleep in his bed, clutching his phone and the hollow knife. He wasn't sure how long he'd managed to stay awake, only that he woke to the vibration of his phone.

A single text message shown on his the screen:

He is coming.

Emmett shut off his phone, then gripped the knife in one hand and the blanket in the other. It was raining outside, and he could barely hear the front door open. His phone vibrated—the trigger from the doormat alarm. Lock pulled the door shut behind him. Then there was the almost imperceptible sound of footsteps approaching Emmett's bedroom door.

He didn't move. He even briefly considered faking being asleep.

Then the doorknob snapped and the door creaked open.

Lock stood in the doorway, silhouetted by the glow of red LED lights from the living room. He stood there silently, staring at Emmett, while Emmett stared wide-eyed back.

Silence stretched on until Emmett couldn't bear it any longer.

"Why?"

"There's an awful lot of *why's*... Do any of them really matter?"

Emmett stared at the murderous silhouette of his roommate—his former best friend. Of course, the questions mattered, but each one Emmett tried to ask felt like bile rising up in his throat. Realization set in, and he knew exactly what Lock meant:

Why didn't you tell me?—
The same reason you didn't tell me.
Why did you join Gnosis?—
It was just a job, at first—same as your internship.
Why did you kill Porcelain?—
Just following orders... See the pattern yet?

Again, Emmett felt like he was staring into a twisted mirror—except that this time, the reflection was far more dangerous.

In the end, Emmett asked the only question that mattered:

"Are you going to kill me?"

Lock scoffed, his face unreadable in the dark. "How else did you think this was going to end?"

Lock walked toward him.

Emmett chucked the blanket toward his roommate and sprung up, ready to plunge the hollow knife into him.

But Lock had already batted away the distraction and lunged forward. Before Emmett could blink, both of Lock's hands were around his throat. He pushed Emmett back against the wall.

Emmett still had the knife in his right hand.

He stabbed Lock in the ribs repeatedly. His first two swings had been wild, but then Emmett tried to aim for his roommate's heart. Warm blood dripped on Emmett's hand with each strike, but the wounds closed as quickly as Emmett made them.

Lock didn't bother to block the knife.

Emmett tried to pull away, but the hands around his throat might as well have been made of metal. His eyes were closed, but he could slowly feel the pressure building around his neck.

Emmett had no idea how many doses of nanites the blade held, but he didn't relent. It couldn't have been more than a few seconds, but each stretched on endlessly.

"Look at me."

Emmett snapped his eyes open and the finality of the situation dawned on him. Emmett's muscles burned—from exertion or lack of oxygen, he didn't know. He'd stabbed Lock dozens of times.

Lock was staring blankly at Emmett. His face was frozen and unreadable—

Until a quiet smile stretched across his face like a dam cracking.

"How else did you think this was going to..."

Lock trailed off, his face twitching in confusion. His grip slackened, but not enough for Emmett to wrench himself away. Desperately, Emmett stabbed Lock in the throat, plunging the blade all the way through and out the back of his neck.

Instead of blood, gray powder fell out.

Lock's voice was hoarse and he gagged like he was drowning on each breath. "What did—what did—?!"

Emmett slipped out of Lock's grasp and tried to back away, but Lock lunged forward like a malfunctioning machine, pinning Emmett to the floor.

He had heard stories about bear attacks. Each victim talked about how sudden and ferocious it was—how powerless they felt. Emmett would've preferred being mauled by a bear.

Lock flailed wildly on top of him—half spasming, half trying to kill him. Spit dripped from his slacken face.

Emmett's leg went first—pain exploded and then his entire right leg went numb. Around the same time, the floor cracked. Lock grabbed Emmett's left arm—his real arm—and pulled. The resulting pop and tear sounded impossibly distant, like it was happening to someone else. Emmett couldn't feel it anymore.

Lock tried to headbutt Emmett, but it was only a glancing blow. His face smashed completely through the floorboards.

But even a glancing blow shot a spike of pain into the side of Emmett's head. His vision swam and body felt impossibly heavy. If he passed out now, he would be dead for sure.

He was pretty sure people in nearby apartments were screaming.

Lock reared back—barely conscious himself—ready to headbutt Emmett again.

For a moment, Emmett thought he heard something like a helicopter, but far quieter than it should be. A thundering *crack* erupted from outside and the center of Lock's chest exploded—leaving a hole almost a foot wide.

Emmett realized that Venture really had been looking out for him, after all.

With the last of his strength, Emmett raised a limp knee and pushed Lock over. His roommate rolled to the floor, still spasming—even with lethal damage, his friend wouldn't die.

As Emmett lost consciousness, he could only hope that Lock was too far away to reach him.

Chapter 51

Serenity

Serenity and Hunter Nine were called in to investigate a disturbance in a block of apartments on the West End. By the time they arrived on scene, the block was already swarming with uniforms—police, firefighters, medics, and some acronym agencies as well. Beyond the congregation of workers, college students littered the rest of the lawn. Almost all were in pajamas, which was fitting because it was three in the morning.

It only took a moment to see why—one of the fourth floor dwellings had a massive hole blown in the side of it.

Hunter Nine brought his ethereal hand down to the lawn without consideration for the crowd, causing several uniforms to shuffle out of the way. She nearly muttered an excuse, but thought it better to get right to business before Hunter tried taking over.

"Who's in charge here?" she asked.

Several more uniforms turned to acknowledge them, but only one woman spoke up and introduced herself as Detective Keely. She had the no-nonsense look of a veteran.

"As for who's in charge, it's a shitshow. It was our crime scene, but there were clearly superhumans involved. One fled the scene, one is dead. We called the DSA then I'm assuming they called you. Corporate goons showed up a few minutes before you. They're upstairs arguing with the DSA about retrieving their property. Hope you have your boss on speed dial."

Hunter Nine stormed off toward the stairs. Serenity nodded to the detective, then quickly followed.

Thankfully, all of the students had been cleared out of the block to make room for the throng of workers. Firefighters and building engineers were examining the ends of the halls, presumably looking for structural damage. Not only had they blown a hole in the roof, but the shockwave might've damaged the rest of the building.

That alone concerned Serenity more than the rest of the scene—it was unheard of for a battle of that magnitude to break out in the middle of a college apartment block between unsanctioned supers. The Summit made a point to track down powerful supers and sweep them up into their ranks. Whoever was involved in this fight—instigator and otherwise—would be getting a visit from the Summit.

The bulk of the workers had gathered in the hallway of the third floor. The colors of medics and firefighters were all but gone now, leaving only a handful of police officers; the scene was dominated by men and women in suits.

Hunter and Serenity waded through them until they reached a line of caution tape marking room 449. Serenity introduced herself and her partner as they stepped into the apartment.

The main living area of the apartment looked like a standard issue college apartment, except for the stretcher near the fire escape. *Someone* was covered up with a white sheet—there was a depression in the center of the body like a hole had been blasted through, but there was no blood on the sheet to mark it. Four pale men in black suits stood guard around it.

The only other things out of place was the broken machinery that surrounded the dining room table. It looked like some of the equipment had been knocked over and hastily swept under the table—presumably by the agents. Serenity stooped down to examine it. It looked like radio equipment, but she couldn't be sure.

Inside, the bedroom looked like a bomb had gone off. There was a hole in the wall as wide as the entire room and part of the floor was mangled, almost to the point of caving in. Two fist-sized holes had been punched completely through. The rest of the floor was covered in broken boards and blood. So much blood that it was hard to tell the original color of the floor.

Serenity had seen enough crime scenes in her time with the Summit—if this had been a true fight between superhumans, it wouldn't have been confined to one room.

Someone had been brutalized here.

While Hunter Nine studied the scene. Serenity walked up to one of the DSA officers that she recognized.

"Special Agent Bernard, glad you're here."

Agent Bernard had been with the Division of Superhuman Affairs since Serenity's mother was a cape. He'd put on a little weight since they'd last seen each other and his thick mustache was completely gray now. In many respects, the man was like an uncle to her.

Despite his professional appearance, Bernard flashed a small smile. "Serenity, wish the circumstances were better." He glanced in Hunter Nine's direction and rolled his eyes without saying a word.

Serenity smirked. "Does the team know what happened here yet?"

Bernard gestured as he narrated. "The struggle looks contained to this one bedroom. Impacts knocked over some things in the living room and the next-door apartment. But we've also got bloody bullet fragments in the bathroom trash. There's no sign of forced entry on the front door, but there *is* on the bedroom door." He pointed to the wall. "Something or someone came through the wall—that's what all this scrap is from. A flying super, maybe..."

Bernard pointed at another hole in the roof. "There's one more thing. A large caliber slug came through the roof, presumably killing one of the combatants. Our men dug fragments out of the lawn. The exit hole was destroyed when the rest of the wall came down."

"A flying super," Serenity said to herself, "or an aircraft of some kind."

Hunter Nine had walked over now, practically seething. "So—where are they? Do we have any leads? Any witnesses?"

"A few students that were outside said they heard the fight, heard a gunshot, then saw the wall break, but they didn't see any super—flying or otherwise."

Hunter muttered something under his breath. "We'll need the names of everyone who lived in the apartment."

Bernard rightly looked to Serenity for permission. "What's your take on this?"

In most superhuman matters, the Summit and its psychics would have final say in any dissemination of information.

Serenity folded her arms across her chest. "Whoever was involved endangered civilians—there's no keeping this quiet. You can tell both of us."

Bernard flipped through an old notepad. "The college shows two seniors in the apartment: Lachlan Harris and Emmett Laraway."

Hunter Nine's ring glowed a sickening green as he stored the information inside it. It was his own magical notepad that could even store limited amounts of memories within it. That was supposedly how the bearer of one of the magic rings of Shelok inherently learned how to use their magic.

Hunter nodded with satisfaction, then pointed to the stretch on the other side of the apartment. "Which one is that?"

Now Bernard looked to the pale men in suits that surrounded it. All four of them stared at Hunter—their blank faces and dead eyes sending a chill down Serenity's neck. It was a challenge: The Summit's authority vs their employer.

The men were corporate goons, and only one corporation employed people that looked like *that*.

Hunter barged up to the group, completely unperturbed by their act. He stopped just in front of them.

"One way or another, the Summit is going to find out which dead guy you're hiding. We'll be following up with their families and any other contacts. Either way, we'll know. But before that, I'll make sure my boss pays a phone call to yours. Then you can explain to them why you've wasted the time of so many fucking people."

The gaunt man in front answered flatly, "Lachlan Harris was an employee. In the event of his death, his remains become property of Gnosis. Will that be all?"

Hunter scowled, but seemed to realize that he wouldn't get any other information out of Gnosis's goons.

Serenity spoke up. "Will you be notifying Mr. Harris's next of kin? Or does that responsibility fall to the Summit or the DSA?"

The man turned his unblinking gaze toward Serenity. "Our responsibility ends with his remains."

"Charming," Serenity muttered under her breath.

Hunter stalked away from the goons and back into the bedroom.

Serenity turned back to Bernard. "Is that really how it is? The DSA is just going to let them take one of the victims?"

Bernard glanced at the goons, then quickly away. They were still staring.

His face was wrinkled in dissatisfaction. "My hands are tied. Same as yours."

"That's not just a victim, though. He's evidence."

Bernard shook his head. "I'm not risking my job for evidence that the DSA can recover later."

Serenity huffed. "Even if the DSA can work their legal magic, who knows what they'll do to his body in the meantime..."

"Sorry," Bernard said with a frown. In that moment, Serenity saw the weight of years on his shoulders. He had the look of a man who'd been caught between organizations like the DSA, the Summit, and Gnosis for far longer than anyone should—like he'd been pulled to and fro and nearly pulled apart by it.

Serenity turned and walked up to the group of Gnosis henchmen. "He hasn't been dead long. I'd appreciate it if you let me read his last memories before they're completely gone..."

Serenity trailed off because she felt a quiet psychic presence from the *supposedly* dead man. It felt like he was in a coma or a state of suspended animation. Still, it was a weak enough presence that Serenity would need to touch him to gain anything useful; he might as well have been dead.

The henchmen stared at her blankly. It had been a stretch to ask, but Serenity took their silence as a reluctant agreement.

She reached out a hand to touch the deceased—

The closest henchman seized her wrist. His speed and strength caught her completely off guard.

Instinctively, Serenity tried to pull her hand back, but couldn't. He merely held her by the wrist, but was so strong that she couldn't move her arm at all.

Serenity opened her mouth to demand her release, but froze. She'd reflexively reached out with her powers and touched his mind.

And it took everything she had not to scream.

HIs mind was a wasteland. Forests of blackened trees that wept blood. All around the world was heavy with emptiness, like air before a storm. And when the wind came, it howled with insatiable hunger—

"Lachlan Harris is ours," The man said, interrupting her power. "His body *and* his mind."

As soon as he released her, Serenity stepped back. She quickly composed herself before walking away.

Bernard asked, "Are you alright…" But Serenity recoiled from his touch. She didn't stop to apologize.

Serenity walked out of the apartment and down the stairs to the open air of the lawn. She put her arms over her head and focused on her breathing.

She wasn't sure if the DSA or the Summit would get Lachlan Harris's body back. All Serenity knew was that she wanted no part of it or anything else to do with Gnosis.

Some minutes later—she wasn't sure exactly how long—Hunter Nine found her.

"What was that about? Bernard said you looked like you'd seen a ghost."

Serenity must've looked worse than she realized; Hunter almost sounded concerned.

Serenity shook her head. She would try to explain to Hunter exactly what she felt, but it was like trying to remember a half-forgotten dream. And it reminded her of what it was like to read the mind of a dead man or someone from a hive-mind—

Someone *empty.*

Chapter 52

The Cost of Doing Business

Light came first. Then the sound of steady beeping.

Emmett had been in and out a couple times before finally waking up. Each time he didn't last long before passing out again. He felt like he was swimming...

This time though, Emmett managed to stay awake.

A small measure of relief washed over him as he took in his surroundings. He was lying inclined in a hospital bed, but surrounded by familiar, sterile metal.

He was in section 006—the biolab. He'd woken up here enough times over the last two months that it almost felt like a second home... Or it might have, if not for recent revelations about Dr. Venture. For now, Emmett pushed the thoughts of betrayal and secrets aside and just breathed. He was still coming off the effects of the sedatives and trying to recall what happened.

He remembered Lock coming back to the apartment and attacking him. He remembered the pain—vividly. Lock had injured Emmett's left arm—his good arm—and his right leg.

Emmett looked down at the white blanket covering his body and apprehension settled over him like a cold fog. He tried to lift his left arm, but he couldn't. Worriedly, he tried moving his fingers and found that they moved, but just barely. He tried to look around the room but the right side of his vision was blurry.

"TINA..." Emmett said in a shaky voice.

"Remain calm. I've alerted Dr. Venture and Clara that you've woken up. They will be here shortly."

A few panicked breaths later, and Emmett heard the door to the room slide open with a *hiss.*

Clara slid a chair over beside his bed and leaned her head on his shoulder. Emmett relaxed at both her touch and the realization that he could feel her hand squeezing his forearm. When she finally looked up at him, her face was a mixture of red eyes and a smile.

"I thought I told you to wait for me before you blew something else up?"

With the mix of things Emmett was feeling, all that came out was his own mixture of a scoff and a laugh. He was just glad to see her.

Dr. Venture stepped into view and cleared his throat, and much of the mirth drained from Emmett's chest. It might have been his imagination, but Venture didn't look much better than Clara.

"How are you feeling?" Venture asked.

Emmett swallowed dryly. "I can't lift my arm."

Venture nodded, then launched into an explanation. "The damage from your fight with Lachlan was *extensive*, to put it plainly. Your left arm was torn off at the shoulder. Both your legs below the knee were crushed. Your skull was fractured. Without your enhancements, you likely wouldn't have survived the trip back to the lab.

"Still, the damage to your limbs was too much to fix with mutagens and nanites. TINA and I were able to fit you with prosthetics similar to your right arm. The procedures are complete, but your nerves are still integrating. Now that you're awake, we'll get you started in the Gray Room to speed along your recovery."

Emmett's mouth was hanging open as he listened. He had known in his gut that things had gone bad at the apartment, but he would've never imagined that they were *that* bad. Both of his arms had been replaced, and almost all of his legs. If not for Venture's prosthetics, Emmett would be a quadruple amputee.

How much of his body was even left?

Venture continued, unperturbed. "Your skull was another problem and part of why you've been out for five days... The blow to your head crushed several bones on the right side of your face... We had to replace your eye. Thankfully, the connection to your ocular nerve is stable and should get better over the next few days..."

Emmett forced himself to focus on Dr. Venture, not the blur on the right side of his vision.

"The blow also caused a brain bleed and swelling—out of all of your injuries, this one was the most dangerous. It took two surgeries and a series of nanites to correct. We'll need to do tests over the next few weeks to make sure your healing has gone satisfactory, but the initial scans look like you're in the clear."

Emmett sighed. This was three times that he owed Dr. Venture his life. But as grateful as Emmett was, he honestly didn't know if it changed how he felt about Venture.

After a moment, Emmett said, "Thanks," and hoped Venture understood.

Venture nodded, then glanced nervously at Clara before saying, "I'll give you two a few minutes to catch up."

Emmett called after him. "Did you tell her what happened?"

Venture paused and nodded before leaving.

Clara confirmed, "He told me everything."

Emmett and Clara stared at each other in silence. Emmett was afraid to speak—it felt like if he did, it would be like pulling the plug on a bathtub. He'd blubber and wasn't sure what would come out.

Clara's lip trembled like she was feeling much the same.

In a way, it felt like an inverted version of what Emmett had felt with Lock. There was so much that needed to be said between them, but neither could give voice to any of it. Neither knew where to start. And it wasn't just then, Emmett had felt something similar with his family too.

Was that really how things were going to be? He couldn't fix things with Lock... But it didn't have to be that way with his family or Clara.

"I'm glad you're alright," Emmett said with a smirk.

Clara scoffed and socked him playfully on the arm. "Me?! I'm glad *you're* alright."

"Venture just put me in a hospital bed, not in some enormous containment chamber."

Clara grinned and shrugged. "You're just not as cool as me."

"What are you talking about? I'm cooler. You have fusion power or something."

"Alright, alright, fine. You're *cooler*." Clara's mirth faded and she glanced at the floor. "...I'm sorry about my dad, and about lying to you about Lock. It wasn't right to keep that from you."

Emmett shrugged. "Secrets are part of the business."

"They shouldn't have to be."

"Yeah, but when has the world made that much sense?"

The pair shared an awkward laugh. Then Emmett asked, "Have you heard from anyone else?"

Clara nodded. "Everyone's licking their wounds, but they're fine. Dad spoke with Athena and reassured her about our conditions. McGuire texted your phone, asking pretty much the same thing, and I texted him back—I hope you don't mind. Also, your family is getting together for another dinner this weekend... or maybe it was next weekend."

Emmett smiled and shrugged. "It's fine. Thanks."

He nearly asked if Lock had texted, but caught himself.

"What... What happened to Lock?"

Clara shifted uneasily. "The nanites you made worked. They eventually froze him when you were fighting, but Lock still almost killed you. Dad had heavy drones on standby and shot him... Dad seems to think that Lock is still alive, though I don't know how he could be between all that. Gnosis claimed his body."

Emmett tried to sit up further on the bed, but failed. "What do you mean?"

Clara just shook her head in defeat. "He had mutagens in his system."

She said it with such finality—like there was no other justification needed. It made Emmett's stomach turn.

Gnosis did this to him. They pumped him full of mutagens and turned him into a weapon. Even though they knew that Mutagen-X would eventually turn him crazy. Even though they knew he would die.

Lock was Emmett's friend. Despite fighting each other, Emmett *knew* that things would've been different.

His friend didn't have to die. It wasn't right.

Emmett clenched his fists, and his words were a quiet threat. "They can't get away with this."

Clara stayed silent. Emmett knew what she was thinking though:

What could he do against Gnosis?

Right now, not much. But even if Emmett couldn't do anything now, he wasn't going to stay a Class 1 super.

Clara asked, "What are you going to do now?"

Emmett sighed. "I guess I'm going to stay here for a few more days because I can't really move. But after that, I don't know. I need some time to think things over and make sure this is really what I want."

TINA chimed in. *"If you decide not to continue being a mask or a cape, then Dr. Venture and I can exchange your prosthetics for civilian-appropriate ones."*

Clara's eyes widened. "Would you really stop? I thought this was what you've wanted for, like, forever?"

Emmett smiled awkwardly. "I want to continue being a mask... I meant, I'm not sure if I want to keep working with Dr. Venture."

Emmett hated the words before he finished saying it, even before he saw Clara's sad reaction.

"Don't worry," Emmett added. "Even if I don't come back to the lab because of your dad, I hope we can still keep talking and still keep patrolling the city... I hope that wouldn't change anything between us."

"You know it would though."

He knew it. Clara knew it—if Emmett left the lab, nothing would stay the same.

For a long moment, neither of them spoke and other realizations seeped in to replace Emmett's turmoil.

"Oh, man... What day is it? What have I missed?"

"It's 3:26, Monday afternoon," TINA said. *"Dr. Venture took the liberty of forging you a doctor's note in the chance that it's needed."*

Clara interrupted. "The bigger issue is your apartment got trashed, and the Summit and the Division of Superhuman Affairs are looking into it." Clara paused like there was something else she wasn't telling him.

"Please, just tell me all of it."

"One of the members of the Summit is coming to pay Dad a visit... and he wants to talk to you, too."

Chapter 53

Venture / Ultimatum

A mixture of cameras, spectroscopes, radio beacons, hyperlight monitors, pressure sensors, and even magical scanners surrounded Venture's lab. All of these extended out across several blocks and covered every known spectrum of existence in a complex web that only an entity like TINA could manage.

Wight had sent word to Venture through official Summit channels that he was going to pay a visit. He'd kept it short and to the point, not giving Venture any hint of what kind of visit to expect.

Venture's apprehension grew as he watched Wight walk the block toward the lab. But he didn't know for certain that something was wrong until Wight didn't ask permission to enter—

He just phased through Venture's front door.

So much for pleasantries...

Wight was the type of super that did everything with purpose, including things like letting surveillance cameras see him or asking permission to enter.

Wight wanted Venture to see him coming and to realize that there was nothing he could do to stop him. Even if Venture couldn't keep him out of the lab, he briefly considered summoning an exosuit—he had a few specifically built to counter Wight's powers, but it would send the wrong message.

Instead, Venture poured a gin and tonic and waited for his guest.

Wight phased through the door to 001 and stepped into Venture's living room. The spymaster of the Summit of Heroes kept a straight face, but his eye was twitching, which meant that he was hiding his irritation. Venture clutched his drink tight and swallowed dryly.

It had been a long time since he'd seen Wight about to lose his temper.

Venture defaulted to awkward humor as a defense mechanism. "You look like you're ready to rip out my heart or my windpipe. Which is it?" Both of those, he could do.

Wight scoffed. "Oh, no. Next time you test me, I'm going to reinstate you back into the Summit. Forcibly. Then you can answer to Amarque and Paragon."

That was worse.

Wight walked over to the bar and mixed himself a drink. "Do you have any idea of the shit storm you're bringing down on yourself?"

Venture relaxed slightly, but still clutched his drink. "I can guess."

"I know all about the scene at the Woods apartments. Is that your idea of lying low and keeping your kids out of trouble?"

Venture took a long sip of his drink to collect his thoughts. "...Is that your idea of maintaining a crime scene? Just letting Gnosis walk off with the evidence?"

Wight smirked—a foreboding look on the spymaster. "Gnosis wants your boy. I have half a mind to give him up as a peace offering."

"That's not a peace offering, that's capitulation."

Wight sipped his drink casually, punctuating his threat. "The Summit wants *you.*"

Venture chuckled. "Those are shit choices, and frankly, I'm insulted. What else can I give you to make you go away?"

"It's not me you have to appease. It's Gnosis, Amarque, and Paragon."

Venture swirled his drink. "I don't give a shit what Gnosis wants."

"Fine. But either way, I'm not going to save you."

Venture paused, then downed the rest of his drink in one gulp. It didn't help what he was about to do..

"I can give you the location of the super who attacked Amarque."

Wight's eyebrows raised and, for a moment, he looked genuinely impressed. "How?"

Venture shook his head. His cellphone tracking techniques had proved fruitful. The super that attacked Amarque had been part of a much smaller operation than the mutagen smuggling one.

Finally, he said, "I got lucky."

Wight scoffed. "Bullshit. Fine. Even if we can't catch the ringleaders, we can make an example of her."

Venture felt a pang of sympathy for the super known as Pythia, but it was gone the next time Wight spoke.

"I want to talk to the boy."

"...I'm not sure that's—"

"I wasn't asking, Magnus."

Venture held up a hand in surrender. "I meant that he's having a heart to heart with someone right now. Give them ten minutes to wrap up."

Wight sighed, but relented.

Emmett *tried* to push himself up further in the hospital bed, but the weakness in his arms wasn't something he could just overcome. Any other time he would've stood.

So he gave up and leaned back on the inclined bed. Both he and Clara eyed the two men that entered. The first was Dr. Venture, looking slightly more disheveled than usual. His lab coat was undone and his hair looked like he'd just smoothed it back and it wouldn't hold for long.

The second man looked... unremarkable. He might've been a little taller than average, and definitely wasn't built like most supers. Or dressed like it. He wore a plain brown sweater and slacks.

The man looked over both Emmett and Clara with an unsettling indifference. He had clearly come here with a purpose, but the way he looked at them made Emmett think he was ready to discard them both.

Even worse was how unsettled Venture looked. He shifted uneasily and sweat beaded on his forehead.

Venture cleared his throat. "Clara, you can go."

"No. She stays." The man spoke calmly but definitively. He didn't look over to acknowledge Dr. Venture at all before he continued, "Clara Venture, Emmett Laraway, the Summit of Heroes knows about both of you. I'm a member of the Summit, and their representative. You can call me Wight."

Emmett froze, and not because Wight knew his name. Wight wasn't *just* a member of the Summit.

"Forgive me if I don't shake your hand," Emmett said as evenly as he could manage, then quickly added, "sir."

"Nerve damage," Venture offered in Emmett's defense.

Wight didn't look like he cared. "Do you know who I am?"

Wight was one of the highest members of the Summit of Heroes. Someone who stood beside supers like Paragon and Amarque and Kronos and Aeon—all of whom could flatten cities. He was also the closest thing to a real-life boogeyman.

No one knew who Wight really was—supposedly not even the other members of the Summit—or what the limits of his powers were.

If Emmett wasn't terrified, he might've tried to convey that he *understood* who Wight was, but all Emmett managed was a nod. He was vaguely aware of Clara nodding similarly.

Wight made a small grunt of approval. "The Summit and the DSA keep their eyes on promising new supers. Magnus did an impressive job hiding you from our notice, but that's over now. Both your powers and your exploits have grown too much for our organizations to ignore.

"Someday you will be offered the choice between staying a mask or becoming a registered cape. One of those choices will take you further than the other."

Clara asked, "But you're not offering us that choice right now?"

"I'm giving you time to come to your senses. The Summit isn't the only group that keeps its eyes on new supers. One day you might get propositioned by an organization like Gnosis, and you won't find them as accommodating."

At the mention of Gnosis, Emmett found his voice again. "They took my friend's body."

"I'm sorry to hear that."

Emmett tried to find the words, but Wight's stare was immutable. He didn't bother asking whether the Summit could get Lock back. But his questions didn't end there—there were more important things to consider.

Emmett asked, "If Gnosis and the Summit know our names, then will our families be alright?"

Wight eyed Emmett as he spoke. "We have surveillance on them now, but I suspect they're safe from Gnosis. But they'll also be fielding questions from Summit patrols about your whereabouts."

"That doesn't make any sense," Clara said. "You already know who we are. Why would you ask them anything?"

Venture chimed in, surprising everyone except Wight. "Because this is also an interview."

Wight sighed. "Don't be so dramatic, Magnus." He regarded Clara and Emmett before continuing. "I extend your father certain courtesies, but those are nearing an end. I kept Clara's secret safe, but I can't hide either of your actions any longer.

"Low-ranking members of the Summit have opened an investigation into reports of an artificer and a cyborg—the pair of which have been involved in a fight with Summit capes, the destruction of a warehouse building, as well as the death of a student and destruction of college property.

"I'm betting you can hide from the Summit long enough to make up your mind about registration. But know this, sooner or later, you will need to choose which organization you work for. Personally, I hope you both choose to join the Summit."

Wight turned and walked away, bidding Dr. Venture goodbye as he phased through the door.

Emmett slumped a little further down in the bed.

Somehow he'd managed to get caught between Gnosis and the Summit of Heroes. And that did not make his feelings about working for Venture any less complicated.

Venture had turned to watch one of the wall screens. He was watching Wight's path through the lab, presumably making sure the ghost actually left.

"Cheer up," Venture said dryly. "Most people don't get that much of a choice. And solo masks don't have long careers."

Emmett turned to Clara, who was staring blank-faced at where Wight had been. "What do you think?" he asked.

Clara sat down on the edge of his bed and leaned forward to rest her chin on her hands. When she finally spoke, her voice felt small as the flame of a candle.

"I don't know."

Chapter 54

Alias, Pythia / Clara

Ash stacked her blueprints and notes on the end of the kitchen table. It was nothing definitive, just potential candidates. Another tech business, a high end art boutique, a low level Summit station, a pub for villains and mobsters...Jobs that could wait a little longer.

Then Ash brought the red velvet cake out of the refrigerator, as well as saucers, forks, and a knife.

The timing was impeccable.

Carter walked out of their bedroom, pulled their robe and rubbed their eyes. They stopped cold when they saw the cake. Their smile widened and they ran over to embrace Ash.

"What's the occasion?" Carter asked, face buried in Ash's neck.

Ash held them tight and almost forgot to answer.

"Nothing."

Carter scoffed and leaned back to stare at them. "What do you mean, nothing?"

"I just... wanted to do something for you."

"Uh huh... This isn't a pre-apology cake for the next job?" Carter's voice was a tumultuous mix of joking and serious.

Still, the accusation hurt. "No. I... don't have another one yet."

Carter must've seen because they rubbed Ash's arms to reassure them. "I know you. You'll figure something out. Now—if you don't mind—my thoughtful partner baked me my favorite dessert, and I should like to try a piece."

Ash snorted a laugh and made a sweeping gesture for both of them to take their seats. Then Ash served them both a slice.

Ash had tweaked the recipe over the last two years, and it tasted like it was finally *right*. Carter sighed in approval.

"You can't keep playing with my emotions like this, especially with cake," Carter said. "I'll get fat."

"It's *happy weight,*" Ash said, savoring a bite.

Carter rolled their eyes and laughed.

Ash's mother used to talk about how she put on weight after meeting Ash's father. *Happy weight,* she called it. Dad made her happy. For a while, at least.

Ash hoped they could do the same for Carter. Recently there had been too much work and not enough cake. Ash resolved to change that.

"We should go to the gym tomorrow," Carter said, gesturing at the cake with her fork. "Burn some of this off."

"Together?"

"You know what I mean. Go together. You do your thing. I do the treadmill."

Ash grinned. "I can do that. What about tonight?"

"*What about* tonight? It's Tuesday night... Unless your idea includes something that has me in bed by nine—"

Ash raised an eyebrow, and Carter pointed to their cake.

"I'm sorry. My partner made me this delicious cake, and I plan to eat all of it because I'm happy."

For a moment, the apartment was filled with laughter. It was probably wrong of Ash to use cake in such a manner, but they were ready to do whatever it took to make Carter happy. To keep Carter happy.

Everything else came secondary.

It felt like things had turned around between the two of them, like a ship righting itself after a storm, or like two stars who'd finally settled into orbit.

In their tiny apartment, Ash and Carter ate cake and laughed, and forgot everything else but each other.

It was just the two of them. Until it wasn't.

Ash froze mid-bite. They were looking over Carter's shoulder at a man standing just inside their apartment door.

He wasn't dressed like a burglar—he wore a drab sweater and slacks, and kept his hands clasped behind his back. He wasn't wearing any kind of mask—not bothering to hide any of his features.

The door had been locked—was *still* locked. Ash hadn't heard it open. Neither of them had.

He was a super, and there was only one reason he was here.

Carter's face wrinkled in confusion. "What's wrong?" They turned around and gasped. In a panic, Carter hurled their saucer and sliver of cake at the super.

Both things phased through him. The saucer shattered against the door. He didn't even flinch.

In the same breath, Ash stood and grabbed the cake knife and stepped in front of Carter. Ash held poison in one hand and leveled the knife in the other. "Who the fuck are you?"

"Ash Harris, the Summit of Heroes knows about you. About your involvement in criminal operations in Belport, including the Donjon club attack, and the attack on Aquarius's headquarters."

The man's face was eerily calm as he spoke, like he knew that there was absolutely nothing that Ash could do. They couldn't run, and they couldn't hide—not anymore.

Ash's heart was pounding so hard it felt like it was going to leap out of their chest. Tears streamed down their face. Carter was hysterical.

It felt like watching the sun burn out.

"I'm a member of the Summit, and their representative. My name is Wight."

Ash listened, but the super's voice felt distant. Carter felt distant. Wight requested they put down the knife and let go of their poison, and Ash complied. They had the building surrounded. Ash heard all this, but barely.

Wight unlocked the apartment door, and Summit and DSA agents filed in to apprehend Ash. Their hands were bound and their heads bagged, and then they were led out of the building while more agents filed in to search the apartment.

Ash was led down the stairs, past the murmurs from the laundromat, and onto the street, then put in the back of an armored car. The last thing they saw outside was Carter was being put in the back of a plain police cruiser.

The doors shut and the clang brought them back to the moment. Ash's new world was tiny and dark. They were alone. Carter was gone—the light had gone out from Ash's world.

It was over.

It was over.

It was over.

Clara dragged her feet on the way from the Gray Room to the living quarters. She'd been training when her dad requested her presence *to talk*.

They'd already discussed her meltdown and reviewed her parts of the warehouse battle. There was only one other thing to talk about, and they'd both avoided the subject.

She found her dad reclining on the couch, drink in hand.

"You've been doing that a lot lately," she said, pointing to the glass. She dropped down on the couch across from him and stuffed her hands in her hoodie.

Venture swirled his drink. "I guess I have been. I assure you, I know my limits."

Clara didn't believe that for a second, but there was no telling that to her dad.

Venture asked, "How are you feeling?"

"I'm fine." Physically, that was the truth. Despite the meltdown, her body had recovered. In every other way though—mentally, emotionally—she felt raw.

"What did you want to talk about?" she asked, quickly changing the subject.

Venture swirled his glass, then tried to meet her eyes. "I'm sorry about Emmett. I should have listened to you; I should have told him about Lachlan. And I'm sorry if my mistakes affect your friendship with him."

That was different. Maybe he was turning over a new leaf. Did it really help anything though? Apologies didn't amount to much after the damage was done. Clara knew that, first hand.

She nodded, but couldn't look her dad in the eye. "Our decisions always affect others, right?" It was a platitude, one her dad was fond of using.

Venture looked dejected, like he'd taken her dismissal to heart.

Clara wasn't sure how she felt about that.

Venture finished his drink and then looked at the ice that was left. "What about you? What do you want to talk about?"

He'd seen right through her.

"I'm sorry too," she said, quietly.

"Why?"

"If Emmett leaves, I'm leaving too."

The ice abruptly stopped. "What? Clara... You can't be serious. Think about your condition."

"That's why I've been training all these years, right?"

Her father was leaning forward on the couch now, aghast. "Where would you go?"

"I'm not going anywhere. This is my home. Belport is my home."

"It's too dangerous."

"If I have a meltdown, I'll jump in the bay."

By now they were both standing and animated, but Venture didn't relent. "You couldn't stay here."

Clara scoffed. "What? Would you run me out of the city?"

"Clara—"

"Would you? ...Dad?"

Venture hung his head. He still clutched the glass, but the ice had fallen out onto the floor.

"I... I really messed up, didn't I?" He walked over to the counter and leaned on it for support. "Of course I wouldn't run you out of town. But the lab is the safest place for you. You know that."

Her dad wiped a tear from behind his glasses.

It had been a long time since Clara had seen him so broken up. Not since Mom left.

Clara leaned on the couch. "I was never going to stay here forever. I'm just moving out a little faster than we thought."

"Emmett hasn't said one way or another yet," Venture said quickly. The way he said it felt like he was still holding on to hope for both her and Emmett.

Clara nodded. She wanted to reassure her dad, but she couldn't bring herself to say anything.

Venture cleared his throat. "It's been a long day... We could put on a movie, or, uh, maybe some anime."

Clara managed a small smile.

"Sure, Dad."

Chapter 55

Funeral for a Friend

Emmett finished his lap around the Gray Room. It had taken a day and a half, but he was walking again despite the fact that both his lower legs and both his arms were prosthetics now.

He could probably even run, but Venture and TINA ordered him not to push it.

Just because his nerves had finished integrating, didn't mean his bones and sinew had. It would be another week before he would be running across rooftops and getting into random brawls with masks again.

Which was fine by Emmett. He had things to do in the meantime.

The most pressing of which was his late best friend's funeral.

Emmett left the Gray Room and walked the long hall to section 001. Venture had said he had something for Emmett—

And Emmett had to say goodbye.

Dr. Venture was standing in the living room, looking thoughtfully at the wall of monitors showing a sunrise over Belport. He snapped back to the present when Emmett entered the room.

"Here," he said, gesturing to a black suit hanging over the couch. "Everyone needs a good suit."

Some of the clothes hanging in Emmett's closet had been destroyed by debris from the fight with Lock. His dress suit was among them. Still, it was a few years old and probably wouldn't have fit anyway.

Emmett walked over and admired it. It was modest but well-made. Emmett didn't know what he had expected, but he was glad it wasn't flashy.

"Thanks."

Emmett meant it, but it didn't change anything. It didn't change the lies or the secrets. Didn't change the fact that his friend was dead—that Emmett was responsible.

Venture must've seen the turmoil on Emmett's face. "You don't have to make a decision right now," Venture said.

Emmett returned a small smile to the man that had been his mentor.

Venture was right. He didn't have to make a decision right now. But Emmett's mind was made up. At the very least, he needed some space.

Venture stuffed his hands in his pockets sheepishly. "I can understand what it's like to learn horrible things about the people close to you. I tell myself that everything I've done is to keep people safe—Clara, even you. But it's inevitable that we'll make the wrong call one day."

Emmett folded the suit over his arm and admired the weight as much as the feeling of it against his skin.

"What then?"

Venture replied, "All we can do is hope that people show us grace and forgiveness. That they give us the chance to make the right choices."

Emmett turned. "Goodbye, Dr. Venture."

Emmett thought he heard both TINA and his mentor say goodbye, but he was already walking away down the hall.

Emmett changed into his suit and stuffed his clothes in his backpack. Then he rode the bus across Belport.

He could've walked. He had plenty of time.

He hadn't ridden the bus much lately, not since he got powers. Not since all of this mess started.

Riding the bus seemed *fitting*.

Emmett sat down with his backpack on his lap. Then he put his earbuds in and put on his old synthwave playlist. *Leaves of Orion* by Starquake came on.

The music helped.

By the time Emmett got off the bus, he thought he was ready. By the time he walked to the church, he knew he wasn't.

His hands were shaking and it wasn't because they were both prosthetic.

The funeral service seemed small, consisting of a dozen family members and another two dozen friends and acquaintances. Emmett recognized some of Lock's friends from the party last month, as well as Lock's sister, Maya.

Emmett had only ever seen a picture of Maya, but the resemblance to her brother was uncanny. They almost looked like they could be twins, except that she seemed far more outgoing and animated than Lock had ever been.

He overheard a bit of her conversations—Maya wasn't moving back in with her parents. She was going to move in with friends. She might even leave Belport and start over somewhere else.

Emmett waited until a lull in the gathering to approach Maya and offer condolences.

She threw her arms around him.

Emmett hugged her while guilt welled up inside him.

"I just can't believe it," she said, finally pulling away. "I hope they catch the villain that did it. Catch him and put him away for good."

Emmett swallowed dryly.

The official story about what happened was that Lock had been murdered by a small-time villain. Of course, the villain was never caught, so the only hypothesis the police and DSA gave was that Lock must have gotten on the wrong side of a villain while bouncing at a club.

The casket at the back of the room was closed. Officially, Lock's body was being held by police for the investigation and he would be interred when it was over.

For a split second, Emmett considered telling her the truth about everything. About Gnosis, about him and Lock...

There was no way he could, of course. Telling Maya any of it would just put her in danger.

So Emmett just bit his tongue and nodded. "I hope they get him too."

Then she was gone, pulled away to another set of condolences.

Emmett took a seat and waited for the pastor to start. All of a sudden, he was glad to not be talking to anyone else—

It didn't last long.

Two of Lock's friends from the party sat down beside Emmett. Manton was a friend from class, and Jessie had also worked at Gnosis—not in the same capacity as Lock.

Come to think of it, Jessie definitely had powers. She'd been showing them off that night at the party. Was she in the mutagen program, had she gotten a hold of a knock-off vial, or had she just been a super all along? Not that it mattered—he couldn't just ask her.

Manton pushed up his thick glasses. "How are you holding up?"

The question shook Emmett out of his trance. He shrugged. "Alright enough."

Jessie interjected with a hushed whisper, "Tell me about it! I'm still in shock. It hasn't set in yet. Hey Manton, have you heard from Carter?"

Manton shook his head. "No. They aren't answering."

Jessie sighed. "I can't get ahold of Ash, either. I hope they didn't forget."

Manton replied, "That's not like them. Something must've come up."

"You're probably right."

Manton and Jessie kept talking amongst themselves and Emmett half-listened until the pastor stepped up to start the service.

The pastor was a weathered man, who clutched the podium until his knuckles were white. Despite looking frail, his voice was steady, and Emmett imagined he'd presided over lots of funerals. That he'd sent many on their way to whatever was waiting for them.

"Lachlan Harris was a bouncer. He was a student. A friend. A son and a brother. I didn't know him as well as some of you, but everyone agreed that he was quiet and hard. Perhaps stoic is a better word..."

Emmett half-listened while the pastor spoke. His eyes flitted from the grieving crowd, to his hands clasped in his lap, to the empty casket, and back again. The pastor invited people to stand and talk about a cherished memory with Lock. A few did, sharing times from when he was a boy, or when someone told a joke and everyone laughed but Lock. Jessie stood and shared a time Lock had escorted her home after a party.

Emmett didn't stand, but he did think about their time together: Nights hanging out on the roof, venting about schoolwork over takeout... But it was hard to look back on those innocent times now that Emmett knew the truth.

They'd both been playing the game. Keeping secrets from one another.

Just a few weeks ago, they'd sat down to watch TV together—the very same night that Lock had killed Porcelain with his bare hands.

Emmett was still angry at Lock for lying to him, but Emmett had been doing the same thing. They'd both been playing the game. Hiding things, protecting corporations...

Emmett clenched his prosthetic fists.

He fucking hated it. All of it.

It wasn't a game. It was a joke. The world of supers and cabals and corporations... Just because the world was at a stalemate between all those powers didn't mean that it should stay that way.

And just because Emmett was a super didn't mean that he had to play by those rules. Maybe he could change something. Just because the game was bullshit didn't mean it had to stay that way.

Suddenly, Emmett realized what he wanted as a super, and he realized just how much further he had left to go.

As if on cue, the pastor launched into a sermon—using the death of Emmett's friend to guilt everyone into going to church. He somehow managed to spend most of the service talking about God rather than talking about the reason they were there. He continued for so long that he put supervillain monologues to shame. Emmett was pretty sure Lock didn't believe in God, but that was beside the point. To Emmett, it felt like one more organization profiting off the back of his friend.

Chapter 56

Moving On

University staff helped Emmett and several other students move into new apartments for the last few weeks of the semester.

It had been a smoother process than Emmett expected—if one ignored the sifting through the wreckage and the memories. While Emmett was there, he searched for any signs of surveillance from the Summit, Gnosis, or anyone else, but he didn't see anyone suspicious. The only other people there were the occasional carpenters and engineers working on rebuilding the damage.

Everyone responsible for what had happened was moving on.

Emmett was moved into an apartment in the Woods, just two buildings down from his old one. Jensen was a digital art major, and Michela was a bio major. They'd filled their apartment with all kinds of art, most being either made by Jensen or by others in his classes. Both were eager to help their new roommate get moved in. Emmett was able to set up his radio locator project in the corner of the living room and the rest of his things moved into the spare bedroom.

Classes and the process of relocating helped to keep Emmett's mind off recent events, at least for a few days. And Jensen and Michela were friendly enough, but it didn't take long for Emmett to get restless.

He made up a story about waiting tables to cover for his late night superheroics. Thankfully, Jensen and Michela didn't pry.

One night, Emmett went back to his old apartment. He didn't bother sneaking in through the caution tape. He just went around back and leapt up the side of the building, using his whip to haul himself up the rest of the way.

He walked the roof, just to make sure he was alone, then he unfolded one of the two lawn chairs that had been left behind. Emmett had neglected to check the roof while packing—the same night as the fight, Dr. Venture had used a heavy drone to transport Emmett's full-sized radio locator to the lab for safe keeping.

The roof looked a little barren without it, but it was fine for the moment. Emmett didn't need it.

What made him crack a small smile was that both his chair and Lock's chair were still there.

He sat down on the roof of his old apartment under the stars for the last time.

It was hard to believe that it was the end of April already. Emmett had been a super for almost two months. He was about to graduate.

Lock was gone.

Emmett never felt like he gave enough thought to the future. For so much of his life, he'd been going through the motions. Get good grades. Get out of high school. Get a job. Go to college. Graduate. Then presumably he was supposed to get another job. Get married. Get a house, and so on.

He was at the threshold of graduating, and it didn't feel quite real. Maybe it was because he'd expected Lock to be there with him. They'd even joked about getting another apartment.

That wasn't going to happen now.

Emmett stared up at the stars and chuckled darkly. "What happened to us, man?"

No one answered.

Emmett wasn't sure how long he stayed there thinking, about the events of the last two months and how things would be different. But finally he said one last goodbye and leapt off the roof.

And left both lawn chairs behind.

That same night, Emmett met Clara and McGuire on a roof on the outskirts of downtown and South Side. A nearby billboard for Pirouette perfume cast a neon glow on one side. His friends hid in the shadow cast by the back of the billboard, but Emmett saw them easily. While McGuire was around, Clara kept using the name Arsenal.

McGuire fiddled with his mask. "There he is and looking all put back together. Knew you would make it."

Arsenal stood up, her new exosuit eerily silent. "I hope you don't mind, but I filled McGuire in on what happened... How are you holding up?"

Emmett shrugged. "I'm alright."

"...*Riiight,*" McGuire replied. "It doesn't even sound like you believe that."

Emmett glanced at Arsenal, but her expression was unreadable behind her helmet.

"It's just that *everything* is going to be different now. I'm going to..." Emmett chose his words carefully, since McGuire was with them. "I need to get a new place and there's no way I can afford to live on my own. I'm not trying to move back home or move into the lab. I need some time to figure out what to do about work."

"Trouble in paradise?" McGuire asked.

Emmett snorted, but Arsenal was deathly silent. "More like trouble with the Doctor."

Arsenal cleared her throat. "You could say that."

McGuire nodded. "That complicates things. Don't you need him for your repairs?" McGuire gestured to Emmett's arm—then his other arm. Then his entire body.

Emmett sighed. "It's not like I'm cutting ties. I just need to figure out what to do now. I guess the biggest thing is to get a job and find a new place to live."

McGuire adjusted his backpack. "You know, I may have a solution for that, but it requires a lot of trust."

"Yeah?"

"A LOT of trust."

Emmett threw his hands up. "Tell me what it is first and then I can figure out if I'm agreeing to it or not."

Arsenal chuckled. "Alright, out with it, McGuire."

McGuire continued, "It just so happens that I have a spare room, and I could get you a job."

"Doing what?"

McGuire thought for a moment. "Something up your alley."

That didn't help Emmett make a decision, but then, they were at an impasse. There was no way to share an apartment and keep their identities secret. It was risky for Emmett to admit to needing a new place and for McGuire to say what he did for work. Both of those facts could narrow down their identities.

McGuire stuck out a gloved hand. "Let's shake on it."

Emmett smirked. There wasn't an easy way to get past that initial hurdle of trusting a fellow super, but he couldn't think of anything else.

"I'm about to graduate from Belport University. That's why I need a new place."

McGuire countered. "I work at a repair shop. You can handle that, right?"

"I'm interested. I was over on the West End."

McGuire nodded. "My place isn't far. It's outside of downtown."

"What about me?" Arsenal asked. "How many rooms do you have?"

Emmett had been so lost in thought that he almost forgot about Clara.

McGuire idly kicked a pebble across the roof, clearly not wanting to answer.

Arsenal crossed her arms in her exosuit. "Don't tell me this is a boys' club and there're no girls allowed."

McGuire held up his hands in defense. "Nothing like that. I *love* the ladies. Not you—I mean, you're great, it's just I figured you and Mod were a thing. Alright, scratch that... It's not about that, it's just... I don't think my mom is going to go for it."

Both Emmett and Arsenal snorted.

McGuire quickly retorted, "Hey, someone else was just talking about moving back home, so I don't want to hear it!"

Emmett waved a dismissive hand and wheezed. "Don't worry. My folks wouldn't go for it either."

Even Arsenal paused. "Yeah, I never asked Dad either."

McGuire's head swiveled comically fast. "The Doctor is your dad?!"

Arsenal shrugged in her exosuit. "Yeah. We're sharing secrets, right? Even if your mom doesn't let girls move in, I still want to be part of the group."

Both Emmett and McGuire replied over one another, before Emmett added, "Of course, you're included. Us tech supers have to stick together."

"Tech supers against the world!" McGuire shouted and punctuated by pumping his fist overhead. Then he promptly fixed his homemade mask again.

Suddenly, a shadow swooped down on them and passed overhead in a blink. Emmett caught just enough of a glimpse to realize that it was a giant bird so dark it looked like it was made out of ink.

It swooped around and landed on a nearby roof, right next to the supers Cherry and Larian. They stood defiantly—Cherry with her hands on her hips, and Larian making spellcasting signs with his hands. A black tree stood ominously behind them.

"Friends of yours?" Arsenal asked, her exosuit humming to life.

"Yeah, actually." McGuire waved to them, and Cherry hesitated before waving back.

Arsenal relaxed, but only a little. "Oh, in that case, hopefully they're here to spar."

Emmett just chuckled to himself. Maybe life after graduation wouldn't be so bad.

McGuire shouted across the roofs, "What are you guys up to tonight?"

Across the roofs, Larian was unreadable as he readied spells, but Cherry laughed. "I thought you'd never ask."

Epilogue

Venture

Venture cleaned himself up in the bathroom mirror while TINA checked over protocols in the case of his absence. Then Venture walked over to his bedroom, left his stained lab coat on the back of the deck chair, and grabbed a sweater. Then a different sweater.

The first one had reminded him of Wight.

He settled on a subdued blue and slipped it overhead before leaving the lab.

"Is everything ready, TINA?"

"I have double checked all systems and readied contingency protocols."

"Thank you."

He'd slowly gotten used to TINA's *appearance* of sentience and adjusted his manners accordingly. Better safe than sorry.

Besides, he felt more comfortable leaving the lab under her care now. TINA's systems had grown even more robust. Now he felt certain that there was nothing she couldn't adapt to in his absence.

Which was good because Dr. Venture was on his way to a meeting. So far, his hosts had played nice, but there was always the chance—however negligible—that Venture wouldn't return.

Venture climbed the final stairs and exited the lab. The midday sun nearly bowled him over, and Venture cursed while his glasses darkened.

He needed to get out more.

Venture sighed, and then he walked across the street to Gnosis's headquarters.

Technically, he was still under their employ, so he wasn't worried about the appearance of this meeting. So what if the Summit or the DSA knew? He didn't work for them anymore.

Of course, Venture's real position was *consultant*—a notoriously flexible label.

The main corridors of Gnosis bore only a passing resemblance to the horrific experiments they conducted. The basement of Gnosis was filled with monsters and blood. The main floors were trimmed in red and lined with abstract paintings, meant to evoke an otherworldly aesthetic.

Dr. Venture walked in the front door and was escorted to an office on the second floor. This room was no different from the rest of the upper floors—even the furniture was a blood red mahogany—but Venture was starting to suspect there was a deeper meaning to the swirling red art that adorned the walls.

To the untrained eye, the patterns were abstract and random, but Venture's eyes weren't ordinary. And he guessed that the patterns held significance for each of the founding members of the Gnosis corporation. Something between fingerprints and self portraits... written in blood.

Venture sat in front of the desk, taking in the intricate swirls on the walls, while he waited for the VP of Gnosis to arrive.

Ichabod didn't keep him waiting long.

There was the slightest wave of pheromones before he entered the room. TINA used nanites to adjust Venture's sense of smell so that he was only vaguely aware of the sensation. Otherwise, he'd be feeling a sense of acute fear and panic. Even that only hinted at the strength hidden within his biology. After all, he was one of the strongest supers in Belport... And one of the strongest of his species.

What most people knew about vampires was based solely on popular culture and the younger of their kind. Elders and ancient vampires were far more strange and terrifying.

Venture knew the truth, and he'd allied himself with them, anyway.

Ichabod entered the office and shut the door behind him, moving with the silence of the grave. He was a lanky giant of a man—pale and gaunt, as was normal for his kind. He'd taken to wearing foundation on his cheeks to blend in better, but neither that nor his jet-black hair made him look like anything but a walking skeleton.

He took a seat behind the blood red desk, sitting straight up at attention.

"It's over?"

Venture nodded and slouched back in his chair. "It's over."

"It was a doomed experiment, but we were able to get data. We'll find a different way forward. Thank you for getting rid of the evidence, both the warehouse and the saboteur."

The super that Venture gave up. "I gave Pythia to the Summit."

"I know."

Venture raised an eyebrow. "You're not worried they'll talk?'

"No."

Ichabod said it so absolutely that it made Venture's skin crawl. Of course Gnosis wasn't worried. They were too powerful to care about the testimony of a lone super—

If Pythia didn't have some kind of accident in the meantime.

Athena had once told Emmett that Gnosis corporation was far older than they appeared. They weren't just a biotech company—even Venture wasn't certain he knew the true extent of their business holdings. Athena was also correct that the Gnosis lineage could be traced back before one thousand BCE... But anything beyond five thousand BCE was conjecture. There simply weren't enough historical records that went back that far.

Gnosis might have some records dating that far back, but they didn't need them. Some of their elders were older than that.

Like everything else, Gnosis and their founders prioritized a *biological* advantage over everything else.

"It won't work," Venture said, surprising both of them.

The eyes of a predator settled on Venture. "Nature doesn't stop trying just because one attempt at evolution doesn't work."

"It wasn't one attempt... How many mutagens did you try this time?"

"A few dozen in Belport. A few dozen more in... other cities," Ichabod said indifferently.

"None promising?"

"None that warrant a letter."

Venture suppressed a smirk. He tried not to take joy in seeing allies fail.

Ichabod continued, "The board wanted to express their gratitude to you for uncovering a weakness of our flagship product. I understand it was your protégé that took down our asset?"

Venture rubbed his chin idly as he lied. "I came up with the solution. He merely used it." There was no reason to put all of Emmett's potential on the table.

Ichabod nodded. "Either way, you may choose your reward."

Venture made a show of thinking about his reply, but truthfully, he didn't care. There was nothing else Gnosis could offer him, and Venture didn't want to tie himself to them anymore than he already had.

Finally, Venture said, "I just want the money to stay the same and our mutual ceasefire to stay in place." He stood up to leave, then added, "And next time you're planning something like this, let me know *right away*. You could've saved us both a lot of headaches."

"Perhaps if you worked more closely with us..."

"Out of the question," Venture said with a sweep of his hand. "I can't be implicated."

Ichabod shrugged, and the gesture looked grotesque. "The future waits for no one, Dr. Venture. Not even you. One day my kind will reign again and no super will stand in our way. The masters of the past will become masters again of the future."

Venture smirked. "The future belongs to technology. It will usher in a new age. One day, we'll drag you—and everyone else—kicking and screaming into the future."

"So long as you don't drag us into the light. ...They call us monsters and machines while calling themselves gods. I'm with you, Magnus Venture, until the reign of the supers is no more. Then all truces will end."

Venture turned to leave. "Until then."

One day, the final war for Earth would come down to tech supers and horrors from humanity's past. Venture was betting on the former.

Then the world would finally be free.

SIMULATIONS

Mod V1.1 vs Katana aka "Sword-girl"

Mod briefly fought against the villain known as Katana during the raid on the mutagen warehouse. The battle inside the warehouse was chaotic and involved several supers, but enough data exists to simulate one-on-one engagements.

QUERY: How would Mod fare against Katana?

LOADING SIMULATIONS...

FIRST MATCH: Mod V1.1 vs Katana, wielder of *Pyre*

Thanks to his prosthetic arm, reinforced skeleton, and suffusion with Mutagen-A, Mod's physical strength is between a Class 1 and Class 2 rating. Physically, he is a match for Katana, who draws similar strength and durability from her magic sword.

Pyre, one of the lost flamebrands of the Solari Dominion, can cut through *most* mundane weapons and armor, though the impact shield designed by Dr.

Venture was able to withstand several direct strikes. However, it will not survive a prolonged assault.

Since upgrading the attachment rails in his prosthetic arm, Mod's versatility has grown dramatically. In that respect, he completely outclasses Katana, whose magical sword has not been fully unlocked yet. As such, Katana can only use basic slashes and a single ranged slash attack rather than its full magic arsenal.

RESULTS:
Scores out of 1,000 simulations...
Mod Victory — 458
Katana victory — 523
Double Incapacitation — 19

CONCLUSION:
Mod's victories hinge on the correct synergy of location, surprise, and flexibility. Indoor locations with debris and varied terrain offer the greatest advantages—any combination that allows Mod to use his full arsenal of gadgets to create openings or to overwhelm Katana.

Katana's victories hinge on open locations where there is little room to hide or maneuver around her. In these instances, she can maintain pressure with her ranged slashes and then finish off a wounded opponent up close.

NOTE: Margin of Error is factored into Katana's victory percentage to account for the chance that Pyre awakens in the middle of battle.

QUERY: Does a fully unlocked flamebrand alter Katana's chances of victory?

LOADING SIMULATIONS...

FOLLOW-UP MATCH: Mod Vi.i vs Katana, wielder of fully-un-locked *Pyre Immensus*

ERROR: UNKNOWN VARIABLES
Pyre Immensus

SIMULATIONS

Clara Exosuit F-3 vs Tendril aka "Hair-girl" [One on One Rematch]

Clara briefly engaged the villain known as Tendril during a heist of mutagen variants. Enough data exists to simulate one-on-one engagements.

QUERY: How would Clara's Exosuit F-3 fare in a one-on-one match against Tendril?

LOADING SIMULATIONS...

FIRST MATCH: CLARA EXOSUIT F-3 VS TENDRIL

Clara's Exosuit model F-3 is optimized to channel her innate power into controlled energy. In that respect, Clara outclasses her opponent in firepower, speed, maneuverability, and flexibility. In most arenas, Clara is able to stay out of reach of Tendril and pummel them from afar.

However, in close quarters and enclosed venues, Tendril's strength and stamina are overwhelming. Even with Clara's additional gadgets, Tendril wins.

RESULTS:

Scores out of 1,000 simulations...
Clara Victory – 782
Tendril Victory – 218

CONCLUSION:

At full power, Clara's Exosuit and firepower are too much for most equally classed supers to overcome. These results come as no surprise.

NOTE: Scores are measured for incapacitation of Clara's Exosuit. Meltdowns excluded from results.

QUERY: How does Clara fare if she's forced to fight at 50% power?

LOADING SIMULATIONS...
"TINA, that's enough. Cancel request."

CANCELLING REQUEST

SPECIAL NOTE: Hopefully Clara won't have to handicap herself much longer.

SPECIAL NOTE 2: Tendril's physicality in confined arenas is impressive. Though the transformation is grotesque, it's surprising that Gnosis does not use this mutagen more often. Reports of its use in civilian and military applications are scarce...

SIMULATIONS

Mod V2 vs Mod V1

Mod's body and capabilities changed drastically between his inciting incident on Champion street and his injuries at the hands of Lock after the warehouse mission. These two events serve as lines of delineation in Mod's capabilities.

From here on, Mod's original Mutagen-A suffusion and prosthetic arm are labeled as V1. Mod's numerous mutagen variants, nanite infusions, skeleton enhancement, and rail attachment system are labeled as V1.1. Mod's quadruple prosthetics and ocular implant are labeled as V2.

QUERY: How would Mod's original V1 body compare to his second iteration of prosthetics and enhancements?

LOADING SIMULATIONS...

FIRST MATCH: Mod V2 vs Mod V1

In every measure, Mod's original version is outclassed by his new upgrades.
Strength...
Speed...

Stamina...

Durability...

Healing factor...

Combat knowledge...

The differences in capabilities are not as stark as the comparisons evident in [Mod V1 vs Lock M-X], but the results are similar.

RESULTS:

Scores out of 1,000 simulations...

Mod V2 Victory — 995

Mod V1 Victory — 5

CONCLUSION:

In every simulation, Mod's second iteration achieves victory over his original body.

Mod V2's prosthetics are too powerful for Mod V1 to overcome. Mod V2's arsenal of attachments and gadgets and the fluidity of their use completely overwhelm and negate Mod V1's capabilities.

By every conceivable measurement, V2 is an improvement over V1.

NOTE: Parameters necessitate that a Margin of Error be maintained for unforeseen circumstances, such as Mod V2 being lured into an environmental trap or succumbing to a similar random hazard.

SPECIAL NOTE: Mod's progress is satisfactory. He has completed the first step... TINA has compiled additional upgrade paths for him to choose from. He needs to choose carefully.

SPECIAL CONSIDERATIONS: [Redacted] and [Redacted] are among the most promising upgrade paths. The latter path necessitates monitoring of his mental state.... TINA thinks it is too much too soon—I don't. Technology will succeed where magic, superpowers, and biology cannot.

Before you check out the next book, please consider leaving an honest review on your favorite store. Nowadays books live and die by the algorithm and even a simple star review can help it gain traction.

And of course, recommend this to anyone else in your life that's looking for a new superhero series!

More Books

Check out SamuelFlemingBooks.com and consider subscribing to the E-mail newsletter for new releases and updates. Social media may change, but E-mail is forever!

If you like the action and intrigue of Mod Superhero, check out these other stories:

A Battleaxe and a Metal Arm — Helesys is cunning, driven-and trapped. Her only ally is a towering barbarian who's as cold as his blade. They're trapped in a mad wizard's endless prison. Together, they'll have to survive impossible realms and find their memories in the process. As her powers come back, Helesys feels confident that the two of them will make it out or die trying... But even death might not be an escape.

Binge the complete series!

If you're looking for more Superhero stories, Progression Fantasy, or LitRPG, there's some awesome communities on Reddit, Discord, and Facebook!

THANKS

Thanks to all the early and constant readers online (in no particular order):

Cronofire, TofuuKnight, Eader, Cosy Curse, Gameknight2169, Bounce, Robort, Vadelent, The Bell Tolls For Thee, Newbage, Venn, Summer-ray17, KorenTiquar, Death Threat Collector, Morris Darkstar, Nomad1791, The Mimic Slayer, Weas97, 3SlicesOfBread, Dead Dragon, IDontKnowItTrueCipres, Arkhron, AI_March, namesare_hard, perfectgeneral, AmagiBestShip, Novitiate, sabbahillel, Khargol, Koooomakimi, georgylijf, Skoonting, Tormented Sage, Mister Bill, Solarus, Slayer_of_boxes, Andrexus Kasnia, Phan_Of_Wafflez, Big Havok, Ogoun, jpx, Jujubeanz, Laovi The Eldritch Banana, Katsurandom, Someonenoone7, Cassanunda, Accent, Linnoquake, Arad127, zorian22, Lionard, Aerodoth, EricTheMeek, playr543, Oroborozs, Doctor_C, Sir ReadsALot, Cestarian, Skylos308, Papa Legba, Down The Dragon's Gate, MilkTheShark, BrunoMaric, Omacron, msng, 3SlicesOfBread, Be3Bee, gaju, Confused_Kano, kilmor, ilyr, Kaywye and more!

A big thanks to Cactus for helping me get started on Discord.

Thanks to all my early supporters on Patreon: BrainError, Oth, Felix Liebgott, Glennen Hopson, Quaternion, Noooooooooooool, Duco Van der Ploeg, jay, Steve McFarland, Ty Tuttle, Kyle, Josh Cothran, Jan L, backrest.puppy390, Charles johnson, Quadrivirus, mafytoogamer, Neorem, Imspinnennetz, and Alexandre Breisse!

About the Author

Samuel Fleming is a Sci-fi, Fantasy, and Horror author.

He grew up in Maryland, spending most of his time swimming and writing. The thing about swimming is that it gives you a lot of time to daydream, so the two hobbies complemented each other well. Idle day dreams turned into stories, some of which stuck with him for years. These days he swims a little less and writes a lot more.

He loves a good story no matter the medium: Books, TV, video games, comics, tabletop RPG's, or podcasts–most of which he attempts to share with his wife and three kids, and occasionally on his blog.

Find him on social media at SamuelFlemingBooks.com